Praise for *The Last of the Firedrakes*

"*The Last of the Firedrakes* is a fantasy novel that will entrance young adult and adult readers alike . . . Political intrigue, danger, and deep characterization make for an interconnected epic. Enthusiastically recommended for high fantasy connoisseurs."

— **Midwest Book Review**

". . . the narrative components echo the classics; the Academy of Magic at Evolon could be Hogwarts, while the Shadow Guards are reminiscent of Tolkien's Ring Wraiths or Rowling's Dementors . . . a beautifully drawn fantasy world."

— **Kirkus Reviews**

"*The Last of the Firedrakes* is a magic-filled romp that carries you back to the fantasy stories of childhood . . . Lovers of classic fantasy will likewise gobble down Oomerbhoy's scrumptious story."

— **Vic James**, author of *Gilded Cage*

"This book is one of those fantasies you want to live in simply because the characters and pace of the story are so very compelling. I fell in love with Aurora, with her plight to understand the circumstances surrounding her parents' deaths and the visions she'd recently been having. One of Oomerbhoy's biggest strengths is her captivating descriptions . . . This story was completely enjoyable and engaged me from beginning to end. I highly recommend it to anyone looking for a classic fantasy."

— **Amber K. Bryant**, author of *Unseen*
and winner of the 2015 Margaret Atwood Writing contest

"*The Last of the Firedrakes* is one of my favorite reads this year . . . I loved this story. The characters were endearing and I rooted for Aurora as she struggled to develop her powers and gain confidence . . . This story is such a fun read. I highly recommend you to check it out!"

— **Sarah Benson**, author of *Born of Shadow*

"*The Last of the Firedrakes* was one of the very first fantasy books I have ever read. The feisty heroine, Aurora, hooked me immediately! I loved watching her blossom throughout her journey. She is a strong and likeable character, yet makes mistakes like every young girl. The vivid detail in this story made me feel as if I was part of the magical world of Avalonia, and I enjoyed the action incorporated in every chapter, especially the forbidden love budding between Aurora and Rafe. This is a must read for every lover of fantasy. I am really looking forward to book two."

— **Darly Jamison**, author of *Strawberry Wine*

THE RISE OF THE DAWNSTAR

OF THE

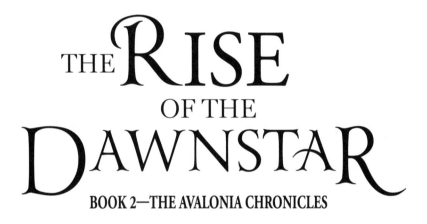

BOOK 2—THE AVALONIA CHRONICLES

by

FARAH OOMERBHOY

ISBN 13: 978-1-63489-934-5
eISBN 13: 978-1-63489-933-8

Library of Congress Catalog Number: 2017931500
Printed in the United States of America
First Printing: 2017
21   20   19   18   17   5   4   3   2   1

Cover design by Scarlett Rugers
Interior design by Kim Morehead

WISE Ink
CREATIVE ★ PUBLISHING

Wise Ink Creative Publishing
837 Glenwood Ave.
Minneapolis, MN 55405
www.wiseinkpub.com

To order, visit www.itascabooks.com or call 1-800-901-3480.
Reseller discounts available.

To my mother, for always believing in me.

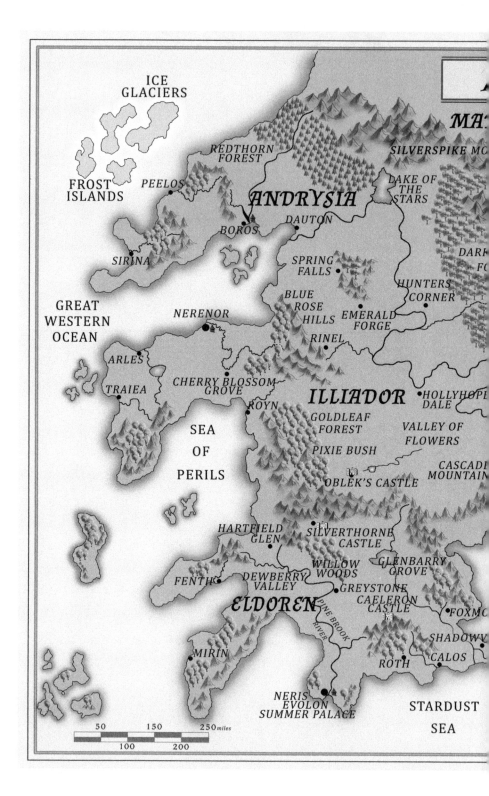

ICE
GLACIERS

FROST
ISLANDS

PEELOS

REDTHORN
FOREST

ANDRYSIA

DAUTON

SILVERSPIKE MC

MA:

LAKE OF
THE
STARS

SIRINA

BOROS

SPRING
FALLS

DARK
FO

GREAT
WESTERN
OCEAN

NERENOR

BLUE
ROSE
HILLS

HUNTERS
CORNER

EMERALD
FORGE

RINEL

ARLES

TRAIEA

CHERRY BLOSSOM
GROVE

ROYN

ILLIADOR

HOLLYHOP
DALE

SEA
OF
PERILS

GOLDLEAF
FOREST

PIXIE BUSH

VALLEY OF
FLOWERS

CASCAD
MOUNTAIN

OBLEK'S CASTLE

HARTFIELD
GLEN

SILVERTHORNE
CASTLE

FENTH

WILLOW
WOODS

GLENBARRY
GROVE

DEWBERRY
VALLEY

GREYSTONE

ELDOREN

CAELERON
CASTLE

FOXMC

MIRIN

NERIS
EVOLON
SUMMER PALACE

ROTH

SHADOWV

CALOS

STARDUST
SEA

50   150   250 *miles*

100   200

PROLOGUE

"WHY IS THE girl still alive, Lucian?" asked a woman's voice from a shadowy corner.

"I'm working on it, my queen." The Archmage of Avalonia swept into the darkened room, his black mage robes, bordered with gold, billowing around him as he walked. Broad-shouldered and regal in his bearing, he raised his right hand; the damp fireplace flared to life, warming the cold stone floor.

The queen of Illiador sat in a red velvet chair, staring into the flames that illuminated her heart-shaped face. The windows were shut against the cold air that had started blowing down from the north, and a dark mist swirled outside as the wind howled, racing through the kingdoms of Avalonia, heralding the coming of winter.

"Then where is she?" Morgana snarled, rising slowly from her high-backed chair and turning to face the archmage. Her obsidian hair was loose and tangled and her emerald eyes were bloodshot.

Lucian bowed and his eyes narrowed as he addressed Morgana. "We have no idea. It is proving impossible to find her with magic. As long as she wears the Amulet of Auraken, I cannot determine her whereabouts."

"Yes, I know. But surely there are other ways to find her?"

"Not with magic."

"Then find her without magic," Morgana hissed.

The archmage's jaw tightened. "I have spies everywhere, looking for the princess. The last we heard, she left the Summer Palace in the dark of night. That was days ago—by now she could be anywhere in the seven kingdoms."

Morgana clasped her hands together and started pacing in front of the fireplace. "She won't get far on a normal horse; at least she doesn't have the added advantage of a pegasus anymore."

Lucian coughed and looked down.

Morgana's eyebrows rose. "What are you not telling me, Lucian?"

"There was an incident in the ruins, after you, um, left. My sources say the princess healed the pegasus."

"How is that possible? The pegasus was dead, I saw it with my own eyes." Morgana paused as she assessed the archmage. "Is her healing power so great?"

"I believe it is. She has the blood of the immortal fae running through her veins. You know how powerful their healers are, and she is stronger still. My sources say the healing she performed on that day was something no one has ever seen before."

Morgana seemed utterly unimpressed. "The Shadow Guard were supposed to kill the pegasus and the princess, but they failed." Her eyes narrowed. "I thought you had trained them all personally? How can a little chit of a girl defeat the deadliest warriors of Illiador?"

"She is too strong," the archmage said, his face almost feral at the thought of the girl who had evaded them for over fifteen years. "The more she uses her magic, the more her power grows. There is no mage who can stand in her way now."

"Rubbish!" The flames in the fireplace leapt and danced as Morgana's anger flared. "There is always a way."

Lucian didn't blink an eye. "Whatever you say, my queen."

She flashed him a glare. "And what news is there from Eldoren? Are you sure your sister and her husband know what they're doing?"

Lucian nodded. "The Blackwaters will take over the throne of Eldoren as you have commanded. The plans are already set in motion."

"That is not enough," Morgana snapped. "I want Prince Rafael dead as well. The Ravenswood dynasty supports Aurora, and none must be allowed to survive. We will strip her of all her allies and her friends. Without proper guidance, the girl is likely to destroy herself. Then we will strike when she is at her weakest."

"What about Izadora? The fae queen will never bow to

your rule, you know."

She gave Lucian a pointed look. "Izadora will have no choice, once I am done with her. My plans concerning Elfi are already underway. You just make sure Aurora never reaches her grandmother's kingdom."

Lucian shook his head. "Forget her, Morgana." He came closer and put his hand on her shoulder. "She is weak and foolish. She doesn't have it in her to be queen. Like you said, she will eventually destroy herself. Concentrate on taking over the other kingdoms first. Once you are crowned High Queen of Avalonia, Aurora Firedrake will become a memory."

"I want her dead, Lucian." Morgana moved away from him and turned to face the flames, dismissing the archmage with a wave of her hand. "I should have called for the Drakaar assassins much earlier. They will find her and kill her, even if you can't."

The archmage's spine stiffened. "But, Your Majesty, the Drakaar are not to be trusted. They will extract a high price for this—remember what happened after you hired them to kill Azaren." He paused and took a step closer, lowering the tone of his voice. "Morgana, let me find the girl. I will not fail, just give me more time."

The queen turned back around to face him. "There is no more time, Lucian. The people have already heard she is alive. You told me yourself rebel factions have sprung up all over Illiador and are searching for her too. We must find her

4

before those troublemakers who call themselves the Silver Swords do. They are the last remnants of Azaren's supporters, and I want them gone. Burn the forests where they take cover, and scorch the villages and towns that conceal them. If anyone is found supporting Aurora, they must be made examples of. My niece must have no place to go, nowhere to hide. Then we will strike and make her wish she had never been born a Firedrake."

The archmage bowed, his eyes like shards of cold steel. "It will be done, my queen."

"See that it is." Morgana gazed into the dancing fire. "If I want to become High Queen over all the seven kingdoms, Aurora Firedrake must die."

1
THE JOURNEY BEGINS

I TURNED OVER in my bed of damp moss and fallen leaves as muted sunlight shone through the trees and woke me to another day. The earthy fragrances of the forest floor lingered as dewdrops danced in the cool morning breeze, dazzling the woods with a myriad of colors, spectacular in the light of first dawn. The weather had become colder as winter drew near—I pulled my thin blanket snugly around me, not ready to get up just yet.

Rafe was sitting on a large rock, his gray eyes intent as he sharpened his sword. I gazed at him, my eyes still half shut. He was wearing a plain white shirt with the top few buttons open, dark leather pants, and high boots, with his customary dagger strapped to his leg. He smiled when he looked up and saw I was awake.

"Happy birthday!" He put down his sword and came to squat down beside me. His dark hair framed his chiseled jaw, and he looked exactly the same as when I had first seen him so many months ago in the dungeons of Oblek's gloomy castle.

I smiled up at him, his big shadow blocking out the sun.

"How did you know it was my birthday?" Even I didn't know the exact date.

He chuckled. "Everyone in Illiador and beyond knows when your birthday is, Aurora. There are some villages and towns in your father's kingdom that still celebrate it as a holiday."

"Oh!" I blushed as I sat up. "I didn't know."

I looked around. "Where's Kalen?"

Rafe stood up. "Our little fae friend has gone to get you a birthday breakfast. He should be back at any moment. Come," he gave me his hand. "We should be on our way soon. We're camped too close to the village as it is."

"Give me a minute." I pulled myself up and brushed twigs and leaves off my dress.

Rafe reached over and plucked a few out of my hair.

"Thanks," I mumbled. I must have looked a sight. I washed my face in a pond nearby and gargled with water infused with mint leaves.

The bushes rustled and Kalen came charging into the clearing where we had camped for the night. Runaway strands of ash blond hair stuck to his forehead as he huffed and put his hands on his knees, trying to catch his breath. "There you are."

Rafe turned immediately. "What's wrong?"

"I heard the village guards talking at the market. They are telling everyone to keep a lookout for the both of you.

Anyone found helping you will be arrested by order of the king."

Rafe swore softly and immediately started saddling the horses. "We need to leave now. My father's guards won't be far behind."

It had been ten days since Rafe had led us through the secret passage and out of the city of Neris. Resourceful as ever, he had procured three horses and led us, without incident, to the foot of the Sunrise Hills, further east into the heart of the kingdom of Eldoren.

Our journey took us along the Emerald Coast, and we slept outdoors, skirting small villages along the way. Many had cozy, comfortable inns, beckoning us to stay and enjoy the quiet serenity of the little villages, but we didn't dare go inside for fear of being noticed. Most of the time we hid in the woods, and only Kalen could go into the nearby farmhouses and village markets to buy food for us while we waited like criminals, hiding amongst the trees and living on the outskirts of civilization.

Our pace was slow; we took back roads and hidden forest paths, constantly stopping and hiding from the guards that patrolled the main trade routes. Market wagons and farmers littered the narrow dirt roads, so we disguised ourselves as poor travellers, blending into the surrounding countryside. Rafe had carefully concealed his weapons under a worn brown cloak Kalen had procured for him at the last market we passed.

———⟨⟩———

At the end of the next day, we rode through the open gates of Roth, a little town not that different from those I had seen before in northern Eldoren. Small, unplanned streets and rickety wooden houses were crammed together at the edge of the forest that extended into the hills, looming like dark shadows in the distance.

"We will stop here for the night." Rafe turned his horse into a cobbled alleyway that led into darkness.

I spurred my horse forward and followed, passing cloaked figures who hurried through the streets, eager to get out of the chill—a biting wind had started blowing in from the north. I tried to maneuver my horse closer to Rafe's, but I could barely see a few feet ahead of me through the thick fog.

"What if we are recognized by someone?" I clutched the reins with one hand and pulled my cloak tighter around me. "Isn't it too risky?"

"Keep your hood on," said Rafe. "This is the only way to get the information we need. Once we have it, we will leave this town before anyone notices us."

"Are we meeting someone here?"

Rafe nodded. "Marcus Gold. I've known him since I was a boy. He may be a shady character, but he's safe and avoids the authorities even better than we do. In any case, he's the only one I know who can give us information about the dagger. We need some sort of plan if we are going to steal it from Morgana. The more we know about it the better." He spurred his horse forward. "Follow me."

We stopped in front of a tavern that desperately needed a fresh coat of paint and didn't look quite as inviting as the Dancing Daisy Inn, where we had stayed when we were passing through the town of Greystone on our way to Evolon. Still, I hoped I would finally get a real bed to sleep in that night.

Groaning, I maneuvered myself off the horse, and Rafe came over to help me down. I was exhausted and my thighs were chafed and aching from riding for what seemed like months.

"Go on." Kalen took the reins from me. "I'll water down the horses and meet you inside."

I smiled at him gratefully, handed him the reins, and followed Rafe into the inn.

The main hall of the tavern was full of rowdy men and women who looked and smelled like they hadn't had a bath for days. Some were playing dice at the tables, their eyes intent and their pockets getting emptier by the minute. Others were drowning their sorrows drinking at the bar. All the tables were packed with people chatting around frothy mugs of ale and eating the sumptuous tavern fare.

No one paid us any attention, but I still fiddled with the

hood of my cloak, making sure my features were covered. The innkeeper passed by me with a huge wooden tray; the delicious smell of freshly baked bread reminded me I hadn't eaten a proper meal in days and I was absolutely starving.

Rafe moved toward the far end of the room, where a man was sitting at a table in the corner, his hood over his head. He spotted Rafe almost immediately and waved us over.

Rafe sat down on the bench and introduced me to the small, thin man before me. "Marcus, I presume I don't need to tell you who she is?"

Marcus shook his head and pulled back his hood. His skin was a warm dusky color and he had a thin mustache over a small goatee, which, in my opinion, made him look a bit like a musketeer.

"It is a great honor to meet you," Marcus said, his voice low but clear. His eyes were shrewd and bright, and they twinkled as he glanced at my amulet, which I hadn't realized was showing.

I smiled at him and tucked it back into my tunic. I had to be more careful; the Amulet of Auraken was the one thing that identified me without a doubt.

"I hope you don't mind, I ordered some food while I was waiting?" Marcus said, when the innkeeper brought three steaming wooden bowls of stew to our table, accompanied by a basket of hot bread and a golden-crusted meat pie for us to share.

"Thank you, Marcus." Rafe picked up the knife and started cutting up the pie. "Go on, Aurora, you must be famished. I know I am."

"I believe you have an interest in procuring what us Brandorians refer to as the Dark Dagger," Marcus said, leaning forward and getting straight to the point while Rafe and I ate.

I nodded with my mouth full.

"We think Morgana has it, but we need to know more about how it works and how the curse can be broken," Rafe elaborated.

Marcus seemed to find this amusing and smiled to himself before he answered. "You plan to break the demon curse on the Dagger of Dragath?"

Rafe did not seem amused in the slightest. "That is why we are here, Marcus. Now, is there a way or isn't there?"

"There might be." Marcus rested his elbows on the table and propped his chin on his hands, fiddling with his wispy beard.

I stopped eating. "And?"

"I have no idea what it is. There is only one person who might know how it can be done."

My face fell. This supposed expert didn't know how to deal with the Dagger of Dragath. "Who?"

"Constantine Redgrave," Marcus replied.

Rafe's eyebrows shot up. "But Constantine Redgrave is

dead."

"That's what everyone thinks," Marcus retorted, fiddling with his beard again. "I have seen him with my own eyes. Constantine Redgrave is still alive and living in exile in Brandor."

I tried to remember my history lessons. "I've read about him at Evolon. He was Archmage during my grandfather's rule, wasn't he?"

"Yes!" replied Rafe. "He was your grandfather's right-hand man, and loyal to your father. If he is still alive he will definitely help us. He is the foremost authority on Dragath and demons. If anyone knows how to break the curse on the dagger, it's him. He was supposed to have died on the same day as your father, the day Morgana took over the throne of Illiador. He must have escaped the massacre at the Star Palace."

Marcus nodded. "Redgrave knows the Star Palace at Nerenor like the back of his hand, and must have discovered a secret way out. If you intend to break into Morgana's palace and steal the dagger, you are going to need his help. I have heard he is working as the mastermage of the Library of Sanria. He now goes by the name Diego Ramirez."

"How do you know all this?" I was not completely sure if I should trust him blindly, though Rafe seemed to. "And why should I believe you?"

"A short while ago, while I was out on a mission in Sanria,

inside the Red Citadel, I overheard a conversation between Redgrave and Gabriel Silverthorne."

I gasped, my hand flying to my mouth. "My granduncle?"

Marcus nodded. "I heard Silverthorne call Redgrave by his real name. They mentioned you."

"What were they saying about me?"

Marcus shook his head. "I don't know. I only had a moment before I had to leave or risk getting caught."

I stared down at my plate. I wasn't sure what to believe anymore. Uncle Gabriel had kept so many secrets from me, revealing only what he thought necessary. I knew he only wanted to help and I was grateful, but it made it more difficult to believe what he said. It did sound like Marcus was telling the truth, though. What would he gain by making it up?

"A word of advice, if I may?" Marcus leaned forward and lowered his voice. "You must proceed with caution, princess. The Dagger of Dragath is an ancient and dangerous weapon, and I don't know how Morgana got her hands on it. But going near the dagger without the proper knowledge is like going into battle with a needle instead of a sword. Go to Brandor and meet the mastermage before you go after the dagger. He will have the information you need. Only then will you have any chance of finding the Dagger of Dragath, let alone breaking the curse."

Kalen suddenly appeared and sat down beside me, his

face instantly giving away his distress.

I put my hand on his shoulder. "What happened?"

Kalen's eyes were wide. "It's the town guards. I was rubbing down the horses at the stables and I heard them talking about a fugitive who was supposed to be staying at the inn."

Rafe pushed his food away and grabbed my hand, pulling me up with him. "We have to leave, now." He moved toward the door and gestured for Kalen to follow us.

Marcus had already put the hood of his cloak up and was heading out the door when it opened. Five armed guards with their swords ready strode into the crowded tavern, blocking our only escape route.

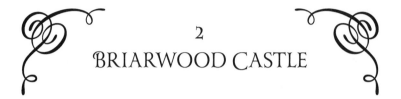

2
BRIARWOOD CASTLE

A HUSH FELL over the usually rowdy room, and no one moved.

The tavern was too crowded for us to use magic and fight our way out—somebody might get hurt, and Rafe knew that. It was just my luck I would get caught and dragged back to the Summer Palace before I got halfway to Illiador.

But it wasn't me they had come for. They didn't seem to know who we were.

The guards moved forward and surrounded Marcus, pulling back his hood and holding swords to his throat. Marcus didn't move, but his shrewd, dark eyes darted back and forth between them.

The captain of the town guards walked into the crowded room. A chill wind followed as he slammed the tavern door.

"Is this him, captain?" the guard holding Marcus asked his superior. His uniform was a dull blue, and mud stains speckled the front of his tunic.

"I believe it is," said the captain, a sly grin spreading across his pockmarked face. He strode over to Marcus, a plain sword held loosely in his beefy hand. "Well, well,

well, if it isn't Marcus Gold, Brandor's most infamous black market trader." His voice boomed across the hushed room as he pushed his straggly brown hair out of his face. He eyed Marcus warily, a cat playing with his prey. "You and your dirty magical items don't belong in my town. You should be more careful of the people you work with. Looks like your last customer didn't mind squealing your whereabouts in the torture chamber."

I winced at the word torture, but Marcus' expression remained unclear as to what he was thinking. The tavern customers shuffled backwards, huddling against the walls and trying to stay out of harm's way. Many of them moved toward the door, but the guards did not let them leave.

Marcus looked the captain straight in the eye. "You have the wrong man."

"Oh, I don't think so." The captain's eyes gleamed almost manically. "There have been bodies turning up dead all over town, and you were seen leaving one of the murder scenes."

My heart had started beating so loudly I was afraid everyone would hear it.

"I have no idea what you are talking about," said Marcus calmly.

"Should we take him to the dungeons, sir?" asked one guard.

The captain nodded, his face hard. "Take him, I will deal with him personally."

THE RISE OF THE DAWNSTAR

As the guards started pulling Marcus towards the door, a thin, gaunt man, who had been sitting at the table next to us, came and stood in front of the captain. He wrung his hands and shifted from side to side as he spoke.

"I saw them, my lord," he said, pointing at us and addressing the captain in a simpering voice. "They were all whispering together in a corner."

"Were they?" said the captain. His muddy boots clumped on the wooden floor as he walked towards us.

I tensed, and my magic flared to life.

Rafe moved slightly, pulling me up to his side and putting his arm around my waist. "Not yet," he whispered. He knew me too well.

I had learned to control my powers to a certain degree—it was a struggle to restrain myself, but I managed to push my magic back down.

The captain came to stand before us as he eyed me warily. His rancid breath made me feel like gagging. His informant scurried behind him.

"What is your connection to the Brandorian spy?" said the captain to Rafe. It was obvious he didn't recognize the crown prince with his hood drawn over his head.

Rafe spoke calmly. "I have never seen him before. We just met him, he wanted directions."

"Liar!" spat the little informant. "I saw them huddled together. They are his accomplices, my lord captain."

"Are they now?" said the captain, moving closer. "Remove your hood, sir," he pointed his sword at Rafe.

Rafe didn't move, but I could sense his magic building up inside him. If Rafe and I unleashed our magic in this tavern, there would be no telling the number of casualties.

The captain glanced at me once and looked back at Rafe. "I said, remove your hood," he enunciated every word. "Let's see what you are hiding under there."

A burst of cold air entered the room. Everyone turned toward the door.

"Marcus Gold doesn't have any accomplices," said a tall, dark figure standing at the entrance of the tavern.

His eyes went straight to Rafe and then to me. For a fleeting second I thought he recognized us. He turned to the captain of the Guard. "They are not to be touched," said the stranger, pulling back his hood, revealing handsome features, framed by a mass of wavy gold hair. He was young and broad shouldered, and looked not much older than Rafe.

"But my Lord Delacourt," said the captain, bowing low to the stranger, "they were conspiring with the criminal."

Delacourt turned his cold blue eyes on the captain. "No, Captain Finley! They were working for me, to apprehend the criminal." His voice was soft, but laced with steel. "In fact, your untimely outburst nearly ruined my carefully laid plans."

"What bull!" the captain's voice trailed off.

"Mind your tongue, Captain Finley," said Lord Dela-court, his blue eyes like ice chips, "or it will be the last time you use it." He pushed back his crimson cloak, trimmed with fur, to reveal a gleaming sword at his waist.

Captain Finley gulped and took a step back. His eyes tightened and he looked like steam was about to start erupt-ing from his ears at any moment, but he moved out of the way nonetheless. His sneaky little informant disappeared into a shadowy corner.

Lord Delacourt dismissed the captain with a wave of his hand and moved to stand in front of me. His face softened, and much to my astonishment he gave me a sweeping bow. "I thank you for your assistance, my lady. I am forever in your debt."

"It was my pleasure," I said, even though I had no idea what he was taking about.

I glanced at Rafe, but he didn't look perturbed; in fact, I saw the hint of a smile playing at the corner of his lips. Was this something he planned? If this mysterious stranger was a lord of the realm, then he must have recognized his prince. But I had no idea who he was; I had never seen or heard of him before.

Delacourt clasped Rafe's hand in his. "My friend, you will stay at my castle tonight—it is much more comfortable than this miserable inn."

Rafe nodded. "We would be delighted, my lord," he said,

with a smile.

"Escort the prisoner and my guests to the castle," said Lord Delacourt to his men, turning and walking toward the door.

"No! Arrest them!" the captain shouted to his underlings. "The magistrate will decide if they are telling the truth."

Three guards rushed forward to apprehend us, but Delacourt raised his hand, stopping them in their tracks. I could feel the rush of magical power concentrated around him; he was a mage.

"But, but, the magistrate . . ." sputtered the captain.

Delacourt turned to the captain. "The magistrate will do as I tell him to do. And I presume you will too if you value your job, Captain Finley."

The captain bowed again, and Lord Delacourt gave me his hand. "Allow me, my lady."

I took Delacourt's hand and walked forward, but I caught a glimpse of the hatred in the captain's eyes. I had made a new enemy, of that I was quite sure.

Outside in the courtyard of the little inn, the horses waited.

Delacourt turned to me, his voice soft. "You can ride with me, my lady."

But Rafe was beside us in an instant and snaked his hand around my waist as he pulled me toward him. "That won't be necessary, Lord Delacourt. The lady will be riding with me."

Delacourt smirked, his eyes twinkling. "As you wish." He jumped up onto his own horse in one graceful leap.

Kalen had retrieved our horses from the stables, but my horse was given to Marcus to ride; meaning I had to ride with someone else. I was glad it was Rafe; I wouldn't have had it any other way.

We followed Delacourt and the guards uphill to a castle that lay on a rocky crag along the side of the mountains overlooking the town below. I sat in front of Rafe as we traversed the rocky mountain road, which cut through the gray stone between the thickly wooded slopes. He wrapped his cloak closer around us and his powerful body protected me from the biting chill of the howling wind sweeping down from the mountains.

"We will be safe at Briarwood Castle," said Rafe in my ear. "For tonight, at least."

"Do you know Delacourt well?" I whispered.

"Yes, Brandon and I were at Evolon together for four years. We lived in the same house at the Academy. The Delacourt family has ruled these lands ever since anyone can remember. The Earldom of Briarwood is one of the oldest titles in Eldoren, passed down through centuries, and Brandon Delacourt is the only heir. He has been away from Eldoren for the past year; last I heard, he had gone north to Andrysia."

I tried to remember if I had seen him before. But I knew I would have remembered him if I had. "Aunt Serena never told me anything about this family, and he wasn't at the palace for the ball either."

Rafe laughed softly at this. "You won't catch Brandon Delacourt dead at a ball. He is a notorious loner, no one ever sees much of him. His family doesn't sit on the council of nobles, and I suspect that's why your aunt didn't put him on your list of family names to learn." He lowered his voice to a barely perceptible whisper. "Earl Delacourt, Brandon's father, went mad almost twenty years ago when his only daughter, Brandon's older sister, flung herself out of that tower and killed herself." Rafe pointed to the tallest tower of Briarwood Castle that pierced the sky, looming over a deadly cliff that dropped hundreds of feet into the rocky base of the hills.

"They say she was like a mother to Brandon after his own mother died in childbirth," Rafe went on. "No one has seen the old earl in over a decade, but we presume he is alive. Brandon is a viscount, but everyone knows he's the real earl, except in name."

"How awful." I clutched the saddle as the horse ambled uphill toward the eerie stone castle. "Why? Why did she do it?" I couldn't shake the image of a young girl flinging herself from the top of the tower. I looked up. It was so high that parts of the castle were still shrouded in mist and cloud.

"Riora was many years older than Brandon, the earl's daughter from his first wife," said Rafe, trying to keep his horse in check as we navigated the narrow road, which fell into a steep drop. "The story goes she was in love with a man who married another. On the day of their wedding she ended her life."

Tears welled in my eyes for the grief the poor girl must have felt; enough for her to end her own life over a lost love. I hoped I would never have to experience that sort of despair in my lifetime.

"So, who was the man?" I asked Rafe, still wondering what kind of person caused the destruction of a whole family without a backward glance.

Rafe shrugged. "I don't know. I was too young at the time. And Brandon never speaks about it." He rode forward as I held on tight. Kalen had to fall behind, as there was not much room to maneuver the horses.

"Stick to the left," Rafe called out to Kalen as the small path leading to the castle became narrower. Walls of jagged rock created a narrow pass we had to navigate before we came to the castle walls. "Follow me."

We rode through the massive gates and into the enormous outer courtyard of Briarwood Castle, where towering stone walls enclosed us in their shadows. Fur-clad guards walked the battlements, vigilant of anyone or anything approaching the mountain fortress. Gray towers speared the night sky, and the moon finally decided to peek out at us from behind low hanging clouds, lighting up the castle in its ghostly glow.

Grooms ran up to take their master's horse as Brandon Delacourt jumped off his steed and strode up the wide steps to the great wooden door of the castle. He stopped for a moment to address his servants. "See that the rooms in the east wing are made ready for my guests." He pushed back the hood of his fur-lined cloak. "I will see them shortly in the library."

"And the prisoner, milord?" said one guard.

Brandon turned his cold gaze on the guard. "I think you are acquainted with the lodgings for prisoners, soldier." His words were clipped. "Put Mr. Gold in the dungeons. I will deal with him later."

Frost hung in the air as the guards, servants, and grooms scurried off to do Lord Delacourt's bidding.

Rafe gave me his hand, but this time I refused to let anyone help me down. I could get on and off a horse on my own. It was time I became more independent. Now that I was wearing my traveling clothes all the time—thick woolen leggings, a warm tunic, and high boots—I remembered how much more comfortable pants were, instead of running around the countryside in flowing dresses, which were extremely impractical for what I needed to do.

My boots slipped on the frosty cobblestones as I stepped closer to speak privately to Rafe. "What are they going to do to Marcus?"

"I will talk to Brandon. I'm sure they have the wrong person. I know Marcus, and he is not a killer."

A guard approached and asked us to follow him.

"It's become too cold," said Kalen, rubbing his hands together and hopping about. "Come on, you two, for once we will have some real food and a warm room to sleep in. Questing is not my favorite way to pass time—all you ever end up with is a very long and tedious journey."

Rafe shook his head and I laughed at Kalen as we followed the guard up the wide stone steps and into Briarwood Castle.

Blending perfectly with the rock face, the stone castle was unfriendly and gloomy, its different parts connected by a maze of corridors spilling out from a big entrance hall. The guard lit a wooden torch and led us to a very long flight of steps. This castle was going to be even more difficult to get around than Silverthorne Castle, which, although larger, had more open spaces, big windows, and light, airy corridors. Here everything looked the same: dull, gray, and dark.

The guard led us to the library where Lord Delacourt was to meet us. A fire had already been lit, warming the vast space. Leatherbound tomes lined the shelves, the higher ones collecting dust, looking as though they hadn't been read in a long time. Normally a library would have me very excited, but tonight my eyes skimmed over the books, more concerned with thoughts of why Delacourt had brought us here and whether Marcus was innocent.

I had gradually become suspicious of everyone. These past few months in Avalonia had changed me, and I finally realized how naïve I had been when I first came here—trusting everyone with my secrets and always looking for the good in people. But that had stopped, and I saw enemies everywhere. Though I knew it was better to be suspicious than to get myself killed, I did wonder if constantly looking for the darkness in people was better than seeing the light.

Brandon Delacourt strode into the library. His doublet and boots were stitched in the latest fashion I had seen all the nobility wearing in Neris. He came up to Rafe and gave a short bow now that we were alone. "Your Highness."

Rafe smiled and stepped forward, clasping Delacourt's forearm. "It's good to see you, Brandon. Thank you for getting us out of that tavern. I wasn't particularly looking forward to hurting my own citizens."

Brandon laughed. He was almost as tall as Rafe, though his torso was big and muscular whereas Rafe's was powerfully built but lean. "Think nothing of it, my old friend."

"This is . . ." began Rafe, looking at me, but Brandon cut him off.

"I know who she is." Brandon stepped forward and bowed

briefly before me. His straight, aristocratic nose complemented his square jaw and the cleft on his chin. He straightened and looked me up and down with a piercing gaze, as if I were a prize mare. His knowing stare made me feel a touch uncomfortable.

"I had heard the lost princess of Illiador was alive, but I didn't believe it until I saw her in person. She looks just like her father." He turned to Rafe. "I must say I was surprised to see you in my town, Rafael. But I could tell you didn't want to be recognized. You do know the king is looking for you? Running away from the palace with Princess Aurora was not your best moment. I'm sure Lady Leticia will not be too pleased either."

Rafe grimaced at this. "No, probably not."

Brandon looked at me and smiled. "No offense, Your Highness."

"None taken." But I was sure I was blushing. "Please call me Aurora." I peeked at Rafe from the corner of my eye. I hated being reminded of Leticia, and it was a quick jolt back into reality. For nearly two weeks, I had had Rafe all to myself and become comfortable around him, secure in the knowledge that he was there. But one day he would leave me, return to his fiancée, and marry her.

"How did you know who I was?" I asked Brandon.

"My spies know what information is significant. They keep me apprised about everything that happens in the capital. I received a raven last night with news from the palace. The council has called for your arrest, Aurora. They are saying you have gone rogue and abducted the crown prince."

"Abducted! Who?" I turned to look at Rafe and burst out laughing. "The royal council of Eldoren has gone mad."

Brandon smiled at my reaction, but Rafe did not look amused.

"And what does Silverthorne have to say about this?" Rafe crossed his arms. "I'm sure my father would not listen to the nonsense ramblings of some insignificant nobles."

"Silverthorne has tried to pacify them, but they will not listen," said Brandon. "There is talk that the Blackwaters have returned to Neris and been given a full pardon by the king. They are the ones out for her blood, and have convinced all the nobles and the king that Aurora is a threat to the whole kingdom."

"How is it possible? The council must know I could never hold Rafe against his will." But an uneasy feeling had settled in my gut. What if what Brandon said was true?

"They have a witness who says you had help." Brandon rubbed the nape of his neck. "They are saying the Black Wolf colluded with you to bring down the monarchy. And the fae are involved in this conspiracy." He shot a glance at Kalen, who was standing quietly behind me, listening.

"Even if the Blackwaters are back," said Rafe, "there is no way my father would pardon them after what they did, and he certainly would not listen to them over the word of the Duke of Silverthorne."

"But he has pardoned them, and he is listening," said Brandon. "What's more unnerving is that many of the nobles are supporting the Blackwaters and not Silverthorne."

"This is absolutely absurd." I waved my hands in the air. "Do you actually believe the Blackwaters?"

"At first I was not sure what to believe. But after seeing the two of you together, I can see that it is not the case." He gestured to the cozy seating arrangement near the library windows. "Come and sit. We can talk freely here. I am curious to know what you are up to, Rafael."

I shot Rafe a worried glance, and he reassured me with a smile. This eerie castle gave me a bad feeling. I couldn't put my finger on it, but I wished we hadn't come here. I was not completely convinced Lord Delacourt was on our side. Although Rafe knew Brandon, and he had saved us from being recognized by the whole town, I still didn't trust him. What exactly did he want with us?

3
FUGITIVE

I SETTLED MYSELF on a comfortable chair with Rafe and Kalen seated beside me. Brandon poured all of us goblets of gold liquid from a crystal pitcher he had on the table, and sat down on the opposite chair. Rafe took his drink with a grateful smile and downed the contents in a few gulps.

"What is this?" I asked when Brandon offered a goblet to me.

"Fireberry whiskey, from the best whiskey makers in the Andrysian Highlands," answered Brandon, looking very proud of his acquisition. "I just returned from there and brought these barrels with me."

I shook my head and put down the goblet. "Sorry, I don't drink." I needed my wits about me at all times now. And I had read somewhere that alcohol could affect your magic.

"As you wish," said Brandon, sipping his drink. "What exactly are you doing here? And how can I help?"

"We need to get to the library of the Emir of Sanria," said Rafe.

Brandon's eyes went wide. "Roderigo Valasis's library?"

Rafe nodded.

"But he is the most powerful of all five Emirs on the Brandorian council," said Brandon. "You know the protocol, Rafael, you can't go into his fortress without an invitation."

"I know," said Rafe. "But there is information we need that can only be found there. We have to find a way to get in."

"What kind of information are you looking for?"

Rafe leaned back in his chair. "That I cannot reveal." He sneaked a quick glance at me. "It is a personal matter."

"I understand," said Brandon. "But do you not think it is better to go back to the palace and let everyone know you have not been abducted? Maybe then your father will call off the hunt."

Rafe shook his head. "Most of the council lords have been against Aurora from the beginning. And if the Blackwaters are back on the council, the most we can hope for is a trial." He looked at me, and his eyes softened. "If we go back, Aurora will get put in the palace dungeons. I cannot vouch for her safety down there. I would not be allowed to see her. If she uses her powers against them, even to defend herself, things could get worse—they would condemn her immediately. The best course is to get her out of Eldoren. Once I get her to safety, I will go back and sort this out with the council and my father."

"I don't agree," said Brandon. "If you don't go back now, there is no telling what the Blackwaters could do."

"I can't leave Aurora to fend for herself, she's not ready."

"I will take her to Brandor and protect her with my life—you have my word, Rafael," Brandon said, glancing at me. "You must return to the palace. Without you the Ravenswood dynasty will fall."

"No." Rafe shook his head. "Silverthorne will have to deal with the Blackwaters until I get back. I will see Aurora to safety myself."

"Maybe we should go back, Rafe," I said, finally interrupting. "We could explain everything to the king, and I can go to Elfi with my granduncle as originally planned." I looked down at my hands. I didn't want to be hunted like a criminal. Now I would be running from Morgana as well as the whole Eldorean Guard. What had I done? All I wanted was to get my mother back, and I had made things worse again. I may not always make the best decisions, but I do so with the best intentions.

Rafe leaned forward and put his hand over mine. "I don't think that is the wisest course, Aurora. I didn't want to alarm you earlier and neither did your granduncle, but . . ." He paused and looked at Kalen. "Kalen, tell her what you saw outside the palace."

Kalen straightened. Hesitating a little, he turned to me. "I didn't tell you this because my mother would hardly let me see you when you were recovering after your battle with Morgana and the Shadow Guard. And later your granduncle asked me to keep it to myself until you left for Elfi."

My heartbeat quickened. "What is it, Kalen?"

"There is unrest in Eldoren among the people. After we brought you back from the battle with Morgana and the Shadow Guard, the people of Neris had gathered outside the palace, protesting and urging the king to send you back to Illiador, to Morgana."

"But why?" *This was unbelievable!* "I defeated the Shadow Guard. I thought everyone hated and feared them?"

"They did, until you defeated them." Kalen got up to pace in front of me. "But now it is you they fear. Anyone powerful enough to wipe out most of Morgana's Shadow Guard is a terrible threat if they go dark."

"But I'm not going dark," I said, standing up. "I never will."

Rafe held my hand and pulled me back down. "We know." He clasped my hand between his and looked at me intently. "But they do not. You have to understand that the common people do not understand our magic."

"But Vivienne said they were calling me Avalonia's savior," I insisted, trying to think back to my last conversation with my best friend.

"In elitist circles, yes," said Brandon, "but only a few mage families think like that. Most have been taught to fear fae-mages, and for good reason."

I remembered the stories the mastermage of Evolon had

told me about some of the fae-mages before me turning to dark magic because of the power it gave them. But I never thought they would think it of me.

"Some of the nobility, and also the Mage Guild, feel the king should make a deal with Morgana to hand you over to her in return for her not invading Eldoren," said Rafe.

"Why didn't you tell me this before?" I was disappointed he felt fit to keep secrets from me.

"I didn't want to upset you," said Rafe. "But now that you know everything, you can understand why it is better not to go back. We will go to Brandor, and then south to Elfi to your grandmother Izadora. I will send word to your granduncle as to where we are."

"Shouldn't we go straight to Elfi if they are hunting us?"

"It's not possible to take that route," Kalen answered. "The seas around Elfi are protected with powerful magic and ancient creatures which live in its depths. No ship can sail through those waters. The only way to enter Elfi is through Brandor and the Gandren Pass in the Wildflower Mountains."

"Yes," Rafe agreed. "Kalen is absolutely right. Your grandmother's magic protects Elfi from the world. That is the only place you will be safe from Morgana while you learn to master your powers. As long as Izadora remains in Elfi, no army will ever enter the fae kingdom. Since we need to go through Brandor anyway, we will get the information we need from the Valasis Library on our way to Elfi."

I nodded. Everything he said made sense. Rafe knew how important it was to me to get that information from Constantine Redgrave, otherwise I would have no hope of finding the Dark Dagger and releasing my mother. The new circumstances made getting to the Dagger more difficult than before. Now that I had a chance to think about it properly, I realized Uncle Gabriel's plan to have me go to Elfi was, in fact, well thought out and for my own good.

I had finally accepted I wasn't going to be able to get my mother back yet, although that didn't stop me from feeling guilty every time I thought about her. Knowing she had sacrificed herself to save me felt like a huge burden I had to repay. But getting myself killed before I gave myself a fighting chance was stupidity.

Brandon stood up. "I'm not sure exactly what you are up to, but I would still like to help. You have come at just the right time. I was about to leave for Calos tomorrow to attend my cousin's wedding. Santino Valasis will be there; he can get you to Brandor and into the Emir's fortress without anyone asking questions."

"Santino Valasis." Rafe raised an eyebrow. "The son of the Emir of Sanria?"

"The very same," Brandon nodded. "I know him well, and I can ask him to help us."

Rafe poured himself more Fireberry whiskey, took a swig,

and sat down. "Then we will accompany you to Calos, and you can introduce us to Santino."

"But how do you know he will help us? What if he turns us in?" I asked.

Brandon laughed, filling up his goblet as well. "You don't have to worry. Santino Valasis is a notorious privateer and trader. If he thinks the cargo is valuable enough, he will take you to the Sea of Shadows if you wish it."

"But if he is the son of an Emir of Brandor, why would he help me?" I was not convinced about the likelihood of receiving aid from a stranger.

"I have heard of Santino," said Rafe. "He is known as the Pirate Prince, and even the most cutthroat pirates stay far away from him. But I have also heard he is a fair man, and the other Emirs fear him. It might not be such a bad thing having him on our side."

Brandon nodded. "Rafe is right. Santino is a deadly fighter and a shrewd man. He is the reason his father holds most of the power in Brandor. Santino is notorious for having an army of mercenaries and pirates loyal only to him, and the port city of Sanria is completely under his control."

"What about Marcus?" I voiced my other concern.

Brandon's face hardened. "What about him?"

"Why have you locked him up?" asked Rafe. "You and I both know that he did not commit those murders. He may be a spy and a profiteer, but he is not a killer."

Brandon rubbed his chin. "He is a cheat," he said finally. "He sold me a magical item that didn't work and then disappeared. That was a few years ago, and I swore if he ever came back I would not spare him. I heard he was in town and I came to apprehend him myself." He paused and looked at me strangely. "Looks like I got more than I bargained for."

"So, if he agreed to give you your money back, would you let him go?" Rafe inquired.

"Perhaps," Brandon answered. "But he may know something about the killings. He is a spy, after all. Why are you so interested in him?"

"Let me talk to Marcus." Rafe put down his goblet and got up from the chair.

"I will send for him." Brandon went over to the door and spoke to the guard standing outside. In a few minutes, Marcus Gold was brought into the room.

Brandon waved his hand. "Leave us."

The guard promptly bowed and scurried out.

Rafe stood beside Brandon. "Marcus, if you cooperate with Lord Delacourt we can clear this up immediately."

"So, Mr. Gold," Brandon began. "It looks like this is your lucky day, since the prince has use of you. I am prepared to let you go on one condition."

"Which is?" said the smaller man, crossing his arms and looking Brandon straight in the eye.

"The object I bought from you so many years ago didn't

work." Brandon clasped his hands behind his back as he circled Marcus. "You will get me one that does. And this time I am coming with you." He stopped in front of his prisoner.

"The object you seek can only be found among the witch tribes of Rohron," said Marcus. "But I cannot guarantee it will work. It depends on the power of the witch who made it."

"What is it you are after, Brandon?" said Rafe, looking perturbed at where this conversation was going. "The magic of the witches of Rohron is unpredictable and rooted in dark power. I would advise against seeking out any of their magical objects."

"It is an object that will let me speak with my dead sister," Brandon elaborated. "It is the only way I can say goodbye."

Rafe was silent, and so was Marcus. Brandon looked so forlorn and I felt bad for him. I went up to him and patted his back. "If there is such an object, I'm sure Marcus can find it." My thoughts whirled with the prospect. Maybe I could speak to my father as well? But first they had to find it, and I had other problems on my plate.

Marcus nodded. "I know where we can get one, but it won't be easy. We will have to go through Brandor—the Illiadorian border is now closed."

Brandon thought for a moment. "We can travel together to Brandor with you," he said to Rafe. "Then Marcus and I can go on to Rohron from there."

"It's settled then." Rafe concluded the conversation. "Tomorrow we leave for Calos and you can introduce us to Santino. I hope he is willing to help us."

The steward of the castle came in to announce dinner was served. Marcus declined the invitation, and since Brandon had agreed to release him from the dungeons, he sent for guards to escort him to a guest room.

Brandon gave me his arm to lead me to dinner, and I took it, not wanting to be rude to our host. He had been hospitable, and it was good of him to warn us about what was happening in Neris. But I did think it was quite the coincidence he was traveling to Calos at around the same time we were. I shook my head as if to shake off the silly thoughts that entered. Coincidences happened all the time, but my intuition kept telling me I was not wrong to be suspicious.

The dining room was a large high-ceilinged hall, with intricately embroidered tapestries lining the cold stone walls. Four places had been set at one end of the massive oak dining table, which was beautifully decorated with flowers and large silver candelabras. A fire crackled in the stone fireplace and I was glad for it.

Brandon held my chair as I sat down next to Kalen and opposite Rafe, looking out at the three large windows shut against the biting chill of the mountain air. Huge brass chandeliers hung from the rafters of the ceiling, generously lit with thousands of candles which warmed the room with their golden glow.

Brandon took his place at the head of the table as white-gloved, liveried footmen stood in a line, each one holding a large platter topped with a silver-domed cloche to keep the food warm. Once we sat down they came over to serve us one by one, opening the cloches with a flourish and revealing the delicacies underneath.

Brandon looked amused at the portions I took on my plate, but I was so hungry and everything looked so good I couldn't resist. There was fig glazed roast pork with a rich red wine sauce, a chicken and leek pie with a buttery crust, honey roasted vegetables, roast venison wrapped with crispy bacon, honey corn bread, lemon curd tarts, and steamed treacle pudding with a honeycomb cream. Brandon raised an eyebrow when I asked for my third helping of treacle pudding. Rafe, of course, was used to my appetite and seemed entertained by Brandon's face when I polished off all the food.

After dinner was done, Brandon walked us to our rooms himself through long drafty corridors to the east wing, as moonlight bathed the old stone castle in a spectral white sheen.

"I know you must be tired, and I won't keep you," he said, bowing to me at the door of my room. "I will send your breakfast up to your room in the morning so you can rest, and take your time getting ready."

Rafe ignored Brandon. "We will leave at daybreak, Aurora. The faster we get on that ship to Brandor, the better."

"As you wish, Your Highness," said Brandon, a wry smile playing at the corner of his mouth.

Rafe's eyes narrowed.

Brandon took my hand gently and brought it to his lips, his cerulean blue eyes never leaving mine. "The journey to Calos is not long. But I do look forward to getting to know you better, my lady."

I could see Rafe scowl behind Brandon. Blushing, I gently pulled my hand away. "Thank you, Brandon. Goodnight, Rafe," I said quickly, and opened the door to my room.

It was big and ornate, with a large, wooden, four-poster bed hung with dark green velvet and trimmed with gold. There were only two windows, and they were shuttered. The castle, although warmed suitably by large stone fireplaces, had a very cold and dismal sense to it. It felt as if the rooms had never experienced any real warmth.

There was a knock at the door.

"Who is it?" I called out, whirling around.

The door opened and two young housemaids came in, with three footmen who were carrying a large wooden tub. They set it down in the center of the room and proceeded to fill it up.

A bath! That would be perfect. It had been days since I'd had a real bath, in a tub, with soap.

The maids insisted on helping me undress. They put me in the hot tub and soaped me with a lavender scented soap from head to toe, washing all the dust and dirt of the long journey out of my hair.

The younger maid, with soulful doe eyes under thick lashes, dressed me in a bright green robe and sat me down in front of the ornate dressing table, brushing my hair until it shone. "How lovely you look, my lady. I was shocked when his lordship asked us to open this room and clean it. It hasn't been used for years." She put the brush down. "Now, however, I can see why he wanted you in this special room."

I turned to look at her and a sudden chill scuttled down my spine. "Why? Who did this room belong to?"

"This was the room of our mistress, the Lady Riora, madam," said the older maid, her nose hooked and a white cap tied under her sharp chin. "Lord Delacourt's late sister."

Orange and gold flames flickered and crackled in the fireplace, which had recently been lit with dry wood, and I wondered why Brandon had put me here. Wouldn't it have been easier to put me in smaller guest quarters? Sleeping in a dead woman's room that hadn't been used for over twenty years seemed too creepy.

I thanked them, shrugging off the eerie feeling that had crept into the room.

The maids had the tub cleared away, just as another showed up with a little silver tray carrying a mug of warm vanilla milk, topped with thick cream and dusted with cinnamon.

Brandon was very generous. But what did he hope to gain by helping me?

I left the candles burning and shot a fire strike at the fireplace to reinforce the flames, and the fire roared to life. At least I was next door to Rafe and Kalen's room—I was glad they were within shouting distance.

I had a few sips of milk and lay down on the plush bed, covering myself to my chin and snuggling under the warm blankets. I stared at the opulent velvet canopy, elaborately embroidered with gold thread and woven to look like stars in the night sky. And realized I was right back where I started.

I was a fugitive once again.

4
MASQUERADE

THE JOURNEY TO the seaside town of Calos would take about four days. Brandon had given us new identities and clothes for the journey. I was grateful we decided to travel by coach and stop at well-kept inns along the way. My thighs ached from all the previous riding, and my bottom was terribly sore.

I peeked out of my curtained window as the carriage rambled along the main road, lurching and bumping over stones as we passed overgrown woods, open fields, and small villages. Weary travellers ambled past and farmers hurried back and forth with their wagons laden with produce to sell in the closest town. Rafe, Kalen, and Marcus rode beside the coach disguised as guards, serving as our escort. I wished it were Rafe who sat beside me instead of Brandon.

While we travelled, Brandon proceeded to tell me more about the area, pointing out important historical sites and giving me more information about the kingdom of Eldoren.

"That one," Brandon pointed to the ruins of what must have once been a grand castle, "was once the largest fortress in southern Eldoren."

"What happened to it?" I scanned the charred structure that remained.

"They say it was burned to the ground over two decades ago by the Prince of the Night Court, a merciless High Fae warrior, who swept down from the sky and wreaked havoc on our kingdom. People in this area still talk about the Dark Prince and his fury and hatred towards the mages."

"Why did he do it?" My voice was almost a whisper.

Brandon shrugged. "I have no idea. But he nearly shattered the fragile peace between our kingdoms. It was only because Izadora, your grandmother, intervened that war between the mages and fae was averted." He paused and leaned back in his seat. "Be careful of the fae, Aurora. Not all of them are like your friend Kalen. I have heard the Royal Court of Elfi is an evil place. Full of backstabbing traitors and High Fae who believe they are so much better than everyone else. Although their numbers have dwindled to near extinction, they still think they are the masters of this world. Your grandmother may be a good queen to her people, but she is known for her ruthlessness and cunning mind, not to mention her vast powers. I would not be so eager to go to Elfi if I were you."

I nodded, trying to assimilate all he had told me about the High Fae and my grandmother's kingdom. Why was he trying to put me off going to Elfi, a place where everyone else wanted me to go? I was not sure what to believe anymore. But I knew I would never forget the story he had told me of the ruthless fae warrior who burned a whole castle and its inhabitants to the ground. An involuntary shiver darted down my spine; I hoped I would never have to meet the dreaded Prince of the Night Court when I went to Elfi.

On the last day of our journey, Brandon turned to me in the carriage. "I hope you don't find this too forward, Aurora. I would love to hear your story. I've heard bits and pieces; mostly rumors that have been spreading since people realized you were still alive. I want to hear what actually happened."

I smiled at Brandon. He was sweet, and he did seem like a good friend who wanted to help. Still, there was something about him that disturbed me. I couldn't put my finger on what it was. I realized I had to be on my guard with everyone I met from now on. I had learned my lesson, and I was more careful with what I revealed and to whom. I proceeded to tell him my story, leaving out big chunks of it, of course. I couldn't tell him about the *Book of Abraxas* and the keys, or about the Dagger and my mother.

Brandon listened intently and cursed the Blackwaters under his breath at the very mention of Damien's name. "The Blackwaters can never be trusted. They are snakes, all of them. Each one worse than the next."

I nodded. "I learned the hard way." I told him about

Damien's betrayal. I had been such a fool, thinking they couldn't possibly be so bad, that they were not truly evil. But I was so wrong.

I wrapped my cloak tighter around me. Brandon had given me a warm green one lined with fur. It was very snug, but it was getting colder by the day and even inside the coach my fingers were frozen. I hid my hands under my cloak to try to keep them warm. "How can the king pardon them after their treachery?"

"It does seem strange." Brandon leaned over to close the carriage window, which was ajar and letting in the chill. "But Devon Blackwater—Damien's father—is the king's cousin, his father's sister's son. They are family after all, and next in line to the throne if anything happens to Rafael."

"But surely the king will come to his senses soon, once Prince Rafael returns and tells him what actually happened?"

"I'm not so sure," said Brandon, crossing his arms. "I wouldn't underestimate the Blackwaters."

"That's what Rafe always says."

"So, it's Rafe now, is it?" said Brandon with an amused chuckle. "I've seen the way you two look at each other. I suspect Prince Rafael has made another conquest."

I sat up straighter and tried to look indignant. "What do you mean?" I knew what he meant, but I felt so stupid when he said it. "We are friends, that's all."

"I meant no disrespect, Aurora, but I can see clearly that

you are more than friends with the prince. A man does not leave his kingdom and family to go running after a girl if he doesn't have strong feelings for her. I've never seen him like this. His duty to his kingdom has always come first. Until now."

"He was just helping me with something." I was not eager to explain myself any more than I had to. "When I go to Elfi, he will return to Eldoren and marry Leticia." I tried to make myself sound like I didn't care, but I don't think I succeeded.

"Probably, but he is not thinking very clearly right now. Rafe's very presence is a danger to you. He is recognized throughout the land, and is much more conspicuous than you would be if you were traveling with someone else."

"Like you?" I said, bluntly.

Brandon shrugged. "I am the likely candidate. I will make sure you get to Elfi safely, I give you my word. But you must be the one to tell Rafe to go back. If you don't do it now, he will lose his crown and Morgana will be one step closer to becoming High Queen of all Avalonia."

I looked down. He was right, I was being selfish. I wanted Rafe to stay with me as long as he could before he went back, but if he did, he might not have anything to go back to. Without Rafe, Brandon was the only other person who could get me to Elfi. No one else wanted anything to do with me. They wanted to lock me up and throw away the key.

"I see you are besotted with him, however much you may

try to hide it." Brandon didn't smile. "But there is no future for you with Rafael. He will never marry you." He looked away. "I know I shouldn't be telling you any of this, and he is one of my oldest friends, but I can't sit by and see such a wonderful girl get hurt by him again."

"How many women has he been with?"

Brandon gave me a half smile. "Quite a few more than I can keep track of, I can tell you that."

"I thought he'd been betrothed to Leticia for years?"

"That part is true, but it didn't stop Rafael from breaking hearts all the way from Andrysia to Brandor."

My face fell and Brandon shook his head. "I am sorry, Aurora. I should not have overstepped my bounds. It is not my place to tell you or Rafael what to do. I can only give you advice on the matter. And I don't want him to know we had this conversation."

"I won't mention it."

"If you care for him, you must convince him to go back as soon as possible," Brandon added.

I nodded, burying myself further into my cloak and ending our talk. Brandon did seem very concerned about Rafe, and maybe he was being sincere about his eagerness to help me. But he didn't mind spilling Rafe's secrets to me, and I couldn't help wondering what Brandon's agenda was. I was going to have to be more careful around him. If he wanted me to trust him, he was going to have to prove himself first.

On the fourth day of our journey we reached Calos, a big seaside town which lay further east along the Emerald Coast of Eldoren. Autumn had come and gone and fallen leaves, in shades of gold and brown, crunched beneath the horse's hooves. Although Calos wasn't anywhere as big as Neris, the capital city of Eldoren, I had read in my books at the Academy that it was a big trading hub and shipping town.

A cold November thunderstorm had washed clean the approaching winter air. The wheels of our carriage clattered over the cobblestones and splashed through muddy puddles as the coach lurched and jolted its way toward the docks. The smell of fish permeated the air with a thick stench and the streets were crowded and bustling with merchants going about their daily business. Warehouses were stocked to full capacity, and traders from all parts of Avalonia were haggling and selling their wares at street corners and along the quay.

Brandon pointed out two massive warships. "We need to stay away from those," he said as our carriage rolled up the main cobbled avenue of the seaside town. "They are part of the royal Eldorean fleet posted here in Calos."

I looked out of the window, studying the area and the ships anchored in the bay. There were whalers from Andrysia, and small fishing boats from the villages and towns on the Eldorean Coast. Some of the big ships were passenger schooners from Illiador and many looked like merchant galleons, which Brandon explained were actually slave ships from the far eastern kingdoms of Brandor and Rohron. I wondered which one belonged to the Pirate Prince, Santino Valasis, and I was intrigued and a little apprehensive about meeting him. I hoped Brandon managed to convince him to take us to Sanria.

"The customs guards here are more interested in making money than checking the cargo," Brandon informed me. "Many a pirate and slaver has dealings with the people of Calos. It is one of the major southern ports, and the main trade here is smuggling slaves and black market items from the far reaches of Avalonia. I'm sure Marcus will feel right at home."

Finally, we stopped at a large whitewashed inn. Brandon opened the door of the carriage, jumping out as I gazed up at the structure. Pretty, wooden shutters opened out to a wonderful view of the azure blue coast of the Stardust Sea. Wisteria cascaded down from every windowsill and the roof was painted a beautiful powder blue, complementing the violet flowers.

Brandon gave me his hand and helped me out of the carriage. My legs were stiff from sitting for so long. And my backside, although not quite so sore as it would be after riding, was still hurting after all the numerous bumps along the road from Roth to Calos.

Calos was an interesting town, rising on one side of a hill

and overlooking the vast coastline. All the streets connected to a main avenue and a maze of houses and cobbled walkways led to the docks.

Brandon got us rooms facing the ocean, and as I stood at my window, the crisp air of the afternoon breeze cleared my head. There was a wooden tub with fresh warm water waiting for me in the center of the room and I removed my clothes, soaked my tired body, and washed off all the grime of the journey. I changed into a simple brown dress with long sleeves and washed my pants, shirt, and doublet, hanging them on the chair to dry. They were the only other items of clothing I had carried with me.

There was a knock on the door and two footmen carried in a big chest, putting it down in the center of the room. "A gift from Lord Delacourt, my lady," said one, as they both bowed.

"What is it?" I was suitably intrigued. Brandon did know how to spoil a lady. I went over to the chest and opened it. Out spilled a variety of beautiful dresses, each more sumptuous and extravagant than the next. Why had he sent me these? Warm milk and a hot bath were one thing, but this! This was too much.

"For the ball tonight, my lady," said the same footman.

"What ball?" Did Brandon expect me to accompany him to his cousin's wedding? Wouldn't that be too dangerous?

"Our orders were to deliver this to you, my lady." The

footman bowed again and they left the room.

I sat down on the edge of the bed and stared at the beautiful dresses before me. What was Brandon up to? We couldn't go out in public—the whole Eldorean guard was looking for me. We were supposed to find Santino and sail for Brandor as soon as we could.

Rafe had warned me to stay in my room and I obeyed. I didn't want to cause unnecessary trouble. He said he had something to do, and I was curious as to what was so important he would wander around the town with the risk of getting caught.

Normally I would have gone looking for him or insisted on accompanying Brandon myself to speak to Santino, but I had lost all confidence in myself and my decisions. Every time I tried to do something I thought was right, it turned into a disaster. Now I had to tell myself time and time again that I should listen to others who knew better. This was my time to learn, not be foolish and get myself killed. I had to stay alive long enough to get to Elfi and my grandmother.

I lay down and took a nap, the fresh sea breeze lulling me into a calm sleep.

When I awoke, it was evening, and twilight was starting to set in. I rose from my bed and stared out of the window at the dusky pink sky that lay above the water. The setting sun had turned the bay into a myriad of red and orange, while ships with colorful sails danced on the waves, bobbing up and down on the shimmering sea.

Rafe came to see me. He eyed the dresses with a raised eyebrow, and I explained that Brandon had sent them over.

"I spoke to Brandon." Rafe ignored the dresses. "It seems trying to see Santino on his ship today will not be possible. He sails for Brandor tomorrow."

"Did Brandon tell him who we are?"

Rafe nodded. "He had to. If Santino finds out we lied to him, we could end up at the bottom of the Stardust Sea. He has spies everywhere, and must already know we are in town. He will not bother us unless we cross him. He is notorious for taking up lost causes." He smiled.

I did not. "But has he agreed to take us with him?"

"You being who you are may be the one thing that will make him agree to take us," Rafe went on. "He wants to meet you, then he will decide."

"Where? I thought you said we couldn't meet him on his ship today."

"We can't, so Brandon has fixed a meeting between us and Santino at the masquerade ball tonight."

"So that's why Brandon sent those dresses."

Rafe nodded. "Choose one and get ready. There should be some masks in there as well. If everything goes as planned, we will be on a ship to Brandor by tomorrow. It is imperative that we convince Santino to help us and leave as soon as possible. This town is crawling with guards, it's only a matter of time before one of us are recognized." He turned to leave.

"Maybe you should go back," I said, remembering what Brandon had told me, before I changed my mind. "I can manage from here on." My throat was so dry I could barely get the words out. "Once we meet Santino and I get on the ship, you can return to the palace and sort this all out with your father. You can't allow Morgana's minions to get control of your kingdom."

Rafe smiled. "I won't let her do that." He came closer and took my hand in his. "What brought this on?"

I shook my head and looked at my feet.

"I'm not going to leave you, Aurora, I had hoped you would know that by now," he said softly. "I don't trust anyone else with your safety, least of all Brandon and a pirate. I will see to it that you get to Elfi myself."

"Because of the debt to my father?"

Rafe laughed and his eyes crinkled at the corners. "No, Aurora. That was an excuse to spend more time around you and not look like a complete fool when you questioned my motives for always turning up when you needed me. I didn't want you to think I was a stalker."

I smiled at this. "And were you?"

"What?"

"Stalking me?" I teased.

Rafe shrugged, but I could see the mischievous gleam in his eyes. "I wouldn't call it stalking."

"Oh! Then what would you call it?"

Rafe pulled me toward him—his hot breath grazed my ear and my legs turned to jelly as he whispered, "Protecting you, my love."

His lips found mine and he kissed me; gently at first, and then more insistently, pressing me firmly against him. My passion flared as I wrapped my arms around his neck, trying to get closer. I knew this was not right, that he was engaged to be married, but I didn't want it to stop.

Still I knew that I had to, and I slowly broke away, trying to steady my breathing.

Rafe stepped back. "Get ready," he said briskly. "I will see you downstairs in an hour."

The ball was to be held at the bride's father's home. He was a cousin of Brandon's father and a very wealthy merchant. The magnificent white mansion was the largest on the hill and overlooked the town and the sea beyond. Terraced gardens were opulently transformed into what looked like a miniature fairyland, with lengths of sumptuous gold fabric draped across the trees like an open tent.

As I walked down the steps on Rafe's arm, no one noticed me. My gold lace mask hid my identity for the night and I had reddened my lips with a bit of magic, keeping with the theme of the ball. Brandon walked ahead, but Kalen and

Marcus stayed behind at the inn.

Beautiful masked women in a myriad of silks and brocades flitted about the gardens on the arm of many a well-dressed gentleman. Plumes and feathers, sparkling with precious gems, made my simple lace mask seem extremely plain. But it complemented my emerald green dress, the tight embroidered bodice of which was suffocating me as I walked.

Rafe was dressed in an unadorned black doublet with a black and silver mask, slightly different to the one he used as the Black Wolf. I gazed up at him as his lean six-foot frame dwarfed me.

"Where do we have to meet Santino?" I looked around as Rafe and Brandon scanned the grounds. Sparkling chandeliers hung from the branches, lighting up the garden, and candles shone on the white and gold fabric-covered tables, decorated with grand flower arrangements.

Brandon led Rafe and me to a man dressed all in black, wearing a silver mask over his short-clipped beard. His hair was dark, long, and held back in a ponytail. Brandon briefly whispered something in his ear.

The man turned his rich amber eyes on me and bowed. "Santino Valasis at your service, my lady," he said in a deep voice, taking my hand in his and planting a lingering kiss, a smile playing on the corner of his full lips.

I smiled and murmured an appropriate greeting.

"I am charmed to meet you," said Santino. "Delacourt

did tell me you were beautiful, but I see mere words do not do you justice."

Against my better judgment, I blushed. Santino was a flirt—he couldn't in truth see my whole face. But Brandon had said he was our only way out of Eldoren and we needed his ship.

"And you know who this is, of course," said Brandon, keeping his voice low and introducing Rafe. "Although I don't believe you have ever met."

Santino clasped Rafe's forearm. "I've heard a lot about you," he said, looking Rafe straight in the eye.

Rafe didn't flinch. "Likewise," he said. "Tales of the Pirate Prince have reached the highest of circles amongst the Eldorean nobility."

Santino laughed. "Yes, I'm sure they have," he replied good-naturedly. "And tales of the Black Wolf have been circulating through Brandor for some time now," he added softly.

"It looks like your spies have been keeping busy," Rafe said.

"They wouldn't be very useful if they didn't," Santino countered with a grin.

Rafe smiled. "Point taken."

A beautiful, olive-skinned women, wearing an extravagant maroon dress with a skirt so big it made her look like a birthday cake, came up to Santino and caught his arm. Her hair was a rich burnished mahogany and she wore a heavy gold tiara that screamed royalty.

"Santino, my darling brother," the woman declared, glancing at me briefly and settling her eyes on Rafe. "Aren't you going to introduce me to your friends?" She adjusted her mask—a feathery concoction of gold plumes, studded liberally with ostentatious rubies.

Rafe looked uncomfortable.

Santino smirked. "I believe you already know the young man before you, Katerina."

Katerina held out her hand to Rafe, her red lips parting in a sensual smile. "Yes, I believe I do," she said, in a heavily accented voice, as Rafe bowed and rather stiffly gave her a peck on her hand, straightening immediately.

I glanced at the two of them. Katerina was gazing up at Rafe as if he were the only man at the ball. How did they know each other? She must have known him quite well if she recognized him with his mask on.

Two giggling women came over and whispered in Santino's ear. He grinned. "I will leave you all to get acquainted. These poor women need a dance partner and I wouldn't want to disappoint them."

Katerina laughed, a deep, throaty sound. "My brother has still to learn how to say no to a beautiful woman."

I smiled as I watched Santino saunter off into the crowd, one girl on each arm.

"My brother said we were to take an Andrysian noble's daughter to Brandor with us," she said to Rafe. "But he did not say who the other passengers were."

"I'm sure he simply forgot to mention it," Rafe said tersely.

"Oh, Santino forgets nothing." Katerina snaked her arm through his. "Take me to dance, Rafael," she cooed in his ear, but still loud enough for me to hear. "It's been so long since you held me in your arms."

Rafe shook his head. "You know I don't dance, Katerina."

But that didn't deter her.

"For me?" She looked at him with her slightly upturned eyes, batting her luscious lashes, while her mouth turned downward in an extremely sexy pout. "I'm sure you can make an exception. After all, we will be spending the next few days squashed together aboard my brother's ship."

I knew Rafe couldn't argue with that. If Katerina told Santino not to take us on his ship, we would be stranded here with no way to get to Brandor except through the desert that separated the two kingdoms. It would take days to find another merchant who would be brave enough or stupid enough to take us.

Katerina pulled Rafe away from me and toward the center of the garden. He glanced back for a moment, but I quickly looked away. I didn't want him to know I was bothered. He was free to do what he wished, with whomever he wished.

Katerina was Leticia's problem, not mine.

Katerina pressed herself against him as they danced, and soon they were lost in the melee of masked couples on the dance floor, locked in romantic embraces and enjoying the freedom the masks gave them to behave in a manner they would not usually attempt.

I was left alone on the side, looking at what I believed to be the love of my life in the arms of another woman, and my heart sank. I had to steel myself against my feelings for Rafe—eventually they would go away, or at least that was what I kept trying to convince myself.

Brandon, who had been talking to someone else, spotted me and came over. "Why are you out here alone, Aurora?" His blue eyes gazed at me with genuine concern. "I thought you were with Rafe."

"He went to dance with Katerina Valasis." I looked over to the dance floor, but I couldn't see them anymore.

"Ah!" Brandon sighed with a note of sympathy in his voice I hated to hear. "I should have warned you about Katerina, but after so many years I didn't think she still wanted him. I should have known better. Rafael does tend to have that effect on women."

"Rafe was with her?"

Brandon nodded slightly. "They courted for a while, when Rafael was on an official visit to Brandor with his father. Santino was away at the time, so he never met the prince, but Katerina fell instantly in love with him."

"What happened?" I wasn't sure I was going to like the answer.

"Rafael did what he always does," said Brandon, and I thought I detected a hint of jealousy in his voice. "He left to go back to Eldoren without a backward glance. And Katerina was left heartbroken."

My face fell. Rafe had been with so many women, and I had to wonder if I was also another one of his dalliances.

Brandon took my hand and placed it in the crook of his elbow. "Come, we can have a walk around the gardens," said Brandon, smiling. "Or maybe you would like to dance?"

"No, let's walk." I shook my head, putting my hand on Brandon's arm as he led me through the meandering garden paths, my thoughts whirling about Rafe and Katerina.

We passed the dancing couples and I saw Santino still swaying to the music with some new woman he had found since I last saw him. She was fawning over him and dancing closely, her voluptuous breasts the center of the Pirate Prince's attention. I smiled. Santino was a complete rake and a massive flirt, but he seemed quite straightforward as far as I could tell. I hoped Brandon knew what he was doing by asking us to trust a pirate, even if he was a prince.

I spotted Rafe at the edge of the formal gardens, near a wooded area of the grounds. He was with Katerina; I recognized the dress. They were deep in conversation and Rafe was holding Katerina's hand in his as they spoke.

My heart slumped in my chest. For some reason this revelation hurt more than seeing him with Leticia. At least I knew he was marrying Leticia out of duty. But this exotic princess, who was clearly still in love with him, broke through my defenses. A dull ache seemed to clamp around my heart. I knew we were only supposed to be friends, but I thought what we had was special. However, the more I discovered about him, the more I realized there was so much I didn't know.

Suddenly there was a commotion in the gardens, voices were raised, and the musicians stopped playing.

"Everybody, please stay where you are," came a loud, booming voice.

I had heard that voice before, and I never thought I would again. I looked over to the steps, and my heart skipped a beat. I grabbed Brandon's hand.

Lord Oblek was standing at the top of the grand staircase, surrounded by at least twenty of Morgana's guards, all wearing the crest of a black rose. I recognized two of them flanking Oblek. Blue Cloaks, the king of Eldoren's elite warrior mages. What was Oblek doing here?

"Stay where you are and no one will get hurt," said Lord Oblek, scanning the garden. "No one leaves the mansion until I have checked your identities, by order of the king."

"Not until you tell us what is going on," shouted one old gentleman.

Oblek grinned at the crowd, a wolfish smile, and stepped to one side.

A black-cloaked figure moved forward, gliding down the steps to the garden. His robes were dark as night with a gold border edging the flowing fabric. He removed his hood, and his dark piercing gaze immediately quieted the garden. No one moved—it was as if he had the power to stop them with a single glance. I recognized the markings on his robes. There was only one mage who wore black with a gold border.

The archmage!

Lucian had come after me himself.

5
THE ARCHMAGE
OF AVALONIA

I FROZE. My legs started shaking and my palms became clammy. I wiped them on my dress. I knew I was only moments away from getting caught and dragged back to Morgana, this time in chains. People had already started removing their masks. It was only a matter of time until Oblek recognized me. There was nowhere to hide.

"I would suggest you do as I say, and remove your masks," said Lord Oblek, addressing the crowd again, his voice reverberating across the quiet garden.

Everyone did as they were told. The mere presence of the archmage was enough to bend them to his will. I looked around. Someone had betrayed us. Was it Santino?

I spotted Rafe, slowly moving through the crowd toward me. Katerina had removed her mask and was clutching his arm for dear life and trying to pull him the other way.

"Once the guards are busy checking people, we will move toward those trees," Brandon whispered, inclining his head toward the wooded area on the far side of the garden.

I nodded, and Brandon caught my hand, squeezing it tightly. "Stay close. I won't let anything happen to you."

The guests started lining up and Oblek checked their identities personally. But I couldn't see Santino anywhere. The archmage walked in front of the guards, and all the mages bowed as he passed by. I hadn't known he commanded such subservience from the mage community.

But how did the king allow him and Oblek to head the search for me? I knew the Blackwaters were involved in this; after all, Lucian was Sorcha Blackwater's brother. But with what Morgana was doing to Avalonia, how could he support them? It hurt to know that the king of Eldoren thought so little of me. I had thought he liked me, and he was always so good to me when I was at the palace. But now he seemed to think I was capable of kidnapping his son and trying to take over his kingdom. It looked like I was a worse judge of character than I thought.

As Brandon and I reached the far end of the garden, a voice behind us stopped us in our tracks.

"Stop! No one leaves until the archmage has seen them," said Oblek.

It was over. There was no escape.

There were too many people. If I used my magic and someone got hurt, it would make them fear me more. And this time it was a fight I couldn't win. The archmage was known for his power over dark magic. I could feel his menacing presence before I turned to face him. I had learned to sense magic around me and in others, and I was slowly getting better at it. But I didn't have to concentrate to feel his power. The air was thick with his malignant presence. It was like black tendrils of a menacing shadow that spread out across the garden.

I finally turned to look at Lord Oblek. Two blue-cloaked warrior mages flanked him, surrounded by four guards.

"Remove your mask, sir," Oblek demanded.

Brandon slowly removed his mask and ran his hands through his thick blond hair. "Brandon Delacourt at your service, my lord." He inclined his head in a perfect imitation of Santino.

"And the lady?" my old nemesis asked, looking straight into my eyes.

"She's no one, my lord, just my, um . . . how should I say . . . companion for the night," said Brandon, winking at the guard who stood behind Oblek.

The guard sniggered at this. And my hackles went up. My magic flared and I had half a mind to stun that stupid grin off the guard's face. But I pushed it back down. It wouldn't do me any good; as it was, they already thought I was a monster.

Oblek didn't believe Brandon's story for a minute. "I still need to see her face." He looked into my eyes. "Remove your mask, madam."

I had no choice. Slowly I bowed my head and untied my mask, finally looking up to face Oblek. He didn't look surprised to see me, as a wide grin spread across his scarred face.

"It is she!" said Oblek loudly, and the guards stepped apart to allow the archmage through.

Lucian stalked toward me with an almost feline grace. He was not what I expected. Tall and impressively built, the archmage had long, obsidian-black hair tied in a ponytail, slightly graying at the temples, the only thing giving away his age.

"The amulet?" said the archmage. "Let me see it." His voice was a soft caress, silky and smooth. He didn't have to raise his voice to be heard, but his tone was one you could not disobey.

Oblek stepped forward, and I took a step back.

The archmage raised his right hand. "Come here." His eyes were dark as night, shaded beneath strong eyebrows, and his fine features, strong chin, and aristocratic nose only added to his regal presence. He might not be a king, but in the mage world he commanded as much respect.

My legs moved of their own accord. Darkness pulsed out of him and tendrils of shadow pressed against my magic as if they were trying to find a way to latch onto it. I struggled to free myself from his hold, but it felt like invisible hands were tugging me forward. His long, elegant fingers clasped the chain around my neck and pulled my amulet from within my gown.

The archmage smiled, a savage grin. "Finally, we meet,

Princess Aurora. I have been looking forward to this for fifteen long years."

"I can't say the same," I said bluntly.

"I'm glad you didn't try to run," said the archmage, ignoring my remark. "Personally, I thought you would—you are known to be quite reckless." He walked slowly around me, his hands behind his back, eyeing me from every angle, assessing his enemy.

I was rooted to the spot. My legs felt like rocks had been attached to them; I couldn't move however much I tried.

He stopped circling and looked me in the eyes. "It would have been futile, of course. The whole mansion is surrounded, you wouldn't have gotten far."

My eyes darted across the garden. How were we going to get out of this? There was no sign of Rafe anywhere; I couldn't see Santino either, or Katerina. If Santino left on that ship tomorrow, we would have no way of getting another person to take us to Brandor. Especially with the guards and Blue Cloaks prowling every inch of Calos. Where was Rafe? Was he with Katerina?

"You have no authority here," said Brandon, squaring his shoulders and stepping forward to stand beside me.

"I beg to differ, Lord Delacourt." Lucian's voice was sweet and silky, but laced with an unmistakable trace of steel. "As Archmage of Avalonia, all mages come directly within my jurisdiction. And if you read the fine print in the treaty of the seven kingdoms, which I presume you have not, if there is a threat to the safety of the Mage Guild, my authority supersedes every ruler in every kingdom."

"I'm not a threat to anyone," I said.

"That's for me to decide," said the archmage. "Bind her hands." He gestured to the guards. "And Lord Delacourt, since you, too, are one of us, a mage with affiliation to the Mage Guild, you are under arrest as well, for assisting a known criminal."

The guards moved forward to hold Brandon and bind his wrists.

"I am not a criminal," I said between clenched teeth. It would be so easy to knock them all down. All I had to do was remove my amulet and unleash my magic, which had built up to a huge pulsating ball inside me. It had been a while since I had used it, and it wanted out.

I pushed it back down, subduing the beast that had begun to wake inside me. For that is exactly what it felt like, a great slumbering beast, one that woke when I took off my amulet. The real Aurora Firedrake, the fae-mage who was not afraid of anyone, who could kill without remorse and bend powerful magic to her will. I knew now that person was buried inside me, waiting for me to unleash her on the world. But I was not ready, I was not strong enough to let her out again. My amulet kept her in check, but not for long.

"Where is Prince Rafael?" one blue-cloaked warrior mage

asked. I recognized him from my time at the palace: Captain Gerard, leader of the palace guards. "Is he with the Black Wolf?"

"Do you actually believe I kidnapped the prince and dragged him halfway across the kingdom?" I snapped at the captain.

"It doesn't matter what I think." Captain Gerard glanced briefly at Lucian.

The archmage smirked.

"The king has ordered me to bring you both back to the palace," the captain continued. "And that is exactly what I am going to do."

One of his men came forward to address Captain Gerard and Lord Oblek. "We have searched the other guests and the Black Wolf is nowhere to be found, my lord."

Oblek turned his eyes on me, took a step forward, and gave me a warning look. "Tell us where your accomplice is. That scoundrel has made a fool of me and my guards for the last time."

"Tell us where he has taken the prince and my king will be lenient with you," Captain Gerard added.

I had had enough. My anger flared, and my magic pulsed through my body. I pushed hard against Lucian's power that was holding me rooted to the spot. The archmage's eyes widened as I shattered his hold over me and walked up to Oblek and the captain.

"I have told you once, Captain Gerard," I snarled softly, looking him straight in the eyes. "I did not kidnap your prince, and I don't know where he is. Maybe you should check the brothels and taverns back in Neris. That is where he usually spends all his time, I hear."

Captain Gerard's eyes went wide, and his face changed to the color of fresh beetroot.

"And as for the Black Wolf," I addressed my old enemy Oblek, "you will never catch him, for he's a better warrior mage than you can ever hope to be."

Lucian chuckled, and his face distorted into what I presumed was a grin. "That's the Firedrake princess all right. My nephew Damien told me she had quite a temper. Exactly like her father, this one."

Lucian raised his hand. Pain shot through my body and I gasped, clutching my chest as I fell to my knees.

"Do not think your innate gifts are any match for mine, little princess," said the Archmage of Avalonia. "I've mastered powers you have never dreamed of, long before you were born."

Dark magic clawed at my body as I tried to defend myself. Lucian smiled calmly as if it were no effort for him. I had no idea how to break his hold over me this time, and his sinister power was suffocating mine.

I could see Brandon struggling to move toward me, but two guards held him back. My vision blurred and I tried to force back the shadows twisting around me. The world started swimming before my eyes, and the pain kept building, until finally my magic weakened and I fell to the ground, darkness forming an ebony veil before my eyes as I lost consciousness.

When I awoke, I was bound and lying on the floor of a dark room. My mouth felt dry and my tongue was like sandpaper. The metallic tang of Lucian's magic remained, leaving a sour taste at the back of my throat. I pushed myself up into a sitting position, my eyes adjusting to the lack of light. Something scurried away beside me, and I drew my legs up closer. I hoped it wasn't rats—I hated rats!

I looked around. I was in some sort of cellar under the mansion—barrels of wine and ale lined the dank walls. I shivered as I tried to use my magic to untie the ropes around my hands, but it didn't work. I couldn't recreate the magic I had performed in the ruins with Morgana, because I never really knew what I was doing.

I slumped back against the cold stone wall, gazing around. I knew it was too much to hope for Rafe to rescue me again; but I hoped he had escaped. If Oblek found out he was the Black Wolf, his cover would be blown and he would not be able to help the fae anymore.

The door opened and Lucian strode in, stopping a few feet away. "Good, you're awake."

"Where's Brandon?" I struggled with my bonds, but they remained firmly in place.

"Don't worry, your little boyfriend is fine," Lucian said, clasping his hands in front of him and eyeing me warily. His stare was cool and calculating. "Well, maybe not fine, but he's alive, at least. You will get him back soon, but first I need to talk to you in private. This position suits you, princess. On your knees and at my feet where you belong."

"Go to hell," I snapped, pushing myself back against the wall. I was still light-headed, and if I tried to stand now, my legs could give way—I didn't want Lucian to realize how much his dark magic had affected me.

He moved closer and, without touching me, pulled me up, holding me against the wall with his magic.

"Oh, I'm sure hell is where I will end up, eventually." A sardonic grin formed on his lips as he held me pinned to the wall. "You should learn to behave better with your elders, princess. Especially those who could give you what you want."

"You and Morgana have been hunting me for months, and planned to kill me," I spat. "I want nothing from you."

"Ah! But you will, little princess," said the archmage, "and you will change your tune when you hear what I have to offer."

"You have nothing to offer me," I snarled.

He glided closer, his voice silky and smooth like a caress.

"I can offer you more than your incompetent Prince Rafael or that rogue the Black Wolf." His breath was warm against my cheek as he spoke into my ear. I tried to move away but his magic held me rooted to the spot. "You and I together would be unstoppable, Aurora. Marry me, and I will make you High Queen of all Avalonia."

Was he serious? Did he think I would marry him to get the throne?

"What about Morgana?" I was eager to keep him talking, while my mind processed this. Would he betray his queen to gain power?

"I will take care of Morgana, you needn't worry about her." The archmage moved back slightly.

"You are just her lackey, what can you do to her?" I tried to goad him. I needed more information, I had to keep him talking.

"You underestimate me, young princess." Lucian's features distorted into a cruel sneer. "I know what Morgana is hiding. I know her secret. I know the real reason she had Azaren killed and why she wants you dead so badly."

She had a secret?

"If you agree to marry me, I will tell you what it is," he said, coming closer.

"And that would conveniently make you High King."

"That is the whole point of the offer." His hand moved to caress my hip. "It wouldn't be a very good deal if I didn't get anything in return."

I recoiled at his touch and forced myself to keep my voice even. "Why not marry Morgana?"

"Morgana will never marry." Lucian scowled. "She plans to rule alone. She will never share power with anyone."

"First," I said, outwardly calm and meeting his gaze, even though my heart was beating faster than usual. "I am barely seventeen, and you are old enough to be my father, so this is very creepy. And in any case, if you were closer to my age, I wouldn't marry you if you were the last man in all of Avalonia."

His features distorted into an ugly snarl and his dark power tightened around my chest making me I gasp for breath. My own magic welled up to fight it, but with my amulet on, the beast remained caged. If I didn't learn to control it soon, there was no telling what would happen when I removed the amulet the next time. I wasn't about to take that chance and kept the amulet firmly on. I fell to my knees, pain shooting through my legs. I took deep breaths and tried desperately to shake off his hold.

Lucian quickly released his grip and turned to leave. He looked back at me with a sneer. "You should also know your dear granduncle, the illustrious Duke Silverthorne, is rotting away in the palace dungeons. There is no one to come to your aid now."

"What?!" I gasped through the pain. What the hell was

going on in Eldoren? "King Petrocales would never imprison his most trusted advisor. You're lying."

"Am I?" A devilish grin spread across his hardened face. "And I suppose you also think I am lying when I say we have an informant who knows where your dear prince is hiding."

"Who?" *Who could have betrayed us?*

"Santino Valasis, the pirate." Lucian looked extremely pleased with himself. "In fact, I'm about to go and meet him now. Once I have disposed of your prince and your so-called rescuer the Black Wolf, you will realize the best option for you is to ally yourself with me. I am your only chance for survival."

I slumped against the wall. If Santino had given us up to Lucian, this was the end. We were done for.

The door opened and Brandon was pushed down the stairs, landing at my feet with a thump. His head was bleeding. I moved to help him, but with my hands tied, I couldn't do much. I looked at the archmage, my hatred for him clearly showing in my eyes.

"You can have my answer now," I ground out between clenched teeth. "I will never marry you, not for every single crown in the seven kingdoms."

He didn't look perturbed in the least. "Think about it," he said, unimpressed by my refusal. "You have till sunrise to give me your answer."

Lucian turned and left the cellar, plunging me back into

shadow as I was cloaked in the room's murky folds.

6
AURORA FIREDRAKE

BRANDON GROANED AND tried to push himself up, but his hands were bound too. His one eye was swollen and the gash on his head was oozing blood, which trickled down the side of his face. I moved closer to him. If I could remove my bonds I could heal him. Again I tried to untie the ropes with my magic, but it wasn't working.

"What did they do to you, Brandon?"

"They wanted to know where Rafe was," Brandon groaned as he tried to sit up again. "But I didn't tell them anything." His voice was hoarse and his breathing was labored. I hoped he had not broken any ribs. "Oblek was not pleased, as you can imagine."

I made a face at the mention of my old enemy. How I wished I could encounter him with my amulet off. One day I would, I promised myself.

"What did Lucian want?" Brandon asked.

"He asked me to marry him." I laughed, despite the circumstances. I still found it absurd, although I could understand the motivation behind it. His offer had thrown me off guard.

Brandon's eyebrows rose. "I can understand his eagerness. After seeing you, any man would be besotted."

I felt bad I had got Brandon mixed up in my problems. "He thinks he can get the throne of Illiador through me," I explained. "His loyalty to Morgana is waning. He wants more power, and Morgana is not going to give it to him."

Brandon nodded. "On my way back from Andrysia, I came across a camp of rebels who call themselves the Silver Swords."

"I've never heard of them."

"Not many people have. They are a secret group of men and women who are opposed to Morgana's rule. They live in the forests of Illiador away from the towns and the capital. Although I cannot say how true this rumor is, but,"—Brandon paused—"there has been talk of Morgana looking to replace Lucian as archmage."

"That's why the sudden offer of marriage happened," I said, my brain churning with this information. "If what you say is true, than Lucian must be desperate. He will have his own agenda now and that makes him more dangerous, because we don't know what he is planning."

"There is something else. I heard Oblek's guards talking when they thought I had passed out. Captain Gerard thinks they came here to find and rescue the prince, but Lucian plans to kill Rafe on Morgana's orders."

I gasped. Kill Rafe! I had to warn him. But how? It was

too late, Santino had betrayed us and Lucian was already on his way to find him. "I thought you said we could trust Santino, but he gave us up the first chance he got."

Brandon shook his head. "I don't understand it. Santino may be a pirate, but he is also a man of his word. If he agreed to take you to Brandor, he would never give you up to Lucian. There must be something more to this."

The cellar door opened, casting a beam of light on the wooden floorboards. Captain Gerard walked down the stairs and stopped before me.

"Is it true?" His voice was brisk. "Is Lucian planning to kill the prince?" He looked at Brandon.

Brandon nodded. "Yes, it's true."

"Then there is no time to lose," he said quickly, glancing at me. "Get up! We have to get out of here before the archmage returns."

I was stunned, but only for a second. Was he helping us? I pushed myself up hurriedly—if Captain Gerard was going to get us out, I was not going to argue. But I still had questions.

"Why help us?" I asked, as he drew a knife from his belt and slit the ropes that bound my hands behind my back. I rubbed my wrists as the blood flow returned.

I moved over to assist Captain Gerard with Brandon.

"My main concern is Prince Rafael's life," said Captain Gerard, as he went to work slicing the ropes binding Brandon.

"And you believe I didn't kidnap him?"

"I do now," said the red-haired captain of the Blue Cloaks. "The prince came to me and told me you are innocent, and that he left the palace of his own accord to help you."

"But how will we leave? We have no ship. Santino has betrayed us."

"My prince has informed me the pirate's ship is ready to take you to Brandor."

"But the meeting with Lucian?" I asked, confused.

"A ruse to get the archmage out of the mansion," said Captain Gerard. "The pirate Santino has not betrayed you. He is working with Prince Rafael to lure Lucian away from here and give you enough time to escape to the ship."

I smiled. I knew Rafe would come up with a plan. He hadn't forgotten me here. It was also a great relief to know Santino was still loyal, and he was waiting for us with his ship ready to sail. At least now I had some hope of getting out of this alive.

"Thank you for helping us," I said sincerely, placing my hand on Captain Gerard's arm. He was a good man and Rafe trusted him, which was good enough for me.

The red-haired captain nodded. "Now that the Blackwaters are ruling the council and Silverthorne has been imprisoned, Prince Rafael needs to go back, or he will lose his throne." He paused and narrowed his brows. "But he won't go until he has seen you to safety. So that is what I am going to do."

Hearing the worry in Captain Gerard's voice made me realize how selfish I had been all this time. When Brandon advised me to convince Rafe to go back to Eldoren, I did so half-heartedly. I should have been more insistent. I hadn't realized how bad things were for him. All this time I was only concerned about myself and my quest to find my mother, when I should have been thinking about the bigger picture. Rafe had a kingdom of his own to protect, and my stupidity could cost him his throne.

"We must go, there is no time to waste." Captain Gerard helped Brandon up and put his arm over his shoulders.

"I can heal him. He won't get far in the state he is in." I didn't want Brandon's injury to jeopardise our escape.

"No! It will take up too much energy," insisted the captain. "I need you to have full access to your magic in case we have to fight our way out."

"I don't get tired by healing, my fae magic is different from yours."

"Make it quick," Captain Gerard conceded, glancing at the cellar door.

I gathered the magic and placed my palms on Brandon; one on his head and the other on his chest, like I had done in the test at Evolon. It was invigorating using magic again, and I remembered what I had been taught, making sure I didn't pull the magic to me.

I could feel the magic of the earth flowing into me in gentle waves, and I carefully guided it through me and into Brandon. My hands started to glow as Brandon's face healed. He groaned and closed his eyes. I could feel his broken ribs joining together and see the bruises vanishing.

Brandon sighed with relief, flexed his arms and stood up. "Thank you, Aurora, that was truly remarkable."

Captain Gerard looked at me, wide-eyed, and smiled. "Looks like I underestimated you, Princess Aurora. I will make sure I never make that mistake again."

I grinned at them both. It was fulfilling to use my powers after so long, and knowing I could call on them whenever I wanted gave me courage for what I was about to do.

Captain Gerard drew his sword. "I will go first. Oblek has stationed his guards here to make sure you don't escape."

"Where's Rafe?" I asked.

"The prince is waiting for you at the docks with Santino and his men—it was too dangerous for him to come here. All the guards would recognize him, and with Lucian intent on killing him, I didn't want him anywhere near this place. But we need to reach the ship before Lucian realizes we have tricked him."

"What about Kalen?"

"Your little fae friend is on the ship waiting for you." He adjusted the grip on his sword. "Let's go."

"Wait," I said, catching his arm. "How are we going to get

out if Oblek's men are still here?"

"Leave that to me," said Captain Gerard. "Most of them are with Lucian. But some are still here, and we may have to fight our way out. You will need to defend yourself."

I nodded, but I couldn't help doubting myself and my abilities. Every move I had made so far was a wrong one; every choice a disaster. And I had no idea how to be the person everyone expected me to be. But the captain was right. I had magic, I was trained, I should be able to do this.

"Wait here," said Captain Gerard. "I will call the guards in and distract them. I want you to stun them enough so they won't wake up for a while."

I flexed my fingers. "I think I can manage that."

"Right." He smiled at me. "Keep your amulet on and your hands behind your back until they come down the stairs."

"But what about you? Aren't you taking a big risk helping me? If Rafe can't sort all this out with his father, you could be heading to the dungeons too."

"My main concern is my prince's life. And he will not go back to the palace without knowing you are safe."

My heart fluttered. Rafe did care about me—I wasn't just one of his many women.

"Ready?" said Captain Gerard.

As ready as I can be.

I nodded and he shouted for the guards.

The door swung open, and three men burst in and ran

down the stairs with their swords out.

I gathered the magic that had been roiling inside me waiting to get out. Raising my hands, I shot two guards with a powerful stun strike as Captain Gerard did the same with the third, and they crumpled before me.

"That was easy," I said.

"Too easy," said Brandon, picking up one of the fallen guards' swords and grabbing my hand. "Let's get out of here."

We followed Captain Gerard into the deserted hall.

"Where are the other guards?" I grabbed my skirt and peered down the long moonlit corridor of the mansion. I wished I had my traveling clothes now. Escaping in a dress was always so cumbersome.

"Keep alert," whispered the captain.

We ran up a flight of stairs and down the corridor to the grand foyer. The big doors to the mansion opened and Oblek and his guards strode in.

His one eye fixed on me. "Going somewhere, little girl?" His voice had a nasty sneer to it. "I had a feeling you would pull something like this. So, I stayed back to make sure you wouldn't escape from me again."

A whole host of guards started emerging from all around us, and I whirled, looking for another way out.

There was nowhere to go but back.

Captain Gerard shot two stun strikes at the guards. One missed and one guard went down. I froze, and my heart rate sped up. This was it—I had to fight, or we would never get out of this alive.

"Keep your shields up," Captain Gerard said, raising his sword and rushing at the guards, slashing and cutting through their ranks.

I had no choice but to follow. I didn't want to hurt anyone, but I had to use my magic. I faced Oblek. He had his hand raised and shot a bolt of light at me. My shield deflected it easily.

Swords clashed as the clang of metal rang in my ears. Brandon swore and shot a fire strike at an oncoming guard; another one rushed at him with his sword and he deflected it, fighting back. Brandon was engaged in close combat, defending me, and Captain Gerard was fighting Oblek, who knocked him down. I gasped as Captain Gerard's sword clattered away across the floor.

Oblek laughed, and raised his weapon for the killing blow.

Captain Gerard looked over at me. "Now, Aurora, do it!" he shouted and dove out of the way.

I knew what he meant. My heart was racing. I wiped my hands on my dress and raised them, focusing on Oblek and his guards. I gathered more of the power stored within me, making me stronger. Even with the amulet on, my magic was fiercer than most.

Oblek's one good eye went wide with terror as my magic

hit him and his guards at full blast, flinging all of them like rag dolls against the far wall. I could hear skulls cracking as they crumpled to the ground in sprawled heaps.

"Nice one," Brandon commented, coming up to me, his eyes twinkling as he dusted off his jacket. "Now I understand why everyone is so scared of you." He grinned.

I scowled. I didn't find it funny. I didn't like hurting people.

"Come on, it's not over yet," said Captain Gerard, getting up and briefly glancing at Oblek and the unconscious guards. "We need to get you to the ship before the archmage comes back."

Captain Gerard led us down a path to the docks where Rafe and Santino were waiting for us.

I ran to them and Rafe caught me in his arms so tightly he nearly knocked the breath out of me. "I was so worried Lucian had hurt you." He looked me over, checking for injuries.

"I'm fine."

Rafe turned to the captain. "Thank you—I am forever in your debt, Gerard."

Captain Gerard nodded. "You need to get out of here now, Your Highness. Before the archmage realizes he's been tricked. He could return at any time."

Just then there was a shout, and I looked back to see Santino's pirates engaged in a fight with Lucian's guards. The

Archmage of Avalonia had arrived, and he was not pleased.

"He's here," said Santino, taking out his knives and twirling them in his hands. "Let's go."

Four guards ran at us from the other direction. Santino shot past me and engaged two of them, whirling around and slashing the throat of one, then stabbing the other behind him without looking. Rafe knocked one off the docks with a push strike and stabbed another in the leg with his sword, kicking him to the ground.

"We need to get to the ship now," Santino shouted over the sound of swords clashing.

Santino's men were flung out of the way as the dark figure of the archmage came into view. His magic swirled like a menacing shadow and clawed its way toward us.

I turned, terror consuming my senses. I couldn't think clearly until Rafe caught my hand, jolting me out of my fear. "Keep your shield up and run!"

"Go!" said Captain Gerard, flinging lightning strikes at the archmage. The sky crackled as Lucian easily deflected them and kept coming at us.

"This way!" Santino called out and we followed his lead, sprinting down the wooden quay to a little boat that stood bobbing at the docks.

"You want us to escape on that?" I said, horrified. We didn't stand a chance.

"Only to get to my ship," said Santino. "I've kept her

ready to sail."

In the distance, I could see a dark pirate galleon waiting on the open sea. Kalen was already there—we just had to get to it.

Easier said than done. The archmage was gaining on us.

Lucian raised his hand, and a shot of red fire blasted through Captain Gerard's shield. The leader of the palace guards screamed and fell to the ground, his uniform in flames. I faltered, and Rafe steadied me. But there was no time to grieve for the fallen. I fortified my shield and ran for my life.

Lucian raised his other hand and a powerful fire strike hit my shield as I ran. I felt a jolt and a slight dent in it, but it held. I tried to gather more power, but I was tiring. Lucian's dark magic had weakened me.

A cry shot through the air and I glanced back for a second to see Captain Gerard, launching his burning body at the archmage as he passed. Lucian was knocked to the ground. The captain's valiant last stand had the element of surprise giving us the seconds we needed, and we took them. Captain Gerard had given his life so his prince could escape.

Running as fast as we could through the coiled ropes and nets, we jumped over wooden crates and sacks to reach the ladder leading to the little boat where Santino's man was waiting to row us to the ship. Santino went first and I followed suit, descending the ladder, my feet slipping on the wet rungs. I practically fell into the boat, but Santino caught me before I went overboard.

"I knew you would fall for me eventually," he grinned, setting me down gently and picking up the oars.

I gave a nervous laugh while Rafe untied the ropes. How could Santino joke in the midst of this?

The sky crackled overhead as Lucian shot lightning strikes in our direction. Santino and his man started rowing furiously toward the ship along with Rafe and Brandon.

"He's trying to sink the boat," Rafe said.

I strengthened my shield and pushed it outward to protect the others too. The chill spray of the water drenched me as wave after wave crashed into the little boat, sending shivers through my body while I struggled to hold the shield in place. The archmage sent out another lightning strike that hit the sailor near Rafe. I felt the tear in my shield as it struck. The sailor screamed in agony and fell overboard.

The little boat lurched on the choppy sea and I grabbed the oars, helping them to row toward the waiting ship. I patched up my magical shield as best I could, but my powers were waning. The archmage's magic could still reach us as we rowed furiously toward the pirate galleon. I could see him and his guards readying boats to follow us.

We were still some distance away from the ship when a fire strike hit one of the oars I was holding. It went up in flames and I dropped it into the churning sea.

"I will shield the boat, Aurora," shouted Rafe. "But my magic cannot reach the docks, it is too far." I could hardly hear him over the din of the waves and the crackling of magic in the air. "We need to stop them from following us."

"I can reach it," I replied firmly. "But I need to take off my amulet."

"Are you sure you can handle it?" said Rafe, the sound of the waves nearly swallowing up his voice.

I nodded, but I was not sure what would happen. I still had to learn control over my powers, but I had no choice right now.

"Do it!" barked Santino. "They already know where you are, the amulet cannot hide you anymore. If they get any closer, we won't stand a chance."

I gathered my magic and stood up in the rocking boat. Bending my head, I removed my amulet. The magical beast within me reared its mighty head, uncoiling like an enormous snake ready to strike. Power rushed into me and courage filled my senses as I started to glow.

Aurora Firedrake had awoken, and I had no control over her.

My heart rate slowed and my emotions shut off. All I could see was the quay swarming with guards getting into boats to follow me and take me back to the palace in chains. My anger flared, and I raised my hands toward the docks as the huge ball of magic that had collected within me was released.

Blazing beams of silver-fire shot out of my palms, hitting the docks in a terrifying display of my unfettered magic. The sky lit up amidst horrified screams, as the whole quay of Calos burst into flames.

The sky crackled overhead as a lightning strike tried to hit our boat, but Rafe's shield kept us from sinking. I tore my gaze from the burning docks to see three boats already in the sea, rowing furiously toward us. Lucian was in the closest boat. His dark magic rippled outward and I felt it as it struck.

Rafe clutched his chest, dropping the shield around the boat, which lurched precariously. I fell sideways.

Santino and Brandon were still rowing, trying to get us to the ship. I glanced hurriedly over at Rafe. His face was distorted with pain as the archmage's magic pierced his chest. I knew how it felt, having experienced it firsthand. The archmage wanted to kill us both, but I wasn't going to let him.

I pushed myself up, bracing my feet on the sides of the rocking boat, and searched for fae magic. Time slowed as the sea responded to my call. I could hear the rush of water inside my head and could feel the fae magic within the water surrounding me on all sides.

I slowly raised my hands above my head, and the sea came with them, lifting the little boat that held the archmage onto the crest of a gigantic wave.

Lucian's hold over Rafe dropped immediately, but I was already too far gone to stop. The pressure of holding up the wall of water was proving too much for me. My body started shaking, my arms trembled, and spots formed before my eyes as I tried to restrain my magic. If I lost control now, the water would engulf us and sweep the ship away.

Rafe pushed himself up and moved toward me, putting his hand on my leg and holding me steady. "I've got you, Aurora, you can do this," he said as he surrounded me with a powerful shield holding me firmly in place.

His presence gave me the confidence I needed and I pushed back at the water, fighting the pressure on my body and pulling more magic into me. I raised my arms higher above my head and my hands started glowing brighter than ever before, lighting up the sky. Gathering the full force of my powers, I brought my arms down in a wide sweeping arc, giving the water one final push.

I could hear the guards on the little boats scream in terror as the colossal wave curled toward the shore. The enormous wall of water rose over the quay and crashed into the burning docks, flinging the archmage and his boat into the watery depths of the Stardust Sea.

The sea churned under us as it adjusted back to its original state. I stood there on the rocking boat, gazing out in horror at the shore of the town I had destroyed.

No one said a word.

Everyone in the little boat looked at me with awe. Or was it fear I saw in their eyes? I wasn't sure.

What had I done? I was a monster. How many people had I killed this time?

"Well, at least you put out the fire," said Santino, breaking the silence, and resuming his job of rowing us to the ship.

I smiled at him, grateful for his dark humor, as exhaustion overtook me and I collapsed into Rafe's arms. I drifted in and out of consciousness, and only vaguely knew where I was when I saw the glow of lights and heard sailors shouting orders as we neared the massive pirate galleon.

At the back of my mind I was excited to have found my water talent. But the pressure on my body to bend the water to my will had almost been too much for me to handle. If Rafe hadn't been there, I would have lost control.

I finally gave in to the fatigue clouding my senses and fell into the quiet oblivion of a dreamless sleep.

7
THE STARFIRE

THE WARM RAYS of the winter sun sparkled through the water-speckled windows of my cabin, waking me to the gentle rolling of the ship. I had no recollection of boarding the vessel and presumed Rafe must have carried me. He must have put my amulet back on as well while I was passed out. It rested like a weight on my chest.

My head felt heavy and my mouth was dry. I groaned as I tried to sit up, my limbs screaming in agony, and I felt empty, as if I had completely exhausted my powers. Thankfully I could still feel a small spark glowing deep within. I knew it would replenish itself, but at the moment I couldn't manage to light a candle with my magic.

The cabin Santino had given me below the quarterdeck was small and compact. A little table was positioned in a corner, flanked by two wooden chairs, and there was a trunk beside the bed. I could hear the shouts of the crew above as they went about their chores.

Somehow, I managed to get up and wash my face with a jug of water left in my room. Feeling a little better, I decided to go above deck.

Santino's ship, the *Starfire*, was sleek and beautifully built. The huge masts soared above me, swaying gently in the salty spray of the wind and piercing the morning sky as the massive ship cruised over the waters of the azure sea.

I looked over to the other side of the deck where Santino was busy, expertly helping his men hoist the immense black sails as they caught the wind. His bronze skin glistened with perspiration and his long dark hair whipped around his face as he shouted orders to his men and adjusted the rigging himself.

He looked toward me and bowed; I raised my hand to wave a greeting. Santino had changed from last night and was clad in a loose white linen shirt with billowing sleeves, half open at the front, on top of tight black leather pants and high boots. A sleek rapier hung at his side, fastened to a belt loosely slung over his hips.

This was a whole different side to the Santino Valasis I had met at the masquerade ball in Calos. This was the Pirate Prince, the scourge of the seas, the man other men only spoke about in awe and women in hushed whispers. He was an impressive specimen, tall and broad-shouldered, with a lean, muscular body.

I noticed some of the crew gaping at me. Santino beckoned a deckhand and passed him the ropes he was holding. Turning on his heel, he strode across the deck toward me and the rest of the crew scattered to their stations at his command.

The wind ruffled his hair as he came up to me and brushed my fingers with his lips. "Good morning, Princess Firedrake." His voice was deep but gentle. "I'm glad to see you are up and about. You gave us quite a scare there when you collapsed after using your magic. It was an impressive show you put on last night. I can understand why Morgana wants you gone so badly. I, for one, wouldn't want to get on your bad side."

My cheeks heated at his words and I mumbled something about not knowing how to control it.

Santino dropped his joking stance and his eyes softened as he looked at me intently. "I have travelled all the way to the Sea of Shadows and beyond," said the Pirate Prince. "And I have never seen anyone do what you did with the water in Calos." He paused, looking out to sea. "I may not know a lot about fae magic, but I am pretty sure the magic you performed last night was greater than most fully trained water-fae. And I have seen many strange and wondrous things in my travels. It has been a while since I have been so impressed with anyone. Your fortitude and courage are extraordinary for one so young, and it is an honor to have you aboard my ship."

"Thank you for everything you have done for us," I said, finding my voice. How was I supposed to respond to such a grand compliment? "I will find a way to repay you one day."

He bowed and kissed my hand, glancing up at me through thick lashes that framed his amber eyes, and winked. "I look forward to it."

I laughed and swatted his arm. "Flirting won't get you anywhere, Santino."

"It was worth a try," he grinned. "I will go and see how our friends are faring. Lord Delacourt is not happy with his lodgings and has been hassling my steward for better quarters." He rolled his eyes. "I don't think he understands the difference between a ship and an inn."

He mumbled something about sons of nobleborn lords. I couldn't help but smile as I watched him jump down two steps and walk briskly across the deck.

Strong arms clasped me around my waist. "I'm glad to see you have recovered, my love," Rafe whispered.

I smiled and turned to face him. "If you hadn't been there . . ."

He put his finger to my lips. "You don't have to thank me, Aurora. I would do anything for you. You know that."

My heart leapt in delight as I gazed up at his sinfully handsome face. "You have already done so much." Brandon's warning rang in my head and I knew I had asked too much of Rafe as it was. "You have to go back, Rafe. Captain Gerard told me things have become much worse in Eldoren."

"I know," he said with a sigh. "I leave tomorrow at dawn. Santino's ship will drop me off a little further down the coast. I can take the King's Road back to the capital from there. I have lost enough time as it is." He clasped my hand in his. "Kalen has decided to come with me—he needs to find out what happened to his mother."

I nodded. "Yes, of course, I understand." It was safer for Kalen to stay with Rafe.

What else could I say that didn't sound childish and selfish? I knew he had to go back and I had to go to Elfi—that hadn't changed. But I had hoped we would have more time.

"Silverthorne is in trouble and the Blackwaters have some sort of strange hold over my father," said Rafe, letting go of me and taking a step back. "I have to return to Neris and find out what is going on."

I held on to the railing behind me for support and kept quiet, letting him talk.

He stood beside me and gazed out to sea. "I've been foolish and blindsided by my feelings for you. I've made a grave error in judgment by helping you leave the Summer Palace when I knew you were not ready. I thought I would be able to convince you to see sense and get you to go back of your own accord. I didn't realize the Blackwaters would take this opportunity to return."

"Never underestimate the Blackwaters, right?" I said, trying to smile. I knew what he was saying was right. He had to go back and I wasn't about to stand in his way. I may have already cost him his throne.

Rafe nodded but didn't smile. He took my hands in his. "Santino and Brandon will see you safely to Elfi."

"What happened to Marcus?" I asked, remembering the little man was not on the ship. "I thought he was coming with us?"

"I have no idea." Rafe shook his head. "Marcus was gone by the time I got back to the inn to get Kalen."

My eyes went wide. "Do you think he was the one who betrayed us to Lucian?"

"That is what it looks like, and Brandon is convinced it was him," Rafe said. "He disappeared as soon as the arch-mage came to Calos. But I have known Marcus since I was a child, and he would never betray me. My old nurse Maggie, the fae lady who you met in the woods, used to trade with him. She trusted him, and she is never wrong."

"I didn't know Magdalene was your old nurse." I couldn't imagine him as a baby. He had the aura of someone who was born fully grown with a sword in his hand.

Rafe smiled. "There are still a few things you don't know about me."

At that moment Katerina Valasis came onto the deck. Her almond-shaped eyes, so like those of her brother, sought out Rafe in an instant, and she waved to him.

I raised my eyebrow. "Apparently, there is quite a lot I don't know about you."

"What's that supposed to mean?" Rafe's eyes narrowed.

"You know what I mean," I said, and forced a fake smile on my face as Katerina walked toward us.

"Rafael, my love, why didn't you mention you were leaving?" said Katerina, pouting and putting her arm through his, virtually ignoring me. "Santino just told me. You know how much I've wanted you to visit my palace in Sanria again." She batted her lashes at Rafe, and I saw her glance at me. "Do you remember how you kissed me behind the fig trees in my father's garden?"

I had heard enough. I turned to walk away when Rafe caught my arm. "Don't leave," he said softly.

Katerina's eyes shot daggers at me. But she behaved as if I wasn't there. "Darling," she said, running her finger over Rafe's chest, "don't you want to take me back to my room to say a proper goodbye before you leave?"

"I think I should go," I said, pulling my arm away.

"Aurora, wait!"

I stopped.

Rafe turned to Katerina, his gray eyes piercing and angry. "Katerina, I told you at the ball in Calos I was not interested in resuming our relationship." His voice was calm but his tone was icy. "The person I love is standing right in front of me." He glanced at me before turning back to her. "And that person isn't you," he said, looking her straight in the eyes.

Did he just say that?

Katerina's ears went red and her mouth fell open. She

recovered quickly, her eyes narrowing, and she slapped Rafe hard across his face. "That's for leading me on for all these years," she said, gathering her skirts and stamping off, presumably to find her brother.

Rafe grimaced and rubbed his cheek. "I guess I deserved that."

I laughed at him and nodded. "Probably."

"Katerina means nothing to me," he said, as he took my hand and led me to a more secluded area on the deck.

"I know that now."

He turned to look at me at me with a hunger in his eyes I had never seen before. "No, I don't think you do."

My breath hitched in my throat.

"I love you, Aurora, and it's about time I tell you the truth about my feelings. I have held it in for so long, hoping it would go away, but it has only become stronger." Rafe put his hand around my waist and drew me to him. "I have never felt this way about anyone. You haunt my dreams every single night, and when I am away from you I feel like a part of me is missing." He lowered his voice to barely a whisper. "I would give my life for you."

My hands had started trembling—I couldn't believe he was talking this way.

Rafe's lips crushed mine. I wrapped my arms around his neck as he pulled me closer, pressing my body and molding it to his. He had never kissed me like this before. My mind and body exploded with pleasure as Rafe held me to him, devouring my mouth and invading it with his tongue.

He broke the kiss, and I gasped to catch my breath as he held me tightly in his arms, breathing heavily.

"There is something else I have to tell you before I go." Rafe moved back and released me from his embrace.

"Is there something wrong?" I tried to compose myself.

Looking around once he said, "Elial Dekela is dead."

"What!" Professor Dekela couldn't be dead. He was the Mastermage of Evolon. "Are you sure?"

Rafe nodded. "Captain Gerard told me he was found dead in his study at the Academy. We don't know how it happened. But now we have a bigger problem."

My eyes went wide. "His key?" Professor Dekela was one of the guardians of the keys that opened the *Book of Abraxas*.

"Yes." He nodded. "His key is gone."

"Did the Blackwaters do this?" My heart was heavy with grief as I remembered Professor Dekela's kind eyes and wise teaching. He had helped me at a time when I needed it the most, and he was also one of my father's supporters. Now there were so few left.

"I suspect they had a hand in this. We know Morgana is after the keys, and we can assume she now has Dekela's key, which is the second one she has retrieved. I have no idea what has happened to Silverthorne's key. I suspect he's managed to hide it from them, otherwise he would already be dead."

"Let me go back with you," I said impulsively. "I want to help you save my granduncle and Eldoren. And I need to find out if Aunt Serena and Erien are safe."

"No, Aurora. I will make sure your family is safe. Go to Brandor with Santino—he will take you to Constantine Redgrave. Get the information we need about the dagger, and then go straight to Elfi. Santino will help you get there, and I believe you can trust him."

"When will I see you again?" I said, trying to keep my voice from trembling. Tears formed in my eyes but I held them back. I didn't want to let him see me cry.

"Soon." He pulled me toward him, enveloping me within his powerful arms. "I promise, I will come back for you, Aurora." I rested my head on his broad chest. I could hear his heartbeat as he kissed the top of my head and smoothed my hair. "Train hard, and master your powers. I give you my word I will return to help you find the dagger and free your mother. We just need more time."

"I will always love you," I whispered into his chest.

"And I you," whispered Rafe, holding me closer. "Forever."

A single tear fell onto his shirt. I brushed the rest away, steeling my heart for the days, weeks, and months to come. Rafe was leaving, and he was taking my heart with him. But this time I was not sure I would ever get it back.

8
THE PIRATE PRINCE

AT SUNRISE THE next day, Rafe left the ship with Kalen and was rowed ashore near the town of Shadowvale, where he could procure horses and ride back to the Summer Palace. Soon Santino's ship would leave the Eldorean coastline and sail eastward into open waters towards Brandor and Elfi.

I stood on the upper deck and watched him leave. This time I wasn't sure he would return. Our kingdoms were separate and so were our destinies. Once he got back to Eldoren they would force him to wed Leticia. He hadn't said anything about what he was going to do and I had no idea if he was going to go through with it or not. His promise to his mother still hung over our heads like an executioner's axe, ready to descend at any moment and sever our love forever.

When I saw him next, if I ever saw him again, he would be married. It was futile to get my hopes up about our chances. Nothing short of a miracle would suffice.

I had gone back to wearing the traveling clothes Kalen had brought back for me from the inn. He had also brought the sword and daggers Rafe had given me. I strapped them all into place. If I was going to be a warrior, I had to start behaving like one, which meant being armed at all times. I started sleeping with a dagger under my pillow, and was ready to use it if I needed to.

Santino was sparring with his men on the deck. I watched with fascination as he moved, surefooted and deadly but still graceful like a dancer. His every move was perfection, his instincts honed by a hard life and superior training. I had never seen anyone fight the way he did, and I had been in a lot of fights since I came to Avalonia. Santino wielded his daggers like they were extensions of his arms. His muscles glistened as his shirtless chest heaved with the exertion of fighting three of his men.

He glanced at me as he threw one of his men over his shoulder and held a dagger to his throat. This was the first time I noticed how handsome he was—I looked away, embarrassed to be caught staring.

Brandon was leaning against the railing of the ship, also watching Santino sparring, and I walked over to stand beside him.

"I'm glad to see you have recovered," Brandon said, his arms crossed, "but shouldn't you be resting?"

"I'm fine," I snapped. I was stronger than I looked and I had been in worse situations. I knew in the back of my mind Brandon only meant well, and my bad mood stemmed from seeing Rafe leave and not knowing when I would see him again. But I wasn't about to admit that to anyone. They would think I was a weak, simpering girl who cried whenever her boyfriend left, and I was supposed to be a warrior queen who was not afraid of anyone. If I didn't act the part, no one was going to follow me or accept my rule.

Brandon didn't give up and turned toward me. "You don't look fine to me, and that is nothing to be ashamed of. What you went through would be too much for anyone to recover from so soon."

"But I'm not just anyone."

Brandon smiled. "I know, believe me." He took my hand in his. "But you still need time to rest and gather your magic. If I am not mistaken, your magic is dangerously low."

I pulled my hand away. "How do you know?"

"Calculated guess." He shrugged. "The point is, you should be resting."

I turned to look out across the horizon. "I told you, I'm fine. I will rest when I get to Elfi."

But I knew my bravado was only a veil. I was drowning in despair and had made so many mistakes along the way. If I had only listened to my granduncle, all this wouldn't have happened. Now a second key had been taken, Professor Dekela was dead, Uncle Gabriel was in a dungeon, Rafe was on the verge of losing his crown, and I was not close to finding, let alone freeing, my mother. I had to make this right somehow, and the only way I was ever going to be able to do that was to master my powers and push myself as far as I could go. I would not give up, not this time.

"Tell me more about Santino," I asked Brandon as we watched the sailors fight.

"What would you like to know?" Brandon kept his voice low.

"If he is a pirate, how does he hold so much power in Brandor?"

Brandon thought for a moment before answering. "He's not a pirate anymore." He turned from watching Santino sparring, placed his hands on the railing, and gazed out to sea. "In his younger days, Santino was indeed a pirate. The most dangerous pirate who ever sailed the five seas."

"So why did he give it up?"

"About a decade ago, there was an incident in Brandor that caused the five families to fight amongst each other, plunging Brandor into the bloody depths of a civil war. Assassinations and killings were rampant in the desert kingdom, and Santino's elder brother was murdered. That was when Santino's father summoned him back. But by then Santino had already amassed an army of his own, consisting of highly trained fighters, pirates, and mercenaries. He responded to the other Emirs with sure ferocity and he subdued the rest of the nobility, bringing peace back to a once-troubled kingdom."

"What happened to the other Emirs and the Council of Five?" This was a whole history of a kingdom I had no idea about; I was intrigued.

"Santino appointed a new council of five, consisting only of noble families who supported him and his father. But everyone knows the council is ruled by Rodrigo Valasis, with the might of Santino's army keeping them in their place."

Santino had finished sparring, and was putting his shirt back on while giving orders to his men.

I squared my shoulders and walked up to the pirate prince. He turned toward me, eyeing my clothes. "Suits you," he said, buckling his sword belt around his waist. "Although I do prefer a woman in a dress."

I ignored his comment. "Teach me to fight like you," I blurted out.

His amber eyes twinkled with amusement as he considered my request. "That could take a while."

"I'm not going anywhere," I said, looking around at the ship. The journey to Brandor would take more than a few days if the winds were in our favor, longer if not, and all I had was time.

Santino grinned. "It would be my pleasure, Princess Firedrake. But I must warn you, I will not go easy on you."

"I look forward to it."

The days aboard the *Starfire* went by quickly, with most of my time spent sparring with Santino on the deck. I made friends with most of the sailors as they stopped their work to watch their captain teach me to fight, and joined in from time to time to assist Santino when he needed more than one opponent to demonstrate what he wanted me to learn.

He taught me moves I wouldn't have even dreamed of, and I was getting better at using daggers. They were my weapon of choice, although Santino did not let me learn with real daggers like Rafe did. We trained with small wooden sticks, making it far easier for me to master some of the moves.

"I don't want to hurt you," Santino said, laughing, when I questioned him on when we would use real weapons.

I was knocked down more times than I could count. But I welcomed the beatings, each one reminding me I had so much more to learn.

"Get up!" yelled Santino, after a particularly hard session. "Your last teacher was surprisingly soft with you."

I pushed myself up from the damp wooden deck. "I guess Rafe was not the right person for the job."

Santino laughed. "No, probably not. I think he must have been more interested in courting you instead of teaching you to fight."

I tried to look indignant, but ended up blushing. "It wasn't like that. A lot of the time was spent on magical training, that's all."

Santino didn't say anything, but gave me a knowing look and went about commanding his ship.

I walked back to my room, a mass of bumps and bruises. But he was right, Rafe had been going easy on me. Giving me time to adjust, but what I actually needed was to be pushed to my potential. I couldn't blame him, and it was endearing to know he wanted to protect me. But the truth was no one could protect me now. I was the one who had to protect myself and everyone else from Morgana, who wanted to destroy everything my ancestors had built.

"How did you become a pirate?" I asked Santino one day after a particularly hard training session lasted the whole morning. I didn't get knocked down as many times as I usually did, so I considered it a good day. We had been sailing for eight days and would be reaching the port city of Sanria soon.

Santino smiled. "It's a long story."

"I'm not going anywhere."

"Well, all that fighting has left me famished. I would be honoured if you would join me for lunch."

I followed Santino to his cabin. Since I'd come aboard this ship, I usually ate lunch with Brandon, who insisted on instructing the cook on how to create Eldorean dishes. According to him, the Brandorian spices were too hard on his stomach. I hardly ever saw Katerina, who stayed in her cabin complaining of seasickness; I was glad she wasn't around.

I was curious as to what the captain's cabin looked like, and it was the first time Santino had invited me here. It was a beautifully crafted space with walls of gleaming wood and polished brass handles. A bed lay along one wall, decorated with sumptuous crimson cushions. A big desk in the middle of the room was littered with ledgers, charts, and what looked like a map of Avalonia. He went about clearing papers off his desk, and the steward came in to lay out an assortment of food on the table in the center of the large cabin.

Santino gestured for me to sit down and offered me some. "Go on—it's a Brandorian recipe, you will love it."

I took the plate and picked up a pastry wrapped like a parcel. I bit into it, and my taste buds exploded. The little pastries were filled with a white salty cheese drizzled with honey and pinenuts, covering a spiced fig centre. They were delicious, though a bit too spicy for me.

"These are amazing." But I didn't take any more. "How do you have such good food here on the ship?"

"My father insists I take one of the cooks from the Citadel with me when I sail." Santino reached for another one. "Also, Katerina would never eat food cooked by a pirate." He grinned and passed me another plate, which had slices of meat cooked in an apricot, fig, and almond sauce, and yet another one with flatbreads stuffed with meat. Everything was fantastic. The food from Brandor was so different from what I was used to in Eldoren.

I smiled. "You never answered my question."

114

"I'm sure you have heard the stories of my mother being a slave of the Emir of Sanria?" Santino began as we munched on a bowl of rose petal nougat for dessert.

I shook my head, covering my mouth and trying to pick bits of sticky nougat from my teeth.

"Well, she was. My father had many slaves, and I lived in the palace with the other children, half brothers and sisters from various concubines. We were educated and trained with the royals and noble children who lived within the palace grounds." He paused for a moment before continuing, "My mother died when I was six."

"I'm sorry."

"Don't be. I had a good life and was treated fairly well. But when I turned sixteen I left the palace, wanting to see the world, so I sailed on one of my father's merchant ships to Eldoren. On the way there, we were caught by pirates. I was put to work on the ship and I learnt everything I could, including how to fight. One shipment of the pirate's cargo was slaves, people from my mother's tribe in Rohron. I freed them and killed the captain, taking over the ship. Soon I was roaming the seas, and merchants paid me a lot of money to carry goods knowing they would reach land safely. No one wanted to take on the Pirate Prince, as I had been dubbed."

"Was that when you went back to Brandor?"

"Yes. My family needed me and I had to return."

"Because of the civil war?"

Santino nodded. "My elder brother Alfonso was the real heir, but when he was killed by the powerful Detori family, I knew I had to return to help my father secure his place on the council." He got up from his chair. "Brandor is still unstable, and Morgana's spies have infiltrated many of the ruling families. You must be on your guard at all times when we are in Sanria. Don't trust anyone."

I nodded. My trusting days were over.

The next day, the *Starfire* sailed into the bay of Sanria, Brandor's wealthiest trading port. Brandon and I stood on the deck watching the massive eastern city come into view, while Santino helped the crew as they bustled about, lowering the sails and preparing the ship to anchor.

There were more ships here than in the bay of Calos. Merchant galleons and passenger ships bobbed on the waves but there were no Eldorean warships in sight, which was a relief.

From the top deck of the ship I could see the Red Citadel rising above the towering walls. Situated high on a hilly plateau and surrounded by acres of woods, the ancient palace and fortress, the home of the Emir of Sanria, was a magnificent structure.

I had changed out of my tunic and woolen leggings into a plain brown cotton dress which Santino had given me. He handed me a thin veil. "Put this on. Women in our kingdom cover their heads and faces while in public."

I put on the veil and secured it with a cloth hairband. It was made of a light gauzy fabric that covered my face and head, but I could still see through it.

A small boat rowed us to shore, and the salty spray of the sea wind brushed my face. The balmy breeze of the eastern coast was a welcome change from the biting chill of the Eldorean winter.

"Travellers and merchants from all over the seven kingdoms come to this city," said Brandon as we traversed the bustling docks lined with ships unloading their wares and merchants inspecting their most recent acquisitions. "Most people will not pay any attention to foreigners here, but it's good that Santino made you wear that veil."

Santino led us to some horses that were waiting for us. There was a palanquin for the ladies and Katerina, already fully veiled, sat down in one almost immediately. I was relieved there was another waiting for me, as sharing with Katerina at this point would be awkward.

Brandon and Santino rode ahead as we were carried behind them through the crowded streets of the outer town. I moved the curtains of the palanquin aside and peeked out at the passing dockyards, custom-houses, street sellers, shops, taverns, and inns along the way. I was fascinated by the innumerable colors of the great, tented, open markets selling everything from jewelry and precious stones to food and weapons as Brandorians traversed various stalls, looking for the best wares of the day.

The cramped areas and dark cobbled alleyways gave way to broader roads and avenues flanked by magnificent white-washed mansions and houses of the nobility, impressive structures stood majestically within open courtyards and gardens alive with fruit orchards.

Soon we came onto the main avenue that led to the Emir's palace on the hill, lined by huge cyprus trees. The Brandorian stronghold was not only a palace but also an ancient fortress built centuries ago with the red clay and brick of this land—thus its name, the Red Citadel.

We entered the massive walled fortress and stopped in the outer courtyard before climbing the grand steps leading up to the palace. The citadel was situated at a strategic point, overlooking the city of Sanria to one side and the deserts that stretched across the kingdom to the east.

We followed Santino through the towering arched entrance into an antechamber where he met with some of the palace officials while I looked around. The inside of the palace was more magnificent than the outside. Geometric carvings inlaid with white, blue, and gold were beautiful in their almost lacelike detail, tastefully adorning the high ceilings. Filigreed walls lavishly decorated with crowns and stars and interspaced with local flora caught my eye. I wondered at the craftsmanship it must have taken to create this wonderful palace.

"This part of the citadel is the more official area," said Santino as he led us into the forecourt of the main palace, through passages lined with white marble pillars and paved with intricate colored tiles. "I will show you to your room."

We passed courtyards sporting beautiful fountains and little pools surrounded by wild myrtle and orange trees, which filled the air with their enchanting fragrances. The different parts of the complex were connected by rosebush-edged pathways, with gates leading to orchards of fig, date, and pomegranate trees which dotted the inner gardens.

"The royal residence is at the north end of the complex. Once you have bathed and changed, I will take you to meet with my father. It is imperative we get his support if I am to help you."

"I didn't bring much with me."

"No matter," said Santino. "I've had your room filled with all the necessities ladies cannot do without."

"Thank you." I was grateful for a proper bath and a change of clothes.

My room in the palace was a beautiful bright space which opened onto a central court with symmetrical doorways framed with glazed tiles and stucco. The low bed could be reached by climbing three steps. It was hung with beautiful muslin curtains effortlessly draped around the massive bed, enveloping it in an airy cocoon.

A flock of maids were waiting to attend to my every whim, bustling about quietly and efficiently getting my bath ready in an enormous mosaic tub filled with rose-scented water. Once I had bathed and washed my hair, they laid out an array of clothes on the bed and started dressing me, draping me in layers of a light gauzy fabric that clasped at one shoulder with a jeweled brooch and flowed around me, bound at the waist with a gold jeweled belt. The flimsy one-shoulder top was long and reached my knees. But the bottom part was slit all the way up to my waist to show a billowing pair of sheer pants, worn underneath and cinched at my ankles. My hair was dried, brushed, and plaited with gold threads intertwined through the strands.

"A lady must always look her best," said the eldest of the maids, still fussing with the last runaway strands of my hair that never managed to stay in one place.

"Don't I need to wear a veil?" I asked, admiring my reflection in the two big gold mirrors that the maids held up for me. I smiled at my appearance—it was not every day I was pampered like this.

"Not inside the private palace."

Santino came to fetch me from my room, and I followed him through the flowering courtyards to another wing of the private residence of the Emir of Sanria.

"My father wanted an unofficial audience with you, and

prefers not to let anyone know who you are or why you are here."

I nodded. It was better no one knew who I was. Once they did, something bad always tended to happen.

"Where's Brandon?"

Santino shrugged. "Brandon said he had to meet someone. I'm sure he will be back soon. He doesn't seem the type to wander the streets of the city after dark."

We came to big silver doors, guarded by the largest men I had ever seen. They were dark-skinned and shirtless with corded muscles and leather straps across their chests. Santino explained they were tribesmen from the eastern reaches of Brandor, warriors trained since birth to protect the Emirs. Each had a deadly-looking spear in his hands and two curved swords hanging at his waist. These were guards you didn't want to mess with.

We entered the vast reception room of the Emir of Sanria, who sat flanked by his personal guard. Santino bowed to his father and I did the same.

The Emir nodded and looked satisfied by my gesture. He beckoned for me to step forward. "I am pleased to see that your newfound royal status has not diminished your respectfulness towards your elders, Princess Aurora."

"I thank you for your hospitality, Your Highness." I knew I was at the mercy of the ruler of every kingdom in which I took refuge. And I had to become smarter, sharper and more cunning if I was going to learn to survive out here. "Your son Santino saved my life and I am forever in his debt."

The Emir looked at his son with a hint of pride in his eyes and turned back to me. "Yes, Santino is always trying to help those in need, quite unlike his reputation as the deadly Pirate Prince."

Santino looked uncomfortable at this unexpected praise, but I was not sure his father meant it as such.

"But," said the Emir, "the fact remains that Morgana is looking for you. And by bringing you here Santino has endangered our whole kingdom." He paused and studied me. "Out of respect for my son, I will permit you to stay here for a day or two at the most, until you are rested and able to resume your journey."

"But Father," said Santino, "she is also a victim of Morgana's crimes. Surely we cannot turn our backs on another ruler in need?"

"She is a ruler of nothing," said the Emir, his voice turning cold. "She commands no army, she has no throne, no crown, no kingdom to go to." He turned his gaze upon me, and his eyes narrowed. "Take my advice, child, go to your grandmother in Elfi where Morgana cannot touch you. Disappear forever and give up this fight. It is one you cannot win. Morgana and the archmage are too strong. Now backed by the Drakaar, they are deadlier still. We have received reports from the northern frontiers. Morgana's army is amassing in the Silverspike Mountains and terrorizing the plains. The dwarves have shut themselves up in Stonegate, and will not stop Morgana's army from moving south. With Silverthorne in the dungeons and the Blackwaters running Eldoren, there is no one capable of standing in her way and stopping her from taking over the seven kingdoms."

"We cannot sit back and permit Morgana to conquer the whole world," argued Santino. "Since when has Brandor backed away from a battle?"

"Since Morgana," said Emir Valasis, lowering his voice. "I have spoken to the other members of the council and we are in agreement. We will accept Morgana as High Queen, and in return she will not attack Brandor."

"Not attack!" Santino paced the floor in front of his father's throne. "That is what she says. But what's to stop her from coming into our kingdom and doing as she pleases?"

"It won't come to that," said the Emir. "Once we swear allegiance to her, she will let us live in peace."

Santino shook his head and stopped pacing. "As long as Morgana is High Queen there will never be peace in the seven kingdoms. And what about Aurora, are you going to give her up to Morgana too?"

I paled.

"I will not go so far as to hand over a child to that monster," said Rodrigo Valasis, an indignant tone to his voice. "But I will not endanger my own kingdom for an untrained, inexperienced princess who may or may not take back her kingdom one day. Morgana is real, and she has an army. In fact, she has more than one army, and she is coming for Aurora. The girl must be on her way before anyone finds out she is here."

Santino bowed stiffly to his father. "We will be leaving for Elfi as soon as I can prepare. I promised to make sure she reaches her grandmother safely, and I am going to keep that promise. We will ride out tomorrow."

I hung my head and followed Santino out of the room. No one wanted to help me anymore, and no one believed I would be able to win back my throne. The worst part was the Emir was right. I was no queen—I had no army, no backing, and no training or experience. My granduncle tried to help me, but I was too stubborn to listen to reason. And now I was alone in a foreign kingdom, running for my life.

But I had to finish what I came here for. I had to meet Constantine Redgrave, the ex-archmage of my grandfather's kingdom. He was the only one who would have some answers about the Dagger of Dragath and my mother.

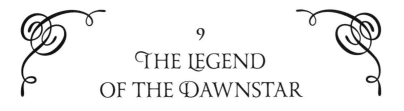

9
THE LEGEND
OF THE DAWNSTAR

"I WILL SEE you in a few hours," said Santino as he escorted me to the royal library, which was housed within the citadel and therefore part of the massive fortress complex of the Emir of Sanria. "I have some work to attend to, but the mastermage will see you now."

"Thank you, Santino—you are a true friend. I appreciate all you have done for me. But I don't want you to go against your father's wishes to help me."

"Don't worry about that. Get what information you need from the mastermage and I will prepare for our journey to Elfi." He left two guards outside the library to escort me to my room once I had finished.

I entered the royal library and was immediately spellbound by what lay before me. Gold-trimmed mahogany bookshelves lined the walls and stretched all the way to the magnificent domed ceiling, carved with intricate designs in white, blue and gold.

The mastermage of the library was a small, frail man with frizzy white hair and a short, trimmed beard. He looked over a hundred years old, but his deep brown eyes were sharp and focused beneath bushy eyebrows. He bowed briefly when he saw me.

"I have been expecting you." He turned, gesturing me to follow him as he shuffled deeper into the massive library.

"You know who I am?" I trailed behind him, passing huge arched windows with ornate stained glass that flashed in the sunlight and lined the gallery that skirted the first floor of the massive room.

He didn't stop or look back. "Did you meet with the Emir?"

"Yes, and he wants me gone as soon as possible."

"Then we have little time." His hand lit up as he opened a small wooden door at the very end of the great library.

I followed him down the spiral steps to a smaller room. Stacks of books were strewn on the floor, and a variety of maps were pinned to one wall. The mastermage was a strange little man. How did he know who I was? Had Santino or the Emir told him I was here already?

"There is still so much you do not know about our world. And it is imperative you understand these things before you go to Elfi," the mastermage said. "We never expected the Blackwaters to turn face so quickly. And neither did we expect the king to support them. Now that Dekela is dead and his key taken, we have bigger problems on our hands."

I froze. "But how do you know about the keys?"

"Because," said the mastermage, looking pointedly at me,

"I am the fourth guardian of the keys."

"Oh!" I shut the heavy wooden door behind me.

"Your granduncle and I have been in contact since you came back to this world. After you discovered Morgana was in pursuit of the keys, Silverthorne was to bring you here on your way to Elfi. I only recently got word from him that you had left Eldoren on your own." He scrunched his eyebrows together as he assessed me. "Although many may think it was a wrong move on your part, I believe it was fate that caused you to flee Neris when you did. And it was the same fate that brought you to me, even without your granduncle. If you hadn't left that night, you might be rotting in the dungeons along with Silverthorne."

I nodded, sitting down in the nearest chair. "I may have saved myself by leaving the city, but my family is in trouble because of me and I can't do anything to help them." I felt so useless, and doubts about my ability to continue this path were slowly creeping in.

"Everyone makes mistakes, Aurora, even you. But this is not one of them. The events that are starting to take place are not your doing. You are but a pawn in a much larger game you have not begun to understand." The mastermage went over to his desk. "Destiny is a strange thing—it may shape our fate, but eventually we all have a choice as to how to use the opportunities given to us."

"But Eldoren has joined hands with Morgana, and it's all

my fault. I should have been there to help them."

"They are scared, and rightfully so. Morgana and Lucian have the Drakaar working with them. If you'd been there, what could you have done? Even your magic could not have held them off. All you would have achieved would be getting yourself killed."

"I could have fought them. I could have saved Aunt Serena and Erien. And what about Penelope? I don't know what happened to her."

"If you had learned to control your fae powers without your amulet, things might have been different," said the mastermage sternly. "But you have barely scraped the surface of your magic, and there is still so much for you to learn." He paused. "Silverthorne is safe for now; he may be in the dungeons, but he is still alive. He will never give Morgana the key, and as long as she doesn't have it, she will not kill him. I have also heard reports that Serena Silverthorne and her son escaped and are not to be found."

"But they could be anywhere. What if they need help? Someone has to find them."

"I have my people looking for them."

"There is something I need to ask you." I tried to word my question correctly.

"I will answer you the best I can."

"I have heard Morgana has a secret." I told him what Lucian had said.

The mastermage shook his head, sitting down in his chair behind the desk, a weariness on his face making him look older than his years. "I do know she has a secret," he said finally. "And your granduncle was also very eager to find out what it is. Unfortunately, I never discovered what she was hiding."

"But what if it is something important? It could help us against Morgana. Shouldn't we at least try to find out what it is?"

"The most important thing for you is to learn to master your fae magic. There is so much more to it you cannot begin to grasp. Going to Elfi should be your first priority."

He was right, I had to stop being so impatient. I could not do everything at once.

"But I still haven't understood why you disobeyed your granduncle's orders and journeyed out into the world alone?"

I cringed at my stupidity and tried to explain about my mother and the Dagger. "That is the main reason I came here, because I need to ask you about the Dagger of Dragath and how I can get my mother back." I couldn't leave without answers.

The mastermage ran his fingers through his messy hair, got up from his chair, and started to pace the room. "I do not have all the answers, I'm afraid. But it is heartening to know Elayna is still alive, and I do believe you are on the right track. After controlling your magic, getting the dagger out of Morgana's clutches should be your highest priority. Without it she cannot release Dragath from his prison, even if she opens the *Book of Abraxas*. Dragath is an ancient being, with powers that stretch back through time. He was the one who created the Dagger, and the only way to break his dark curse is with ancient magic."

"But Uncle Gabriel said ancient magic doesn't exist anymore?"

"That is the common belief," he nodded, getting up and walking over to the crowded shelves. He came back with a large, worn, leatherbound book. "But what Silverthorne did not tell you is there is still one last piece of ancient magic left in this world."

"There is?" My eyes widened. There was a way to free my mother, and I had come to the right place.

"Yes." The mastermage opened the book. "The *Vironion Codex* and other sacred texts and scrolls over the centuries speak of a weapon that contains the last of the magic of the ancients."

"A weapon!" It sounded very powerful, and a little far-fetched. But if there was a way to combat Dragath's magic, I had to find it. "What is it?"

"It is known as the Dawnstar. This legend has been told many times over, in different ages and by different seers. Although this is not the original version but a copy of what is written in the *Vironion Codex*, it will suit our purpose."

Flipping through the pages, he ran his fingers over some of the symbols, reading them and muttering to himself. "Ah!" he said, stopping and smoothing the page he was looking for. "Here it is, the legend of the Dawnstar." He read from the page in front of him. "A weapon of unimaginable power, created from the blood of the ancients. The Dawnstar remains Avalonia's last defence against the darkness."

He shut the book and opened another one. "I don't know all the details, but the *Sarabine Chronicles*, an older text of legends and prophecies, mentions it as well." The mastermage read aloud from the page he had opened to. "The last of Avalonia's ancient magic resides within the Dawnstar."

He closed the book.

"What exactly is the Dawnstar? Is it a sword, a jewel? A ring? How do I find it?"

The mastermage shook his head. "I regret to say I have no idea. The witch tribes also mention the Dawnstar in their ancient scrolls, as do the fae. But no one has ever seen it or knows what it looks like."

"What do the other texts say?" I was curious to know more about this legendary weapon, Avalonia's last defense against Dragath's magic.

"The answers you seek lie in Elfi. The whereabouts of the Dawnstar are buried somewhere within the pages of the Fae Codex. Only the Elder Council of the High Fae and the Queen of Elfi have access to it." He paused and gave me a pointed look. "The magic of the Dawnstar is the only power that can break the curse on the Dark Dagger. It is, in fact, the only way to get your mother back."

"How will I know what I am looking for?" There was so much I didn't know, and so much more I had to learn.

"You will know when you see it. I cannot stress enough how important it is for you to master your magic and control it. Get the High Fae to show you the Codex and it will lead you to what you seek. If Dragath is ever released, you will find yourself in a nightmare from which you cannot awake."

I shivered involuntarily at this. "And the *Book of Abraxas*? Where is it now?"

"It is in Elfi, protected by the fae. But eventually Morgana will find out where it is and come for it. When that time comes, you must be ready to face her. She must never get her hands on the book. It contains magic from a time we cannot comprehend. If opened, it will give her unimaginable power."

I nodded. I was trying to remember everything I had been told about the *Book of Abraxas* and suddenly realized that wasn't very much at all. "Professor Dekela told me the book was a dark grimoire."

"It is much more than that, Aurora," The mastermage shook his head and frowned. "The *Book of Abraxas* is neither dark nor light. It has been called a dark grimoire and can indeed be used to do unspeakable things, but the book is also called the *Book of Power*, by those who know its true purpose." He paused. "But power corrupts. As it did to the ancient fae lord who had the book created for his own ends, which resulted in Dragath coming to this world."

I gasped. "The book brought Dragath to Avalonia?"

"The magic written in the *Book of Abraxas* gave the fae lord a great power, to rip apart the veils between the worlds as no one has ever done before. He summoned Dragath from an ancient world, a dark world that is a prison for ancient evils that cannot be contained anywhere else. Although the fae lord had the knowledge of the book, he did not have sufficient power to bind Dragath to his will. Dragath broke free and killed him, claiming the book for his own. Using the knowledge within the book, Dragath created the Dark Dagger. Morgana already has the dagger; if she gets the book as well, there is nothing we will be able to do to stop her from releasing him."

I nodded. I knew that this was what Uncle Gabriel was trying to prepare me for. If only I had listened earlier. I had to find the Dawnstar before I went looking for the dagger. It was the only way to battle Dragath's magic and break the curse imprisoning my mother.

"Go to your fae kin. Your grandmother and the Elders of Elfi will have more answers about the Dawnstar. The High Fae are an ancient race and the knowledge they possess dates to a time far beyond the age of mages. Work hard and master your fae magic so when Morgana comes for the book, you will be ready to remove your amulet and face her." He looked at me closely. "For if Elfi falls, there is nowhere in this world where any of us will ever be safe again."

I must have looked as horrified as I felt, for the mastermage smiled and his eyes softened. "This is your destiny, Aurora. It is what you were born to do. But your fate is not set in stone and is still to be decided. It all depends on the path you take. Choose wisely. The future of this world rests in your hands."

I got up from my chair. "Great! As if I didn't have enough on my plate already."

The mastermage chuckled. "I'm sure you can handle it."

"I have no doubt she can handle anything," said Santino from the doorway.

I whirled around.

Santino was leaning on the doorframe, his hands crossed across his chest. He looked regal in his court attire, his jeweled robe open at the front but covering his leather pants and carefully concealed weapons.

I smiled as Santino walked in and closed the door behind him. "The Emir has requested her appearance be changed for the remainder of her stay here," Santino addressed the mastermage.

I rolled my eyes. "Not again."

Santino's lips curved slightly as he turned to me. "It is a

better option than being confined to your rooms. At least this way you can accompany me to the banquet tonight, which is being held in my honor."

Santino was right, it was a better option, and I did want to see the rest of the palace and the people who lived here. I could have done it myself, but my magic still felt weak after using it in Calos.

"Fine," I said, moving to the standing mirror in the corner of the room; it was dull and blotchy but it suited my purpose.

"I will wait for you upstairs in the library. I have a book I need to consult." Santino closed the door behind him.

I nodded and turned back to my reflection. "Go ahead," I said to the mastermage, "but please let me choose how I am going to look."

"Tonight you can be whomever you want to be," said the mastermage kindly. I explained to him what I wanted.

"But what about the servants? They saw what I looked like." I remembered the maids who had helped me get ready.

"The servants are all loyal to Santino. They will not bat an eyelid when another girl turns up in your room instead of you. They will think Santino simply got bored and replaced you."

"Does he do that a lot?" I eyed the mastermage in the mirror.

The mastermage was smiling. "Do what?"

"Get bored with a girl and replace her so soon."

"Frequently," the mastermage grinned and rolled up his sleeves to perform the transformation. "Santino is not the type to be tied down to one girl for more than a few days. Every girl in Brandor has tried, but he will not marry. Says he hasn't found the right one."

"Poor fellow." I felt sorry for the Pirate Prince. "He must be very lonely."

The mastermage chuckled. "I don't think he sees it that way."

I stood in front of the mirror as the mastermage worked his magic on me. It was like watching myself in a Disney movie, and the mastermage was the fairy godmother. Without the swirling stars and sparkling wand, of course.

He ran one hand in the air inches from my face, and my eyes changed color from green to a deep azure. My lips became fuller, changing to a voluptuous shade of red, and my skin darkened to a golden bronze. He smiled and waved his hand around my head, and my dark locks lightened into a shining sea of spun gold which fell about my shoulders and sparkled in the candlelight. I was too spellbound to do anything else but stand there and watch myself being transformed. He made it look so simple, and I knew how difficult it was for a mage to transform a person's features and have it hold for a length of time.

"Done," said the mastermage, going back to sit on the

chair behind his desk. "Go! Have a good time at the banquet; no one will recognize you now. I have some work to complete—I will see you there later."

Santino was waiting for me. His dark amber eyes smoldered as I walked toward him and he grinned. "I still prefer the real you, but I guess this will do for the night."

I swatted him on his arm. "Don't tease, I hate it when I have to change my appearance."

"Did you find what you were looking for?" Santino asked as we walked to the banquet hall.

I nodded. I didn't want to say too much; I had to be careful what I revealed and to whom. I made a note to ask the mastermage if I could trust Santino with this information. He had a huge network of spies and could be an asset when it came to finding out what Lucian and Morgana were up to.

The banquet hall was a grand domed room, elaborately decorated with carved walls and an enameled ceiling. Rows of low rectangular tables lay around the room, forming a square with the center of the hall empty for the entertainers to display their arts.

I looked around for Brandon and found him reclining on a luxurious pile of cushions, a gold goblet in his hand, eyeing the scantily clad dancers wearing gauzy veils as they whirled and gyrated their hips to the music.

Santino stopped to say hello to a few of the guests, and I went to speak to Brandon.

I sat down on the edge of a cushion next to him. "Where have you been?"

He sat up straight. "Excuse me, my lady, do I know you?"

I clapped my hand over my mouth. "Oh, I forgot to tell you, I had to change my appearance," I whispered.

He looked at me more closely. "Aurora?"

"Shhh, not so loud. The Emir wanted me to be in disguise, and he wants me to leave tomorrow."

Brandon's eyes darted to the door. "So soon?"

I nodded. "Yes, he thinks it's too dangerous having me in Sanria. Do you think Morgana or Lucian can find me here? That is, if he is still alive."

Brandon took a deep gulp, draining the contents of his goblet. "Oh, he's alive."

"How do you know?"

"Just a guess." Brandon shrugged, signaling the attendant with the wine jug to top up his cup. "He's the Archmage of Avalonia, I don't think a little water is going to stop him."

Could Lucian still be alive? Was he that powerful?

"There you are, Delacourt," said Santino, sitting down beside me. "I was afraid you might have been robbed by thieves in a back alley somewhere. I was about to send guards looking for you. The streets of Sanria are not safe after dark."

Brandon scowled at Santino. "I can take care of myself."

Santino laughed and brushed off Brandon's surliness.

I turned to the food that had been laid out. Meats and poultry stuffed with or dressed in figs, almonds, and dates were placed in the center of the long tables, along with seafood and rice cooked in saffron; spiced, candied fruit concoctions with cinnamon; and honey-infused rice pudding. There were more exotic-looking dishes I couldn't name but couldn't resist trying. We would have to leave tomorrow, and the journey was a long and tedious one. I was not looking forward to it.

Brandon wasn't eating, he kept refilling his cup with wine and gulping it down like water. Why was he in such a bad mood?

At least Santino was so funny and easy to talk to that the hours passed easily. Brandon had left at some point during the night, presumably to sleep off all the wine. He was going to have a pretty bad headache the next day, I was sure.

The last of the guests trickled out of the hall, many of the men accompanying the women out or to their beds.

Santino stood up and held out his hand. "Come, I will escort you back to your room. We have a long journey ahead."

I took his hand and followed him out of the great hall into the gardens. I took in the night air, drenched in the heady smell of orange blossoms and wild myrtle. Santino stopped but didn't let go of my hand.

"Aurora."

I turned towards him. "Yes, Santino."

"I want to apologize for not being able to offer you refuge here for a few more days. But I want you to know I will make sure you reach your grandmother's kingdom safely."

"It's already too much to ask, and you have been so good to me already." I looked down. "I don't know how I will repay your kindness."

Santino touched my cheek with the back of his hand, a gentle caress, running it down to my chin and under it, tilting my head up to look at him. "I'm not doing this out of kindness," he said, holding me spellbound with his dark gaze.

I didn't know what to say. Santino was handsome, there was no doubt, but I loved Rafe and I still wasn't over him, and I wasn't sure I ever would be. In any case, it was too soon.

"Santino, I . . ." I began trying to form the words, but he cut me off.

"Your hair is darkening and your eyes are changing back," he said abruptly.

"What!" I said, touching my hair and my face. "How? The mastermage said the transformation would last until I left." I looked at my hands—my skin had started changing back too.

"This can only mean one thing." Santino unsheathed his sword, turning on his heel. "The mastermage is in trouble."

He grabbed my hand and started running. "We have to get to the library."

We dashed to the massive library, through the wide arched doors, and down the main aisle.

The sight that lay before me stopped me in my tracks.

The mastermage was lying on the floor, blood seeping from the wound in his stomach, running like a river of red onto the white marble. His attacker was nowhere to be found.

Recovering quickly, I went to him and fell on my knees. He was still alive, clinging to his last breath.

"Can you save him?" Santino came up behind me, keeping his voice low.

I nodded solemnly, but I wasn't so sure. I had no idea how much damage had been done to the internal organs. But I had to try. I placed my hands on his chest and tried to find a drop of magic to begin the healing, but my magic would not surface. I tried again. I could feel a hint of it within me, but I needed more. I needed to remove the amulet for this sort of healing. I closed my eyes and willed my magic to surface, but the mastermage abruptly grabbed my hand.

My eyes snapped open.

"You will not do this, Aurora." His voice was low and raspy. "My time has come—even you cannot save me now. Have you forgotten what happened when you tried this with your pegasus?"

An image of Lilith flashed before my eyes and I lowered my hands. He was right, he was too far gone. If I tried to heal him I could open another portal, and something worse than Lilith could come through.

Santino kneeled beside me and gently took the other man's hand in his. "Who did this to you, Diego?"

The mastermage coughed and blood splattered onto his chest. He could barely speak, but he wanted to say something.

"They are here," the mastermage's voice cracked, and I had to strain to hear his words. "You need to . . . leave . . . now."

"Who, who's here?" I asked.

"The Drakaar." His eyelids fluttered.

"What!" I gasped. "How did they find me?"

"Dela . . ." he had another coughing fit and tried again. "It was Delacourt."

I looked at Santino, who was pacing behind me. His knuckles were white as he gripped the hilt of his sword and scanned the empty library. "That traitor."

"But why?" I asked, still not comprehending Brandon had betrayed me. "What does he have to gain?"

"The key," rasped the mastermage, clutching my hand. "He took the key, Aurora."

Santino's head snapped back to look at me. "What key?"

"No!" I shook my head as my heartbeat sped up. One more key to the *Book of Abraxas* was gone.

The mastermage grasped my hand. "Go to Elfi . . . find the Dawnstar . . . It is the only way. . ." He closed his eyes, and breathed his last.

"We must leave," urged Santino, putting his hand on my shoulder as I let go of the mastermage's limp hand. "There is nothing you can do for him now."

A low growl sounded and my blood ran cold. It was coming from inside the library. I could feel a dark presence moving closer and I knew what it was before I saw it.

Terror struck me. Drakaar assassins, the dark sorcerers who killed my father, had finally come for me.

This time there was no one to save me and there was nowhere to hide.

10
THE DRAKAAR

A DARK FIGURE emerged out of the shadows and my legs nearly gave way under me. A creature out of my worst nightmare, half man, half beast, towered above Santino. I would never forget those burning red eyes and razor sharp fangs. Its leathery wings spread out behind it, ready to pounce on its prey.

I recognized it immediately. A gorgoth! The vile henchmen of the Drakaar.

Santino slashed at it with his sword, but the gorgoth growled and blocked the blow, flinging him out of the way. I gathered my magic and aimed a fire strike at the creature. Power blasted out of my hands and sizzled as it struck. My magic only made it hesitate, and it kept coming for me.

I ran to help Santino, pulling him up with one hand and scorching the gorgoth with all the power I could muster.

Santino recovered and grabbed my hand. "Run!"

We sprinted through the towering bookshelves and deserted corridors of the massive library. The creature was fast and gaining on us; its growls echoed through the room.

"This way." Santino pulled me through a door, which led

out into an open courtyard.

What I saw before me made my blood run cold.

The palace courtyard was a mess. A group of guards had engaged in a bloody battle with four gorgoths that flew through the terrifying melee, slicing open necks and chests with their sharp fangs and deadly claws. Bodies lay strewn on the ground as guards fell under the massive strength of the demon creatures.

Santino removed a dagger from his boot and swiftly threw it at the closest gorgoth, hitting his target in the eye. The gorgoth screamed and fell to the ground, thrashing but still alive. Another gorgoth was surrounded by spear wielding guards and Santino raised his sword, rushing into the throng.

But the magic I felt moving towards me was not coming from the gorgoths, and I turned toward the darkness that threatened to engulf us all. Four hooded figures stood perfectly still in the middle of the courtyard, watching their henchmen wreak havoc on the Brandorians, and I paled.

The Drakaar.

The sorcerers of Dragath removed their hoods and what I saw in front of me sent a shiver down my spine. Their faces were sharp and angular, human-like in their outward appearance, with the pale white features and blond hair of the northerners. But what I saw in their eyes when they looked at me made my magic recoil as if it wanted to hide. Dark black pools that seemed to have devoured whole worlds gazed at me. Their necks and parts of their faces were covered with black tattoos that glowed with a strange magic, depicting ancient symbols that swirled over their pale skin. The power they radiated was nothing I had ever felt before, not even with Lucian.

Not human.

One Drakaar smiled when he saw me—a feral grin with a terrifying glint of teeth, revealing elongated canines that could tear out my throat with a single bite. He reached out his hand toward me and latched onto my magic like a blood-sucking leech, sucking the very lifeforce out of me. I struggled to get my power back under my command, but it would not obey me.

There was a flurry of shouts and screams as Santino's mercenaries entered the fray. On Santino's orders, they battled the remaining gorgoths, who slashed and dismembered palace guards three at a time. Santino continued shouting orders to his men, clear and precise instructions on how to kill the gorgoths.

He ran up to me amidst the chaos. "You must remove your amulet, Aurora."

I hesitated. I was not ready, I had not mastered my control yet.

"Now!" he shouted as he ran ahead, already engaged in a fight to the death with a gorgoth that had felled at least ten of his men. Santino swerved and danced around the creature, never giving the creature a chance to get a hit in. His sword flashed lethal in his right hand as he slashed the back of the gorgoth's knees and then its wings with the dagger he held in his left. The gorgoth crashed to the ground as Santino took a running leap, pouncing on the creature and burying his sword up to the hilt in its chest.

One of the Drakaar raised his hand, and I could feel the ancient hum of dark magic as tendrils of dark shadow lashed out at Santino, picking him up and flinging him against the far wall.

I had seen enough. I had to do something, I had to overcome this fear. I was a warrior trained to fight, but I knew this was a battle we could not win. If I could muster enough power to hold them off, I might be able to get us clear of the citadel with our lives intact.

I removed the chain from my neck, and both my hands shone with silver-fire as my fae magic awoke and responded, unbound by the fetters of the amulet that held it in check. The darkness hit my shield and tore against it, trying to find a way in. Raising my hands, I released the silver-fire that rose in my veins, lashing out at the sorcerers of Dragath with everything I could muster.

But the Drakaar only hissed and faltered momentarily, my magic hitting a shield that absorbed my silver-fire into the blackness as if it was never there.

As the sparks abated, the first of the Drakaar smiled, his canines flashing like daggers in the moonlight. "You have power, little princess, but not the skill or the experience. You still do not know how to use your fae magic, and I will enjoy killing you slowly."

The Drakaar sorcerer raised his hand—I could feel a crushing weight around my shield, pushing against it and threatening to shatter it completely. An ancient evil seeped out of his very pores, feeding on the terror that lay thick in the air, suffocating all hope and light, replacing it with despair, pain, and sorrow.

I drew more magic into me to strengthen my shield, but the sorcerer's power was more formidable than I had anticipated. The other Drakaar added their sorcery to the assault, and my legs started shaking. I fell to my knees. The pressure of trying to hold my shield against the crushing darkness was too much.

"There will be no escape this time, Aurora," a familiar voice drawled. I looked up. Brandon stood in front of me surrounded by the Drakaar sorcerers, a satisfied smirk on his handsome face. "There is no one who can save you now."

My anger flared and I wanted to strangle him. My magic blazed in response and I threw a stun strike at him, but the Drakaar were shielding him, and he remained unharmed. Silver-fire started to form in my palms as I desperately tried to gather my magic.

Brandon looked at my hands with no remorse whatso-ever. "I wouldn't do that if I were you." His cold blue eyes were like shards of ice.

I heard a cry and Santino fell to his knees. One Drakaar had his hands outstretched, his magic concentrating on Santino, pinning him to the ground and awaiting orders.

We were surrounded.

"Why, Brandon?" I ground out through clenched teeth, my hands continuing to glow. "Why did you do it? Why betray us?"

"Curb your magic, Aurora, or the Pirate Prince dies," said Brandon sharply.

I hesitated, then reduced the glow in my hands, although not completely.

"You won't get away with this," I stated, but I could see Santino out of the corner of my eye, struggling with his magical bonds.

"Oh, but I already have."

"What has Morgana offered you?" I had to keep him talking—maybe I could stall until some backup came. "Land, titles?"

But I could hear screams coming from inside the palace, and I knew the gorgoths were keeping the guards busy. No one was coming to help us.

"You think I did this for money?" Brandon paused. "So like your father. Clueless to the feelings of others or too selfish to care."

"My father? What does my father have to do with it? He's dead."

"Yes, he may have died, but not before he ruined my sister's life and took her away from me."

My hand flew to my mouth as realization dawned. Rafe had told me the story of Brandon's sister, the poor girl who leapt from a castle window and killed herself over a man. But I never knew who the man was. Until now.

"It was my father," I choked on the words. "The one your sister was in love with?" That's why he put me in her room at Briarwood Castle. It was some sort of sick game he had been playing.

Brandon nodded, his lips a thin line. I could see the pain in his eyes every time his sister was mentioned. He must have loved her a great deal, and I almost felt bad for him.

"Yes, he told Riora he loved her, but when your mother came along he discarded her without a backward glance," he snarled.

"No!" I shook my head, I didn't want to believe it. "My father wouldn't do that. He was a good man."

"Foolish girl." Brandon stepped closer, his jaw tightening. "Your father was a coward and a liar. Now he has left his daughter behind to pay for his crimes. I was lucky to have met the archmage on my travels through Illiador, and he offered me a chance to finally get my revenge on your family."

"You told Lucian where we were in Calos too." It all made sense. That was why he was so concerned about how my magic was recovering. "It wasn't Marcus who betrayed us. It was you all along."

"Yes." Brandon nodded. "Getting rid of Marcus Gold wasn't difficult. It was that insufferable Captain Gerard who spoiled my carefully laid plans." He paused, eyeing me warily. "When I realized your powers were stronger than the archmage, I had to change my strategy. I sent word directly to Morgana as to where you were, and that your magic was weakened from using it in Calos."

The Drakaar were still circling and holding Santino down with their sorcery.

"I have what I came for," Brandon grinned, taking out the triangular key from his pocket. "The Drakaar, however, I called specifically to take care of you."

He seemed to be enjoying this. *How could I ever have trusted him?*

I gathered my magic and let it build up. If I was going to die today, I would go down fighting.

"Don't do it, Brandon. You have no idea what Morgana is going to do with that key." I tried to reason with him. "She is going to destroy our whole world."

"I don't care." Brandon turned to walk away. "I got what I wanted, and I will be placed in a high position once Morgana becomes High Queen." He stopped and turned back, almost as an afterthought. "I do regret having to kill the mastermage, though," he added. "But the silly old man kept the key on a chain around his neck. It was the only way."

He looked at the Drakaar. "I'm done with her. She's all yours."

My heartbeat quickened. I had to stop him from leaving with the key. Raising my hands, I gathered my magic. The sky crackled and shimmered as I shot a lightning strike at Brandon, but the Drakaar were still shielding him and he disappeared into the shadows.

Santino lay pinned to the ground, struggling to get up as Drakaar shadows circled him. I couldn't project my magic past theirs to shield him, and the darkness was reaching for me and snaking around my shield, trying to break through.

I whirled and shot consecutive bolts of silver-fire at the Drakaar; they recoiled and hissed as it struck them but only stopped momentarily. My fae powers held them back, but not for long. Silver-fire was the only thing that made them hesitate; mage magic had no effect on them whatsoever. Sweat formed on my brow as I struggled to control my wild magic without my amulet, but the dark sorcery of the Drakaar was too strong, and I had no idea how to get past their shields.

The leader of the Drakaar, the one who spoke to me earlier, reached out his hand, which looked more like a claw. Out snaked a shadow that solidified into a horrific creature similar to a gorgoth but without wings: a shadow demon. It lunged for me, pushing me to the ground as it clasped me in its talons, reaching out and suffocating my magic.

I struggled to focus. I couldn't die here. I had so much to do. There were so many people who were depending on me. I had been foolish and naïve all this time. If only I had learned to wield my fae powers properly.

But it was too late.

The Drakaar unsheathed a deadly-looking black sword from the scabbard on his back and stepped forward. "Once you are dead, little princess, Morgana will give us what we need to release our lord from his prison. And when he is free, even the High Queen of Avalonia will bend to the might of Lord Dragath."

A resounding screech, unfamiliar yet oddly comforting, made me look up. Even the Drakaar glanced up and faltered. What I saw next left me speechless and awestruck as the last spark of hope in my heart struggled to stay alive.

A brilliant flash of light burned through the night sky, drowning out the light of the moon. Out of the swirling clouds above emerged four massive griffins, creatures of myth and legend, with the bodies of lions and the heads and wings of eagles. On their backs rode four magnificent fae warriors, armed and deadly, holding swords flashing with silver-fire.

They leapt off the griffins before they touched the ground, and the shadow creature holding me in its grasp shrieked in fury as a blazing sword of silver-fire sliced through it. It exploded into black shards that dissipated in the light.

The fae warriors took up a fighting formation, surrounding me and shielding me from the Drakaar. The first warrior to reach me, the one who had killed the Shadow demon, looked to be the most lethal. I never knew the fae to look like this. His hair was long and dark as night, his face was the epitome of male beauty. Tall, lean, and corded with muscle, with unmistakable fae ears, he radiated power like nothing I had felt before.

He turned to glance at me and his bright sapphire eyes glowed with silver sparks, like stars in a twilight sky.

I pushed myself up and stood on wobbly legs, willing my hands to stop shaking. I gathered my magic and shielded myself.

The big fae warrior turned his back to me as he faced the leader of the Drakaar. "Ah! Raziel," he said with a smirk, seeming utterly unimpressed with the dark sorcerer. "It's been a while." He stepped forward with his deadly sword flashing silver in his hand, confidence rolling off him in waves. "You dare to come so close to the borders of Elfi?"

"Tristan," hissed the Drakaar, taking a step back, his eyes darting to Tristan's companions who stood around us, perfectly honed warriors. "Stay out of this, it has nothing to do with you."

But Tristan didn't flinch. "That is where you are wrong,

Raziel." His sharp eyes narrowed. "Princess Aurora is under the protection of the queen of Elfi. If you want her"—he twirled his sword deftly in his hand and assumed a fighting stance—"you will have to go through me."

"Hey!" said a red-haired warrior on my left, glaring at Tristan. "What about us? Do we look like chopped liver to you?"

Tristan turned his head slightly, and I could see the feral grin curling his lips. "Them too," he added, jerking his head towards the rest of his companions. "Cade here would love to add your head to his collection."

"So be it," said Raziel, raising his hands.

The Drakaar called for the gorgoths, and the creatures swooped down to defend their masters. The fae warriors fought them with strength and agility I had never seen before, whirling and slicing through flesh, bone, and shadow.

I heard a resounding screech and the griffins descended on the gorgoths, tearing at their limbs and wings.

All around me more Shadow Demons had sprung up, but the fire-fae warriors led by Tristan sliced through them with their flaming swords, cleaving through the darkness and leaving nothing behind. The Drakaar kept summoning more demons, but they were no match for the fae warriors of Elfi.

So that's how they do it. This is what I still had to learn. Now I finally understood why I needed to be trained by the fae.

I was completely mesmerized at the way the fae warriors used silver-fire. But out of the corner of my eye I could see a shadow demon moving on Santino, who, although alive, could not fight its magic.

I raised my magical shield and dove for Santino's sword, which lay on the ground beside me. I pushed my magic into it and it lit up, channeling my silver-fire into a blade of pure light. The magic within the blade made it lighter and easier to handle than a normal sword, and I allowed my magic to take over as I ran at the shadow demon attacking Santino. Raising my sword as I had seen Tristan do, I sliced through the creature. It burst into black shards of shadow that vanished in the light of my concentrated silver-fire.

Tristan was beside me in a flash and glanced over briefly to check my sword, which had started to fizzle out. "Your silver-fire is not strong enough. If you don't concentrate, it won't hold." He moved to take care of the other demons.

My grandmother must have sent them. But how did they find me?

I tried to infuse more power into the sword, but only bursts of magic sparked through the metal and faded. It wasn't as easy as it seemed.

Tristan looked like an avenging angel, his long dark hair whipping in the wind and his sword twirling and flashing in his hand as he swiftly beheaded two of the Drakaar. It was a pleasure to see them fight—even Santino could not move with the lethal grace and surety of the fae.

"Don't let Raziel get away," shouted Tristan to his red-haired companion, who stood over the severed head of one of the Drakaar.

But the Drakaar called Raziel was already gone, and so was the third key to the *Book of Abraxas*.

11
TRISTAN NIGHTSHADE

I KNEELED BESIDE Santino, who was thankfully still alive with no deep wounds. I placed my hands on his head and chest, assisting the healing. My magic flowed more freely, and I concentrated on knitting muscles and tendons, along with healing the cracks in his ribs. Santino was strong and he grimaced as his body mended.

Tristan came to stand beside me. He didn't offer any advice or help, just sheathed his sword in the scabbard strapped to his back and watched me as he scanned the surroundings, each move smooth and lethal. I wondered if he ever let his guard down.

"Thank you for what you did for us," I said, looking up to address the tall warrior once I finished healing Santino.

Tristan shrugged. "Just doing my job."

I helped Santino stand up. "What about the other gorgoths in the palace?"

"The griffins will have taken care of them." Tristan crossed his arms as he watched me warily. "Where did you learn to heal like that?" He glanced over at Santino, who was picking up his sword.

"At Evolon."

His brows scrunched together. "You learned this healing from mages?"

I shook my head and fidgeted under his sapphire gaze, adjusting my clothes, which were ripped and revealing too much. "I had a fae teacher."

His shoulders relaxed. "That explains it," he said, and moved away to speak to one of his companions, a fair-haired fae warrior with long hair, a green tunic, and high leather boots, who looked as deadly as Tristan. He eyed me warily as Tristan spoke to him in hushed tones.

Santino approached the fae warriors, his hand out-stretched. "Brandor is forever in your debt."

Tristan turned to face him. "It was nothing." He grasped Santino's forearm, nodding his acknowledgement of the debt as if it were an everyday occurrence.

"A man of few words." Santino winked at me. "I like him." Santino didn't seem to be fazed by the big fae warrior who towered over him. "I would like to offer you a place in my humble abode to stay as long as you wish. Anything your heart desires will be brought to you: food, jewels, women." He grinned at his last offer.

Tristan's mouth quirked to the side in what I think was a smile. "Thank you, but we must be on our way."

"As you wish," said Santino, "but at least rest and have something to eat before you leave." He looked up at the sky.

"Dawn will soon be upon us, and I am sure you must be famished after all that fighting."

Tristan nodded and turned his attention to me, his eyes narrowing. "Get your things ready, princess. We leave at first light."

The fair-haired warrior who stood beside Tristan put his hand on his shoulder. "Why do we have to take the *half-breed* with us?" He flicked a glance at me. "We should go back and send someone else to get her. As it is we had to save her. Now she will slow us down."

I bristled and my spine stiffened. *Half-breed.* Penelope had mentioned some of the noble houses of the fae looked down on anyone who was not purebred, but the animosity I felt coming from the fair-haired warrior was palpable.

Tristan looked me over and spoke to his companion as if I weren't there. "Our orders were to escort her to her grandmother, Aiden. She will have to keep up. It's not my problem if she collapses when she reaches Elfi."

Aiden nodded at Tristan and gave me a sharp look. "It would be a good riddance."

The fae warrior with short russet-colored hair walked up to us. He was dressed the same as the others and his twin swords were already sheathed on his back. "Aiden and Tristan can't help being rude," he said, smiling at me. "Think nothing of it, they're huge snobs."

Tristan scowled at his companion.

I nodded, but kept my mouth shut as I studied them all.

"I apologize," the red-haired fae said before bowing briefly. "I'm Cade. And you already know these two." He jerked his chin towards the two scowling warriors. "And that one," he pointed to the fourth warrior, who was still surveying the premises, "is my brother, Farrell."

"You look alike." I glanced at Farrell and smiled. At least one of them could speak without grunting in monosyllables or caustic remarks.

Cade stood up straighter. "We're twins but not identical, thank the Great Goddess. I got all the looks, as you can see."

I laughed. Cade was sweet, and at least one of them had a sense of humor.

"Enough, Cade," said Tristan. "Go get your things, princess, we leave at—"

"First light, yes," I said tightly. "I got it the first time." I'd had enough of his rudeness. And I didn't want to prove Aiden right by letting them know I needed to rest. I pushed my shoulders back. "I will meet you back here when the sun rises."

Tristan's eyebrow rose at my tone, but he said nothing.

Cade laughed. "I like her." He glanced at Tristan. "She may liven things up in Iris. The Royal Court has become so boring of late."

I hoped I had sounded remotely regal as I spun on my heel and sped off into the palace.

Santino followed, practically running after me because I was walking so fast. "I can't believe they are actually here." His eyes looked a bit wild.

I looked over to him and slowed my pace. Santino fell into step with me as we traversed the ornate corridors of the Red Citadel. "Who? You mean Lord Rude and Lord Obnoxious over there? You heard Tristan, my grandmother sent them."

"But these are not any fae warriors, Aurora," he said, hardly able to contain his excitement. "That is part of Queen Izadora's Elite Guard. The immortal High Fae knights of legend, the last of the fire-fae warriors of Elfi." I had never seen him so worked up. He was usually calm and composed in everything he did.

"I thought all of the fae knights were gone." I tried to assimilate what I had learned about the fae so far from Penelope and Kalen.

"Not all of them," said Santino. "Tristan Nightshade is a legend. Although he is one of the youngest, he is also the fiercest of Izadora's warriors, and the deadliest. They say his silver-fire can burn mountains to ash. Many of the Drakaar over the centuries have lost their heads to Tristan's blade."

"Centuries?" My eyes grew wide. "How old is he?"

"Around three hundred, I would say, give or take a few years."

"Three hundred years! But he looks in his early twenties.

How do you know all this?"

"I have studied the fae, as they are our direct neighbors and I need to protect our borders. But even if I hadn't, all Brandorians have grown up on fae stories. Everyone knows about Tristan Nightshade, Prince of the Night Court."

"The Prince of the Night Court?" I gasped, and an image of the ruins I saw when I was traveling to Calos flashed before my eyes. He was the one Brandon told me about; the merciless High Fae warrior who burned a mage fortress to ruin, killing everyone inside. He sounded like a monster. I shivered involuntarily. If Tristan hated mages so much, my grandmother must have quite a hold over him to get him to rescue me and take me to Elfi.

I sat down on the edge of my bed, my thoughts reeling. I had read a little about the fae courts in passing at the library at Evolon; it had been part of my research for my fae studies class. As far as I knew, there were three grand courts of the High Fae: the Day Court, the Night Court, and the Royal Court. The Day and Night Courts were ruled by a grand duke or duchess; and my grandmother, the queen of the fae, and her Royal Court presided over both the Day Court and the Night Court from the capital city of Elfi, known as Iris.

"I will leave you to change and pack your things." Santino stood up. "I must go check that the fae are well taken care of."

I nodded and tried to gather my thoughts before I proceeded on the last leg of my journey. I had no idea what to expect when I reached Elfi. The fae were steeped in tradition and old magic, and were much more powerful than the mages. Brandon had warned me against them, and although he had betrayed me, I knew there was some truth to what he had said about the High Fae. I would have to proceed very carefully from now on. My focus had to be learning to master my fae magic and understanding how to control it without my amulet. But I knew I had more to learn if I was going to be half as good as the fire-fae warriors.

Soon Santino returned to tell me that the fae warriors were ready and getting impatient to leave. Two maids accompanied him with trays of food.

"I wanted to make sure you ate something before you left," Santino said. "It will be a long journey to Elfi."

I went over to the breakfast tray and popped some berries and dried fruits into my mouth while Santino apprised me of his father's plans. After this attack on the palace, the Emir had forbidden him from escorting me to Elfi, as Santino was needed in Brandor. The fae warriors were more than capable of protecting me on our journey. But I was uncomfortable around them. I wished Erien, Vivienne, or Kalen were here if Rafe couldn't be. I needed a friend, someone to talk to, and these fae warriors didn't look too friendly. After what I'd heard about them, I was not sure what to expect anymore.

I had already changed into my traveling clothes and tucked my hair under the hood of my cloak as I moved about my room, gathering the last of my things and picking at my breakfast tray. I couldn't resist eating the whole bowl of fresh clotted cream, drizzled in honey and candied fruits, a traditional Brandorian breakfast.

"Give me five minutes." I couldn't find the second dagger given to me by Rafe, and I didn't want to leave without it.

"What did the mastermage mean about the key Brandon stole?" asked Santino as he helped me look for the missing dagger.

Santino had proved he could be trusted, so I told him briefly about Morgana's search for the *Book of Abraxas*. He needed to know what was at stake, what Morgana and the Drakaar were truly after, but I did not tell him about the Dawnstar. He didn't need to know about it yet, not until I knew more about it myself.

I had to begin thinking strategically. If Santino could convince his father and the other Emirs to stand against Morgana, we could have a chance to defend Elfi. Brandor was the bordering kingdom, and Morgana would have to go through Brandor to get her army to Elfi, if it ever came to that.

Santino listened carefully, not saying a word until I had finished. He ran a hand over his mouth and short beard.

"My spies have heard rumors Morgana's people have been looking for ancient magical artifacts. But I never suspected this was what she was after." He started to pace. "But this may be what we need to get my father to stand against Morgana. He would not be so foolish to let her get her hands on the *Book of Abraxas*."

I nodded. "Yes, exactly. If we can get the kingdoms to unite against Morgana, we may have a chance."

Santino stopped pacing and gripped the windowsill. "I have heard of a rebel group that hides in the Darkwood on the border of Illiador."

"Yes, Brandon mentioned them; the Silver Swords, I think they call themselves."

"Precisely," said Santino. "You are surprisingly well-informed." He turned to face me. "I had some of my spies infiltrate the rebel camps. It seems most of the rebel leaders are comprised of the common people brought together by remnants of noble houses who were loyal to your parents. When Azaren and Elayna were killed, the survivors of your father's court hid in the Darkwood, biding their time and helping the people of Illiador who were tortured by Morgana's Shadow Guards."

"Where are you going with this?" Could the Silver Swords help us? Would they?

"Ever since word you had returned reached the rebels, plans have been made to gather an army."

"What army?"

"Your army, Aurora. For you to lead, and take back your kingdom."

I knew it was coming to this, but the reality hadn't struck me until now. "And who leads the Silver Swords?" I had my own suspicions about who it was.

"My latest intelligence has revealed Duke Gabriel Silverthorne is the leader and commander of the Silver Swords." Santino's eyes never left my face.

"I thought as much," I muttered. Uncle Gabriel was quite a resourceful fellow. "I hope Rafe manages to free him from the dungeons."

"Prince Rafael is in touch with the rebels—they will help him free the duke, if it can be done."

"How does he know them?" Rafe had never mentioned it.

"Rafael has been working for your uncle for some time now, taking messages back and forth between Silverthorne and the Silver Swords. The Black Wolf was his cover."

I shook my head. "But why didn't he tell me any of this?"

Santino shrugged his broad shoulders. "I don't know why he kept it from you. But I'm pretty sure he and Silverthorne had their reasons and would have told you eventually."

This was what Uncle Gabriel and Rafe were planning all along. I wished I had listened and trusted my uncle when he said he had a plan, although the mastermage had pointed out it was fate which sent me from the palace that day. Otherwise I might have been captured along with Uncle Gabriel. Or worse, already dead.

"I have my people in touch with Rafael. I will aid when I can to help free your uncle. You concentrate on mastering your powers, until we can get you in contact with the Silver Swords. I have sent more spies on the lookout for your cousin and aunt."

"Thank you so much, Santino—you have helped us a lot. And I know I've said this before, but I appreciate everything you have done. I am forever in your debt."

Santino moved from the window, but he didn't come closer. "And I in yours."

I hung my head. I still had reservations. "I don't know how much help I am going to be to you. I have failed at everything I have tried to do so far. Why would the rebels follow me? Why would anyone follow me? I've proved nothing so far except my own naivete. My magic is still too wild, and I am not sure if I will ever be able to master it completely. Maybe I should take your father's advice and disappear entirely. I will never be strong enough to stand against the Drakaar, and Morgana will never stop hunting me. I am no queen, and I'm not sure if I ever will be."

I had never truly realized the magnitude of what we were up against until I met the Drakaar and the High Fae. These were warriors and magic-wielders with centuries of experience under their belts. I was facing immortal, hardened killers, with magic that threatened to suffocate all hope and light from this world. My only hope was a legendary weapon that may or may not exist.

Santino came to stand before me and took my hand in his, looking me straight in the eyes. "Do you know what happened on the night when the Silver Swords heard about your battle with the Shadow Guards?"

I looked at my feet. "I was told many people called me a monster and beseeched the king of Eldoren to send me back to Morgana."

Santino smiled. "A few of the Eldorean rabble, no doubt." He lifted my chin with his finger to look at him. "But in Illiador, in your kingdom, in the rebel camps and in the streets of various towns and villages, fires were lit all the way from the Darkwood to the shores of the great Western Sea, passing the word that their Queen, Aurora Firedrake, had finally returned and was coming to take back her kingdom. Music and dancing flowed through the streets for the first time in a decade as fires lit up the skies over Illiador."

He grasped my arms gently. "You have given them hope, Aurora. A reason to live on, to fight for their freedom from Morgana's tyranny." Santino's sharp eyes narrowed. "Do you know what your people are calling you?"

I shook my head, a knot in my chest clenching as an unfamiliar feeling rose and took hold.

Santino smiled, his amber eyes twinkling. "It looks like

you have a new title, *Aurora Shadowbreaker*."

The knot in my chest got tighter, and tears pooled in my eyes as I took in what he was saying. Listening to Santino speak about the Silver Swords, about men, women, and children, my people, who were willing to follow me into battle and help me fight for my right to my father's throne, humbled me to such an extent a tear finally leapt free and fell on my cheek. A single spark of hope ignited in my chest.

My decision was crystal clear.

I would fight for my kingdom. I would fight for my parents and everyone who had ever believed in me. I would fight, because that was who I was. Aurora Firedrake was not a monster curled up inside of me waiting to be set free whenever I took off the amulet. She was the strength within me, the one who would never back down even in the face of death. My magic was not a burden to be bound and stifled. It was a gift, it was my destiny; it was what made me *Aurora Shadowbreaker*.

I had kept that part of me hidden for so long, because somewhere deep down I was afraid of what I was truly capable of. It was time to embrace my fate, move forward, and grow into the woman I knew I could be, one whom my parents would be proud of.

Aurora Darlington was gone. Nothing in the world was going to change that. I was Aurora Firedrake, and I was born to be a queen.

The people of Illiador needed me, my people needed me, and this time I would not fail them.

12
IRIS

Dawn had arrived.

I finished packing my little leather satchel, I didn't have much to take with me. I carefully sheathed my daggers in place and strapped the sword Rafe had given me on my hip. "I'm ready."

Santino walked me to the gardens where the fae and their griffins were waiting. I stared in awe at the mighty creatures, their gold feathers glinting in the light of the rising sun. The fae warriors were pacing in front of their massive mounts, eager to get in the air.

They stopped when they saw me. Tristan's eyes darkened as he looked me over. "I am glad you had the sense to change into appropriate riding attire, princess."

I glowered at him. "I'm not completely new to this, you know."

"You could have fooled me." He turned to check the saddle on the griffin. "We must be on our way—the longer we are away from Elfi, the longer the kingdom remains unprotected."

"Modest much?" I muttered under my breath.

172

Tristan turned and glared at me.

I rolled my eyes. Of course he could hear me with that immortal fae hearing of his.

"So, who am I riding with?" I looked around. Aiden ignored me, and I was glad for that. Cade and Farrell smiled and got on to their mounts.

"Griffin riding can be dangerous for an inexperienced rider like yourself," Tristan answered. "Your mount has been arranged." He jumped onto his griffin's back in one fluid motion.

I drew my brows together. "My mount?"

Just then a musical tinkling voice filled my head. *Do not fret, little princess, I am here.*

My heart leapt, and a broad grin spread across my face. Snow!

I looked up. The white pegasus flew out of the sky, her iridescent wings bigger than before, and landed amidst the griffins, stamping her hooves and shaking her magnificent mane.

I ran to Snow and hugged her neck. It was so good to have her back. "I missed you," I said through our bond.

"*I did too, little princess,*" said Snow. "*Get on, these griffins look like they are raring to go.*"

I smiled, and Santino gave me a leg up as I jumped onto Snow's back. The fae had fitted her with a beautiful light leather saddle, which was far more comfortable than riding bareback as I had been doing until now. I said goodbye to Santino and waved once as Snow broke into a canter, spread her massive wings, and shot into the brightening sky. The griffins leapt into the air after us, quickly forming a formation around Snow and me.

We flew over the vast deserts of Brandor and onward toward the towering Wildflower Mountains surrounding Elfi. The wind whipped through my hair as Snow easily kept pace with the powerful griffins and their riders.

I told Snow all that had happened, and she updated me on what she knew about the state of affairs in Eldoren. It was much more convenient speaking to Snow in my head; we were traveling so fast our voices could not be heard over the sound of the wind. "Has there been any news about Aunt Serena and Erien?"

"Not that I've heard."

"And Rafe?"

"The prince got back to the palace a day ago. He was the one who informed me where you were and sent me to you."

"Is he all right?"

"He was when I saw him." Snow soared on the wind as we rose higher and higher into the clouds. *"He also sent word to your grandmother about what happened. When you removed your amulet, we could sense your exact location. That is how the fae warriors and I found you. Prince Rafael has been worried about you, and wanted to make sure you got to Elfi safely."*

My heart shifted and the familiar ache returned. I missed Rafe and his cheerful confidence. He was my anchor in a sea of troubles, and when he was around I knew he always had my back. Even when he was far away, he watched over me. I wished I could go back and help him.

———∼∼∼———

We left the desert behind us, the endless sand dunes of Brandor giving way to patches of foliage and tufts of trees as we approached the base of the Wildflower Mountains. The slopes spread out in all directions as far as the eye could see, guarding Elfi from the outside world.

The sun had started to set as Snow and the griffins climbed higher over the towering peaks, soaring through the clouds and flying into a narrow gorge past thickly forested mountain slopes. Finally, we emerged in a lush valley covered with a carpet of wild green grass and heather, strewn abundantly with wildflowers.

In the middle of the hidden valley, the magnificent fae capital city, Iris, came into view. It was the most breathtaking sight I had ever seen. The Crystal Castle was built into the face of the mountain. Slender towers spiked through the night sky and glittered brilliantly as the moon rose overhead, dazzling the whole city with its silver light. Clear streams cascaded down from the mountains around it, sparkling as if the water itself was filled with stars.

A massive wall enclosed Iris, protected by powerful magic. The fae warriors could not fly over the city. We landed in the valley outside the city gates where twelve proud centaurs stood at attention. Half-man and half-horse, the fae creatures bowed low when they saw who were riding the griffins. Most of them had their long hair tied back from their rugged faces, and each of the centaur guards wore two massive swords strapped to his back alongside a quiver of arrows and held a massive yew bow. Six of them moved forward to open the city gates for Izadora's elite band of warriors.

As the great golden doors to the fae capital opened inward, the fae riders got off their griffins. I did the same with my mount; the griffins and the pegasus were not allowed inside the city.

"*I will be gone for a while,*" said Snow. "*I must journey to the Old Forest and find out what happened to my family.*"

I hugged Snow and patted her neck. "I understand. I hope you find them. Be safe, and come back soon."

"*I will,*" Snow said in my mind as I walked forward, surrounded by my escort, and entered the fae city of Iris.

We strode through the cobblestone streets and up the main avenue to the Crystal Castle. A towering white stone structure embedded into the mountain, with outer walls made entirely of a rock hard fae crystal found only in the southern mines of Elfi, the fae queen's palace gleamed in the distance as the moon rose over Iris. Opulent mansions of the nobility descended into the valley from the foothills of the castle, surrounded by flowering grottos and shaded paths that led down to the city, which spread out in a wide semi-circle around the palace.

Most of the High Fae shuffled out of the way as the fae warriors passed. Others would gawk at Tristan and move over to the opposite side of the street. He sauntered like a stealthy predator, his sapphire eyes constantly scanning the crowd for threats.

We crossed white marble bridges shimmering above small streams and glittering waterfalls that ran down from the mountains. Glass orbs floated through the air, lighting up the city. A haunting melody rose to my ears as fingers danced on harp strings in the starry night, filling the city with their lilting song.

Here within the confines of their own land, protected by the magic of their queen, the fae seemed to move about their lives without fear. I was glad to see one place that was still safe from Morgana's evil, which had started to claw its way into every kingdom in the north and west and was now looking to the east. Eventually she would move south to Elfi; it was inevitable.

"How things have changed," Aiden muttered to Tristan as Cade and I followed behind them, past the palace gates and through the vast open halls of the Crystal Castle.

Tristan glanced at him. "What do you mean?"

"How can you be okay with this?" Aiden asked, obviously unconcerned that I could hear him. "I thought you hated mages?"

"I do hate mages," said Tristan. "But she's only half mage and not a threat. She's weak and her magic isn't strong."

"Not strong?" Aiden looked incredulous. "She's Aurora Firedrake, the most powerful fae-mage to be born in thousands of years. You've heard the stories about her!"

"Exaggerations," Tristan shrugged. "She can't be as powerful as they say she is. I saw her fight, she's untrained and clumsy with her powers."

"She could be here to spy for the mages." Aiden's voice was low but dripping with malice. I could still hear him and he knew that. "Did you think of that? The queen is taking a big chance letting this one into the city. She could turn on us at any time."

Tristan nodded. "It's possible. No mage can be trusted. But the queen wants her here and there is nothing we can do about it right now." He lowered his voice, but I could still hear him faintly. "Hopefully she will be gone soon and we won't have to see her ever again."

Aiden looked back at me and scowled. "I hope so."

I scowled back at him and stepped closer to Cade, who coughed and flicked a glance at me. His eyes pitied me, and I knew he too had heard what Tristan and Aiden had said. Did all of them hate half-fae? Maybe Cade did too and was keeping quiet about it.

We entered the throne room, a grand hall lined with marble pillars and huge arched windows fitted with fae crystal that glinted in the moonlight. I followed Tristan and the others, their boots clumping loudly on the smooth marble floor. At the very end of the room, standing before her throne, was Izadora, Queen of the Fae, my grandmother.

She stood regal and elegant on a raised dais, dressed in a gown of pure silver that flowed around her body like a shimmering mist. I thought she was the most beautiful woman I had ever seen. Her hair was the color of spun gold, entwined with silver cascading down to her feet. Her eyes were the most startling shade of gold, and she radiated a glow unlike anything I had seen before. On her head, she wore a crown of pearls set within a carved circlet of silver. The queen of the fae was over a thousand years old, but she didn't look a day over forty.

All the fae warriors bent their knees and bowed when they saw her.

"We have done as you asked, Your Majesty," Tristan said, his voice low. "The princess is safe."

My grandmother looked me over. "Thank you, Tristan, you all may go. Aurora and I have much to discuss." Her voice was cold.

The fae warriors turned and left the room without a word. Izadora's gold eyes met mine and I smiled, stepping forward to hug my grandmother.

Immediately a wall of magic slammed into me and knocked the breath right out of my lungs.

"We do not show affection in my court," said my grandmother with an immortal stillness, as I stood gasping for breath. "Kindness and love, which the humans prize most, is a weakness. It is a noose around your neck waiting to strangle the life out of you." She paused, assessing me. "I know you have grown up in the human world, and I don't know why your mother chose to send you there. But let this be your first lesson. Life is hard, and everything comes at a price. The sooner you learn that, the better. Understand you are not here because of some grandmotherly affection I feel towards you. You are here for a purpose, and that is all."

I was reeling from shock. I thought my grandmother would be happy to see me. But she was as cold as the winter snow, an ice queen without emotion. What exactly was I getting myself into? But it was too late—I was here, and this was my last chance to prove myself.

I clenched my fists and straightened my spine. "Then why did you send the fae warriors to bring me here? You should have let the Drakaar kill me."

"Don't be so dramatic." The queen of the fae waved her hand and turned to go and sit on her throne. "You have your uses, and I do not let my feelings get in the way of what has to be done. The mages have created a mess I must now clean up. Morgana has ruled long enough, and I cannot let her reign of terror continue, not when she dares to threaten the borders of my kingdom."

"And what about the other kingdoms?" I spat out. Didn't she care about the rest of the world? Was she so heartless that she would let others suffer if she could help them? "People in Illiador are dying, children are being torn from their parents, terrors unimaginable walk in the northern kingdoms, and you sit here on your comfortable throne and tell me you have decided to stand up to Morgana because she threatens your safe little part of the world?"

Her immortal stare was cool and calculating as she assessed me. "The rest of the world is not my concern."

"Morgana killed your daughter. How can that not be your concern?" I snarled.

"Killed?" Izadora said coolly, her one eyebrow arching in a perfect bridge.

My mouth dried up. *She knew!*

"You knew my mother was not dead, but trapped in the dagger. And you did nothing about it?" I struggled to keep my voice even. I could not let my anger take hold of me; not here, not now. I clenched my fists. "You left her to rot inside it for fifteen years."

"Elayna knew what she was getting into when she married your father." The fae queen's voice was icy and without a drop of affection. "I warned her against marrying outside the fae court, and she married a mage of all things. She thought she was in love, and gave up her immortal life to save her mortal *half-breed* child. She deserved her fate."

"How can you say that about your own daughter?" My body shook as my magic tried to break free. I dug my nails into my palms and willed myself to stay calm, pushing it back down. I never imagined my grandmother could be so cold-hearted. "No wonder my mother left you—at least she had a few years of real love." I tried to keep my voice from breaking.

"And what did it get her?" my grandmother snapped, her gold eyes flashing.

I pursed my lips, my blood boiling, but I held my anger in check. She was an immortal and much stronger than I was. I could not let my anger get in the way of what I had to do. I needed her and she needed me. And I had to make the most of what I had.

"One day, I will free my mother," I vowed.

"Without my help, you will never succeed in defeating Morgana or getting close to the Dark Dagger," said the queen, coolly. "While you are in Elfi, you will abide by my rules. Remember you are only here because I permit you to remain."

I pursed my lips and contained my anger. I could not afford to lose Izadora's help.

"Be not mistaken," the fae queen continued. "You are not

my heir, nor will you ever be named such until you prove yourself. You are a fae-mage and thus a *half-breed*," she sneered. "The High Fae will never follow you. Fae-mages are abominations of the natural order of things; your powers are unpredictable and largely unmapped territory. Your magic needs to be controlled and given direction. Containing it will eventually end badly for you and for the rest of the world. Therefore, I will allow you to stay in Elfi and train with my warriors. The magic within this valley is concentrated with all the powers of the fae. It is only here you will be able to tap into your true potential, and find the real depths of your powers if you so wish. Once you are ready, I will provide the resources you need to take back your father's throne and end Morgana's rule for good."

Izadora's help would be invaluable when it came to the final battle to retake Illiador; without her and the fae warriors of Elfi, even if I secured the Silver Swords' assistance, I would only be leading a band of rebels to their death. If I made it to that point. This was an offer I couldn't refuse, and she knew it.

But she needed me too. If I refused to fight for my throne, Elfi would eventually be swallowed up by Morgana's growing empire. I knew the fae queen valued strength above all, and she wanted me to prove I was worthy to be her heir, I would do it. Starting now.

"I will do as you ask," I said, crossing my arms. "But I

have one condition."

Izadora smiled for the first time since I met her. It looked more like a feral grin, but it was a smile all the same. "So, you are not as dimwitted as you seem."

I ignored the deliberate jab and waited.

"What is your condition?" The smile was gone, replaced by a cunning look.

I chose my words carefully. "If I do as you say, remain in Elfi and do everything to master my powers, I want you to help me rescue my mother from the Dagger of Dragath."

The fae queen's gold eyes flashed, her knuckles white against the throne she gripped.

I waited, holding my breath. I willed my heart to stay calm. Had I gone too far? Would she burn me to a crisp?

Finally, Izadora's eyes softened slightly, and she nodded. "Yes. If you do exactly as I command while you reside in Elfi, I will help you break the curse on the Dagger of Dragath and release Elayna."

As she ended her last word, I felt a magical bond pass through us.

"What you felt was a magical oath binding. I am bound by my oath to help you, but only if you manage to keep yours."

I nodded. "Thank you." And we were bound until one of us broke our oath.

The doors opened and the fae guards stood at attention

as Tristan walked in.

"You sent for me, Majesty?" he drawled, inclining his head.

"Tristan here will make sure you don't get up to any trouble," Izadora said to me.

Tristan scowled.

"I expect her to remain alive while she is in Elfi." She gave Tristan a warning look. "You know how the rest of the court hates *half-breeds*, and I don't want any so-called accidents. I have a use for her, and she is under your protection until it is done."

Tristan nodded, his eyes shooting daggers at his queen, but she chose not to notice. I was taken aback momentarily; I thought all the fae loved their queen. I guess I was wrong, and I didn't blame him.

"She will start with the novices tomorrow," Izadora continued. "You will oversee her training."

Tristan's hands were balled in fists. "I do not train novices."

"You do now. Get Cade or Aiden to help you—I've heard she's quite a handful." The queen of the fae waved her hand to dismiss us. "Now go! I've had enough of her for one day. She looks like her father."

13
THE CRYSTAL CASTLE

"I'M NOT A bloody nursemaid," Tristan muttered, storming out of the throne room.

I followed but kept my mouth shut. The fae prince didn't look like he was in the mood for chitchat. But I still had to stay close to him, whether or not he was a bad-tempered ass. I was unnerved to find out I was not truly safe, even in this palace. My grandmother had made it quite clear I was under Tristan's protection, but I didn't know how far the hatred toward *half-breeds* went. If Aiden was any example, I suspected I was in for trouble here. I had to be on my guard at all times—I couldn't slip up, not anymore. I had to prove to my grandmother and the High Fae that I was worthy of the name I bore.

He looked back at me, and his eyes narrowed as I ran to keep up. "Are you always this slow?"

"Are you always this grumpy?" I was fed up with his constant surliness. "You could at least try to speak civilly to me."

He stopped and turned, his jaw clenched. "Just because the queen has ordered me to be your guard dog doesn't mean we are friends. Izadora didn't order me to be polite, and I will speak to you however I wish."

Cade fell into step with us. "There you are. How did it go?" He looked genuinely concerned.

Tristan ignored him and kept walking.

I glanced at Cade. "Not great."

Cade put his hand on my shoulder. "If it helps, Queen Izadora's not nice to anyone."

I shook my head. "It doesn't help, but thank you for trying." I smiled at the big fae warrior; Cade was the only one in this place who had been nice to me.

"Cade, watch her and don't let her out of your sight," Tristan growled. "I'll be back soon."

"Where are you going?" Cade called after him.

Tristan didn't answer. He stalked off into the night, like a wild panther on his way to his next kill.

"Is he always this bad tempered?"

"Only for the last twenty years or so." A half smile curved his lips. "Izadora knows Tristan hates mages. Putting him in charge of your training is her way of reminding him that he has to obey her."

"Why can't he refuse?" I was intrigued to know more about Tristan.

He shrugged as he escorted me through the palace. "It's not for me to say. You should ask him yourself."

"He hardly speaks to me. I don't think he is going to tell me his life story."

Cade chuckled. "He's not so bad, once you get to know him." We climbed the stairs to a tower. "Give him time, he'll come around."

My room was situated in a high tower away from the rest of the castle, and could only be reached by climbing an endless line of stone steps to the top. It was sparse and round, with three arched windows that looked out over the city and the hidden valley of the fae all the way to the huge mountains that surrounded Elfi. Although the rest of the castle had windows fitted with clear crystal, my room was open to the elements, its loose muslin curtains hardly a deterrent to the howling wind that swept down from the mountains at night.

I thanked Cade, who informed me he would be on guard at the bottom of the stairs until Tristan returned.

My tower room had a small curtained alcove that housed the bath and toilet. I washed in the porcelain basin with the jug of water that lay beside it. It was too cold to have a bath anyway. I shivered and lay down on the bed, my stomach growling. I didn't want to walk all the way down the stairs of my tower to find the kitchens, so I decided to wake up early and have breakfast instead. I covered myself with the thin blanket and tried to get some sleep.

I was not sure what to expect when it came to my training. I had seen the fae fight with a lethal grace and surety I was sure would take me a lifetime to achieve. Their magic was powerful and more complicated than the magic of the mages.

I thought back to when I first reached Avalonia and Silverthorne Castle. When Uncle Gabriel found out who I was, he was so kind to me, and immediately accepted me back into the family. Aunt Serena and Erien had been nothing but sweet and helpful, though they didn't need to go out of their way to include me and make me feel accepted.

In this fae land, under my grandmother's rule, I was an outsider, a *half-breed*, someone they looked down on. In Elfi I was not a princess, I was a warrior who had a task to do, and I would not back down.

The next morning, I awoke as soon as the sun ascended over the valley and lit up the Crystal Castle. I washed and wore the clothes laid out for me on the chair by some unknown person, then descended the seemingly endless steps from my room to the main hallway of the palace.

I fidgeted with my new clothes, a basic cotton tunic over a white shirt and green skintight pants with my sword hanging from the leather belt around my waist. I wore my old brown boots, which were still in good condition, and wandered around looking for the kitchens.

I smiled at two fae ladies who passed me in the hallway.

They were wearing lose chiffon gowns, clasped on one shoulder with a gold star. Both sniffed when they saw me, stuck their noses in the air, and hurried on. I moved along quickly, lowering my head and looking at my feet as I walked.

I bumped into a wall. Well, at least I thought it was a wall, it turned out to be Tristan. I looked up through my lashes at him, cringing inwardly. I probably wasn't supposed to walk the halls of the castle alone.

He glowered at me, his dark eyes flashing. "What part of stay in your room don't you understand?"

I glared back at him. "No one told me I had to stay in my room."

Cade came running up. "Oh good! You found her."

"Didn't you tell her to wait in her room until one of us came to get her?" Tristan snapped at Cade.

Cade shrugged, his hands in his pockets. "Not in so many words, no. How was I supposed to know she would wake up so early and start wandering around the castle? The high ladies of the Royal Court don't rise until noonday."

"She's not a high lady, she's one of my novices," said Tristan.

"Since when do you train novices?" Cade raised an eyebrow.

"Since Izadora commanded me to train her and make sure she doesn't get into any trouble."

Cade looked me over. "She's fine, so what's the problem,

Tristan? Relax. The only trouble she has right now is you."

Tristan rolled his shoulders and the silver swirls in his eyes died out. "Why were you down here anyway?" he asked me, trying to temper his tone. "I was coming to get you—we are to begin your training today."

"I was hungry," I said sheepishly. "I didn't eat last night, so I was looking for the kitchen."

Tristan turned his head to glare at Cade. "You didn't feed her?"

"I'm not a dog," I snapped. "I don't need to be fed. Just point me to the kitchen and I will get it myself."

Tristan scowled, but Cade chuckled and linked his arm with mine. "Come on, I'll take you to the kitchens. I hear the cook is making pastries for tonight's feast. And no one makes better pastries in all the seven kingdoms than Guido."

"Fine, I will see you both on the training ground after you stuff your faces," muttered Tristan as he stalked off.

Cade rolled his eyes as we walked to the kitchen. Small men and women with big ears and hairy feet bustled around the cavernous room that lay within the mountain. Brownies! Or house sprites, as they were called in Elfi. I had met a few of them in Pixie Bush with Kalen. He had mentioned they were very good housekeepers; I guess they were good cooks too.

Delicious aromas of freshly baked bread and warm hand-made pastries wafted toward me; my mouth watered and my stomach growled loudly. The whole kitchen stopped working and turned to stare at me.

Cade chuckled. "I guess you weren't exaggerating when you said you were hungry."

I blushed all the way from my head to the tips of my toes. *How embarrassing.*

A house sprite in a white apron, his big ears popping out of something resembling a chef's hat, came up to us. "Lord Cade, I have your sugar cream rolls ready," he said, holding out a plate of freshly baked pastries.

Cade took them and popped one in his mouth. "Thank you, Guido, these are my favorites." He held the plate out to me. "Try one."

I took one and bit into the golden-brown pastry. A thick vanilla and lavender flavored cream oozed out of the lightly sugar-dusted pastry. "These are amazing."

Cade nodded, a big grin on his face.

The little house sprites kept coming up to me to sample all the various cakes and pies. But I knew I couldn't eat too much, as Tristan probably had a hard training session planned. I hated passing up the rest of the sugar cream rolls and raspberry pastries, but I took one cinnamon swirl to tide me over till later.

I nibbled on it as Cade escorted me down to the training grounds. We traversed the flowering walkways and terraced gardens down the mountain, occasionally passing a satyr or a dryad tending the various plants, flowers and trees. Foxgloves and daisies dotted the area where marble statues spouted water into shimmering fountains.

The training grounds were situated near the soldier's barracks at the foot of the castle, a whole area stretching all the way to the eastern wall of the city. The grounds were already full of young fae warriors practicing with glinting swords and staffs. At the far end a group of archers were going about their daily practice routine with targets set up on one side of the grounds.

A tall fae warrior who looked much older than Cade and Tristan, his white hair combined with fading gold, stood watching the novices sparring, his powerful arms crossed across his chest.

"Who is he?"

"That's Erik, the leader of Izadora's Elite Guard," Cade answered. "He usually stops by the training ground every day at this time to watch the novices sparring. If he finds one with potential, he takes them on to train them himself. He is the eldest and most experienced of Izadora's warriors and our old teacher."

"How many of you are there in the Elite Guard?"

"Seven," said Tristan, before Cade could answer.

"Only seven? I thought there would be more of you."

Tristan glared at me.

Cade laughed. "It's not an insult, Tristan. She doesn't

know much about the High Fae, so it's understandable she wouldn't know how many are left."

Tristan rolled his powerful shoulders. "We are the last of the fire-fae warriors of Elfi," he explained finally. "For centuries, our numbers have dwindled almost to extinction, and fae with the ability to produce silver-fire are rarely seen. Your mother was the only fire-fae to be born in the last century, and then there's you. Only one of the Elite can teach you to master this ability. It is our only defense against the dark magic of the Drakaar and their demons."

A group of fae boys and girls, some older than me and some younger, were sparring with staffs in the center of the field. Tristan thrust a staff into my hand. "Let's see what you can do. I presume you have learned basic fighting skills?"

I nodded, not sure of myself. I had never fought with a staff, but Santino had taught me to fight with sticks, and I had learned a few basics with swords and daggers when I trained with Baron Tanko and Rafe at Evolon. I adjusted my grip as I stood at the edge of the field, watching the others and wondering which one I would have to spar with, when a sudden blow to the back of my knees dropped me to the ground and the staff clattered out of my hand.

I cursed under my breath and looked up, shielding my eyes with my hand.

"Get up!" growled Tristan.

I pushed myself up and picked up my staff, turning to

my attacker. A young girl about my age, with hair like the noonday sun tucked behind her unmistakable pointy fae ears, stood before me.

She started circling me, lithe and nimble, the staff twirling effortlessly in her experienced hands.

Thwack! She hit my arm with the staff.

I held my staff with both hands and tried to block her next blow. Again and again she hit me—arms, back, legs. She was too fast, a blur. I could hardly see her, let alone anticipate her moves.

A blow to the stomach knocked the wind straight out of me and I doubled over. She kicked me hard and sent me sprawling backward, the staff clattering out of my hand as I fell.

"She's useless, Tristan," the girl said as I tried to get up. "She can't even hold onto her staff."

"Again," barked Tristan, coming over and helping me adjust my grip. "Keep your legs wide, one foot slightly behind the other to brace the blows. I expect you to have improved by the end of the day." He turned to leave.

"Where are you going?" I adjusted my stance as he had suggested. "I thought you were supposed to train me."

"I am to oversee your training, Aurora," said Tristan, his eyes cold. "Heal yourself and start again. I want you to spar with Skye for the rest of the day. There is a problem in the outlying villages I must go and check out. I will be back to inspect your progress."

He turned and left. Cade gave me a pitying look and hurried after Tristan.

Skye came at me again, and I raised my staff, gripping it firmly with both my hands. My arms shuddered as I blocked her blow.

She smiled, her violet eyes flashing. "So, you do know how to fight."

We sparred for the rest of the day. I kept healing myself and getting up, only to be beaten down again. But I didn't give up. I pushed myself and studied how Skye moved, graceful and surefooted, never missing a step. At the end of the day, after hours of trying to defend myself against the beatings, I collapsed on the ground and lay down, my chest heaving from the exertion. I was a mass of cuts and bruises.

Skye came up to me and put out her hand. "You did well." She smiled and her face lit up. "Sorry about the beatings, but Tristan told me not to go easy on you."

"I didn't expect you to." I clasped her hand and pulled myself up, my legs a wobbly mess. I touched my face and winced. I hadn't healed my lip, and it was still bleeding. I ran my finger over the wound and the bleeding stopped, the cut on my lip closing as if it was never there.

Skye's eyes went wide. "Your healing power is very advanced. And it's a good thing too. I don't think it would be a good idea to go to the feast tonight looking like that."

"What feast?" Cade had mentioned a feast as well.

"There is a gathering tonight, I presume to welcome you to court," said Skye as we walked back to the palace.

"But I have nothing to wear." I was not in the mood for a feast or a ball or any of the other court stuff. I was done with all that frivolity. I had a job to do and I was exhausted.

Another girl with flaming red hair and a voluptuous body came running up to talk to Skye and whispered in her ear.

Skye's eyes went wide and she turned to me. "I have to go, sorry." She grimaced. "Apparently, my mother has arrived in Iris for the feast and is on a rampage because I wasn't there to greet her. I'd better go and sort her out."

She turned to the redhead. "Brianna, please help Aurora find something to wear tonight. She recently arrived and has no formal clothes."

"Of course." Brianna smiled, her green eyes studying me like a cat's. "I'll have something sent to your room right away."

"Thank you."

Tristan and Cade fell into step with us, emerging unexpectedly out of the shadows. Brianna's face lit up when she saw Tristan, but he didn't notice her.

"How did she do?" Tristan asked Skye.

"I'm right here, you can ask me yourself," I said tartly.

Skye laughed. "Give her a few days, Tristan, it's all too new for her. See you later at the feast, Aurora. Come on,

Brianna." She ran off with her friend toward the palace.

Tristan glared at me, and Cade grinned.

"Skye's sweet," I said as they walked me back to the palace.

Cade nodded. "She's the only one in the family who is."

"Who is her family? She said something about her mother arriving and going on a rampage."

Cade chuckled. "So, Andromeda's back, is she?"

Tristan nodded. "She came in today for the feast."

"I was wondering why Aiden decided to go on patrol today."

Tristan shrugged. "I guess it was the lesser of two evils."

"Skye is Aiden's younger sister," Cade explained. "And their mother is the Grand Duchess of the Day Court. She has a terrible temper, and when she comes to town even Aiden runs for the hills. Skye is the only one she listens to."

"Where is Skye's father?"

"The Grand Duke of the Day Court has been ailing for some time," Tristan answered. "Andromeda rules the Day Court in his name."

The Grand Duchess of the Day Court didn't sound like someone I wanted to meet.

"I will meet you at the bottom of the steps in an hour," Tristan snapped when we reached the stairs to my room. "Don't be late."

I was too tired to argue, and although I had healed myself, my body still ached and my limbs were sore. I could barely make it up the stairs, and my legs were like jelly when I finally reached the top. Surely this couldn't be the only empty guest room in the castle. I wondered why my grandmother had put me up here.

Someone had laid out a plain green cotton dress on the bed. It was virtually unadorned and part of the stitching had frayed, but it had little flowers stitched on the neckline and cuffs. Brianna must have sent it. I couldn't be bothered to be fussy, so I put it on. It looked like a sack, but at least it was loose and comfortable. I brushed my hair and tied it in a ponytail. I didn't have a flock of maids here to help me get dressed, so it was the best I could manage.

Tristan was waiting for me at the bottom of the stairs, arms crossed and legs apart. I could feel his powerful magical presence before I reached the landing. He looked dazzling in his midnight-colored doublet lined with silver thread. His long black hair was tied back in a ponytail enhancing his fae ears, upon which rested a thin silver circlet, and his high black boots shone with shadows of the night. The Dark Prince, devastatingly handsome in all his glory, stood before me, but he did not look pleased.

He glowered at me. "Are you going to the feast wearing that?"

"It's what Brianna sent me," I answered, holding my head high. "I don't have anything else to wear." I softened my tone, biting my lip.

Tristan cursed under his breath. "Come with me." He turned abruptly and stalked off in the other direction.

"Do you always have to walk so fast?" I ran after him. "Where are we going? I thought the Grand Hall was the other way."

He kept walking. "It is."

We stopped in front of a huge wooden door at the very end of the corridor. It was intricately engraved with the flora and fauna of these lands, a lot like the carved chest I had seen in Rafe's room at the palace before we left. I missed Rafe and wondered how he was. There was no word from Eldoren as far as I knew, and I had no idea what was going on in the other kingdoms.

Tristan knocked once, and a strong female voice bade us enter.

Tristan gestured me forward and closed the door behind us. The room was big and airy. At its center was a large four-poster bed, hung with light muslin curtains dyed a beautiful black with silver swirls that lit up as the moonlight touched them interwoven in the fabric. An elderly fae lady sat beside the fireplace warming her hands.

She turned to look at us and her sapphire eyes sparkled with silver stars, so like Tristan's. She was older than any of the other High Fae that I had come across since I had arrived in Elfi. Her presence was powerful—I could feel the magic of the night rolling off her in gentle waves, as if it were she who commanded the stars to shine forth. Her hair was white and elegantly coiffed and she wore a small silver tiara set with diamonds that sparkled as if she wore the stars on her head.

She was certainly of the Night Court and Royal.

"Grandmother," Tristan bowed formally.

"Tristan, my boy, to what do I owe this pleasure? I thought I would see you directly at the feast." She stopped and turned her eyes to me. Her eyebrows went up when she realized who Tristan had brought with him.

Tristan's grandmother looked me up and down. "What is she wearing?"

Tristan scowled. "That's what I said."

I glared back at him.

"Aurora, may I introduce my grandmother, Rhiannon, the Dowager Duchess of the Night Court," said Tristan formally, remembering his manners.

"Pleased to meet you." I inclined my head in deference to her rank. "I had nothing else to wear," I explained. "And Brianna said she would send me something."

"Brianna Darkvale is a jealous little vixen," snapped the Dowager Duchess, getting up from her chair. "Her father is a Count of the Day Court and thinks a marriage between Brianna and Tristan will be advantageous to their family. Of course, my son, Tristan's father, refused the match, but she still thinks it will happen. She's a troublemaker and no good, stay away from her."

I nodded and flicked a glance at Tristan, who had taken up his favorite pose, arms crossed and feet apart, glaring at me. I rolled my eyes; he had issues.

"Who cares what Brianna Darkvale thinks?" Tristan said to his grandmother. "Can you fix it?"

She clicked her tongue. "Obviously! Otherwise you wouldn't have brought her here."

My spine stiffened and I looked down at my clothes. How would she fix this?

The dowager walked up to me slowly and touched the dress. Within her dark blue eyes, silver sparks swirled as the magic of the night cloaked me. She moved to let me look at myself in the mirror.

Within seconds and with only a touch, the plain green dress had been transformed with powerful fae glamour. The gown that adorned my body was like liquid night, low-necked with thin straps holding it up, flowing about my body, emphasizing every curve. Within the fabric, silver stars sparkled and swirled in an endless dance inside a midnight sky.

My mouth fell open. It was by far the most beautiful dress I had ever seen. The dresses of the Eldorean nobility paled in comparison.

"There! Now you are dressed appropriately for the Royal Fae Court." The Dowager Duchess smoothed her already perfect hair in the mirror. "And close your mouth, Aurora, you look ridiculous."

I pressed my lips together.

Tristan came up behind me, looking at my reflection in the mirror. "I think you forgot something."

"Oh! Yes." The dowager frowned. "I guess I did."

She waved her hand, and a silver circlet studded with tiny diamonds appeared on my brow.

I turned to face Tristan, hoping to get some reaction other than a scowl. "What do you think?"

Tristan shrugged. "It suits our purpose." He didn't scowl, at least.

14
THE HIGH FAE

THE GRAND HALL was noisy and bustling when we arrived. Tristan offered me his arm—I took it gratefully as we stepped forward into the throng of fae nobility and my grandmother's Royal Court. The chattering stopped when we entered, everyone turning to look at the half-fae princess on the arm of the Prince of the Night Court.

The hall was beautifully lit with floating orbs of fae-light that moved about the room as if in an intricate dance. Lilting music wafted down from the first-floor gallery that ran overhead and looked out onto the gardens where the musicians played under a starlit sky.

Whispers followed us as I walked, clutching Tristan's arm as he escorted me forward toward where the queen sat, surrounded by simpering fae nobility. Dressed in all their finery, the fae court glittered in varied hues of gold and silver. A myriad of luscious silks, flowing chiffon, and rich brocades lined with intricate embroidery flowed about their bodies in various styles. Graceful and elegant, the High Fae ladies were all so beautiful, with long hair sparkling in diverse shades of day and night. Stunning jewels twinkled on their necks and hands, glinting in the fae-light.

My grandmother eyed me carefully as I followed Tristan's lead and bowed my head before her. Her crown of pearls glowed in the light of the fae orbs, which hovered above her for her personal use. From the corner of my eye I spotted Brianna standing to the side, the expression on her face giving away her hatred for me. I guess she was upset her plan hadn't worked.

I ignored her as I stood before the queen.

My grandmother did not smile, but nodded once and returned to speaking to the lady seated next to her. She wore a gold diadem, and her azure eyes were piercing as she eyed me.

"Come." Tristan steered me away from the dais. "Andromeda doesn't like to be interrupted when she is speaking to the queen."

"That's Skye's mother?" I glanced back at the dais where the Grand Duchess had resumed her conversation with my grandmother.

Tristan nodded. "And Aiden's."

The rest of the High Fae watched me from a distance and whispered in hushed tones, all the while looking straight at me so I had no illusions as to whom they were discussing.

"What did I do now?"

"Let them stare, you have nothing to fear from anyone." Tristan went to talk to his grandmother, who had entered the room.

Skye came over wearing an ivory gown trimmed with gold flowers. "There you are." She gave me a broad smile. "I thought Brianna would send you something to wear, I guess she forgot."

"She didn't forget, she sent me something that would not have been appropriate." I chose my words carefully.

Skye raised her eyebrows. "I see. Well, you look amazing. You're so lucky, I never get to wear black or red. The colors of the Day Court are so dull. Everyone is talking about you wearing the colors of the Night Court. Even my mother." She gestured to the Grand Duchess of the Day Court, Andromeda, who was still talking to my grandmother at the high table. "She's not going to be pleased that one of our family is wearing Night Court colors to their first feast."

"Family?"

Skye looked at me and narrowed her eyes. "We are cousins, didn't you know?"

I shook my head—no one had told me this. "No."

Skye's eyes softened, realizing I was new here. "Your grandmother was married to my father's uncle, your grandfather, and he was the Grand Duke of the Day Court before my father. When he died, there was no male heir, so my father became the next Grand Duke."

This was news to me. Skye was my cousin, which meant Aiden was also family. I didn't like the thought of that.

Cade saw us, waved, and approached. He looked me over and grinned. "Tristan is a clever fellow, I can tell you that." He winked at me. "Dressing you in the colors of the Night Court. Brilliant move."

"I still don't understand what the big deal is? I know I missed something."

Skye's turquoise eyes grew wide. "You don't know what he's done for you?" She gestured to my clothes. "What all this means?"

I shook my head.

Cade chuckled again; he seemed to find the whole situation very amusing. "Everyone knows your grandmother has not yet proclaimed you as her heir, therefore not providing you with her full protection. Which is why she has Tristan keeping an eye on you, since the Royal Court is a dangerous place for a High Fae, let alone a young half-fae princess."

My spine stiffened. "I know that." Izadora had made sure she didn't give me any preferential treatment, and the rest of the court knew it.

He paused, looking around, and lowered his voice. "Tristan knew what he was doing when he took you to his grandmother, the Dowager Duchess. In glamouring you and dressing you in the colors of the Night Court, she has made a statement, putting you under her protection. She has publicly announced that she has accepted you as Izadora's heir. Everyone will think twice before they dare to harm you."

My mouth fell open. "Is she so powerful?"

Cade nodded, his face serious. "The Dowager Duchess of the Night Court is one of the fae elders who sit on the Royal Council. No queen can rule Elfi without the backing of the fae elders and Izadora knows it."

Tristan had done this for me, and he knew exactly what would happen if his grandmother dressed me for the feast. I smiled to myself as Cade led me to the long table where Tristan was already seated. At least I wouldn't have to worry about Brianna anymore.

I sat down beside Tristan, with Cade on the other side next to Skye.

The long, rectangular tables were sumptuously laid with a variety of silver platters of honey roasted vegetables, creamy seafood stew, and fish braised with apples, nuts, and berries. Big bowls of candied walnuts, sugared almonds, and apricots appeared suddenly in front of me.

More and more food kept appearing out of nowhere—it was difficult for me to keep up. On top of that, if I didn't pick something right away, the food in front of me kept disappearing and ending up on another part of the table, only to be replaced by something more delightful.

Desserts started materializing when the rest of the food had finished. I eyed the towers of fresh pastries and delicate little lemon and lavender cakes, which were like billowy clouds of golden sponge generously topped with dollops of scrumptious buttercream icing and decorated with edible flowers picked from the palace gardens. I took a few more for my plate before they disappeared. These gave a whole new meaning to fairy cakes.

Green-liveried house sprites wandered between the tables, carrying heavy silver pitchers and filling up crystal goblets with an excellent sparkling berry juice while the High Fae chatted and enjoyed themselves at the feast. Looking around, I realized that there wasn't much of a divide between the courts here. Only the Queen and the others of the Elder Council sat at the high table on a raised dais. The rest of the High Fae mingled regardless of which court they belonged to.

Cade and Skye were engrossed in an animated conversation. I leaned over to Tristan. "I thought the Day and Night Courts were rivals?" I asked between mouthfuls. "They all seem very friendly with each other."

Tristan nodded, taking a sip from his goblet. "The distinction between the courts is now merely symbolic. It is more of a political arrangement. The Grand Dukes of the Day and Night Courts have hereditary titles and lands, which they rule over in the queen's name. Many of the High Fae families have hereditary magical abilities too, suited to their court. There are some fae creatures who can only be controlled by or pay allegiance to the Night Court, and some who would not speak to them or fear them. The same goes for the Day Court. Both have different strengths, and the queen uses them to her advantage."

"Thank you for everything you have done for me," I said sincerely. I hadn't thanked him yet for making sure I had the support of one of the Elder Council.

Tristan nodded, and his lip quirked, showing the hint of a grin.

"So, you do know how to smile, Prince Tristan?" I said teasingly.

Cade overheard what I said and laughed, spluttering the contents of his goblet all over the table.

"On occasion," Tristan scowled at us, and went back to frowning at his plate.

I giggled to myself. Under that rough demeanor, the Dark Prince of the Night Court was not so bad after all.

The next morning the Crystal Castle lit up at dawn and sent beams of rainbow-colored light dancing about my room. Cade was waiting for me at the bottom of the stairs when I came down.

"Where's Tristan?" I asked, as Cade led me down a flower filled open corridor, past a secluded courtyard towards the gardens. "I wanted to go to the kitchen to get a bite to eat before going down to the training ground."

"The Dowager Duchess has asked to meet with you."

Cade stopped in front of an ornately carved door. "She has requested your presence at breakfast."

We entered the vast room overlooking the flowering gardens of the fae palace. This was part of the dowager's suite of rooms. How big was this castle? It seemed to be almost endless, with rooms and stairs appearing in places where I could have sworn there were none yesterday. There were some passages extending far back, right into the mountain, and I wondered where they led.

Tristan was already seated at a small round table in the dowager duchess' breakfast room, talking earnestly with his grandmother. Daylight filtered in through the soft white curtains that fluttered in the morning breeze. He rose when he saw me, scowled as usual, and held a chair for me to sit down.

"You're late," said the dowager. "I expect you to be here on time in the future. We have a lot to do."

"Sorry," I mumbled, sitting down. *I wasn't that late.*

Cade pulled up a chair and sat down too, reaching for the hot pastries that lay in a basket in the center of the table.

The dowager swatted his hand. "Cade, where are your manners?"

Cade looked sheepish and dropped his hands into his lap as the dowager gestured for the pastries to be served. House sprites appeared out of nowhere, dressed in black and silver livery, and filled my cup with creamy hot chocolate.

211

Tristan glared at Cade, sipping quietly on his hot chocolate, and I rolled my eyes. "Can't you be a little more cheerful?" I asked, exasperated with his moodiness.

Tristan ignored me. His grandmother smiled.

"I spoke with your grandmother and the other elders last night," said the dowager after she had a sip of her hot chocolate. "And although Tristan will continue training you as a warrior, there are other skills you require to fully master your powers. So, you will come to me every afternoon, and I will oversee the rest of your magical training."

I didn't know what to say—this was much more than I could have hoped for. The dowager was an Elder Fae, possessing knowledge I could never hope to gain without her. She was a bit abrupt and strict, but she had given me her protection and I was grateful. Maybe I could ask her about the Dawnstar? I had to wait until the exact right time.

I thanked her, finished my breakfast, and ran down to the training grounds with Cade and Tristan. Skye was already there sparring with two other girls. She waved when she saw us and sauntered over, her hips swaying.

"Hello boys!" she said, and Cade blushed. "Back for another beating, Aurora?"

"Yup." I picked up my staff, and Skye grinned.

Aiden sauntered over. "So, the *half-breed* thinks she's strong enough to spar with the High Fae," he sneered, drawing his sword from the scabbard on his back. "Let's see how good you are, princess."

Tristan stepped between us. "Leave her alone, Aiden. Once she's trained you can have your way and fight her. But for now, she only spars with whom I say she does."

Aiden looked like he would stab Tristan right there. But he lowered his sword and narrowed his eyes when he looked at me. "Your dear protector won't be with you all the time, *half-breed*." He stalked off, his blond hair blowing in the wind.

I shivered at the menace in his voice; it reminded me of Damien's taunts and threats. I was stronger and more in control of my magic than when I faced Damien at Evolon. But Damien was only a student—Aiden was a full-fledged High Fae warrior, a member of the Elite Guard and a prince. If he was going to come after me, there was no way I would win that fight. It was best I stay away.

"We're going down to the city this coming full moon," said Skye, dismissing her brother and twirling her staff deftly in her hands as we walked to our positions. "It's in a few days. Want to come?"

I shook my head. I didn't want to make the same mistakes I had before.

"Come on, Aurora." Skye leaned her staff on the ground. "It will be fun. Tristan and Cade are coming. There is a new troupe playing at the theater."

My eyes widened. "You have a theater?" I had never come

across one in other kingdoms in Avalonia. And if Tristan was going I would be safe. I glanced over at him. He was standing with his arms crossed, looking at me. Well, glaring would be the more appropriate term.

"The very best." And quick as a flash, she knocked me down.

"Oww," I cried, as I hit the ground, but I managed to hold on to my staff this time. "I wasn't ready." I pushed myself up and positioned myself to defend against her blows.

Skye smiled briefly and shrugged. "You need to be faster." She came at me again.

The whole morning went by in a flash, sparring with Skye while Tristan looked on and barked orders at me as I was bruised and beaten repeatedly.

"Get up," shouted Tristan. "Again."

I healed myself and pushed myself up, only to go down again. But I didn't let the beatings deter me; in fact, my determination grew with every blow.

After a quick lunch I picked up from the kitchens, I spent the rest of the afternoon walking in the gardens with Tristan's grandmother. We sat down on a smoothly polished stone bench in a flowering gazebo overlooking a little fountain.

"I want to hear your whole story," said the dowager. "Start from the beginning, and don't leave anything out."

I recounted my story for the hundredth time. When I told her about healing the pegasus and my encounter with the archmage in Calos, she raised her eyebrows but didn't interrupt. Finally, I told her what my grandmother had said, but I didn't tell her about the Dagger, the *Book of Abraxas*, or the Dawnstar. I would ask her about them another time.

I was not under any illusions anymore; I knew everyone who befriended me had an agenda, and the politics between the High Fae Courts was as complicated, if not more so, than in any of the other kingdoms. At least Tristan had made sure I could move about the castle unharmed. The dowager's protection saw to that. I wondered if he did it so he didn't have to watch me all the time, or if under his scowl he cared what happened to me.

"I can already see your magic is powerful, Aurora, but stupidity can get you killed. The water magic you performed in Calos was virtually impossible to do."

"I don't understand what you mean. It wasn't difficult to tap into. I felt the magic within the water, and it responded to my call."

The dowager nodded. "Yes, but when using water magic, especially on the sea, you need to be very careful and very experienced. You are a conduit for the water, not the water itself. You must isolate the water you are using. Connecting to the water like you did was very dangerous—it could have drained your magic completely, turning your body to liquid and trapping you beneath the waves, never to return."

I looked at her in horror. I had no idea what I was doing, and I was lucky to get this far. Fae magic was vast and complicated and I had barely scratched the surface.

"I hear you are experienced in healing, so we will leave that for now," the dowager continued. "Tristan will help you hone your fire and warrior skills. Since you have found your water talent, I was going to start with that. But after hearing your story about Lilith and the portal you opened, I think we should concentrate on your spirit magic, which is the rarest and most dangerous if something goes wrong."

I nodded.

"What you did for the pegasus should not have been possible. Opening a portal to another world is a rare talent, and usually you need at least ten experienced spirit-fae to combine their magic to open one. Your mother had that power, but even she should not have been able to do what she did for you that day when she opened a portal and sent you through. Now that I have met you and heard what you are capable of, I suspect your own magic aided your mother. It was your magic that made it possible for a single spirit-fae to open a portal of such magnitude. Your magic is more powerful than anything I have seen before, but for someone your age, such power can be detrimental to your mental health. You need discipline and you need training, otherwise you will never be the queen your people need you to be."

As soon as I finished with the dowager, I ran back down to the training ground. Tristan was expecting me, and I didn't want to be tardy and give him another reason to glare at me. The sun was setting on the hidden valley of the fae and the Crystal Castle had lit up in orange and pink hues when I reached the grounds.

Tristan was shirtless in the middle of the training ring, his corded body perfectly chiseled like a statue of a Greek god. I tried not to stare as I stood on the sidelines watching him fight six fae warriors at once with only a staff. He was magnificent, a lethal fighting machine. And although I had seen him fight before, I was mesmerized by his moves. Lithe and surefooted like a jungle cat, Tristan twirled his staff, knocking down three warriors at one time, and he didn't seem to break a sweat.

Three more came at him, and he deflected the blows easily and expertly, knocking the other staffs out of his opponents' hands in the blink of an eye. All around him fae warriors were lying on the ground, bruised and groaning.

He stopped when he noticed me and frowned. "You're late."

Behind him I saw Cade and another warrior moving towards Tristan. Cade put his finger to his lips. But before I could decide whether to warn Tristan or not, he turned swiftly, knocking them both down, his staff twirling faster than the mortal eye could see.

Cade groaned as he hit the ground. "I thought I had you this time."

"You are going to have to do better than that, my friend." Tristan gave Cade his hand and his lips curved slightly.

At least something amused him.

Cade pulled himself up. "One day I am going to get you."

"I look forward to it." Tristan dismissed him.

Cade pretended to scowl like Tristan as he walked over to me, but he wasn't doing a great job of it. I couldn't help laughing. Cade was too funny.

"How did it go with the dowager?" Cade asked me, putting on his sword belt.

"She's nice. I like her very much, she's direct and tells it like it is."

"That's probably the first and only time anyone has described my grandmother as nice," Tristan snorted, coming up to me and thrusting a staff into my hand.

Cade laughed, obviously unable to sulk for more than a minute. "Most High Fae run when they see the Dowager Duchess. Even Izadora takes care not to get on her bad side."

"But I don't understand why my grandmother needs the fae elders to support her?" I gripped my staff and leaned on it. "I thought she was an absolute ruler in Elfi?"

"She is," said Cade, "but only as long as the Elder Council support her as queen. Every thousand years a new queen is chosen. And Izadora's thousand years as ruler is nearly up. Of course, she does have another hundred years or so left, but for an immortal a hundred years is not much time. If she doesn't choose an heir soon and get the support of the Elder Council, the elders will choose for her."

"What happens to the queen after a new queen is chosen?"

"The old queen can choose to join the council of elders, or they can retire to the temple on the Forgotten Isles and join the priestesses of the Great Goddess," said Cade.

"Who was the last queen before my grandmother?"

"You've already met her," Cade replied, a smile tugging on his lips. "Rhiannon Nightshade, the Dowager Duchess of the Night Court, Tristan's grandmother."

Thwack. Tristan's staff hit me.

"Ouch," I ground out between clenched teeth, clutching my arm and glaring at Tristan. "What was that for?"

"Stop chatting." Tristan twirled his staff. "Do you think Morgana is going to wait for you to finish your conversation?"

I gripped my staff and attacked Tristan. He whacked my staff out of my hand and hit me behind the knees with his, sending me flying to the ground.

"You are too slow, your defenses are dismal, you have no concentration, and you are as weak as a newborn colt," Tristan said calmly. "When you fight, you need to have complete awareness of the space around you. Use your fae senses, tap into the magic of the ground under your feet and the air moving around you, use what you can, connect to it, and plan your attack. Only then will you be able to improve your fighting skills."

"Fine," I said, pushing myself up, wiping blood from my lip and picking up my staff. "Again."

And Tristan smiled.

15
THE ANCIENT FAE

WHEN THE DAY of the full moon arrived, Skye told me to meet her at the bottom of the stairs of my tower that night. Although I was exhausted after training, which got more intense every day, after much deliberation I decided to go with her to the theater.

I changed into a plain blue dress she had sent over for me and walked down the stairs to meet her. It was lonely having no friends here, and I told myself Tristan and Cade would be there if anything went wrong. Aiden would not dare attack me while Tristan was around.

I heard voices at the bottom of the stairs and I stopped—my name had been mentioned. It was Skye.

"Aurora needs to get out, Tristan. You can't keep her in the tower forever," Skye was saying. "I know you are supposed to protect her, but it will be nice for her to see the city. She's trying hard to win your approval, go easy on her."

"There's no need to invite her to come with us." Tristan's voice was tense. "I see enough of her already."

"Fine," Skye huffed. "I don't think she's coming anyway. I told her to meet me here a while ago. You must have tired her out too much at training today."

The voices drew away, and I hung my head, walking slowly back up the endless flight of steps to my room.

I ignored Tristan the whole morning at breakfast and spoke only to Skye and Cade. I kept my interaction with him to a minimum, and if he asked me something I answered in monosyllables. It may have been childish of me, but his refusal to see me as a friend and equal was upsetting to me. Tristan didn't seem to mind; in fact, I think he was happy I wasn't chattering in his ear all the time.

During those first few days I spent more time with the dowager as she showed me how to use my spirit magic properly and create portals. It was hard at first and brought back memories of Lilith. But I knew I had to do it—I couldn't make another mistake—so I practiced as much as I could.

"Close your eyes and imagine where you want to go," said the Dowager Duchess in our first lesson. "In the beginning the process is slow. But once you get used to it, moving through portals will be like stepping through a doorway. Reach for your magic and guide it, concentrate on where you want to end up. Choose a place close by in the castle." She paused. "But be careful—only create a portal to a place you have been before, or things can go drastically wrong."

I gathered my magic and projected it outward, thinking of my room and imagining myself there. Slowly a spark ignited in front of me, growing larger and expanding outwards, swirling like a ball of mist. From within it I could see a faded version of my room.

"Good, now step through it. But remember to close the portal after you reach the other side or anyone can follow you through."

I stepped forward, my heart hammering, and I clenched my fists as I entered the portal. My body lurched as I was thrown forward and in a split-second I was in my room.

I was sprawled on the floor, but I waved my hand and closed the portal behind me. I smiled; I had done it. No more walking up and down steps for me, which was a relief.

Another portal opened and the dowager stepped through, elegant as ever without a hair out of place. "That was adequate," she said, smoothing her dress, "but we are going to have to work on your landing. It would be quite inconvenient for you to step out of a portal and find yourself sprawled at the feet of your enemy."

I pushed myself up and straightened my hair. The magic needed to create a portal was complicated, but it was easier than I expected. It would take a little while to get used to, but I quite enjoyed having the freedom it gave me.

"Is this your room?" The dowager turned up her nose at the unmade bed and sparse furnishings. "Without crystal in the windows?"

I hung my head. "This is where my grandmother put me."

"But why haven't you decorated it yet?" she said, a puzzled expression on her immortal face.

"I didn't know I could," I looked around. "There isn't much I can do here anyway."

"Nonsense," said the dowager, waving her hand—all the furnishings in the room vanished. "You're fae, are you not? You have the gift of glamour. Use it. How do you think the rest of the rooms in the palace are done up? When I come to stay at court, I do up the room given to me how I please. As does anyone else with enough glamour. You can even change the size of your room—the castle adapts to the space."

"I don't understand." I glanced around my empty tower room. "How can I make it bigger if there is no space?"

"Make your own space." The dowager waved her hand again. The room started expanding, the walls moving outwards and swallowing up parts of the mountain, revealing a massive open space to do whatever I wanted with. "There, that's better."

I looked around, wide-eyed. "But I'm not sure I know how to do that."

"This kind of glamour may be difficult for other fae," said the dowager. "But for spirit-fae like us, glamour is easier and more complex in the way it is woven. Imagine what you want in your room and connect it to your magic, the same magic you use when you open a portal."

"But is it real? What if I sit on something I created and it disappears?"

"It can be as real as you want it to be," the dowager explained. "You can recreate anything that you have seen, and make it solid. Mind you, this only applies to inanimate objects—you cannot create a real flower or a plant, but you can create an image of it that looks and feels and smells the same while the glamour lasts. But it cannot grow or bear fruit like a real plant. Although," she paused, "a powerful earth-fae could do it. But that kind of magic hasn't been seen in centuries. If your grandmother put you here, it wasn't to make you uncomfortable—she probably asumed you would do up your room however you wanted and couldn't be bothered to do it herself." She turned to leave, but stopped, looking around the space. "This room is the easiest to guard and has the best view, you know."

The dowager waved her hand and opened a portal. "Try it out. I will see you tomorrow for breakfast. Please be on time—tardiness is such a disagreeable quality."

She stepped into the portal and disappeared.

After she left, I practiced using glamour and made myself a bed. It was a perfect replica of my bed in Silverthorne Castle. Now I knew exactly how I wanted my room to look, so I went around the space recreating my old room. Calling up my magic, I scanned my memory for the way the furniture and the curtains that adorned the room looked, adding simple touches that made the space brighter. Smooth white stone floors, a dresser with a big mirror stood against one wall, and a big four-poster bed was draped with white and gold curtains. I looked around. Perfect! This was the most fun thing I had done since I got to Elfi, and glamour had proved to be quite an interesting way of exercising my magic.

Tristan made me practice my sword moves each day until every muscle screamed in protest. But I kept going. No real skill was learned the easy way. We trained alternately with staffs and swords, and I was slowly getting better at both.

"How's your archery?" Tristan asked me after we had finished a particularly long training session.

The novices were still training; experienced soldiers walked through the sparring pairs, adjusting grips and showing them different moves. The archers were practicing with targets set up at the far end of the field.

"Not bad," I said truthfully as he escorted me back to the palace. "At Evolon I had a little while to learn the basics."

"Do you have air magic?"

"I'm not sure." I thought back to the times I had used my fae magic without my amulet. "I think I hovered a bit once or twice when I used my silver-fire."

Tristan raised an eyebrow. "Air magic is a great asset to an archer. Most High Fae have earth magic and air magic; they are the most common magical talents we possess, although most of the air-fae can't do more than create a gust of wind. Archers are chosen from among the air-fae—their ability to manipulate the air gives them a better chance at accuracy. Maybe I should add archery to your training sessions."

After that, Tristan began my archery lessons. The fae bows were different from what I used at Evolon, but I would manage. I was quite good at archery when I trained with Baron Tanko, but I never got a chance to practice much outside the Academy.

Tristan thrust a quiver of arrows at me and I strapped it on. He handed me a sleek-looking yew bow. It was light, beautifully carved at the ends with flowers and vines, and far easier to use than the ones in Evolon. "Let's see what you can do."

I nocked the first arrow, my muscles straining, making sure to keep my elbow up as I had been taught.

"Concentrate with your fae senses," Tristan said softly, standing behind me and adjusting my grip on the bow. "Use the air around you, and find the quickest way through it to your target."

I took a deep breath and did as he instructed. I could feel the air guiding me and connecting to my magic as I released the arrow. I tried not to break the link, but the wind shifted slightly and I was thrown off. The arrow hit the target a little to the left of the bullseye.

"Not bad. I want you to get used to the bow—keep practicing. Once you have mastered using air magic for the arrows, we can add silver-fire to it."

"It's about time," I grinned at Tristan. "But when can I practice using silver-fire with my sword like you do?"

"When I believe you are ready." Tristan ended the conversation.

I practiced archery whenever I had time in between my other training sessions. I spent my mornings with Tristan, Cade, and Skye sparring in the training field and my afternoons walking in the gardens with the dowager.

Sometimes we would go to the library and come back with a stack of books for me to read as the dowager taught me the various intricacies of fae magic and guided me through understanding the political world of the fae. There was so much information in the castle library, famous throughout Avalonia for its extraordinary collections of books and ancient scrolls, and I devoured book after book about fae history.

One evening I met Tristan at the training ground for our usual sparring practice. "Follow me," he said when he saw me.

"Where are we going?" I ran after him. "I thought we

were supposed to be training."

"We are." Tristan gestured to the centaurs to open the city gates, which led out into the valley.

Once we had exited the city, Tristan broke into a jog.

"Where are you going?" I shouted.

"Let's see if you can keep up," he shouted back.

I groaned and broke into a sprint. I soon caught up with him, but every time I did he would go a little faster. My heartbeat quickened as the muscles in my legs burned, but I pushed forward.

"You need to hone your senses," said Tristan as he ran, his voice even. "You are stronger and faster than you know. Your fae blood gives you endurance and strength that no mage could ever hope to have. When you fight, when you run, use your magic, feel it as a part of you. You are fae, the elements are at your command."

Didn't he ever get tired?

I pumped my arms and pushed myself to increase my speed. I opened myself to the fae magic that lay around me and felt the earth beneath my feet reaching up to meet me. My senses sharpened as I concentrated, each step guided by the earth on which I ran. I knew where the stones were; I knew where to place my feet as if the ground itself were telling me where to go. The air around me whispered, and my pace sped up. It was as if the air was assisting me, giving me more power in my lungs, pushing me forward at a speed I had never reached before.

We headed for the forest that led up to the hills. Tristan ran through the trees, sure-footed and nimble, without missing a step. I ran faster than I ever had, jumping over fallen logs and zigzagging through the trees. We were running at an incline, but I pushed myself further, my fae magic giving me extra strength and speed.

"Oww!" I tripped over a fallen log and landed smack on my face.

Tristan was beside me in an instant. "You need to maintain your connection to the elements as you run. If you hesitate or lose concentration, this is what happens."

It seemed like ever since I'd got here I had spent most of my time lying flat on my face. I groaned as my muscles screamed in protest, but I pushed myself up and healed my scraped knees and palms; the pain subsided but didn't go away completely. I had to admit fae healing was convenient.

"Maybe we should go back," Tristan said, looking at the sky. The sun had started to set behind the mountains and the valley took on a dusky glow. Birds chirped high in the trees as they settled in for the night, and the crickets seemed to be trying to outdo their chatter. "It will get dark soon, and we don't want to be outside the city walls at night. I can also understand if you are tired; demi-fae do not have the same endurance as the High Fae."

"Demi-fae sounds better than *half-breed*," I said, as I followed him back down the hill into the valley.

Tristan nodded. "Demi-fae is the politically correct term," he said, slightly embarrassed as we traversed a rough path through the trees. "But some of the nobility believe the fae should not intermarry with other races."

"Why? Why not be tolerant?" I tried to keep up with his pace.

"Many are," said Tristan as we neared the city gates, "but as you know, our numbers have been rapidly decreasing over the centuries. The High Fae who are left are only a handful, the last remnants of a long-forgotten world, when the lands of the kingdom of Elfi stretched far beyond the Old Forest and beyond the great Southern Sea."

"It did?" I had never heard this version of Avalonian history before.

Tristan nodded as the centaurs opened the southern gate for us to enter. "It was in the age of the ancients," he elaborated. "Before the Demon Wars, the mages did not rule Avalonia. It was the High Fae who were absolute lords of this world. This was before Dragath came, before Auraken Firedrake defeated him and trapped him in what many thought was an eternal prison. The Ancient Fae, as they are now called, were more powerful than anything any of us have ever seen—even the Elder Fae."

"What happened to the rest of the kingdom? I have never seen this mentioned in any of the books the dowager made me read."

"You won't find any information on the Ancient Fae in those books. Most of our older texts were destroyed during the Demon Wars," Tristan said as we passed the fae guards and climbed the big sweeping staircase to the palace. "But there is a story about an ancient queen etched into the walls of the great library."

"There is? I've never seen it."

"That's because it is in a much older part of the library than you usually frequent." He paused, as if reluctant to continue, and finally said, "Come. I will show you."

I followed him to the castle library. As usual, it was mostly empty, except for a few house sprites who wandered around cleaning continuously. Occasionally a member of the High Fae would come down to get a book, or read silently at one of the tables positioned between corridors.

Tristan led me past my usual reading shelves into passages I had never been in before. The library was seemingly endless, running deep into the mountain in long winding corridors that descended further down into catacombs which housed some of the older texts.

Tristan stopped in a shadowy corridor and lit up his hand with fae light. I did the same as I followed him deeper into the mountain. This part of the library had no books, only smooth stone walls and endless passages leading into darkness.

He went over to one wall and held up his hand. The fae light shone brightly as beautiful etchings came into view; ancient frescoes thousands of years old hidden under the Crystal Castle. The original colors had faded as time had passed, but most were still visible.

"They say the Crystal Castle was built on the ruins of an Ancient Fae fortress that was destroyed by Dragath during the Demon Wars," Tristan said. "These walls are part of the original structure."

I drew in a sharp breath. "These are beautiful," I whispered, gazing at the intricately rendered paintings of long dead fae warriors fighting a hideous demon. I knew who the demon was; my granduncle had shown me a similar painting in a book at the Summer Palace. But this fresco showed a dark-haired queen in full fae armor fighting Dragath with twin swords of silver-fire flashing in her hands.

"Dragath," I whispered.

Tristan nodded. "During the Demon Wars, the last of the Ancient Fae queens, Illaria of the house of Eos-Eirendil, also known as Illaria Lightbringer, fought Dragath and his armies for hundreds of years. But when Dragath created the Dark Dagger and trapped all Illaria's fire-fae warriors within it, the rest of Illaria's forces were defeated and Elfi fell."

I looked at the etching of the ancient fae queen, and I couldn't understand why this story sounded familiar. Illaria Lightbringer was a name I had never heard before, but somehow, I knew I had to find out more about her.

"Avalonia was plunged into chaos," Tristan continued, "until Auraken Firedrake arose—a fae-mage with unimaginable magic, equal to that of the ancients—and saved our world. But the rest of the fae lands, south of the Old Forest—a whole civilization once lush and prosperous with a huge population of fae—are now a wasteland, an ancient world destroyed by the darkness of Dragath."

"What happened to Illaria Lightbringer?"

"The legends say Illaria fought alongside Auraken in the final battle. She used up the last of her ancient magic to save Auraken so he could defeat Dragath. The mages tend to leave her out of the stories. They want Avalonia to forget the Ancient Fae and the powers they once possessed, but the High Fae still remember Illaria Lightbringer and the great ancient dynasty of Eos-Eirendil. She is the real hero of this world. If not for her, Auraken Firedrake would never have been able to overcome the darkness."

Illaria Lightbringer was a true queen, a legendary hero, giving her life to save this world. The thought gave me hope. If I could be half as courageous as her I could be a great queen.

"After Dragath fell," Tristan went on, "Illaria disappeared, and the last of ancient magic left this world forever. No one knows what actually happened in those final days, but she was last seen riding into battle on the back of a dragon."

My eyes went wide, and I could feel them lighting up. "Are there dragons in Avalonia?"

"Not anymore." Tristan shook his head and moved over to the opposite wall. "When ancient magic disappeared from this world, so did the dragons." He held up his hand as a beam of light fell on a lifelike etching of a dragon's head. Parts of the original colors were still visible and I could see purple scales glistening as the fae light illuminated the fresco. The dragon's eyes seemed to glow with an unearthly radiance as I moved closer, running my fingers over the magnificent work of art.

"Where are they now?"

Tristan shrugged. "No one has seen a dragon in over five thousand years. The legends say the dragons were powerful, immortal creatures born with their own powers. They were also very intelligent and greatly knowledgeable about ancient magic. They were once our greatest allies and fought beside the fae in the Demon Wars."

Tristan moved away from the wall and the ancient paintings retreated into the shadows.

"I thought dragons were dangerous creatures?" I asked as we walked back to the main library.

"They are," said Tristan, "very dangerous. But there was a time when a few rare Ancient Fae could speak to them with their minds and summon them to our aid in times of need. Dragons cannot resist the call of a powerful dragonlord, even if they don't want to help, they have no choice. Normally dragons didn't interfere in the wars of the world except when called upon or summoned by a dragonlord."

"So why can't we call them to help us?" I asked, my mind whirling with the possibilities of dragons. "We need to find a dragonlord to help us."

Tristan shook his head. "There are no dragonlords left in Avalonia. Illaria Lightbringer was the last of them. Many have tried to summon a dragon over the years, but failed. There is no one who has that kind of power anymore, and no dragons are left to call to our aid."

My heart was heavy; if Illaria Lightbringer could not defeat Dragath, even with the help of dragons, I knew I never could. So I had to make sure the *Book of Abraxas* was not opened and Dragath never released. Because if Dragath ever returned to this world, that would be a battle we could never win.

Not without ancient magic.

I had to find the Dawnstar. It was our only hope, and time was running out.

16
THE FAE CODEX

THE WEEKS THAT followed were filled with training from dawn till dusk and sometimes late into the night. In the evenings Tristan and I would run in the valley and the hills outside the city, and I would return exhausted with barely enough energy to eat and portal myself to my room.

It had been a little over a month since I arrived in Elfi, and not a day went by that I didn't think of Rafe, Uncle Gabriel, and the rest of my friends and family. I had asked my grandmother and Rhiannon about them a few times, but no one seemed to have any answers. I had no idea what was happening in Eldoren, and I needed to get back to help them. But I was not done here. Not by a long shot. I still had so much to learn and so little time to do it.

Tristan continued to train me, but as soon as the training sessions were over he left. The conversation in the catacombs was our only one. Skye never asked me to go out again. I started to feel so alone, with no one to talk to and no real friends. Even Snow had gone away to see her family and wouldn't be back for a while.

When I was in my room, I read what I could and studied

the books the dowager had chosen for me. But slowly all the confidence I had gathered so far began to disappear. I missed my friends Vivienne and Kalen; I missed Rafe and Erien, and Uncle Gabriel and Aunt Serena. I missed my old friend Penelope Plumpleberry and her appropriate advice, there whenever I needed it. Now I was alone, in a palace with no warmth, no laughter, no fun—just endless feasts and social backstabbing between the courts. I didn't know how long I could keep this up.

But I had to remain here and I had to learn; that was all that was important. At least that's what I kept telling myself, every time I saw Cade, Tristan, Skye, and Brianna on their way out of the castle for some entertainment. I would watch them from my window until they were out of sight, swallowed up by the fae lights that hovered and swirled over the city, illuminating Iris in its ethereal gleam.

On top of all my physical training with Tristan, I practiced creating portals and learning to use my spirit magic. I could open and close them at will, but the dowager never let me open one leading outside the city. It was forbidden, as it was a direct threat to the safety of the citizens of Elfi. The magic surrounding Iris prevented anyone from opening a portal into the city. For an enemy to enter, one had to be created from the inside.

I took care to visualize the places I went to properly before I released my magic. I didn't want to make any mistakes with this. After what happened with Lilith, portals scared me, and my heartbeat sped up every time I used one. But I learned to control my fears, because I had no choice. I had to do this if was going to improve. There was no easy way to get through it.

"Once you take off your amulet," said the dowager, during a rigorous portal session where I had to create as many consecutive portals as I could within one minute, "you will be able to access your powers more freely."

I disappeared, entering a portal and appearing behind her. "And when will I be able to do that?"

She turned to face me. "Soon. Once I am satisfied that you have learned control over your powers, Izadora said she will allow you to remove it."

"What about Morgana?" I wanted to be able to take off my amulet and find out the true extent of my powers. But at the same time I was scared of what would happen if I couldn't control it again. The amulet was all that prevented her from finding me.

"Morgana already knows where you are," said the dowager. "The Drakaar must have informed her that the fae came to your aid. She's not stupid, she knows the safest place would be to take you to Elfi, to your grandmother. Izadora's powers protect this kingdom, and as long as she can hold the wards secure, Morgana's army won't be able to enter Elfi. But that doesn't mean Morgana won't try. And you must be ready to face her when she does."

I knew she was right. My time here in Elfi was limited. I needed to learn more about the Dawnstar. The mastermage had said that I must find it, that it was the only way to break the curse on the Dagger. The dowager was an Elder Fae—if anyone had information about the Dawnstar it would be her.

So I told her about my mother and what the mastermage had explained about the Dawnstar. The dowager listened silently, but I could see the interest that sparked in her eyes when I mentioned the ancient weapon.

"I didn't think that anybody in the mage world still remembered this old legend," said the dowager softly. "But it is not possible the ancients have left behind some sort of weapon, one that contained the last remnants of ancient magic, or we would have found it by now. No such weapon actually exists. The Dawnstar is a myth, a story told to give us hope."

I shook my head. "No, no, it can't be. There has to be some truth to these legends, something more to this." I couldn't give up. "Without the power of the Dawnstar to break the curse on the Dark Dagger, my mother will be trapped inside it for eternity." I tried to keep my voice even.

The dowager's eyes narrowed. "So you are telling me Morgana is in possession of the Dark Dagger and has Elayna trapped within it?"

I nodded. "Yes, and Duke Silverthorne thinks she plans

to use it to release Dragath from his prison."

The dowager stilled. "Does Izadora know?"

I nodded.

"Then we have less time than I thought. I shall have to increase your training, and I will speak to Izadora about removing your amulet."

"Thank you," I nodded, "but the mastermage specifically told me that I need the Dawnstar if I am to break the curse on the Dark Dagger. I have to find it. Is there any way I can see the Fae Codex?"

The dowager shook her head and looked around, making sure we were not being overheard. "I'm afraid that is impossible. The Fae Codex can only be seen by the queen and the fae elders. No outsider has ever touched the Codex, and none ever will."

There had to be a way for me to get a glimpse of that Codex. "But you have seen it?" I remembered what Cade had told me about the dowager. "You were queen of Elfi before my grandmother, weren't you?"

The dowager nodded. "Yes, I have seen it, and I can tell you that you should stop asking questions about it. Do not under any circumstance mention this to the other elders." She got up and gestured for me to walk with her, lowering her voice. "None of the Elder Council will be pleased to know you want to see the Codex."

"Why?"

"There are secrets in the Codex dating back to the Age of Ancients that could prove extremely dangerous to the security of Elfi should it ever fall into the wrong hands."

"Then surely there must be something in the Codex that mentions this ancient weapon?"

The dowager stopped walking and looked at me sharply. "Ancient magic is gone and it will never return. Don't waste your time on trying to find something that isn't there—concentrate on mastering your own magic. The Dawnstar doesn't exist. There is no legendary weapon left behind by the ancients."

I hung my head as I walked beside her, my thoughts an absolute mess. How could this be possible? I was counting on this, the mastermage said it was the only way to fight Dragath's magic—without it I would never be able to free my mother. And although my grandmother promised to help me free her, I was under no illusions she would keep her promise. The fae were known to find loopholes in their oaths, and I knew how sharp my grandmother was. If she had the power to free someone from the Dark Dagger, surely she would have freed the other fire-fae warriors and rebuilt her army.

Something didn't feel right. I had to find out more before I gave up this quest for the Dawnstar. But I decided to take the dowager's advice and keep quiet about what I was looking for.

———— ~~~ ————

Whenever I found time to go to the library alone, I searched for anything that mentioned the Dawnstar. Once I got used to the eerie space, I began to feel more comfortable and had a good idea which corridors led where. So I continued searching for any mention of it, day after day, but I never found anything.

Once the dowager was satisfied I had adequate control over my spirit magic, she wanted to explore my water talent. At first it was hard, separating droplets of water from the rest, letting them float upward, and joining them together to create a ball.

"Good," she said, as I stood beside a fountain in the garden and manipulated the water within it. "You can mold the water into any shape you want, like you do with glamour."

I fashioned the water into the image of a bird, a sparrow made of liquid, and guided it around the gardens. A noise startled me, and the water sparrow burst into droplets that drizzled down on the head of a gnome busy pulling up weeds at the far side of the terraced gardens.

"Sorry," I called out.

The gnome sputtered and swore at me, but when he saw the dowager standing at my side he bowed his head and got back to work.

"Good," said the dowager, "but your concentration is weak. Now I want you to try something different. Move the water from one fountain to another."

Extending my magic, I lifted droplets of water and deposited them in the other fountain.

"Now turn it to ice."

"What?" I tried to focus with the water but it splashed out of the fountain, spraying the little gnome gardener again.

"Sorry, sorry," I shouted, holding up my hands.

"Let's try it once more, shall we?" said the dowager, a smile playing at the corner of her lips.

I repeated what I had done before, moving the water from one fountain to the other.

"Now push your magic into it and lower the temperature," the dowager instructed.

I willed the water to freeze. To my excitement, it did just that, slowly forming a perfect little ice bridge between the two fountains.

"That was impressive." The dowager inspected my work. "Usually fire and water don't go well together, and the gift of ice less so."

She waved her hand and the ice bridge that I had created disappeared, melting back into the fountains.

"You're good with water magic too," I pointed out.

She gave me a wry chuckle. "Yes, I suppose I am. They didn't call me the ice-queen for nothing. But I don't possess fire magic like you do. For a fae to be born with both ice and fire in equal fury is quite remarkable. Your mother didn't have water magic. You and Izadora are the only ones who have all five powers of the fae. The fire-fae are less than a handful, and the water-fae are nearly extinct." She paused and lowered her voice. "I have spoken to Izadora about removing your amulet while you train."

"And?" I held my breath.

"She has agreed. But only while training, mind you. She feels it is safer for you to keep it on at other times."

I nodded. Finally!

I started using portals all the time after that. I told myself it was practice, but it was also a much quicker way for me to get from the training field and back to the palace for my magical training with the dowager. I was determined to do my best. I had a purpose in life, a goal, and I would not back down or run away as I might have done before.

Now that I could remove my amulet for longer periods of time, I began to discover depths to my magic I didn't know I had. I could feel a change within me, not only physically, but mentally as well. As I trained with my fae powers, my hearing heightened, and so did my sight. In the few weeks I had been here, I was more aware of everything around me, I needed less sleep, and I didn't get so tired anymore. I ran up the stairs to my room, clearing them two at a time. I could have used a portal to get there, but I looked at it as part of my training, only making me stronger. Although I pushed myself to what should have been my limit, I could still do more.

One night Skye came to see me in my room. That was the first time she had come up to the tower.

"Nice room," she said, looking around when I let her in. "I like how you have decorated it; love the reading nook and window seat." She went over to the windows to glance outside. "What a beautiful view, Aurora. This is amazing!" She stared out over the hidden valley of the fae. "I've never seen the city from so high up. Look, you can see the whole valley."

I let her talk and sat on my bed, wondering why she had come and was being so friendly all of a sudden.

"Skye," I said slowly, "why are you here? Is there something wrong?"

She whirled around. "No, no," she smiled and came over to sit beside me. "I thought you might want to come down to the city tonight with us?"

It was sweet of her to make the effort, but Tristan had made it very clear some time ago that he didn't want me tagging along on his excursions to the city. "I don't think Tristan would be so pleased if I joined you."

"What! No, of course he doesn't mind," said Skye quickly. "Why would you think that?"

I told her what I had overheard Tristan say the last time

she had asked me to come out with her.

Skye's face turned the color of a fresh tomato. "I wondered why you never came down that day. And why you never mentioned it or asked to join us again."

I looked at my feet. "It's okay, I don't want to come where I'm not wanted."

Skye laughed. "You've got it all wrong," she said, her eyes twinkling. "It's not that Tristan doesn't want you around. The problem is that he does, and he hates that. He's the one who sent me to get you today."

"Why didn't he ask me himself?"

Skye smiled. "He didn't think you would come if he did."

I scrunched my eyebrows together. "I don't understand."

"As soon as Tristan got to know you, he became extremely fond of you. I've never seen him like this. He talks about you all the time. But you know how he hates mages? Knowing you are half-mage and having you constantly by his side brings back too many bad memories, reminding him of a time he would rather forget."

"Why does he hate mages so much?" Ever since I had met him, I was curious to know more about Tristan. He never opened up to me about himself, and the only time he would speak at length was if I asked him a question about fae history.

"When your mother lived in Elfi, Tristan's mother Selene, the Grand Duchess of the Night Court, was her best friend."

"I never knew that. Tristan hasn't mentioned it."

Skye nodded. "They were very close. While Elayna was meeting your father in secret, Selene met and fell in love with one of your father's courtiers who had accompanied him to Elfi."

My eyes widened. "No wonder Tristan wants nothing to do with me. He must blame my family for his mother's infidelity."

"That's not the half of it," Skye went on. "Tristan's father, the Grand Duke, found out about the affair and in a fit of anger exiled his wife from the Night Court. Selene went to the queen to seek refuge, but Izadora accused her of encouraging her daughter to defy her and marry a mage. So she refused to help."

I held my breath. I could tell already I wouldn't like where this story was heading.

"That's when Selene decided to leave Elfi and journey to Illiador and seek refuge with your mother, the only friend she had left."

"Where was Tristan? Why didn't he do anything?"

"Tristan was away at the time at a training camp, deep in the Old Forest, and couldn't be reached," said Skye. "My mother says Selene was too ashamed to face him anyway, when he got back and heard what had happened he went after her."

"Did he find her?' My voice was a whisper.

Skye hung her golden head. "It was so tragic," she sniffed. "Selene was a kind soul, a healer, she was not equipped to endure such a journey alone. Tristan's mother managed to almost reach Illiador, but on the way she was set upon by a group of soldiers."

My blood went cold.

"She was raped and murdered, Aurora, by a whole garrison of warrior mages." Tears formed in Skye's eyes as she recounted the horrific tale. "Tristan found her, but he was too late."

I sat still, barely breathing. "What did he do?"

"Tristan's rage knew no bounds. He killed the whole garrison of mages and razed their fortress to the ground."

"The mages have a different version of the story," I said, as I remembered the ruins of the fortress I saw in Eldoren on my way to Calos. Brandon told me about the merciless fae warrior that swooped down from the sky and wreaked havoc on the mages. I knew it was Tristan that had destroyed the fortress; Brandon had said it was the Prince of the Night Court. But until now I never knew why he did it.

Skye nodded. "I'm sure they do. The mages asked for Tristan's head; otherwise they would threaten war against the fae. Tristan's father was willing to give him up, but it was Izadora who made a deal with the mage king of Eldoren. Your grandmother saved his life."

"What kind of deal?"

"To keep Tristan bound to her under oath and control him. If he breaks his oath, his life is forfeit to the mages."

I shook my head. I couldn't imagine the pain he must have had to endure, but at least I was starting to understand him a little better. "It must have been such a difficult time for him."

"It was," Skye nodded. "Tristan had to bring his mother's broken body back to Elfi to lay at his father's feet."

"What did his father do?"

"The Grand Duke, Kildaren, knew he had made a mistake, but he couldn't admit it. Ever since then Tristan's relationship with his father has been strained. He barely visits the Night Court, and then only on his mother's death day to put flowers on her grave."

I closed my eyes, trying to remove the pictures of Tristan's mother from my mind. The world was such a gruesome place, and I couldn't blame Tristan for hating mages after what had happened.

"I'm not supposed to be telling you this," said Skye sheepishly. "Tristan doesn't like to talk about it. If he finds out I told you, he will have my head on a stick."

"I won't say anything. I don't want Tristan to fight with you."

Skye laughed, breaking the somber mood. "Oh, Tristan wouldn't hurt me," she flipped her mass of golden hair over her shoulders. "Cade would kill him if he even touched me."

She paused. "Well, he would try."

I smiled. "So, you and Cade . . ."

Skye nodded, she was beaming from ear to ear. "Isn't he the cutest thing you ever laid eyes on?"

"He's very sweet."

"The winter festival is on in Iris and all the best entertainers and troupes are in town," said Skye. "The theater is overflowing. But I managed to get us some seats. Best ones in the house," she winked at me. "Being a princess does have its perks."

I laughed at this. It was nice to have friends and a little distraction in the face of everything I was supposed to achieve.

She got up. "So are you coming with us or not?"

I grinned. "Wouldn't miss it."

I put on my boots and followed her out the door. Tristan and Cade were waiting at the foot of the stairs when Skye and I came down from my room and the Dark Prince smiled when he saw me.

The city was spectacular at night as we walked down the hill along small flower-lined paths, over marble bridges and terraces that spanned the cascading waterfalls beneath. Iris was bustling as we traversed the wide roads and turned into smaller alleys. This part of the city was where many of the demi-fae lived: the artisans, the shopkeepers, the merchants and traders, the entertainers.

Tristan led us to an open area, a beautiful garden surrounded by a wall of trees right in the middle of the city. I had seen this from my room in the tower and always wondered what it was. Now I knew it was the theater.

Fae-light danced over the open space as couples or groups sat under trees or on mats spread out around the circular stage, which was placed right in the center of the garden. Secluded benches dotted the park, but Skye had got us a place right near the stage. Vendors walked around with trays of delectable snacks, and I couldn't resist the little lemon tarts and fresh roasted chestnuts. Tristan bought me a few, and Cade picked up two ice-sticks dipped in berry juice for himself and Skye. We settled ourselves on a large mat Skye had kept ready for us.

The performers were all very good, showcasing an operatic rendition of the War of the Courts. Apparently Elfi had suffered civil war many centuries ago, when the Day and Night Courts were pitted together in a bloody war for power. It was easy to follow the story and the music was beautiful, haunting and full of emotion.

I didn't realize how cold it was that night; even with my cloak on I shivered and rubbed my arms.

"Come here," said Tristan gruffly, and pulled me closer to him, enveloping me in his strong embrace and wrapping his cloak around my shoulders.

For a moment I froze, unsure what to do, but he was so

surprisingly gentle that I leaned back and snuggled into the warmth of his chest to watch the rest of the play, although I was no longer fully concentrating on it. Heat coursed through me as he held me close. His warm breath grazed my neck as he whispered snippets of fae history, explaining from time to time what was happening on stage.

I couldn't understand what I was feeling. I loved being close to Tristan, although I realized that the attraction was purely physical. He was very handsome, there was no doubt, and his body was chiseled and honed into perfection through hundreds of years of being a warrior. I knew it was wrong, but being away from Rafe for so long was difficult, and I had absolutely no idea what he was doing or if he would ever come back for me like he said he would. Still, I felt guilty, but I didn't want to push Tristan away. I wasn't sure how he would take it.

His change of behavior toward me had been gradual, but this was the first time he let his guard down. He was finally treating me like a person and not as an outsider, and I was glad he was more comfortable around me than when we first met. However, I would have to be more careful to make sure I didn't lead him on.

Aiden came over during a break in the performance. Brianna was hanging on his arm, unashamedly falling all over the prince of the Day Court. He looked most uninterested in her but didn't seem to mind her tagging along.

"So you brought the *half-breed* to the theatre," sneered Aiden, glancing at me but addressing Tristan and Skye. "What a waste."

My spine bristled but I held my tongue. I had come here to enjoy myself, not get into a fight with an idiot.

I caught Brianna sneaking looks at Tristan more than a few times and somehow that didn't sit well with me. I had noticed before that Brianna had a thing for him, and it was so obvious she was trying to make him jealous by flaunting herself with Aiden. But Tristan didn't seem to notice or care; he completely ignored her whenever she was around.

"Oh, go away Aiden," said Skye. "Aurora's our friend, and if you don't like it you don't have to sit with us."

"I don't sit with *half-breeds*." Aiden's eyes burned a hole through me. "The stench is unbearable."

Tristan was up in a flash. "Say that again, Aiden . . ."

"And you'll what?" spat Aiden, itching for a fight. "Fight me? Your own brother Elite, for her?" He gave me a disgusted look, as if I weren't fit to wipe his boots.

I stood up. "No, he isn't going to fight you," I said, willing my voice to stay calm. "But since you obviously want to fight with someone, I'm sure I can oblige."

A ball of silver–fire formed in Aiden's hand.

I gathered my magic and the water rose up from the fountain behind Aiden. I released it in a well-aimed jet, dousing the fire in his hand. "Grow up!"

Aiden was startled, but drew his sword. "You're dead."

Tristan stepped in between us, facing Aiden. "Try it," he snarled, his voice laced with steel. Power rippled out from him as the Dark Prince's hands started to glow.

Aiden lowered his sword. "You can't protect her forever, Tristan." He turned on his heel and walked away with Brianna scurrying after him. He seemed to have forgotten she was there.

"Forget him," said Skye, putting her hand on my arm. "He thinks he's better than everyone else. But he's all bark and no bite, he would never hurt you and go against your grandmother's wishes. He knows what she would do to him if he did."

I was about to say something about terrible upbringing and bad manners, but I remembered she was Aiden's sister and I let it go.

"I'll see you later," Tristan said to me, his eyes swirling with silver sparks. "Cade, make sure Aurora gets back to the palace safely."

"Aren't you going to watch the rest of the performance?" I asked.

"No," said the Dark Prince as he stalked off into the shadows.

We sat back down and watched the rest of the show, but I wasn't paying attention as I thought about Tristan and how gentle he had been with me before Aiden came. The fae prince was an enigma, but he was a warrior without equal, and under that rough demeanour and permanent scowl he was a good person. Now that I had discovered his troubled past, I had started to understand him a little better. I was glad we were friends.

I didn't care what Aiden thought. The old me would have cried and pondered over why I was so disliked. But quite frankly it didn't make a difference if Aiden liked me or not. It should have upset me much more, but it didn't. I had finally realized not everyone could love you, or like you, for that matter. What was important was how much you loved yourself. I didn't care if Aiden thought I wasn't good enough, because I knew I was much more than that.

That was the first night I walked up the long flight of steps to my room smiling as I recounted the evening. Aiden had tried to spoil it but he couldn't take away the joy I felt being around friends and enjoying myself without the constant threat of Morgana looming. For one night I had felt like a normal teenager again, and I was grateful to Skye and Tristan for including me.

17
THE HOUSE
OF ÆOS-EIRENDIL

WINTER WAS UPON us, but the hidden valley of Iris remained at a moderate temperature, only cooling down at night when the wind blew from the ice-capped mountaintops. Tristan had been away for the past few days. He had told me there had been attacks in some of the outlying villages and he had to check it out with Aiden. During this time Cade was in charge of my training. He was not as hard a teacher as Tristan and, I managed to get quite a lot of free time to myself.

I continued to search the library for any information about the Dawnstar, but there was still no mention of it in any of the books I came across. Maybe the dowager was right—maybe the Dawnstar was a myth, a legend that didn't exist.

I had nearly given up all hope of finding anything when one night after an easy sparring session with Cade, as I walked the deserted corridors of the vast library, a faint murmuring caught my attention. I went deeper into the labyrinth, down a flight of rough stone steps to a corridor of books I had not checked before. Most of the library was lit up with floating balls of fae-light, which seemed to follow me and shine appropriately every time I took out a book to check its contents.

The murmuring got louder and, as I skimmed my fingers over the spines of rough bound volumes and massive tomes of fae politics, I could swear I heard someone whisper my name.

"*Aurora.*"

I whirled around, but the corridor was empty, one side continuing into darkness and the other leading back to where I came in.

Another whisper: a little louder, a deep baritone. "*Aurora, this way.*"

My hand went to my throat; I recognized the voice. It was the same deep voice that had helped me in the ruins when I fought Morgana. It was back.

My heartbeat sped up as I slowly moved toward the voice, further and further into a part of the library where I had never been. The fae-light that hovered above me fell back as I rounded a dark corner.

I called up my magic and a ball of light started to swirl in my hand. The corridor in front of me lit up, and I spotted a table placed along one wall with a few worn books on it. I walked toward it and ran my hands over the top one, clearing the dust that had collected, obscuring the title.

These books had obviously been sitting here for a long

time, unopened and unread. I checked the title on the first one: *The Great Noble Houses of the Ancients.*

A book on the Ancient Fae!

I thought Tristan said all the older texts were destroyed in the demon wars. I held my hand up, lighting the pages before me as I sat on the rickety wooden chair and started to read.

This book was very informative, giving information about all the noble houses, their sigils, lands, and titles, who they married, which houses were the most powerful. Finally I came to the page listing the house of Eos-Eirendil. It was the longest ruling house during the Age of the Ancients. At the end of the page on the bottom right hand corner was an illustration of the symbol of the house of Eos-Eirendil: a twelve-pointed star surrounding a rising sun.

A sun and a star! What did this symbol mean?

I flipped to the last page, where there was a glossary of house symbols with their ancient meanings written in the common tongue. I ran my finger down the list. *The house of Elfer-Sirundel, the house of Kiare-Edentren* . . . I stopped at the house of Eos-Eirendil and began to read.

"*The house of Eos-Eirendil, known in the common tongue as the house of the Star of the Morning.*" I smoothed the page and read it again.

My heartbeat sped up as I pushed my chair back and stood up. The Star of the Morning! The Dawnstar! It had to be.

The Dawnstar must somehow be connected to the House of Eos-Eirendil. Maybe the Dawnstar had something to do with Illaria Lightbringer. This had to mean something. It was definitely too important to ignore.

I heard a shuffling at the far end of the corridor and my heart skipped a beat. Everything was so quiet, but within the eerie silence, I thought I heard a low growl. The hair on the back of my neck stood up, a chill scuttling down my spine. I didn't wait to see what was moving out of the darkness; I turned and fled down the corridor.

I sped up, but my senses were all over the place as fear rushed in. I tried to feel the magic around me, something, anything, but I could not connect to it, and I bumped into tables and slid around corners as I ran. I must have taken a wrong turn somewhere, because I ended up in a completely unfamiliar corridor, with three more branching out in front of me.

I was lost, alone in the vast library. I turned to go back and froze.

From within the darkness of the library, a pair of glowing red eyes blocked my path and a flash of white teeth caught my eye. I didn't wait to see any more—I spun on my heel and fled down the nearest corridor.

I calmed my racing heart and willed my lungs to breathe. I pulled off my amulet as I ran, calling up my magic and sharpening my senses as I sped up. I could hear the padding of footsteps behind me, occasionally clicking and scraping like claws grating on the stone floors.

Further and further I ran, down into the labyrinth that stretched out under the palace. My eyes adjusted to the darkness as I pushed myself to my limit to get away from that thing. I chose a corridor and sprinted down it, turning again into another longer and darker one, trying to throw the monster off my scent. I could still hear the creature, an angry growl echoing through the lonely tunnels.

I kept running, the muscles in my legs screaming to stop and my heart beating frantically, when I came to a cross-roads. *Which way?* I couldn't run deeper into the maze of tunnels. I would never find my way back.

The scraping got louder; the creature was coming.

"Take the first tunnel on the left," said the deep voice in my head.

I didn't have time to argue and didn't wait to turn and see if the creature had found me. I veered left, running as fast as I could, and emerged in what looked to be a massive cave under the mountain. I lit my hand, holding the ball of light up in front of me, casting shadows against the walls.

The domed ceiling curved overhead, and the walls were smooth as if they had once been a part of some fae-made structure. There was a door at the other side. I ran to it.

It was massive and made entirely of stone, carvings of vines and creepers etched into the rock face, creating what looked like a door—but there was no way to open it. In the center of the stone door was a star with a sun within, the sigil of the House of Eos-Eirendil.

The Star of the Morning! I gasped as I ran my hands over the symbol.

The door would not budge.

I stepped back. I was trapped, and there was no way out of this cave except the way I had come in, back to the creature that hunted me in the labyrinth. I turned just as it came into the cave, blocking my only way out.

It was a monster straight out of a nightmare, with a long gnarled snout and gleaming fangs that shone white in the darkness. Its body was a twisted mass of limbs and muscle, covered in coarse dark hair the color of shadows. Deadly claws snicked out from its massive paws, which scraped on the stone floors as it moved forward. Its red demon eyes gleamed when it saw me.

"Face the creature," said the deep voice only I could hear, startling me into action and breaking the hold of the mind-numbing fear that had me in its grasp. *"Show the werewraith what you can do."*

"But I have no weapons," I said hurriedly. I was not prepared for a fight when I came down to the library.

"Your magic is the greatest weapon of them all, Aurora Shadowbreaker."

I willed my powers to surface as the werewraith snarled

and pounced.

Raising my arms, I called forth silver-fire that blasted out of my hands, slamming into the creature. The werewraith screeched, growled and fell back, embers of silver-fire singing the hair on its back, but the flames were doused by the shadows the creature emitted. It had the same sort of resilience as a gorgoth, a creature made of dark magic, and it didn't stop coming for me.

"You need concentrated power to defeat the werewraith," said the voice, its tone still calm while I was panicking. *"A sword of silver-fire should be able to cut though the creature's defense."*

"But I don't have a sword," I screamed in my mind.

"Then create one," said the voice with a touch of irritation. *"You're fae, aren't you? Use your glamour."*

I had no choice but to follow the instructions of the voice. My palms were sweating while the creature moved forward, warily this time, assessing me. It knew I could hurt it, and I could use that to my advantage.

Glamour was easy after I had used it to decorate my room, and I willed a sword into existence, fashioned on the sword Rafe had given me. It flashed in my hand, and I pushed my silver-fire into it as I had done when I fought with Tristan against the Drakaar and their demons.

My sword lit up, silver-fire coursing through my veins and creating a blade of pure power. I grinned at the werewraith, my insecurities disappearing with the appearance of my magic.

My senses honed in on the creature as it pounced. But this time I was ready. I leapt out of the way at the moment it expected to clamp its teeth down on my flesh. I ducked and rolled, jumping up in a flash. I didn't think, and this time I didn't hesitate. Whirling around, faster than I ever thought I could, I brought my flaming sword down on its neck. The power of my magic sliced through flesh and bone, severing the dark creature's head from its body.

"That was very good," said the voice as the flame in my sword flickered. *"But you'd better get out of there. Werewraiths usually hunt in packs."*

"How?" I whirled around. There was no way out of the cave except the way I had come. A low growl sounded in the distance as more werewraiths entered the tunnel leading to the cave where I was.

"Create a portal," said the voice.

I didn't want to waste any more time. I could hear the creatures—in a few seconds they would be in the cave. My heartbeat sped up again. There was no way I could fight more of them on my own. I had to go.

I threw my magic out in front of me, picturing my room in the castle. My power swirled and grew, forming a portal as the first werewraith entered the cave.

It growled, spotting me.

I ran, pushing myself faster with all the energy I could muster, and flung myself through the portal.

I landed on my knees. Spinning around immediately, I raised my hand. I saw a flash of red eyes and heard a muffled growl as the portal closed. The eyes disappeared and the darkness of the cave dissipated.

I fell onto my back, my chest heaving from the exertion. I was safe.

I ran down the stairs to see the dowager. I had to tell someone what was down there in the library. It was late and I knocked on the door, hoping she was still awake.

I was relieved to hear her voice. "Come in."

The dowager was seated near the fireplace, reading and sipping on a cup of her favorite rose tea. She raised her eyebrows when she saw me. "What happened to you?" She set her book down on the side table. "You look like you've been sweeping chimneys."

I told her what had happened with the werewraith, but I didn't tell her about the voice or the door I had found.

"The mountains surrounding this valley are ancient, and the library was built thousands of years ago." The dowager got up from her chair. "No one knows how far down it goes, and in some places the catacombs run deeper into the mountain where the older texts are kept. There are places down there that have remained untouched for centuries, and there are areas in the walls where the wards could have become weak. It is possible some creatures can slip through from time to time." She went to the door and spoke to someone outside.

When she came back, she sat down beside me and held my hands. "Don't worry, I have sent for Erik. The Elite will check out the catacombs. If there actually is a pack of werewraiths in the tunnels, they will take care of them. For now, try to get some sleep. Don't go into the library until we have cleared it of any threats."

I nodded. I wasn't going to go back there any time soon. Thinking about those red eyes and the flash of teeth sent shivers down my spine.

I got up to leave.

"Although I would like to know what you were doing so far down in the catacombs," said the dowager. I froze. "But we can talk about that tomorrow."

I thanked her and hurried to my room. She had called a pair of palace guards to escort and guard me until Tristan got back. Not that they were of any help. I could probably knock them both out with my magic if I wanted to. They were not going to deter a werewraith, that was for sure.

That night I barely got any sleep. I tossed and turned in my bed, picturing red eyes glinting through the darkness. *I was running down unfamiliar corridors into a dark cavern within the mountain. I came to an ancient stone door. On it was the symbol of the Star of the Morning, a symbol of the House of Eos-Eirendil. I knew there was something behind it, something I needed. I pushed at the door with all my might but it wouldn't budge. Behind me I could hear low growls—the werewraiths. I pushed at the door again, looking over my shoulder at the snarling teeth that moved through the shadows. I had to get through that door. I pushed and pushed, the creature growled and leapt . . .*

I woke up, sweat coating my brow. I had never been so scared in my life. At least with the Drakaar and Morgana I knew what I was facing. But this monstrous creature that hunted me through the library was more terrifying because I had no idea where it came from. It shouldn't be here, under the castle. What else was down there under the mountain? There were so many questions whirling around in my head I couldn't get back to sleep.

The dowager said the Dawnstar didn't exist. But I realized there was so much she wasn't telling me. Maybe I was on the wrong path, looking directly for the Dawnstar when what I should have been looking for was more information on the house of Eos-Eirendil and Illaria Lightbringer instead.

The sun hadn't risen, but I ran down to the training ground before the others woke up and practiced my moves until my muscles were sore. Tristan was back and I was more than warmed up when he came to find me. It was quite obvious he had already heard what had happened in the catacombs. Erik or the dowager must have told him.

"Do you have a death wish?" he growled, side-stepping my blow, which should have hit him in the stomach. "What were you doing in the catacombs? Werewraiths have poison in their bite. You could have been killed."

"If you had let me train with silver-fire by now, I would have been better prepared." I twirled my staff deftly in my hands.

His eyes narrowed. "That's because I didn't think you were ready yet."

"There's no more time, Tristan. If I don't learn how to use all of my powers now, I will never be ready."

He nodded. "You're right," he said unexpectedly, walking over to the sword rack. "Now pick a sword."

"I have my own," I said, and pulled out my sword from a glamoured scabbard on my back. Only a few powerful spirit-fae, like my grandmother or the dowager, could see through it. I knew all fae had the gift of glamour. But it was only the rare spirit-fae who possessed the powerful glamour used to conceal things from other fae. I was never going to be caught unarmed again.

Tristan's lips curved upward. "You've been using your glamour quite well." He sounded impressed. "I must admit I didn't see through it."

That was interesting. Tristan didn't have spirit magic, but

then not many of the High Fae did. Spirit-fae were as rare as the fire-fae. I grinned and looked at the sword Rafe had given me. It was a beauty, and I would be silly not to use it.

"Let me see that sword." Tristan took it from me almost reverently. "Where did you get it?" He turned it around in his hands, inspecting the blade.

"Rafe gave it to me."

Tristan smirked. "Yes, I heard you have a mage suitor. The illustrious prince Rafael Ravenswood no less." He paused, running his finger over the blade from top to bottom. "This is dwarven-crafted."

I nodded. "He had it specially made for me."

"In the old days, the dwarves created swords like these for the noble fae families, forged in the magical fires of their mines in Dragonsgate. Those fires were said to be started by dragons, and they still burn until this day. But the dwarves don't make these anymore. Except on a few rare occasions."

"Why?"

He shrugged and gave the sword back to me. "They have distanced themselves from the fae for centuries. The dwarves hardly ever come out of their mountain cities in the Silver-spike. I don't know how he got them to make one for you."

I shrugged as we walked to the middle of the field. "What makes this sword so special?"

"The steel forged in their magical fires is the perfect conduit for our silver-fire," said Tristan, taking up a fighting stance. "Other blades work too, but eventually they burn out. A dwarven-made sword will never burn up, no matter how hot your silver-fire gets." He shot a glance at my sword. "You can take an army of Drakaar down with that."

I shifted my feet and adjusted my grip. I never knew how precious this sword was. And I was thankful Kalen brought it on the ship for me when we escaped Calos. I came so close to losing it, but I never would again. It would be a constant reminder of everything I had ever taken for granted.

"A sword like that needs a name," said Tristan.

I grinned. "I was thinking the same thing." And I knew exactly what name I wanted. "I will call it *Dawn*."

"Perfect." He smiled, and I must say he was even more handsome when he did, which was saying something.

———

That afternoon I went to see the Dowager Duchess of the Night Court for our lessons.

"Erik has checked the catacombs and there is nothing there," she said as we walked through the flowering gardens and over a small marble bridge that spanned a sparkling waterfall. "The werewraiths must have gone back to wherever they came from."

"But what if they come back?"

"The wards have been reinforced under the mountain. Nothing will get through again. But I would like to know what you were doing so far down in the catacombs." She sat down on her favorite ivy-covered bench in the gardens, overlooking a little pond. A few satyrs were tending the flowers and watering plants as little gnomes wandered about finding weeds, digging them up and eating them. "The books down there are older than me, and most of them are written in the old language of the fae. You wouldn't be able to read them even if you wanted."

"I was looking for information on the Dawnstar," I said finally. "But I found something else." I told her about the book I had found, but I didn't mention the voice that led me to it

Rhiannon's eyebrows rose. "Illaria Lightbringer died five thousand years ago," said the dowager. "I didn't know there were any books left on the ancients. Where exactly was this book you found?"

I explained the location.

"That is very far down in the catacombs, Aurora," said the dowager, narrowing her sapphire eyes. "I would suggest you don't go back down there again. Although the wards may have been reinforced, there are things that are best left alone."

"Like the door with Illaria's symbol on it?" I dared to ask.

"You found a door?" Her eyes narrowed. "What door?"

I described it and told her my theory about the Dawnstar being hidden behind it.

"I thought I explained to you that the Dawnstar is only a myth," said the dowager.

"But the mastermage told me it is the only thing that can release my mother from the dagger." I couldn't let this go. "There has to be some truth to the stories."

The dowager shook her head and put her hand on my shoulder. "I know this must be hard for you to accept, Aurora. But the Dawnstar is not behind that door. We will find a way to release Elayna from the dagger. But first we have to get it back. That should be your first priority."

"But the door?"

"Is out of bounds," said the dowager, ending our conversation. "Do not speak about it to anyone."

I nodded, but I couldn't stop thinking about it and the symbol of Illaria's house. The dowager said the Dawnstar was not behind the door. However, I knew there was something else down there and I had to find another way to discover what it was.

18
SECRETS

FROM THEN ON I took the dowager's advice and stayed away from the catacombs. I started waking up before the sun rose, and would run down to the training field to practice my sword moves before the others started.

Tristan was so impressed with my glamour he increased my training sessions. In addition to creating a sword of silver-fire, he showed me how to create flaming magical arrows, which was great. This way I would never run out of ammunition. He also made me practice creating daggers of silver-fire that I could throw at an enemy. I spent hours every day alternately shooting flaming arrows and daggers at targets he had set up. I practiced until my arms were sore, sometimes not taking a break for hours on end.

There were times, late at night when I was practicing, I would see Erik, the leader of the Elite, standing at a distance watching me as I trained, but he never approached me or acknowledged me when he passed by.

One night after a hard training session, as I reached the door to my room, I lost my footing and slipped, thumping my way halfway back down the steep stone steps. I groaned, bruised and battered in places I didn't want to think about. I gathered my magic and healed myself. Bracing my hand on the wall, I pushed myself up.

The wall gave way.

A rough white stone block moved inward, revealing what looked like an age-worn doorknob. I twisted it slightly to see if it moved. It did. And the whole wall groaned as I pushed against it, revealing a dark passage leading into the mountain.

A secret passage! I called forth my magic and a dense ball of light glowed in my outstretched palm. I walked forward, but didn't close the door behind me completely. I wanted to see where it would lead. I knew I shouldn't, but the lure was too much for me to resist. If I couldn't find my way back, I could just create a portal to my room. That thought gave me courage as I rounded a corner into another dark corridor. It was musty and cobwebs lined the smooth stone walls.

This passage was old, older than the rest of the castle, and I shivered as I felt a cool breeze coming from the left. I walked toward it when I heard a murmuring of voices, two people having a conversation. There was a light at the end where the passage veered off to the left. A gap in the stone looked out into another part of the palace—I put my eye to the space, peering through.

It was the throne room. I was high above, looking down on it.

"I hear my granddaughter has been fighting werewraiths in the catacombs, Rhiannon," the queen was saying. "I thought the wards deterred anyone from using those tunnels?"

The dowager was pacing in front of the throne. "I don't know how she got through them; she shouldn't have been able to do that. I've already had Erik check it out, and I went into the catacombs myself to reinforce the wards."

"Yes, I know that." The fae queen's tone was sharp. "You should have told me about this immediately. I had to wait for Erik to inform me."

"I took care of it, Izadora," said the dowager.

My grandmother gave the dowager a long look. "What was she doing down there anyway?"

I held my breath, and my shoulders tensed.

"She's been looking for the Dawnstar."

To my surprise the queen laughed. "That old legend? Where did she dig it up?"

"A mastermage told her it was the only thing that can release her mother from the Dagger."

"It probably could, if it actually existed," said the queen gravely. "Did she find the door?"

The dowager nodded. "Yes, and she thinks we are hiding the Dawnstar there."

"Foolish girl," said my grandmother. "If we had the Dawnstar we wouldn't be in this predicament. In five thousand years no one has ever found this supposedly ancient weapon, and no one ever will because it doesn't exist. Even the Codex can be wrong on occasion."

"That is exactly what I told her," said the dowager. "And it is better she believes that or she will be distracted from her true purpose." She gave my grandmother a hard look. "But we both know the Codex is never wrong, Izadora."

"It may as well be, for all the good it's done us," snapped my grandmother. "Has she spoken to anyone else about it?"

The dowager shook her head. "No, I told her to keep it to herself."

"Good. No one else must find that door. Or all our plans will be for nothing."

The dowager's eyes narrowed. "I know that. But we have a bigger problem. Those werewraiths were not down there by accident. Only a powerful spirit-fae could have broken the wards and let the werewraiths into the castle. Someone who knows Aurora goes down to the library practically every night."

Izadora gave the dowager a pointed look. "Make sure Tristan stays close to Aurora. Morgana is cunning. I wouldn't put it past her to find a way into Elfi. We may not have the Dawnstar, but we have something equally as important hidden behind that door. Make sure it's secure," the queen said, getting up from her throne. "Tell Erik and the Elite to be on extra alert. I fear we have a traitor in our midst."

The dowager nodded and left the throne room.

I ran back through the secret passage to my room, my heart galloping. Those werewraiths were looking for me! They weren't down there by accident, as the dowager led me to believe. But at least I finally had some answers about the door under the castle.

My quest for the legendary weapon of the ancients had come to a dead end. I had been so excited to find the door and so sure the Dawnstar was behind it. But after what I overheard in the throne room, I finally realized I had to stop wasting my time looking for a mythical weapon that didn't exist and concentrate on getting the dagger back from Morgana. I would have to find another way to free my mother from it. But I did still wonder what else my grandmother and the elders were hiding down there under the mountain.

I stayed away from the library, and didn't dare go down to the catacombs, but I couldn't stop thinking about what my grandmother had said; there was a traitor in the castle. Someone had deliberately let those werewraiths loose.

Could Morgana have someone within the castle working for her? Aiden's words rang in my head. Would he defy his queen to get to me? Could he be the traitor?

After that, Tristan didn't leave my side. Training sessions were more intense and I continued to push myself as far as I could go. Every part of me had become stronger—I could run for hours in the hills and woods that surrounded the valley and still have energy to practice archery or sword moves after I was done. My control over the powers I possessed started to increase day by day, but I pushed myself further and continued to learn all I could before my time ran out. Morgana would not rest until I was dead, and I wasn't going to make it easy for her. If Aiden did come after me, I would be ready.

"Why does the council have to choose a new queen every thousand years?" I asked Tristan one evening, walking back through the valley after a particularly hard run. "I always thought the succession was by birthright, until Cade told me the queen chooses an heir, or the Elder Council chooses for her if she is undecided."

"Cade is right. In the days of the ancients, our queens did rule by birthright. The royal house of Eos-Eirendil was the most powerful, ruling the fae for thousands of years. Ancient magic ran in their veins, but the last of that power died out with Illaria Lightbringer."

"Didn't she have any children?"

Tristan shook his head. "No, she was the last of her line," he said, looking away. "Although there are some people who believe she conceived a child and brought it up in secret."

"Why would she do that?"

"Illaria lived most of her life during the Demon Wars. Those were dark and terrible times for the fae. Everyone was afraid of who Dragath would take next."

"What happened to the child?"

"No one knows." Tristan shook his head. "After Illaria died and Auraken Firedrake founded the seven kingdoms, the fae were left with these lands. For generations the fae elders have searched in secret for the child, but they've never found anything."

"So then how did my grandmother become queen?"

"Those of the fae elders who remained founded the Elder Council and chose a queen from the most powerful families left," Tristan explained. "There was outrage among the fae and Elfi went through years of civil strife, until the council decided to choose a new queen every thousand years depending on the power of her magic, thus balancing the power between the Day and Night Courts."

"Has there ever been a fae king?"

"No. There are only the Grand Dukes who preside over the Day and Night Courts. That still remains a hereditary title, as I explained before."

"So after your father, you will become Grand Duke of the Night Court," I stated. I already knew the answer.

Tristan nodded once as the centaurs opened the gates to let us enter the city. "And Aiden will be Grand Duke of the Day Court."

"Do you think he could be the one who let the werewraiths into the tunnels?"

"Why would you think that?" Tristan's tone was sharp. "Aiden would never go against the queen's wishes."

I told him what I had overheard my grandmother and the dowager talking about. But I didn't tell him where I had heard it. I decided to keep the passage a secret for a while longer.

"My grandmother did inform me there was a traitor in the castle," said Tristan finally, "but it can't be Aiden."

"How can you be so sure after everything he said?"

"I know him. He may hate you, and try to rough you up a bit, but he would never betray his queen."

I held my tongue. Tristan obviously wasn't thinking clearly. His loyalty to his friend was admirable, but I was sure Aiden had something to do with the werewraiths. I would have to be more careful and keep an eye on him. Empty threats or not, something was going on, and I needed to find out what it was before Morgana found another way to get to me.

Twilight was upon us, and the city lit up as the full moon rose overhead, bathing the valley in its silver gleam.

Cade ran up to us as we entered the palace. "Izadora has summoned you." He looked at me. "You have a visitor."

I put my hand to my chest. "Me?"

Cade nodded. "She just got here from Eldoren, apparently."

"She?" My heart started galloping. "Who is it?"

Cade shrugged. "I don't know. I was sent to bring you to the throne room." He started walking down the garden path back to the palace. "Come on. You know Izadora will not be pleased to be kept waiting."

I waved goodbye to Tristan and ran after Cade. Who would have come all the way to Elfi to see me? And why?

My grandmother was seated on her throne, with robes of silver flowing over an ivory gown. I bowed my head briefly before the queen of the fae, and Cade left.

"You sent for me?" I said, straightening in front of my grandmother.

"Indeed I did." Izadora's face was a stone mask. She looked to the side, and a figure emerged from the shadows.

Standing right below the throne was Penelope Plumpleberry.

She smiled and my mood lifted instantly. She looked exactly the same. It had been so long, and I was so happy to see a familiar face. I moved forward to hug her and almost immediately stopped in my tracks.

Magic swirled around Penelope as her height increased and her face changed in front of my eyes. A tall and beautiful fae lady stood in her place. Her golden locks reached her waist and her face was striking, with full lips and a small, slightly upturned nose. Her fae ears became more prominent, elegant and pointed, but her wide almond-shaped eyes were still a beautiful bright blue and sparkled when she looked at me. She was unmistakably High Fae.

I knew those eyes; they were still the same. "Penelope?" I said, my voice barely a whisper.

Penelope nodded and opened her arms. I hesitated but only for a moment. Stepping forward, I hugged Kalen's mother.

"But how? Why do you look different?"

"It's a long story." Penelope hugged me tightly. She was taller than I was.

My grandmother cleared her throat. "That is enough hugging for one day. Life in the outside world has made you soft, Penelope."

Penelope moved away and smiled at the queen. "When did you become so bitter, Izadora?"

I was taken aback. I had never heard anyone speak to the queen of the fae like that. But she didn't seem to mind.

"You've been away for a while, little sister," said my grandmother. "Things have changed."

Sister! Penelope was my grandmother's sister?

Penelope raised an eyebrow. "I can see that."

"But what were you doing living in Illiador for so many years?" I was still trying to get over the shock of seeing her like this.

"She's Elfi's most trusted informant." The fae queen's lips

curved in an amused smile.

I looked at Penelope, my eyes as wide as saucers. "You're a spy?"

My grandmother smiled, enjoying my confusion.

"For the last fifteen years Penelope has been my eyes and ears in Illiador," said the queen of the fae. "I sent her there to assess the situation after your mother disappeared. She has been gathering information on Morgana and you all this time."

I didn't know what to say. For a glamour like this to hold for over fifteen years and remain undetectable by the most powerful mages was an extraordinary use of fae power and could only be achieved by one of the most powerful spirit-fae. I always assumed Penelope was a lesser fae, but it turned out she was not who she seemed at all.

"I will explain everything," said Penelope gently. She glanced briefly at her sister. "But this is not the right time."

Izadora waved her hand. "Go, get settled. I'm sure you have much to discuss."

Penelope turned to leave.

"I expect to see you and Aurora in the council chamber at the next meeting," my grandmother added. "The whole Elder Council will be attending. This is the time to cement alliances. War is coming and we must be ready."

Penelope inclined her head, and I bowed and followed her out of the throne room.

"Penelope, what's going on?" I asked as I fell into step with her. "Why are you here? Has something happened? Is Rafe all right?"

"We can't talk here." Penelope glanced around. "Follow me."

We walked in silence, through great arched corridors and up two flights of stairs to a suite of rooms that looked out over the gardens. Penelope knew exactly where she was going—it was obvious she had been here before. She probably grew up in this palace. I couldn't believe it. Penelope was my grandmother's sister, my grand-aunt, and I never knew. A spy. What was going on?

Once we were within the confines of the room, Penelope spoke. "Come and sit down, Aurora." She patted the seat beside her.

It was still a little strange seeing Penelope like this, and I had to keep reminding myself that she was the same person who had helped me those many months ago when I was new to this world. It would take time, but I would get used to it eventually.

I sat down beside her and thought back to the fight with the Shadow Guard. The blow to Kalen's head should have killed him. At that time I was so caught up with healing Snow I didn't stop to think how Kalen had survived it. Now I knew—he was High Fae, and had extraordinary healing.

I had many questions, but first: "How are Rafe and

284

Kalen?"

She didn't smile.

"Has something happened? Is Uncle Gabriel all right?"

Penelope nodded and shifted in her seat. "Yes, for the moment."

"What aren't you telling me, Penelope?"

Penelope cleared her throat. "When Rafe and Kalen reached Eldoren, the Blackwaters were ruling the council and Duke Silverthorne was still in the dungeons."

I nodded, urging her to go on. "Did Rafe get him out?"

She put her hands in her lap. "It's a long story."

"Tell me." Why was she being so cagy? What had precisely happened in Eldoren?

"Prince Rafael tried for days to get the council to listen and release your granduncle, but they wouldn't budge."

"What about the king? Surely Rafe's father would listen to him. Listen to reason."

"The king of Eldoren is not what he seems. That's why I left; the situation has become worse than I thought." She took my hand in hers. "I'm afraid Lilith didn't go far to find the body she needed."

"What?" I pulled my hand back. "What do you mean?"

"She has killed King Petrocales and taken over his body. The outer shell may look like the king, but the creature that lives beneath the flesh is none other than the dark queen. There was a point when she let her guard down and I discovered who she truly was. Her magic is back. Lilith and the Blackwaters have complete control of the Eldorean Council and the king's army."

My hands flew to my mouth. "No!"

This was all my fault. I was the one who brought Lilith back. It was because of me that Rafe had lost his father, and probably his kingdom as well. He would never forgive me for this.

"Once I realized what had happened, I knew the prince was no longer safe in the castle so I went to Rafael and told him what we had discovered. At first he didn't believe me, but he learned the truth himself soon enough. He managed to escape the palace guards and took us with him." Penelope wrung her hands together. "There was no time to rescue Silverthorne. The dungeons are too heavily guarded. We were lucky to get out of the palace alive."

"What about Rafe?" My mouth turned dry. "Where is he now? Why didn't he come with you?"

"We managed to make it to Silverthorne Castle. We found your Aunt Serena and Erien. They had escaped from the Summer Palace when Silverthorne was taken, and were rescued by the rebel group known as the Silver Swords. The rebels are using Silverthorne Castle as their base in Eldoren."

I stood up. "We have to help Rafe," I said, balling my hands into fists. "We cannot let Morgana take his throne too."

Penelope raised an eyebrow. "There is nothing you can do from here. Prince Rafael needs an army, and the last time I checked you still don't have one."

I sat back down in my chair and hung my head. "I don't know if I ever will."

Penelope took my hands in hers and looked me straight in the eyes. "I know I have kept secrets from you and it will take a while for you to trust me again. But I want you to know I had no choice, I had to do my duty. And keeping my identity a secret until you were ready was essential to my mission. I wish I could have told you sooner, and believe me, I thought about it many times, especially when you ran away from the Summer Palace." She looked away briefly. "Maybe if I had, you would have done things differently."

"I should have listened to you."

She gave my hand a small squeeze. "We all make mistakes, Aurora, but it is what we learn from them that makes all the difference. I am here now, and you are not alone anymore." She leaned forward and hugged me. "We will find a way to get your mother back, and I promise you we will find a way to help Rafe. But first there is still much to do here in Elfi."

I hugged Penelope back. I was glad she was here, but I was not so sure how much to trust her with anymore. I had to be careful and wait to see how far Penelope's loyalties lay towards her sister.

"There's more," said Penelope.

"Whatever it is, it's fine. Just tell me. It couldn't really get any worse."

But I was wrong.

"I explained Rafe's present situation to you," said Penelope.

I nodded, waiting for her to continue.

"Although he has the backing of Silverthorne's army, they are completely outnumbered. All the other nobles have rallied to the Blackwaters either by choice or by force. Rafe does not have enough soldiers to wage war on the king's army and the nobles of Eldoren combined. The prince is backed into a corner and he has no other option. He spoke to Santino about getting his army or at least part of it to help him take back his throne. But Santino had to get the consent of his father to take his troops into Eldoren to join Rafe." She paused. "The Emir agreed, but only on one condition."

"Which is?" I said, my eyes narrowing. I didn't like where this was going, and my heart sat heavy in my chest as I waited for her answer.

"Prince Rafael has to marry Katerina Valasis," said Penelope. "That was the condition set by the Emir. He wants his daughter to be queen of Eldoren, thus gaining a foothold in the west."

"And has Rafe agreed?"

Silence.

"Has he agreed?" I asked again, slowly and more sternly.

I had to know.

Penelope shook her head. "I don't know. I left before he decided anything. Kalen stayed back to help him. And with the state of the world as it is right now, I didn't want my son to come on such a perilous journey."

"But he hasn't rejected the offer?"

Penelope shook her head. "No, he hasn't."

"What about Leticia? How come he's not bound by his vow to his mother ?"

"Leticia has married Zorek Blackwater in her quest to become queen." Penelope had a disgusted look on her face as she spoke. "She has released Rafael from his vow and the engagement."

"Do you think Rafe will marry Katerina?" I asked, my voice small.

"With the state Eldoren is in, I don't think he has a choice but to accept the offer. If he does go to Brandor, it will be to marry Katerina and get an army to take back his throne."

I didn't know what decision he would make, but for now it looked as if I was nowhere on his agenda. Penelope said he didn't have a choice but in the end we always have a choice. How foolish I was to think he would keep his word and come back for me. Brandon may have been a traitor, but he told me Rafe had done this many times to a dozen different girls. I was stupid if I thought I was different, that he loved me like he said he did. Rafe was not who I thought he was, after all.

I went to my room and lay down on my bed. A light mist rolled down from the mountains, swirling in and out of the windows in a lazy dance as I gazed out at the starlit sky. It made sense that he would take the offer. Penelope was right—I had no army, I could not help him take back his throne. I couldn't even take back my own throne.

I cried myself to sleep that night, pining for my lost love. Everything I had dreamed of, everything I had wished for, was an empty shell. All my castles in the sky came crashing down around me as reality reared its untimely head.

I tossed and turned as images of Rafe and Katerina flitted through my mind, teasing me and taking pleasure in my misery, until the light of the morning sun warmed the floor and awoke me to another day.

I was done.

I had to forget about Rafe. Never again would I let myself love someone so completely that they would have the power to rip my heart to shreds as Rafe had managed to do. He hadn't accepted as yet but the fact he was considering it made me feel sick.

As I lay in my bed watching the sunrise, I realized it was my own fault. I had brought Lilith back, and Lilith killed Rafe's father and took his throne. Now the Blackwaters were in complete control of Eldoren, and it was all because I didn't have the sense to listen and trust there were others who might know a little more than I did. I was rash and foolish, and so excited I had magic that I never thought about all the consequences my actions would bring.

I dressed quickly and ran down to the kitchens, picked up freshly baked honey cakes and proceeded to the training ground.

I didn't feel like talking to anyone. I wanted to be on my own.

Tristan was already practicing and waiting for me. Wordlessly, I picked up my staff and ran at him. Tristan sidestepped and sent me sprawling to the ground. I jumped up, my muscles faster, stronger. I opened myself to the magic around me and shifted my feet; bracing myself, I blocked Tristan's first blow.

He grinned. "Finally."

But I was not in the mood to joke.

I twirled my staff, knocking Tristan's out of the way, and thrust. He blocked me again but I kept going. Everything was happening in slow motion when I concentrated. I could see the blow coming before it did, I could feel my muscles responding as I used every move I had learnt so far to fend off Tristan. Again and again I struck, my blood roaring in my ears as I twisted and turned, ducked and jumped, blocking and avoiding blows faster than I ever thought I could move.

Finally I got one strike in, hitting Tristan in the stomach with the end of my staff. Tristan glared at me and knocked me down, disarming me.

The fight was over.

He stood over me and gave me his hand. "Much better. I think you are finally ready to accompany me on a scouting mission."

I stood up, brushing the dirt off my tunic. "It's about time." The fight had not brightened my mood, and I scowled at Tristan. Who for the first time didn't scowl back.

"What's wrong? Why the sour face?"

"It's nothing. I've had a bad night, that's all."

Tristan came closer, and put his finger under my chin, tilting my head up to look at him. His dark eyes bore into mine. "Tell me. Did someone hurt you?"

I shook my head. But then I couldn't hold back my tirade and I told him all about Rafe and what Penelope had said about him marrying Katerina Valasis to save his kingdom. Tristan listened without interrupting; we were lucky there were very few soldiers training on the field that morning so we had some privacy.

Finally he spoke. "So let me get this straight. Your perfect prince was courting you while he was engaged to another, now that he is free to marry whomever he wishes, he is contemplating marrying someone else."

I nodded and hung my head. It sounded worse when

Tristan said it like that. "He hasn't decided yet, but he hasn't said no either."

"Well, all I can say is that he is an idiot. If he doesn't think you are worth fighting for and gives up so easily, then he doesn't deserve you anyway. He sounds like a coward to me."

I smiled at that. It felt good to talk to someone who didn't know Rafe personally and who didn't think he was the best thing to happen to this world since Auraken Firedrake. In fact, Tristan didn't think much of him at all.

Although I was so angry with Rafe, I heard myself defending him. "He's not a coward. This is the only way he can gather an army to take back his kingdom."

"Is that what he is telling you?" Tristan's eyes narrowed. I could see the silver swirls that lit up the darkness within them. "There is always another way, Aurora. And if he truly loved you, then he would find it."

I looked down at my feet. "The truth is, it was my fault he lost his throne in the first place. I don't think he wants anything to do with me anymore."

"Well, that's his loss then, isn't it?" Tristan went over to the rack and drew a sword. "Forget him and concentrate on your training. We don't have much time left." His sword lit up.

I drew my own sword, pushing my magic into it. It lit up as well, burning with fae-fire. I knew Tristan was right, but it still hurt to admit it. I had my own life and my own throne to take back. Rafe was doing what was best for him and his people, and I had to do what was best for mine.

19
THE ELDER COUNCIL

LESSONS WITH THE dowager were cancelled for the meeting with the Elder Council. I was nervous about meeting the other fae elders. As a group they held as much power as the queen, if not more. I had to tread carefully around them, and I would need their support if they were going to give me a fae army to help me take back the throne of Illiador.

The doors to the council chamber opened and I entered a sunlit room overlooking the city. Big arched windows were hung with light muslin curtains fluttering in the breeze. In the center of the room lay a huge table upon which rested a massive, detailed map of Avalonia.

I moved forward to look at it and smiled. It was a beautiful rendering, with towns and cities painted in vivid colors and mountains so lifelike they rose off the page. My grandmother sat at the head of the table; the rest of the council members were seated on the two sides. Penelope was already there and stood beside the queen's chair next to her sister. My grandmother beckoned for me to come forward—the council members eyed me warily as I passed them.

"I have called this meeting today to discuss the situation in the west," said my grandmother. "Penelope has returned with some disturbing news, and the time has come for us to address the threat of Morgana."

"Why should we care what a western queen does in her lands?" said one council member, an old lord from the Day Court. His name was Silias. The dowager had pointed him out while he was walking in the gardens during one of our lessons. "This is not our fight. We don't have that many trained warriors." He pointed at me. "She should go home and take her fight away with her."

The queen looked at the old lord, ice in her eyes, and he shrank back. "Tell them what you have found out, Penelope," she said, not looking at her sister.

Penelope stepped forward slightly to address the council. She told them everything, about Morgana's quest for the *Book of Abraxas* and her plan to release Dragath.

The council was quiet as they listened to Penelope speak.

"But has she the power to release him?" inquired another fae elder, a slender silver-haired high lady. "From what I understand, Auraken Firedrake's magical prison is unbreakable."

"We believe," said Penelope, "that Morgana possesses the Dark Dagger of Dragath."

A gasp went up from the council and I could see a hint of terror in those immortal eyes, but they all held their tongues and let Penelope finish.

"We all know the concentrated power of hundreds of immortal High Fae that lies within the dagger can indeed break the spell on Dragath's prison," said Penelope. "But first she needs the book to learn how to control him."

The council members nodded and I could see many of them had not expected this news. They, more than anyone, knew the threat of Dragath was real. They knew what he and his demons could do. Their whole civilization had nearly been destroyed by him once. And the Dark Dagger was every High Fae's worst nightmare. All of them knew the stories of how Dragath wiped out Illaria's whole army with it. If he ever rose again, Elfi was doomed. There was no Illaria Lightbringer or Auraken Firedrake to protect them.

There was only me.

Rhiannon, the Dowager Grand Duchess of the Night Court, spoke. "Then we must make sure Morgana never gets her hands on the book. If she has the keys they are useless to her without it."

"That is exactly why the book is safest in Elfi," said Elder Silias. "I don't know why mages were made guardians of the keys. We should have been protecting the keys too. They have failed in their task."

"Not all of them have failed," I said quietly, finally speaking up. "Duke Gabriel Silverthorne still has his key. He will never give it to Morgana."

"From what I understand, Gabriel Silverthorne is rotting

away in Morgana's dungeons," said Silias. "He will break. They always do."

I didn't know what to say as doubt crept in. What if he was right, what if they had already broken Uncle Gabriel and had the fourth key? They could be coming for the book right now.

"Gabriel Silverthorne will never give up," Penelope said softly. "He will get out of the dungeons eventually, of that I have no doubt. He is the most resourceful mage I have ever met. Do not underestimate the mages just yet; they are not as weak as we perceive them to be."

"We can argue about this for centuries," said the silver-haired fae elder, "but we don't have that luxury. Something has to be done. We cannot sit around waiting for Morgana to come to Elfi with the Dark Dagger and take the *Book of Abraxas*."

"That is not the only reason she will come," said Lord Silias, standing up and leaning on the table for support. "Morgana will come for her." He pointed one long pale finger at me.

I clenched my fists and held my tongue, reminding myself for the umpteenth time that if the fae threw me out I would have nowhere to go.

"Enough!" said the queen of the fae, standing up slowly. And the room went silent. "We are not sitting here doing nothing, Dyanara." She looked pointedly at the silver-haired fae elder. "Plans have already been set in motion. When Aurora is ready she will lead a fae army to Illiador and take back her throne. We will end Morgana's rule once and for all."

"And when will she be ready?" said Dyanara. "We have received word that Morgana's army is already moving south towards Elfi."

"And what about the Dark Dagger?" said Silias. "We cannot send our remaining warriors into battle only to be swallowed up by the dagger's evil curse. No fae can touch the Dark Dagger without being pulled inside. Morgana will obliterate our race completely."

"That is why we need Aurora," said Izadora. "Being half fae, she is the only one of us who can touch the dagger without being trapped—her mage side anchors her to this world." She paused and flicked a pointed look towards me. "I do not trust anyone else with it. We cannot let another mage get their hands on the Dark Dagger to use against us in the future. That is why Aurora is here and training with us. When she is ready she will lead our army against Morgana and retrieve the Dagger of Dragath."

So that was her plan. She was afraid of the dagger and needed me because I could touch it. It only worked on the High Fae. Which is probably the reason my grandmother had hesitated to get the dagger back until now; she always intended for me to be the one to get the dagger for her. She was a cunning ruler and a master strategist. I never realized she needed me more than I needed her.

"How do we know she won't use the dagger against us?" said one of the elders who had not spoken until now. I recognized him from the feast, but I didn't know his name. "She is half-mage, how do we know her loyalties lie with us and not with them? How do we know she will not keep the dagger for herself or give it to the mage council to use as a sword over our heads forever?"

"You think I haven't thought of that?" said the fae queen, her eyes narrowing. "Aurora will show her loyalty to the fae before she gets our army."

"And how are you going to ensure that?" asked Dyanara.

"Aurora will marry one of the High Fae," Izadora announced.

"What!" I blurted out, unable to stop myself. "That was not our agreement."

Izadora raised her eyebrows. "Have you forgotten your oath? You said you would do everything I asked." Her gold eyes flashed. "If you do not marry into a powerful fae family, our army will never follow you into battle. It is the only way to ensure their loyalty, and yours."

"And who am I supposed to marry?" I said, crossing my arms and narrowing my eyes. This was going too far, but if I refused outright, my oath would be broken and I would never get her help.

My grandmother looked back at me, unflinching. "You will marry Prince Tristan before the spring festival of Ostara is over, and you will become a princess of the Night Court. Your children will be more fae than mage, and *they* will be my heirs."

I found Tristan stalking the hallways and ran up to him.

"Did you know?" I asked, falling into step with him.

He flicked a glance at me but didn't smile. "Yes. Your grandmother summoned me before the council meeting and has expressed her wish to have us wed before the spring festival."

"And you agreed?" My hands balled into fists. "She can't force us to marry."

"She can." Tristan sighed sharply and stopped to look at me. "And she has. If it makes you feel any better, I don't wish to be bound by wedlock to you, but I had no choice either. I too am compelled by my oath to do as she commands."

"I can't get married. We can't get married. I don't want to marry anyone, not yet, I'm only seventeen." I was babbling, and my brain was screaming in protest that I had no other way out. I didn't want to be forced to marry. Rafe was not an option but I still did not want to marry anybody else.

"I don't have time for this," Tristan growled and resumed walking. "There have been reports of attacks on the training camps in the southern range of the Wildflower Mountains."

"What sort of attacks?" I asked, running after him.

"Werewraiths."

"Then let me come with you," I said, finally catching up with him. "I know how to fight them, I can help."

Tristan's eyes narrowed. "Fine," he said abruptly, "you need to practice anyway. Just don't get killed."

"I'll do my best," I grinned, despite the situation. At least Tristan didn't coddle me like the others did. I had to learn to make my own decisions, and I knew I could fight werewraiths. I was fire-fae, this was what I was made for. Only concentrated silver-fire could kill a werewraith. The other fae would be defenseless against them.

"But I'm not taking you into the southern mountains without backup."

My spine stiffened. "I can be your backup."

"You are not going to be watching my back. I will be watching yours. The mountains are treacherous and there are creatures living there that are more ancient and dangerous than any you have come across. I would prefer not to have my potential betrothed killed before the wedding. Cade is my backup."

"And who is Cade's backup?" I huffed.

"He doesn't need any," said Tristan, walking into the armory. "He has me."

I rolled my eyes. Tristan was afraid of nothing, and I was

glad to have him on my side. As a friend he was great, and once you got used to his moodiness and temper, he wasn't so bad. But marrying him was something altogether different.

I would have to find a way to get out of it without breaking my oath to my grandmother.

20
THE TEMPLE

DAWN BROKE OVER the snowy peaks of the Wildflower Mountains, bathing the hidden valley of Iris in its warm glow. Most of the castle was still asleep when Tristan, Cade, and I began our journey to the southern mountain range.

Two griffins were waiting outside the city gates, but Snow wasn't back yet, and I was disappointed. I missed my pegasus, and hoped she was okay.

Tristan helped me onto the griffin and jumped up behind me, taking the reins as I held onto the light saddle. The griffin tensed, spread its massive wings, and with a jerk pounced into the sky. It was so sudden; I would have fallen off if Tristan weren't holding me. I guess griffin-riding was different from riding a pegasus. The griffin stretched its massive wings as it caught a strong wind and we soared over the clouds toward the southern slopes of the mountains.

The griffins were faster than the pegasus, and by noon we had reached our destination. The sun was high in the azure sky as we descended into a clearing within the thickly forested southern range of the Wildflower Mountains. The cold wind bit through my clothes and the ground was wet and muddy from the melting overnight frost. The winter had not abated, though spring was creeping closer. Still, Elfi was far warmer than the northern kingdoms, and the temperatures in lands like Andrysia and Kelliandria were well below freezing in the winter months.

The training camp was in full swing. All around us fae of all shapes and sizes were training with swords and shields, staffs, bows, spears, and other deadly-looking weapons. The clash of steel and the smell of sweat filled the air as High Fae moved among the warriors and inspected the rigorous training. Demi-fae were the bulk of the army; they had been recruited from all over the kingdom along with fae creatures like centaurs, nymphs, and other elementals.

When they came of age, the best warriors in the towns and villages were sent to these camps, which were situated all over the Wildflower Mountains at regular intervals. They were then trained and recruited as soldiers and sent back to their respective courts, where they either joined the Grand Duke's guard or army. The best of these were recruited to defend the Royal Court, and the city of Iris.

In one corner a group of dryad warriors, tree maidens with green skin and flowing hair, practiced archery with the centaurs and satyrs. Many of the warriors stopped training, and turned to look at the fire-fae warriors as we flew into the camp.

"The latest sighting of the werewraiths was nearest this

camp." Tristan jumped off the griffin and helped me dismount. "I will talk to the commander, and find out what I can. In the meantime"—he paused, looking at Cade—"take her to the guest lodgings. I will meet you there." He stalked off into the crowd of training warriors, who quickly moved out of the way to let the Dark Prince of the Night Court through. In the training camps he was more than a legend, the greatest fire-fae warrior of the Elite Guard. I noticed many of them whispering in hushed, awed voices as their eyes followed him around the camp.

Cade led me to the far end of the clearing. Mud and rock gave way to the surrounding forest, at the edge of which rested a few small stone houses, lodgings for the warriors. Tents were also laid out among the trees, as the camps got more crowded with new recruits brought in to train for the upcoming war.

The little stone house Cade led me to was rustic to say the least. Four wooden pallets lay on the cold stone floors, covered with blankets and furs, while a small fire flickered in the fireplace. I moved closer to warm my hands. It was a dismal blaze; I shot a small fire strike at the dying embers, the flames roaring to life.

"Much better," said Cade. "Mage magic is definitely useful for a few things."

I had learned during my time here that the magical fire of the fae was different in that it couldn't create a living flame as mages could. Silver-fire burns as much and can destroy demons, but it cannot produce the warmth of a real fire and a golden flame.

The next night we sat by the flickering fire in the tiny cottage, warming ourselves after a particularly long day trying to track the werewraiths through the forest. "They must have moved on," Tristan said, putting his sword to the side as he packed a small saddlebag. "The camp commander says there is another camp close by that was attacked; we will check it out next."

Just then I heard a commotion outside.

Tristan jumped up, his sword in his hand, and rushed towards it. I grabbed my sword and followed him as the commander of the training camp charged up to him.

"Your Grace," he shouted, his face flushed. "Your Grace, the temple on the south face of the mountain has been attacked by werewraiths. The patrols just came in. Half my men are dead."

"Let's go," Tristan growled, glancing at me.

The griffins were waiting and Cade had already mounted. I jumped up and Tristan followed, settling himself behind me on the back of the massive beast.

"The centaurs are already on their way there," shouted the commander as the griffin crouched, spread its massive wings, and shot into the sky.

"Werewraiths would never attack a temple of the Great

Goddess on their own. They are being controlled by some-one, a powerful spirit-fae," said Tristan in my ear as we flew over the forested mountains, down to the southern slopes.

"Who could it be?" I shouted over the sound of the wind. "And why target the temples?"

"When they were randomly attacking training camps, I wasn't so sure what they were after," said Tristan, his breath warming my neck. "The training camps are situated in such a way as to guard the temples. Now I know what they want."

"What is it? What do they want that the priestesses have?"

"The Fae Codex," said Tristan flatly as the griffins flew lower toward a great stone structure covered in vines and creepers, jutting out through the towering trees.

I heard a blood-curdling scream from the forest, and a great roar followed. The two griffins swooped down toward it and landed in front of the temple. Cade and Tristan had already jumped off before we reached the ground.

I focused my power and jumped right after Tristan, land-ing on my feet nimbly as a cat. I took off my amulet, my fae senses taking over as my powers blazed to the surface. Unsheathing my sword from the scabbard on my back, I ran toward the temple. Screams and snarls were coming from inside and I practically flew up the great stone stairs, taking two steps at a time.

The temple was a mess, the main hall littered with bodies of priestesses. It was as we feared: a pack of werewraiths were wreaking havoc, tearing and slashing and spilling priestess blood all over the stone floors.

The werewraiths turned toward us, new arrivals to their bloodbath. Their red eyes glowed and their twisted bodies stunk of rot and decay, a foul stench I couldn't forget having smelt: the smell of death and darkness.

I pushed my magic into my sword and it lit up, silver flames licking at the steel. Tristan lunged at the nearest creature, and the carnage began afresh as the elite warriors sliced through shadow, bone, and muscle, twin swords blazing in each hand.

Blood roared in my ears as I created a dagger of silver-fire and flung it at the werewraith coming at me. It thrashed to the ground and I raised my sword, slashing its neck.

Another werewraith leapt. I lifted my left hand and shot a beam of silver-fire at it, pinning it to the wall. It fought and snarled and tried to push itself free. I ran toward the creature and slashed across its chest. It screamed and fell as I ran the flaming sword through its back. It burst into black ash, disappearing into the shadows.

Tristan and Cade had finished off the rest of the pack. But a few of the werewraiths escaped and the centaurs hunted them down, galloping into the thickly forested mountains.

Tristan came up to me and inspected me closely. "Are you all right? Did they bite you anywhere?"

I shook my head. "No, I don't think so." I looked myself

over and put my amulet back on. Whoever was after the Codex was powerful, and I had to be careful. Without my amulet I was too exposed out here in the mountains. Anyone with enough spirit magic could easily find me.

"Werewraith poison is incredibly strong." Tristan bent down beside a fallen priestess. Her green robes were spread out beneath her mangled body like a patch of summer grass, stained with blotches of dark blood that seeped from her many wounds.

"She's gone." He bowed his head. "We were too late."

There was a groan from the far end of the hall, near the altar stone. A priestess was still alive.

I rushed over to her. Blood seeped from the slashes on her chest and I could see the darkness of the poison that ran beneath her skin, a cobweb of black nearing her heart.

Tristan put his hand on my shoulder. "You cannot heal her," he whispered, bending down beside me. "The poison has already reached her heart."

There was a flicker of movement as she raised her small hand, placing it delicately on mine. "Abraxas," she said, forcing her words out in a hoarse croak, hoping she was heard. "Find him. Destroy the book." The priestess breathed her last and her hand fell limp. It grew cold as her life slowly slipped away.

I looked at Tristan, confusion apparent on my face. "What did she mean?"

Tristan took my hand. "Come, we can discuss this back at the camp."

There was a howl in the distance. Cade ran up to us. "Let's go, there is another pack out there."

"We need to leave, Aurora," said Tristan, pulling me up by the arm. "Now."

We exited the temple and ran down the steps.

A shadow stopped us in our tracks.

A small hooded figure was standing at the bottom of the stairs. Tristan and Cade simultaneously stepped in front of me, their swords and magic ready.

The figure removed her hood as the moon shone overhead. An old, weathered face with long white hair looked back at me.

"Maggie?" I gasped, moving past my companions. "Is that you?"

The figure nodded, and a familiar voice said, "We meet again, *Aurora Shadowbreaker*. Follow me, we haven't much time. I will explain everything."

Tristan held me back. "We don't know if this is a person you know or a shapeshifter," he said, his eyes flat, his muscles ready for anything. "Who is she?"

"There is more than one pack of werewraiths in these mountains," said Maggie calmly. "And creatures far more dangerous than them too. We cannot talk freely here." She paused, her violet eyes flickering with silver swirls. "But the warrior is right, this is not my true form."

Magic started to swirl around her as she spoke. Her long white hair changed into strands of spun gold, while her wrinkles disappeared and her skin became flawlessly beautiful. She grew in stature as her body changed, shedding the tattered robes to reveal golden feathers and the body of a massive owl with the head of a young woman. But her eyes remained the same, violet swirls tinged with silver stars, and I recognized Maggie within them.

Tristan's eyes widened. "You're an Alkana?"

"What's an Alkana?" I had never heard of them before.

Tristan shook his head as if he couldn't believe what he was seeing. "She is one of an ancient race of beings, powerful seers. They can take on any shape or identity, but if they reveal their true form to a person, that means they will help them."

Maggie chuckled. "Right you are, my boy," she said, spreading her wings. "Come."

And we followed her into the darkness of the forest.

21
THE ALKANA

THE THICKLY FORESTED mountains were quiet with an almost eerie silence as we flew over their darkest parts, following the Alkana. The griffins kept a steady pace, scanning the forest for threats.

Once Maggie had revealed who she was, Tristan and Cade looked at her with a mixture of awe and reverence. For an Alkana to reveal her true form to a fae was considered the highest privilege.

"Where is she taking us?" I whispered to Tristan as the griffins descended into a small clearing deep in the forest.

"I don't know. But we need some answers, and the Alkana's knowledge of all things ancient is vast beyond belief," Tristan said as we dismounted. "The Alkana are immortal and have been around since the Age of the Ancients. They also have a powerful gift of seeing the future."

We came to a cottage hidden among the foliage. It was an exact replica of the cottage where I met Maggie for the first time, during my journey through the Willow Woods in Eldoren. The Alkana flew down from a nearby branch, changing in midair to her old fae lady form, and we followed her inside.

The hut smelled of lavender and vanilla, familiar and comforting.

Maggie sat down on a chair by the fire and tried to warm her hands. "Close the door, Prince Tristan."

Tristan closed the door behind him and leaned against it with Cade beside him. He never questioned how she knew who he was.

"Come here, child." She held out her hand to me. "Be a dear girl and brighten these flames, they seem to have gone cold."

I shot a small flame at the fire and it roared to life.

"Much better," Magdalene said as I knelt down beside her on the small fur rug. "The draft does make my old bones ache dreadfully."

She had told me once that she was over a thousand years old, but I never thought to ask how many years older.

"But Maggie, if you are an Alkana," I said, "why were you disguised as Rafe's nurse when he was young?"

The Alkana turned her violet eyes on me. "It was imperative that the Prince of Eldoren trusted the fae and had personal ties that would shape his character into the king he is meant to be. It was all a part of a much larger plan."

"Which is? The last time we met you told me my destiny was set before I was ever born, and that my choices would determine the fate of all Avalonia."

Maggie smiled. "You have a good memory."

I smiled back. "It's not something you are likely to forget." She might be a mythical bird woman in her true form, but to me she was still Maggie. "So how is Rafe a part of this plan?"

Maggie chuckled. "I see his impending marriage has not dulled your feelings for Prince Rafael," she said, flicking a glance at Tristan. "Do you trust them?"

I looked over at Tristan and Cade where they were leaning against the door. Tristan glared at me.

I looked away and nodded. "Yes, I trust them."

"Good," said Maggie, leaning back in her chair and joining her hands. "I watched you fight at the temple tonight—you have become a fine warrior, my girl. But I fear the worst is yet to come. Now tell me, what would you like to know?"

I had so many questions, and they all tumbled out of my mouth at once. "The priestess told me to find Abraxas and destroy the book. What did she mean? Is that actually possible?"

"Anything is possible," said the Alkana. "But the magic of the *Book of Abraxas* prevents it from being destroyed, except by the one who wrote it."

"So who was Abraxas?"

"Abraxas," answered Maggie, her eyes swirling with silver, "was an Elder Dragon, one of the seven dragons in ancient Avalonian legends."

My mouth fell open. "Abraxas was a dragon?"

Maggie nodded. "The oldest and most powerful of all the Elder Dragons."

"But why did Abraxas write the book?"

"An ancient dragonlord bound Abraxas with powerful magic and compelled him to write down all the knowledge of the Elder Dragons in what we call the *Book of Abraxas*," said Maggie. "That is how he released Dragath into this world."

"But the dragons are gone. Defeated by Dragath in the demon wars," I said, glancing at Tristan and stating what I had been told. "How can we destroy the book without Abraxas?"

Maggie's eyes turned silver and her voice deepened. It was the voice of the Alkana. "The dragons were indeed defeated by Dragath in the demon wars. But there was one dragon Dragath could not defeat."

I gasped. "Abraxas is alive?"

Maggie nodded. "Yes, the mighty dragon still lives."

I opened my mouth to ask another question, but the Alkana raised her hand.

"Dragath had the book, and the knowledge of magic that could bind Abraxas and take away his powers," she continued. "Even with the book, Dragath could not kill Abraxas, because that is the one thing not written down anywhere: how to kill him. He deliberately left it out when he wrote the book. So Dragath could only bind him using the power of the book and trap him in a magical prison, just as he trapped the fae in the dagger."

"So where is he now? How do I find him?"

"The ancient magic that binds Abraxas is very complicated, as the Dark Dagger is. Dragath bound the great dragon in a magical prison in between worlds, a fate worse than death for an immortal. The same magic that can break the curse on the dagger can also break the bindings on Abraxas wherever he is and summon him."

My eyes widened. "The Dawnstar!" I said, finally understanding what she meant.

The Alkana smiled, her eyes swirling silver. "Yes, the ancient magic of the Dawnstar is the only way to free Abraxas."

Tristan, who had been silent all this time, spoke. "I've heard the stories of this ancient weapon Illaria Lightbringer supposedly promised the world, but it is only a myth. No one has ever found it in five thousand years. We cannot search for something that doesn't exist."

The Alkana turned her head to Tristan. "The Dawnstar is real, Prince Tristan. Just because no one has ever found it doesn't mean it doesn't exist."

"Then how do we find it?" I asked. "I don't even know what this ancient weapon looks like."

"Right now we have bigger problems. We don't have time to run around looking for a weapon that can't be found," Tristan interrupted. "Someone is after the Fae Codex, and we need to find out why."

Maggie nodded. "Yes, Prince Tristan, you are right. There are difficult times ahead, and all of you must prepare yourselves for the worst."

"What do you mean?" The Alkana never seemed to give a straightforward answer. "Why do they want the Codex?"

"The Codex holds many secrets," said the Alkana gravely. "But the most important one, the one I believe they are searching for, is the location of the *Book of Abraxas*."

My eyes widened. It all made sense ; that's why the priestess wanted me to destroy the book. "So whoever is behind the attacks on the temples is probably working for Morgana. They are trying to steal the book?"

Maggie nodded.

"Do you know who it is?" I held my breath.

"No," said Maggie. "Contrary to popular belief, the Alkana do not know everything. But whoever it is must be powerful enough to hide themselves from me."

"Is there anything more you can tell us?" I said. "We need to know where the book is hidden if we are going to protect it."

"Go back to the Crystal Castle, Aurora," said Maggie. "The answers you seek lie there. Your grandmother will need you now more than ever. Morgana is coming and I fear the worst. If she gets her hands on the *Book of Abraxas* all will be lost."

"So are you saying the *Book of Abraxas* is in the Crystal

Castle?"

"Yes," said the Alkana, "and so is the person who wants to steal it."

It was as if a switch had been flicked in my mind. "The door!" Now it all made sense. "That's what my grandmother and the elders are hiding behind the door in the catacombs—the *Book of Abraxas*."

Maggie smiled. "Clever girl."

"But if someone was searching the catacombs for the door, they must already know it's there." I told her about the werewraiths I had encountered in the library. "Why kill the priestesses for the Codex?"

"The chamber is protected by powerful magic and the door is sealed by ancient spells," said Maggie. "Whoever is after the Fae Codex knows that only the Codex can tell you how to open it."

"But why does the door have Illaria's symbol on it?" I asked.

"According to the Codex, that chamber was once part of a massive stronghold destroyed by Dragath in the demon wars," said Maggie. "The elders had the Crystal Castle built on top of the ruins of Illaria Lightbringer's ancient fortress, and hid the *Book of Abraxas* in the safest place they knew."

"Is the Dawnstar there too?" I held my breath. I had to know for sure.

The Alkana shook her head and her immortal eyes looked

weary. "No, child, the Dawnstar is not in Illaria's chamber."

"Then where can I find it?" I urged her to continue.

"That I cannot reveal. The magic that protects the Dawn-star prevents me from telling you where it is."

Tristan stepped forward and addressed the Alkana. "Thank you for your help." He turned to me. "We must return to the castle immediately, Aurora. There is no more time to waste."

We left the southern mountains at dawn and flew back to the capital. The centaur guards opened the doors to the city as we got off the griffins and walked to the castle.

"Did you know the book was hidden here in the castle?" I said softly to Tristan.

He shook his head. "I had heard stories of a chamber under the castle which supposedly belonged to Illaria Light-bringer. But that door has not been opened for centuries. The queen and the elders have wards down there to prevent anyone from finding it. I had no idea that's where the elders were hiding the book."

"But I found the door."

"I don't know how you did that," said Tristan. "We must warn the queen. If someone is after the book we must find out who it is and stop them."

The castle was all a-bustle when we got there. House sprites, usually so discreet, were running about helter-skelter getting the palace ready for what looked like another feast, which had obviously been planned at the very last minute. Tristan stopped a house sprite to ask him what was happening, and the little fellow jumped when Tristan put his hand on his shoulder.

He composed himself. "A feast, your Grace. The Grand Duke, your father, has just arrived. He's in the throne room with the queen."

Tristan swore under his breath and stalked off. I had to run to catch up, and he slowed down enough for me to fall into step with him. I smiled. At least we were making some progress—usually he would have stormed off without a backward glance.

"You didn't know your father was coming?"

Tristan shook his head. "He's probably heard Izadora has ordered us to marry."

"Do you think he will be against it?"

Tristan shrugged but his shoulders were tense. "I will meet with the dowager first; she will know what is going on. I also need to inform her of what we've found out. Go and find Penelope, we will need her help. Meet me in the throne room. We need to speak to Izadora together."

I nodded and went looking for Penelope, but she was not in her room. I wondered why the Grand Duke of the Night Court had come to the palace. It obviously wasn't a scheduled visit. I knew I shouldn't eavesdrop, but the lure of the secret passage was too much for me to resist.

I found the loose stone and moved it away, listening in case there was anyone coming up the stairs, then turned the handle. Pushing open the door, I entered the secret passage connecting different parts of the Crystal Castle. I found the place where I could see into the throne room and peered through the stone.

"My son will not marry that *half-breed*," sneered the Grand Duke, crossing his arms as he stood before the queen of the fae.

Tristan's father was a powerful man, tall and well built; I could see his warrior stance as he spoke to the queen. His midnight black hair was long and tied at the nape like Tristan and he wore a silver circlet on his head.

"That *half-breed*," said my grandmother, her golden eyes hard, "is my granddaughter. Her powers are equal to that of any High Fae. When she takes off her amulet she is stronger still. You would do well to curb your tongue while in my court. Tristan will marry who I say he will marry. Or have you forgotten our bargain?" She smiled. I knew that smile; the Grand Duke was in trouble.

Tristan's father paled visibly, his alabaster skin taut on his high cheekbones. "You will regret this, Izadora." His eyes narrowed.

"I regret many things, Kildaren. But I always do what is best for this kingdom. As should you." My grandmother rose slowly from the throne. "I will announce their betrothal tonight at the feast."

I ran back to my room. I had heard enough. I had to talk to Penelope about everything I had found out and meet Tristan in the throne room.

Penelope was still not in her room. The guards then found me and informed me I had been summoned.

My grandmother was seated on her throne, a grim expression on her flawless face. Kildaren was gone and the dowager, Tristan, and Penelope were already standing below the steps. I bowed before the queen and her gold eyes flickered as she regarded me.

"The Codex is gone." Izadora's voice was sharp, cold. "Whoever has it knows Elfi's deepest secrets. If this person is working for Morgana . . ."

"If this person is working for Morgana," Penelope interrupted, "they know where the *Book of Abraxas* is hidden and will be going after it."

"Penelope," said the queen sharply.

"No, Izadora, Aurora should know the truth. You cannot keep secrets from the ones who must protect the book. I told you this would happen, I told you Morgana would stop at nothing to find it, and you didn't listen. You thought we had more time, that she would never find a way into Elfi, but she has."

"I know that," snapped the queen, standing up and walking slowly down the three steps toward us. "That is why we cannot wait any longer. Aurora and Tristan's betrothal must be announced tonight."

"Tonight?" I tried to find any excuse to stall it. "Can't it wait? We have more important things to do than have a feast when someone is after the book."

"I have waited too long as it is," the queen said. "We must prepare the army immediately and move to defend our borders. You must be perceived as one of us, or, as I explained before, the High Fae will not follow you into battle. The Grand Duke of the Night Court is here too, so it must be done now."

Tristan was quiet. But I could see the dark swirls forming in his eyes.

"The feast will begin at sunset." My grandmother moved her hand in front of her and formed a portal. "Don't be late."

She stepped through it and immediately shut it behind her.

22
THE BETROTHAL

THE GRAND HALL was spectacular. Fae balls of light danced over our heads as usual, in time to the music wafting down from the upper gallery where the musicians sat, playing a lilting tune. The High Fae milled about the room, dressed in all their finery, drinking from crystal goblets and dancing, oblivious to the threat of darkness that had fallen over their peaceful kingdom, the darkness that had followed me here.

The queen was seated on the dais in her customary place. To her right sat the Dowager Duchess and to her left the Grand Duke of the Night Court, Tristan's father. Power surrounded him and his dark eyes studied me when I walked in.

Erik stood behind the queen, his long silver hair tied back from his face, his arms crossed and legs slightly apart, seemingly bored. But I knew the lethal power that lay beneath that calm exterior. I had never seen Erik fight, but the way Tristan and Cade spoke about him, I didn't have to. I could guess why he was the leader of the Elite.

Penelope was seated at the far end of the table speaking to a council elder. I couldn't see Tristan anywhere. I was alone as

I walked up to the dais and bowed before my grandmother.

I had taken to glamouring my own clothes. The dress I had created was made of dull gold, similar to the one I wore in black but not nearly so revealing. My grandmother raised her eyebrows when she saw what I was wearing and I thought I saw a flash of approval in her eyes.

I saw Cade leaning against the wall surveying the room. In his fancy clothes he still looked like a warrior. A deep maroon doublet with gold buttons complemented his flaming hair. He was very much of the Night Court, and looked it.

I walked over to him. "Where's Tristan?" I looked around.

"Eager to see your betrothed?" Cade joked.

I shrugged. "Just asking."

Cade chuckled. "I don't know, actually. I haven't seen him. But Skye told me they were going to announce your betrothal tonight."

"Maybe he's not coming. He doesn't want this marriage any more than I do."

"That won't stop them," Cade snorted, jerking his head towards the dais where my grandmother and Tristan's father sat. "Tristan told me why they want you both to marry. It is a strong alliance, and marriages within the High Fae are rarely ever spontaneous. Most of the noble families are very strict about who they marry. It all depends on political alliances."

I nodded. Most of the nobility were like that. I knew one day I would have to face this issue, but I never thought it would be so soon.

My eyes scanned the room. Everyone was here; well, almost everyone. Andromeda had not come, and Aiden was nowhere to be seen either. In fact, there were no Elite here today besides Erik, who was always at the queen's side, and Tristan and Cade.

"Cade, where's Farrell?" Something was wrong. I could feel it nudging at my senses.

Cade shrugged. "He's out on patrol—apparently there were some other attacks in the Day Court lands. Aiden took Farrell, Brice and Daran too."

I had seen Brice and Daran with Erik; they were much older than Tristan and Cade, part of Izadora's elite guard.

That was strange. Why would Aiden need four Elite for a patrol? He and Farrell would have been enough to check out the threat. My grandmother would never send out four Elite unless the threat required so many fire-fae warriors. The last time she sent four of them was to retrieve me from the Drakaar.

Tristan appeared at my side, put his arm around my waist, and gave a small squeeze. He had a way of sneaking up on me. Since my grandmother had told Tristan about her decision for us to marry, there was a new bond between us. Knowing we didn't want this but didn't have a choice had somehow brought us closer.

"Don't look so worried, it's not like she is going to announce your death sentence." He didn't smile, but his eyes held a trace of humor.

I knew he meant to lighten the mood, but I could tell he was as tense as I was. With everything that was happening with Morgana, this was not the time for a frivolous feast. On top of that, getting betrothed to each other was not a small step, and although it wasn't a death sentence, with our choice taken away from us it was a sentence all the same.

I swatted his arm. "That's not why I'm so tense." My eyes darted around the room. "Something's wrong."

Tristan's eyes narrowed, but he didn't brush me off like Cade did. Immediately his stance changed and he scanned the room for threats.

I spotted Skye standing at the far corner of the hall with Brianna. I tried to get her attention and waved to her. She saw me but pretended not to, and turned her face. *Strange*, I thought, but I had other things on my mind.

My grandmother stood up; the room quieted and the music stopped.

"I have an announcement," she began, and held out her hand to me. "Aurora, Tristan, come here."

I moved forward, but I could tell something was wrong. She looked pale, the light and power fading from her eyes; I could sense it. Tristan moved with me, his eyes troubled.

Then my world collapsed.

The light went out from my grandmother's eyes and she

fell to the ground.

Tristan and I ran towards her. The queen of the fae was lying on the floor, her eyes closed, her power cut off. I could feel the wards around the city and the rest of the hidden valley falling apart. Only Izadora's magic held them in place, protecting Iris from the outside world.

Erik was already protecting his queen, his great sword in his hand, daring anyone to come any closer. Rhiannon and Penelope were crouched beside Izadora, checking for life.

I ran onto the dais. Erik eyed me warily but let me pass.

I fell down on my knees beside my grandmother's limp body. "Is she alive?"

The dowager looked up when she heard my voice and nodded. "For now. She's been poisoned. We must get her the antidote and fast. Werewraith poison works swiftly."

Suddenly the High Fae ladies began screaming and the men started shouting. Chaos broke out in the grand hall as I turned to see a swirling cloud of dark mist form in the corner of the room where Skye and Brianna were standing.

A portal—someone was opening a portal inside the palace. It could be from anywhere. There were no wards protecting the city anymore.

A dark-robed figure with eyes like black pits, the eyes of a demon, stepped out of the portal and looked straight at me.

Raziel! The Drakaar were inside the Crystal Castle.

The leader of the Drakaar grinned, his sharp canines

flashing, and more hooded figures followed. Terror crept up my spine as low growls sounded from the first floor gallery and the stench of darkness grew, as werewraiths appeared in the grand hall and pounced on the unsuspecting High Fae.

All hell broke loose.

Penelope took over. "Rhiannon, Erik, take Izadora and get her somewhere safe," she snapped, with an authority in her voice I hadn't heard before. I realized why my grandmother depended on her so much.

She turned to Tristan. "Cover me, I'm going to close the portal. Aurora, with me, I need your help to do it."

Tristan's sword lit up with silver-fire. "This time they've gone too far," he snarled, assessing the room. He put his hand on my shoulder. "You can do this."

I nodded as he leapt off the dais and ran toward the Drakaar.

My hands shook as I removed my amulet, put it in my pocket, and took a deep breath. I was ready. If I was going to face Raziel tonight, I was going in with my full power. I willed a replica of my sword into existence and my unbound magic flared to life, lighting it up in an incandescent beam.

The dowager created a portal to take Izadora to safety at the same time as two werewraiths pounced on the dais. Erik roared, his flaming sword slicing through the werewraiths in midair, reducing them to ash. He picked up my grandmother gently and stepped through the portal as another werewraith jumped between the portal and the dowager.

I ran at the werewraith. Its foul stench filled my nostrils as its twisted body bunched, ready to attack. Power rippled through my veins as my unfettered magic awoke in full force.

The creature snarled and pounced.

Focused, controlled, I raised my flaming sword and sliced it down on the creature's neck. Silver-fire tore through contorted flesh and bone. The reek of rot and darkness filled my nostrils as the werewraith screamed and shrieked, dissipating into black ash.

The dowager nodded her thanks and followed Erik into the portal, closing it swiftly behind her.

At least they were safe.

Jumping off the dais, I followed Penelope and Tristan and ran toward the Drakaar.

Tristan's sword flashed in his hand as he cut through the werewraiths smoothly and precisely. Cade was at the other end of the room, defending the guests and ushering people out of the hall through the side doors leading to the gardens. We had to get past the Drakaar to close the portal or more creatures could keep coming through.

A werewraith snarled and readied itself to pounce on Penelope. My senses honed in on the creature, and I could feel time slowing down as everything became sharper. I moved in front of her, raising my sword of silver-fire, and sliced it down, striking bone with a crunch and searing through decaying flesh. The werewraith fell to the ground and I swiftly beheaded it.

Just then a Drakaar extended its hand, dark magic hitting my shield. Shadows engulfed me as I turned to face it, a dagger of silver-fire forming in my left hand. I threw it at the sorcerer of Dragath; he staggered as my dagger buried itself in his chest. He looked down and sank to his knees, shock apparent in his eyes.

The tattoos on his neck and face started swirling as his magic reached out to attack. I wasted no time, lunging at him; raising my sword, I sliced downward, severing the Drakaar's head from his body.

But there was no time to stop, no time to breathe. The blood pounded in my ears as I ran.

Penelope was making her way toward the portal with Tristan, and Cade was still on the other side of the room. Three werewraiths had backed a bunch of fae against a wall, with no way to get out.

I had to help them; everyone else was busy.

I flung my unfettered magic at the dark creatures with one hand, hurling all three against the wall and pinning them there. I pulled forth more of my magic, drawing on the well that lay open within me, and pushed harder. The werewraiths screeched and even the Drakaar faltered to see what had made their creatures scream.

Instinctively I drew on my mage magic, mixing it with

the silver-fire so that flames of gold and red licked through my body, creating a moving, writhing blaze that flared out of my hands. I focused my power and the flames grew as I created my own brand of magic, engulfing the screaming werewraiths, reducing them to ash and smoke.

So I didn't need a sword to kill them, after all.

Tristan was a distance away, fighting two Drakaar and defending Penelope so she could close the portal. I ran to help them when a wall of dark magic crashed into me out of nowhere, flinging me to the ground. I lost my grip on the sword and it fell to the side, clattering away on the cold marble floor.

"Aurora," Tristan roared and moved toward me as three werewraiths pounced on him from behind, pinning him to the ground. He twisted and plunged a flaming dagger into a werewraith's eye, and it fell back. But another one had sunk its teeth into his arm.

"Tristan," I screamed, reaching for my sword, just as Raziel picked me up by my throat and slammed me into the wall.

Pain tore through me as my head hit stone. The room swam before my eyes as I tried to focus my powers and heal myself.

"So you finally learned to wield your magic properly, young fae-mage," sneered Raziel, his eyes a bottomless pit of darkness. "And it seems you have created your own magic too.

Quite impressive. But too late. Morgana's army is coming, and the *Book of Abraxas* will be hers soon. Izadora will die a painful death, and you, my little princess, will join her."

The crush of his power at my throat held me pinned to the wall. There was a great weight suppressing my magic and refusing to let it surface. An old power was feeding the Drakaar lord's magic, and the ancient darkness tried its best to smother my light.

I looked over at Penelope—she was backed up against a wall. Tristan was still defending her and had fought off the werewraiths. But he was weakening, I could see it; the werewraith's bite had poison in it. How long he could hold out before the poison took hold, I didn't know. He tried to get to me, but two Drakaar and three werewraiths stood between us.

"The time has come for you to die, *Aurora Shadowbreaker*," sneered Raziel. "Once you are gone, all of Avalonia will kneel before the might of Morgana's army, and Dragath will rise once more." Shadow demons appeared beside him and he raised his dark sword, swirling with the blackest of magic, ready to plunge it into my heart. He was enjoying tormenting me, letting me know Morgana had won.

But she hadn't won, not yet.

I shut out the sneering voice and calmed my racing heart. I plunged down within, deep into my well of magic, unbound, unfettered, raw, and powerful. Further down I went, to a place I had never been before, and awoke the real Aurora Firedrake—the queen that I was meant to be.

Courage and hope infused my magic as an enormous power roiled up inside me, uncoiling itself from depths I never knew I had, and pushed itself to the surface. Without the amulet binding me, I had to focus, to not allow it to get the better of me. I had to control it; I *could* control it.

My eyes went flat as all fear fell away. I stared straight into the eyes of the sneering Drakaar and said in the voice of a queen, "Morgana and Dragath will never force Avalonia to its knees. Not as long as I am still alive."

I started to glow as power filled my very pores and Raziel's eyes widened in terror; his magic could not hold me back any longer. I pushed at the wall of suffocating ancient darkness and shattered it. My unbound power reared its mighty head, as twin swords blazing with silver-fire appeared in my hands.

Using all my strength and the swiftness of my fae senses, I brought my arms up in wide sweeping arcs, slicing them across Raziel's neck, severing the Drakaar lord's head from his body.

The other two Drakaar turned in shock to see their commander fall. Tristan took the opening and, with the last bit of his strength, swung his sword at the other Drakaar's head. Tristan's foe dropped to the ground.

But I was not done.

I flung out my arms, pushing my magic at the remaining werewraiths in the hall, mixing mage magic with my fae-fire, creating the flame that could reduce a werewraith to ash. The werewraiths screamed in fury as a wall of silver and gold flames engulfed them. Fur and flesh burned with an acrid stench and dissolved into smoke.

But there was still one Drakaar left, moving backward toward the portal, and toward Penelope who was trying to close it.

Tristan had fallen, the werewraith poison in his blood draining him of strength and magic.

From across the room, I lifted my hand and caught the Drakaar in a magical hold, picking him up, his legs dangling a foot above the ground. His eyes widened in shock at the strength of my powers.

I spoke clearly so the Drakaar could hear me as I walked towards him. "Tell Morgana what happened here today." I fortified my hold over the Drakaar, crushing his darkness with my light. "Tell her Raziel is dead, and that the fae will never bow to her. Tell her to prepare for the fight of her life. Tell her Aurora Firedrake is coming to take back her kingdom and her throne."

I gathered more power and flung the Drakaar backward through the portal. Waving my hand in front of me and weaving an intricate web of magic as I had been taught, I closed the portal and the swirling mist disappeared. The

Crystal Castle was safe.

23
TRAITOR

THE GRAND HALL was streaked with blood and ash, and the bodies of High Fae that didn't get away from the were-wraiths and the Drakaar were strewn haphazardly around the room. Cade had managed to get most of the fae out of the hall and into the gardens. Now palace guards were rounding them up and questioning them. No one had seen anything, and we still had no idea who had opened the portal.

I ran to Tristan as he lay on the ground. He tried to push himself up when he saw me.

"I can heal you," I said, kneeling beside him.

Penelope came up behind me and knelt down to inspect his wounds. "Werewraith poison is not expelled that easily. If you try with your magic, you could cause it to spread faster."

"The dowager said there is an antidote." I tried to remember what I had learned about werewraiths and their poison.

Penelope nodded. "There is." She put Tristan's arm around her shoulders, and I helped her by taking the other. "Come, help him up. We'll take him to my chambers and I will make the antidote."

"But he won't die, will he?" I asked, thinking of the priestess in the temple.

Penelope shook her head. "I hope not. Werewraith poison is resistant to most magic and can kill an immortal. But some of us healers always keep a small amount of ingredients for this antidote. It must be freshly made or it cannot work."

Although I tried not to admit it to myself, I didn't know what I would do if anything happened to Tristan. I had come to depend on him so much, and despite everything he had become my friend. He was the only one I could trust. I wasn't in love and I wasn't under any illusions that I was. Rafe had destroyed that part of my heart. But Tristan was intelligent and handsome, a warrior without equal, and he was the Prince of the Night Court, with an army to match. Being married to him wouldn't be so bad. If I had to marry any of the High Fae and had a choice, I would have chosen him.

"What about my grandmother? Where is she?"

"Somewhere safe," said Penelope. "Don't worry about that now. Rhiannon knows what to do. She is also a skilled healer—she will do what she can to save Izadora's life."

Cade ran up to us and took Tristan, carrying the massive warrior to Penelope's chambers.

"Who could have done this?" I asked Penelope as Cade laid Tristan gently down on the bed.

"I don't know," she said. "The wards around the whole kingdom have fallen. The city and this entire valley are exposed. The Elder Fae will put up what wards they can, but without Izadora, they won't hold long."

Tristan groaned, and I rushed to his side.

"I will make the antidote immediately." Penelope turned to a wall in her room and waved her hand.

The wall fell away to reveal a small secret room, walls stacked with books, and shelves overflowing with vials and bottles and small crystal decanters with liquids of every color swirling within them. A small wooden worktable was in the center of the room, covered with pewter and copper bowls of various sizes along with curious implements.

"I will need your help, Aurora. This potion is difficult to make and your magic can speed up the process." Penelope started taking down books from the shelves and skimming through them. "We must complete it before the poison reaches his heart."

I proceeded to help her measure out liquids and heat them with my mage fire. She added powders and herbs and instructed me on what to do. Cade sat with Tristan while he went through the pain, a silent grimace the only indication of the agony he was in. Werewraith poison burned the fae from the inside; I could only imagine what it must feel like. And for this poison to take down Tristan and my grandmother, it must be very deadly.

But who would have wanted to harm my grandmother? It had to be someone on the inside. Skye was standing near the portal when it opened. But as far as I knew she had no spirit magic, nor did Brianna. And if it wasn't one of them, then who?

Penelope created the potion and fed it to Tristan. He could barely drink, and we had to force the liquid down his throat.

I looked at the fallen warrior who lay so still and pale on the bed. "Now what?"

"Now we wait," said Penelope. "We cannot do any more. It all depends on the immortal's resistance to the poison."

Sometime before dawn I fell asleep on the chair beside Tristan's bed. A sharp knock at the door woke me and I looked over at Tristan, who did not seem any better. Had the antidote worked? I had no way of knowing.

Penelope answered the door, and Tristan's father walked in, followed by three of his personal guards from the Night Court: huge fae warriors dressed all in black, with a silver star emblazoned on their chests, their hands resting on the massive swords at their waists.

He ignored me and spoke to Penelope, but he didn't go closer to see or touch his son. "How is he?"

"It's too soon to tell," said Penelope. "I have administered the antidote, but we need to give it a day to work. He is strong, do not lose hope."

The Grand Duke of the Night Court narrowed his eyes. "I will have my own healers look after him."

"He can't be moved," I interrupted. "Tristan needs to rest. And there is no better healer here than Penelope."

He turned his sapphire eyes on me. "I will decide whose care my son will be under. And you, *half-breed*," he said with a sneer, "have absolutely no say in what happens in this kingdom. Penelope is under arrest," he said, gesturing to his men. They came forward and caught her by the arms.

"For what?" I said aghast, moving towards Penelope. "She was the one who helped me close the portal and fight the Drakaar."

"That's because she was the one who opened it in the first place," said the Grand Duke. More warriors came into the room to make sure there was no trouble.

I turned to look at Penelope—it couldn't be true, I didn't believe it.

"This is ridiculous," said Penelope, shaking her head. "Why would I let the Drakaar into the palace and poison my own sister?"

"People have done worse things in their quest for a crown," said the Grand Duke.

Penelope snorted most inelegantly. "You know I don't care about the crown, Kildaren."

"People change," said the Grand Duke of the Night Court. And I realized there was some history behind that look. Penelope must have known Tristan's father when she lived in Elfi.

Kildaren turned to me. "You are expected at the council meeting today; we will decide what to do with you next."

"You can't have a council meeting without my grandmother."

"Yes, we can," said the grand duke. "The elders have supported the motion to convene the council today, due to what has happened." He turned to his guards. "Take Countess Penelope to the dungeons." He walked out of the room.

"Penelope," I said, moving closer. "I will speak to the council and tell them you did not do this. I will find the one who did."

She nodded. But the guards didn't give me a chance to say anything more as they dragged her out of the room and to the dungeons that lay deep under the Crystal Castle.

I left Tristan with Cade when the guards came to take me to the council chamber. He still hadn't woken up, and I needed him by my side right now. I hoped he would recover soon. Rhiannon and my grandmother were gone, and I didn't know where they were or when they would return. I was alone against the whole fae council. There was no one who would support me now. What were they planning to do to me?

The council chamber was all abuzz when I walked in. Everyone was trying to talk at once and there was no order to the proceedings. Andromeda had arrived and was seated at the head of the table where my grandmother usually sat. Skye stood behind her mother's chair and I tried to catch her eye, but she looked down. Beside the Grand Duchess of the Day Court, seated on a similar chair, was Kildaren. It looked like they were calling the shots, and the elders didn't seem to mind.

They made me stand at the foot of the massive table, which depicted the map of Avalonia. All the elders were seated in their places, their faces grave and pale. But I also noticed there were guards stationed all over the room, behind every pillar, in every corner. My grandmother never had guards attending a council meeting. Why were they here?

Andromeda noticed where I was looking. "The guards are here for our protection," she said with a haughty stare.

She was so full of herself and deluded. If the Drakaar came back, those guards would not stand a chance. Even I could take them out if I wanted to.

"Your grandmother has become weak, more concerned with getting your kingdom back than with doing what is best for Elfi," Andromeda continued to speak. "But she is still the queen, and poisoning the queen is treason."

"Penelope did not poison my grandmother," I said, my hands balled in fists. "You should be looking for the culprit closer to home."

"What's that supposed to mean?" said the Grand Duchess of the Day Court.

"What I mean," I said, looking at Skye, "is that the only people near the portal when it opened were Skye and Brianna. Penelope was at the other end of the room."

"Nonsense. A powerful spirit-fae like Penelope could have easily opened it from across the room." Andromeda paused and stood up, resting her elegant fingertips on the great wooden table. "Penelope has spent too many years outside Elfi, and we don't know what she was doing all this time. She is the only one who could be in contact with Morgana and carry out this kind of elaborate plan."

"What plan?"

"Morgana's army is camped at the borders of Elfi," said Andromeda.

"Already?" I gasped. The last I had heard they were still outside Brandor.

"It is not a whole army, but part of it, led by Lucian the Archmage," said Kildaren. "She has been hiding them secretly in Brandor. The Emirs have given them free passage through their lands."

I shook my head, unable to think clearly.

"Don't you think it strange the Drakaar attacked the palace shortly after Penelope came back to Elfi?" Andromeda asked.

My head was whirling. I refused to believe Penelope was working for Morgana. "No, Penelope couldn't have done this."

"Foolish girl," said Andromeda, banging her hand on the table. "Your grandmother is gone. The wards around the kingdom have fallen—only her power was keeping them in place. Rhiannon is not here to reinforce them. That's all Lucian needs to move his army into Elfi. Soon they will be at the gates of the city."

Penelope did send Rhiannon with my grandmother. Did she do it to get them out of the way so Lucian could invade Elfi? It made sense, but I knew Penelope, and she was one of the most humble people I had ever met. She was not interested in power. Was that also an act? Penelope had lied to me before and was an expert on disguising her actions and motives. She was a spy, after all—Elfi's best, my grandmother had said. Would she betray her own sister to take the throne? Would she betray me? It certainly looked like she already had.

The Drakaar had been there for a purpose, to kill me and take the book. But if Penelope was working for Morgana and wanted to kill me, she had had hundreds of chances to do it from the first moment I got to this world. It didn't make sense; there was a piece of the puzzle missing.

"We have made a deal with Morgana," Andromeda went on. "She has agreed not to invade Elfi if we give you up to her."

"What! You can't trust Morgana, you know it's not only me she's after. She wants the *Book of Abraxas*, and she already has three of the keys. She will destroy Elfi in her search for it."

"No, she won't," Andromeda snapped, looking around at the Elder Council.

Everyone was quiet and let her speak. They had agreed to this already, and none of them stood up for me.

Andromeda looked me straight in the eye. "Because we are going to give her the *Book of Abraxas*."

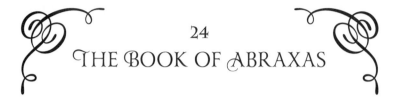

24
THE BOOK OF ABRAXAS

I COULDN'T BELIEVE she had said that.

"You want to give her the *Book of Abraxas?*" I repeated. "This is madness! You are condemning the world because you are too scared to fight Morgana."

The elders were quiet, their immortal faces grave. I glanced back and forth, studying them. They had all resigned themselves to the fact that Morgana had won.

They were giving up.

"Once Morgana has the book and you, she will leave us in peace," said Andromeda. "The High Fae have never been concerned with the workings of the mage world. Why should we care what happens to them now?"

"You are all blind," I said, gritting my teeth at their stupidity. "Morgana is a cunning liar—she will use the book to release Dragath from his prison. And when she does, do you think he will leave Elfi alone? Do you think Dragath won't come back here with the Dark Dagger and finish what he started so many thousands of years ago?"

There was a murmur from the elders as they whispered to their neighbors. The Elder Silias stood up. "When Morgana has you and the book in her possession, she will withdraw her troops from the foothills of the Wildflower Mountains and leave us in peace," he said. "When and if she releases Dragath, she will be able to control him with the book and will not allow him to attack the fae. Morgana has given us her word."

They had been taken in by Morgana's lies. I knew she would not keep her word. She wanted absolute power, and with the *Book of Abraxas* she would have it. How could they be so blind? My grandmother, Rhiannon, and Penelope would never allow them to do this.

And then it hit me.

I looked at Andromeda's smirk and the face of Tristan's father and I knew. They had planned this. They poisoned my grandmother so Lucian's army could come into Elfi. Her son Aiden had taken four fire-fae warriors out of the city that day so there would be less opposition to the Drakaar. They expected me to die at their hands. They blamed it on Penelope so she too would be out of the way. One of them had to have opened the portal. Did Skye know what her mother was truly planning? Was she part of the conspiracy too? I needed proof, or the elders would never believe me.

"When Tristan wakes up, he will never stand for this." I looked at his father. "Does he know you are planning to give Morgana the book, and give me up as well?"

Kildaren leaned back in his chair, putting his fingertips

together. "Tristan is an immortal; soon he will forget you and move on. My family cannot be married into a line of *half-breeds*," he sneered. "As for the book, Tristan will understand it is for the good of our kingdom. We cannot stop Morgana from coming here and taking it."

"I can stop her," I whispered softly. "I just need more time."

"There is no more time," snapped Andromeda. "There is nothing you can do. Your powers may be strong, but they are not strong enough. There is no magic that can stand against her army. Morgana's troops are already at our borders and more will be coming once the winter snow thaws in the north. We will meet with Lucian at the Gandren Pass in the northern mountains and hand you and the book over to him."

I tried to get them to listen to reason. "If you want to give me up to her, fine. I'll go without a fight. But you cannot give her the book." I looked around at all their pale immortal faces, and I could see the fear in their eyes. "I understand you are scared. But there is a way to make sure she never gets her hands on it."

Kildaren's sapphire eyes narrowed. "How?"

"We destroy it," I said slowly.

Andromeda laughed, and so did some of the elders. "Foolish child. No one can destroy the *Book of Abraxas*, except Abraxas. And the last time I checked, Abraxas died five thousand years ago in the Demon Wars."

"No, he didn't," I said, shaking my head. "Abraxas is alive. Trapped in a magical prison between worlds."

Some of the elders gave shaky laughs. Others remained silent.

But the Elder Silias explained slowly, "Abraxas is an Elder Dragon, the most powerful dragon to have ever lived. If he were alive somewhere, there is no one who could summon him. And if they could no one can control him. Dragons are not tame creatures; they look down on most of our kind. The only ones they respect enough to speak to are the drag-onlords. And there are no magical bloodlines left that can command an Elder Dragon. Izadora doesn't have that power and neither do you."

Andromeda gestured to the guards to come forward. "You are confined to your room for the night so you can prepare yourself for your final journey," she sneered. "We leave to-morrow. The Gandren Pass is a day's ride from here."

The guards came forward to catch my arms.

I glared at them. "Don't think about touching me if you value your lives," I growled with all the courage I could muster.

The guards stopped in their tracks and looked at An-dromeda for further instructions. They had seen me fight in the grand hall that night, and didn't look very keen to take me on right now.

"Well," Andromeda said. "We would rather not have a scuffle here. I'm sure you can walk without assistance." She snapped her fingers and four more guards came forward. "Escort Princess Aurora to her room. And make sure she stays there. You are lucky I'm not putting you in the dungeons, only because I don't want you anywhere near that traitor Penelope. So don't try to do anything stupid and run away—I hear you are quite proficient at that. And don't think you can create a portal out of your room. The Elder Fae have warded the castle, including the dungeons. Your spirit magic won't work here anymore. If you do anything to jeopardize this treaty with Morgana, Penelope will die before she ever gets a trial."

The guards bowed. I didn't.

I turned on my heel and stormed out of the council chamber. Andromeda was a bitch, but she was clever. And Tristan's father wanted to get rid of me for obvious reasons. He didn't think I was good enough for his son. If I could prove they were the ones who poisoned my grandmother, maybe I could convince the Elder Council to stop her from giving over the book.

I wanted to go and see Tristan, but the guards wouldn't let me—they took me straight to my tower room. I hoped he was okay—at least Cade was with him. I had to get a message to them to tell them what was happening.

I ran up the stairs to my room and slammed the door

while the guards formed a barricade at the bottom of the stairs. I sat down on my bed and took a deep breath. I refused to believe Penelope was guilty; she had helped me so many times. If only I could get into the dungeons and speak to her. I had to know for sure she wasn't behind this.

That night I waited until the castle was asleep. I knew I could not portal myself out of the room, but there was another way. I silently thanked my grandmother for putting me in this specific room, probably the only one that had a secret passage. This time I was not going to run away; this time I was going to make things right.

I crept slowly down the stairs, listening for any sign of the guards, and pushed open the stone door to the secret passage as slowly and quietly as I could. I had to shut it completely behind me. I didn't want the guards to come up the stairs looking for me only to find the way into the passage. I lit up my hand and a ball of light formed in my palm. Holding it up, I peered down the dark corridor beyond.

I walked forward, my heart hammering in my chest as I passed the crack that looked down to the throne room. No one was there, and my grandmother's throne sat empty in the vast cold hall. I ventured further down the secret corridor. I wasn't exactly sure where it went, but today I was going to find out.

Slowly descending into the depths of the mountain, I followed the passage. If I could find a way into the dungeons,

I could speak to Penelope and figure out the truth. Finally I reached the end of the corridor—a dead end. I looked for a loose stone, and after moments of searching I found the secret handle. The door groaned slightly and opened as I stepped out into another long dark corridor.

This wasn't the dungeon. I was back in the catacombs.

This part of the library didn't have any books, just smooth stone walls and endless dark tunnels cleaved into the depths of the mountain.

"Which way?" I asked the voice in my head, but there was no answer. There was no way of knowing when it would appear. Before this I had tried to contact the voice, but it had been quiet for a while. It only seemed to speak when I was in trouble. I was going to have to find my way to the dungeons on my own.

I was startled by the sound of people talking in the distance. I immediately put out the light in my hand and let my eyes adjust to the darkness. My fae senses became sharper as I moved slowly toward the sound and peered around the corner.

It was a small chamber with two corridors leading out from the other side, running deeper into the catacombs. Andromeda was talking to Skye, surrounded by at least a dozen Day Court guards in blue uniforms with golden stars emblazoned on their chests.

"This is the place," Andromeda said. "Once I leave with

the council and Kildaren to hand Aurora and the book to
Lucian, the wards around the castle will be removed. That
is when you will open a portal here, bring our army into the
city, and take over Iris."

"But what about the Elite?" asked Skye. "They are loyal to
Izadora; even Aiden takes his role as protector of the queen
very seriously. Getting rid of Aurora is one thing, that's the
only reason he agreed. But deposing Izadora, I'm not sure
how he will react."

"Aiden will do as I tell him," Andromeda snapped. "By
the time he finds out the truth, Izadora will be dead, and I
will be queen."

My heart felt heavy. Skye was very much involved in her
mother's plans. I expected this from Aiden but not Skye. I
thought she was my friend.

"What about Erik and Tristan? They will never agree to
this," Skye said.

"Erik is gone and Tristan is injured," Andromeda replied.
"None of the other Elite have the guts to oppose me."

"But Izadora may return at any time once she has recovered, and so will Rhiannon," Skye insisted.

Andromeda shook her head. "No, they won't. I have already taken care of it." Her face contorted with a malevolent
smile.

"What have you done now, Mother?"

"I've already found out where Rhiannon is hiding Izadora while she recovers," said Andromeda. "The werewraiths under my control are on their way to finish the job. Izadora is too weak to fight, and Erik cannot take on four packs of werewraiths on his own."

Skye gasped. "Four packs! Is that necessary? Isn't poison enough?"

Andromeda shook her head. "There is a reason Izadora is queen. She is too powerful—werewraith poison will not kill her, but the werewraiths can while her magic is too weak to fight back."

"It will be a bloodbath," Skye whispered.

Andromeda grinned, as feral as the werewraiths she commanded. "I want to see if Erik is as good as he claims. Let him show us if he can protect his precious queen."

"This is treason and murder, Mother," said Skye, still arguing with Andromeda.

"It must be done, Skye," reasoned the Grand Duchess. "For the good of our kingdom. Izadora and Rhiannon will never agree to give the book to Morgana. This new alliance will save our people from a war we cannot win. Morgana has an army ten times stronger than ours. All we have are insufficient fire-fae warriors, a handful of griffins, and an army consisting of a few hundred High Fae warriors and *half-breeds*." She paused. "Morgana has promised her support for my rule. By the time the festival of Ostara arrives, Elfi will have a new queen."

I was right! Andromeda was aligned with Morgana. She was the traitor. Did the Elder Council know she was planning to take over Elfi?

"I hope you know what you are doing," said Skye.

"Just make sure you follow the plan," commanded Andromeda. "We only get one chance at this."

Skye nodded and walked off through one of the tunnels toward the library.

I had heard enough. Andromeda was going to kill my grandmother, the dowager, and Erik. Penelope was in the dungeons and Tristan was injured. She had rid herself of anyone who could stop her from taking the throne. She thought she was getting rid of me, too, but that's where she was wrong.

I had to go back and warn the elders. If I could make them see Andromeda was the traitor and planning to take over Elfi as queen, they might stop her from giving Morgana the book.

I moved backward into the shadows of the catacombs and froze as cold steel pricked my back. Guards appeared behind me, their swords out, cutting off any hope of escape.

"Well, well, if it isn't our little *half-breed* princess," Andromeda taunted, emerging from the shadows. "How did you get out of your room?" She glanced briefly at a guard who looked terrified and didn't have an answer.

"Doesn't matter." She waved her hand and the guard

clutched his throat, dropping to the ground. She ignored him as she spoke to me. "You're here now, and that's what's important."

"You're a traitor, Andromeda," I said, gritting my teeth. "And I'm going to make sure the Elder Council knows exactly what you are planning." My hands started to glow as my magic awoke. I could not let her get away with this.

"Well, we can't have that, can we?" Andromeda inspected her nails. "I have a better idea."

A low growl sounded through the catacombs and a flash of red eyes stopped me in my tracks. White teeth flashed as four werewraiths appeared beside her.

I took a step back and a ball of silver-fire formed in my hand as I prepared myself for the worst.

"Don't worry, they are not going to attack," said Andromeda, still calm and composed. "Unless I tell them to, of course. But I have other uses for you." She turned to the guards. "Put on the cuffs."

The guards approached me warily. I frantically considered a variety of ways to get out of this situation, but all of them would involve killing a lot of people. If I did manage to fight and kill the werewraiths, killing fae guards who were only following orders was quite another thing altogether. I couldn't do it. That was not who I was. I wasn't a murderer, and Andromeda knew that. I would have to find another way out of this mess.

The guards snapped identical black cuffs on my wrists and the light in my hands went out.

My eyes grew wide. "What's this?" I inspected the cuffs and scrambled to reach my magic, but it would not respond. It felt as though someone had cast a veil over my powers.

"This, my little *half-breed*, is blackened iron from the foothills of Mount Khatral," Andromeda answered.

My heartbeat sped up. I had seen this metal once before; the Drakaar had swords made of it.

"It can only be found in the heartland of Maradaar," Andromeda went on, "and Morgana was kind enough to send me some; a gift from the Drakaar. It is quite effective when it comes to suppressing fae power. She knew you would not go quietly.

"Bring her," she ordered the guards and turned, walking down a dark passage, deeper into the catacombs.

The guards grabbed my arms, pulling me along behind her. Andromeda had the werewraiths there to keep me in check. And with the cuffs blocking my fae magic, I could not fight them.

Further and further we went into the hidden part of the catacombs. The werewraiths led the way, and they knew exactly where to go. They must have been scoping out these passages for a while under Andromeda's orders. I knew exactly where she was taking me.

We reached the cave under the mountain, and I followed

Andromeda to the door. It was the same as I had remembered it, with Illaria's symbol etched into the stone.

"Illaria Lightbringer's secret chamber," Andromeda whispered reverently as she ran her hands over the symbol. "Finally."

Andromeda put her hands on the symbol and spoke in an ancient language, her eyes glowing as she recited what she had learned from the Codex.

The massive stone door to Illaria's chamber groaned and slowly opened inward.

I stepped through the threshold, following Andromeda into an enormous chamber with a curved roof almost a hundred feet high. The fae guards spread out behind me, blocking the door, but the werewraiths refused to enter.

Andromeda held up her hand and a ball of fae-light lit up the chamber. The walls were covered in a series of ancient symbols and scripts etched into the stone. At the far end of the huge room lay a flight of steps that led upward to what looked like a stone altar with a book propped on it.

The *Book of Abraxas.*

Andromeda turned to me. "The Fae Codex was very informative, I must say. No wonder the queen and the elders hid it away. But I found it eventually. Did you know this place once belonged to Illaria Lightbringer? And according to the Codex, she hid the last of her ancient magic in a powerful weapon and locked it in this very chamber."

She knew about the Dawnstar! But the Alkana had said the Dawnstar was not in this chamber! Why would the Codex say it was?

I looked around. "What weapon?" I needed her to keep talking while I figured a way out of this.

"Of course no one ever found what the Codex calls the Dawnstar," Andromeda continued. "The chamber was empty when the Elder Fae discovered it and built this castle on the ruins of Illaria's fortress; I suppose the Codex can be wrong on occasion. The elders thought they were so clever, hiding the *Book of Abraxas* in a place that is supposed to hide something else."

"If the elders have given you access to this chamber," I asked, "why did you need to steal the Codex and kill all those priestesses?"

Andromeda turned her cold eyes on me. "I wasn't sure if they would agree to give the book over to Morgana. Losing the Codex made them realize Morgana could get to them at any time. They are cowards; without Izadora and Rhiannon, the Elder Council is weak. I simply made sure they had no choice."

"You framed Penelope and tricked the elders."

Andromeda's lips tightened. "Yes. Framing Penelope was unexpected but worked out nonetheless. She made it too easy, turning up in Elfi when she did."

Andromeda walked up to the altar and picked up the *Book*

of Abraxas, running her fingers over the symbol in the center. It was not a big book. Bound in brown leather, it looked so harmless. However, I had learned from experience that importance was merely in the eye of the beholder. Knowledge was the greatest weapon of all, and those who understood this were the ones who held all the power. Once Morgana fit the four magical keys that opened the book into the triangular symbol, all would be lost.

"Don't do it, Andromeda. Morgana will destroy Elfi once she has the book."

"No, she won't," Andromeda smirked. "Morgana is sitting tight on her throne in Illiador and fighting a war on many fronts. She doesn't have time to battle the fae. I will give Lucian the book, and he will withdraw his troops from Elfi. But I've decided not to play all my cards yet. I don't want you around when I meet with Lucian; too many things could go wrong. Once I am crowned queen, I will keep the second part of my bargain and give you up to Morgana. Until then, I think I will keep you locked up here where there is no chance of you getting out."

"No!" I gasped as I struggled to get a hold of my magic, but I couldn't reach it. The black cuffs were powerful and the darkness clung to my spirit, willing it to break. I still had my mage magic and my hands were not tied together, so I shot a fire-strike at Andromeda.

It sizzled as it struck skin, but Andromeda didn't flinch.

She turned her icy blue eyes on me. "How quaint." Her grin was feral. "Did you think your puny mage magic could hurt a High Fae?"

I had no weapons or fae magic, but I had to do something. I ran at Andromeda and tried to snatch the book away. She raised her hand, and her magic slammed into me with such force that I went flying across the room. I crashed into the wall, my head hitting the stone, and I slumped to the ground. I had no fae magic to heal myself and the pain was excruciating.

"Soon I will be queen, and there is nothing you can do to stop me." Andromeda's face swam before my eyes and her cruel laugh dissipated as she closed the big stone door behind her.

The chamber was plunged into darkness as I gave in to the pain and passed out.

25
ILLARIA'S CHAMBER

I GROANED AS I pushed myself into a sitting position, leaning against the wall. My head was throbbing and my mouth was dry as I tried to find some fae magic to heal myself, but it was gone. I didn't know for how long I had been passed out, and I had to find a way out of the chamber before Andromeda gave the book to Lucian. I had to warn the elders. I knew Lucian would never pull back his army. Once he had the book, he would attack and the fae would not be able to stop him.

The black cuffs were still on my wrists, cutting off my power. I touched my head and my fingers came back sticky. There was a lot of blood. But there was no time to think about that now.

I reached for my mage magic and was relieved when it responded. Concentrating, I slowly created a ball of light, swirling it around in my fingers. I held up my hand, dimly lighting up the room. I leaned on the wall for support and looked around.

There had to be a way out of here.

I went over to the massive door and pushed at it, but it

did not budge. The chamber was sealed shut. I was trapped. Without my fae powers there was nothing I could do.

I held up the light and inspected the door more closely. The carvings on it were the same on the inside of the chamber as they were on the outside. I ran my fingers over the carved vines and creepers and over the symbol in the middle: the sun and the star, the sigil of Illaria Lightbringer's house.

The blood on my hands smeared across the door. Inside the carving of the sun within the star was a series of smaller symbols. How had I not noticed this earlier? I traced the lines with my fingers. It looked like an ancient script written within the circle. Where had I seen this before?

I gazed at the symbols, committing them to memory. But as I ran my fingers over the last figure, I stopped, my mind clamoring. My heartbeat quickened as I went over the markings again, and I smiled. It was a grin, really—I had seen these symbols my whole life.

I removed the Amulet of Auraken from my neck. I still wore it when I wasn't training or fighting, as a reminder of my parents. I looked at it closely and there it was, as clear as day. I held it up to the door, next to the small round sun that lay at the center of Illaria's symbol.

A perfect match.

The markings on the door were the same as on the Amulet of Auraken. What did Auraken Firedrake have to do with Illaria Lightbringer?

I touched the amulet to the door; it fit into the grooves of the symbol as if it were meant to be. The amulet started to glow, and my blood smeared on the door moved through the ancient stone script like veins, swirling through Illaria's symbol. I watched, mesmerized, as the door lit up and the Amulet of Auraken shimmered in the centre of Illaria's star.

I took a step back. What was happening?

Behind me a voice spoke. "Finally, you have come, *Aurora Shadowbreaker*. I have been expecting you."

I jumped in fright. The voice was unfamiliar yet familiar at the same time. But this was not the deep male voice that had helped me before. This voice was soft and kind, the voice of a woman. It was not the Alkana, but the power in that gentle voice made the magic within me hum and vibrate as if in answer to some secret call.

I turned around slowly, and my blood turned to ice.

Standing in the center of the massive chamber was the specter of a beautiful High Fae lady. Light touched her alabaster skin from the inside and she shimmered like a mirage in a desert of darkness. A silver crown studded with pearls rested atop her hair, a gleaming stream of darkest ebony. Her eyes were the color of emerald, and her silver robes and pointed ears gave away her lineage. But her face! I gasped; it was like looking in a mirror. And I knew instinctively who she was.

"Illaria Lightbringer," I whispered. She looked exactly

like me, or rather I looked exactly like her.

The specter gave a slight nod.

"But you're dead how can you be here?"

The ancient queen smiled. "The Immortal fae never die unless killed by specific weapons. We simply leave this world for a better one. On occasion we can return when needed for a greater purpose."

"But how can you speak to me? Are you real?"

Illaria laughed. "Yes, I am real, as real as I can be. The magic I preserved in this chamber permits me to speak to you through the veils between the worlds. For thousands of years I have waited for the chosen one to open the chamber." She paused, taking a step closer. "You, *Aurora Shadowbreaker*, are the last heir to the ancient fae house of Eos-Eirendil."

My hands trembled—I had to hold them together to stop them from shaking.

"How can I be your heir? My grandmother Izadora never mentioned she was descended from you."

"That's because she is not descended from me, and neither is your mother. Only you are."

"How is that possible?"

The ancient queen's eyes swirled with magic as she spoke. "Auraken Firedrake was my son," Illaria Lightbringer explained. "The first fae-mage ever to be born in Avalonia."

My eyes widened at the implications. "But that would make you . . ." I trailed off.

"Your great-grandmother, from your father's side," said Illaria, smiling. "Many times removed, I may add."

"But why did you keep this a secret for so long?"

The specter stepped forward slightly. "In the days of Ancient Avalonia, a union between a mage and a fae was unheard of, and for a High Fae to marry a mage . . ." She paused. "As you can imagine, there was no option but to hide Auraken's true identity from the rest of the world, or he would have been killed before he came into his powers."

She moved slowly toward me, gliding over the stone floors. "Avalonia is in turmoil. If Morgana opens the book and Dragath returns, you must be the one to stop him from taking over the world as he did once before."

"How can I stop him? I can't get out of this chamber to stop Andromeda. My fae magic is blocked, and if Morgana gets the book I can't fight her. I don't have ancient magic like you did."

Illaria stopped before me, looked me straight in the eyes, and held out her hand. In her palm was a ring: a carved, red stone depicting the head of a dragon, set within a plain gold band. "Take my ring, *Aurora Shadowbreaker*, and become the queen the world needs you to be."

I stared at my ancestor as my heartbeat sped up. "Is the ring the Dawnstar?"

"No, the ring is not the Dawnstar," said the ancient queen.

I took the ring and held it up. It glowed faintly as if in recognition. "Then what is it?" I was confused. "If I am going to go up against Morgana and Dragath, I need your ancient weapon. My magic is not enough."

"It has taken over five thousand years for all of my powers to manifest together within one person." She put her hand on my shoulder. A warm light infused my magic with a power I had never felt before. "You are my legacy, Aurora, the weapon I promised the world."

The chamber lit up.

"You, *Aurora Shadowbreaker*, are the Dawnstar."

There was a pause in the threads of time as my whole world tilted.

"I'm what?"

"You heard me," Illaria removed her hand from my shoulder and took a step back. "I hid the Dawnstar in a place the elders would never think to look: in the bloodline of the mages. You are the last heir to the ancient house of Eos-Eirendil, and your magic is like nothing the world has ever seen before." Her voice lifted. "The time for the Dawnstar to rise has come, *Aurora Shadowbreaker*. Wear the ring and free the great dragon. He will be your guide in mastering the magic of the Ancient Fae and will be invaluable to you in the battles to come."

"Abraxas!" I exclaimed. "Is he in the ring?"

"No, young fae-mage. The ring is part of his prison, but

he is not within it. When Dragath trapped Abraxas in between the worlds, I managed to preserve a link to him, a part of his consciousness, within this ring. With it you can contact the dragon, and he will hear your call through the veil. If your summoning power is strong enough to break the curse and free him, Abraxas will come, wherever he may be."

"How do I summon him?"

"That I cannot reveal." Illaria started to retreat into the shadows. "You must find the magic to break the curse yourself. The Dawnstar has been within you all along, but how you use the power that you have been given is entirely up to you. When the time is right, you will know what to do."

"How will I know when the time is right?" I called out. "Wait!"

But the specter of the ancient queen dissolved into darkness and disappeared.

I slipped the ring onto my finger. It felt warm and the glow got brighter.

"It took you long enough," said the familiar deep voice only I could hear.

"It's you!" I cried, aghast, looking at the ring. "You're Abraxas?"

"A fine observation, Princess Obvious," said the voice of the great dragon, already familiar in my head. *"But we have work to do. So quit dawdling and let us get out of here."*

"Why didn't you tell me it was you?"

"Because that is not how the magic that binds me works," Abraxas replied. "It took every last bit of power I had left to speak to you when you called for help in the ruins with Morgana. At first I was surprised I heard your call, but when I did, I knew who you were. So I tried to help. I had to keep you alive long enough to free me. The closer you were to the ring, the easier it was for me to contact you. When you came to Elfi and to the castle I felt your presence, but only for moments when I could speak through the curse. It also prevented me from telling you the truth about this chamber." He paused for a moment. "Time is of the essence, Aurora. We must leave now."

I shook my head. "My fae magic is bound by these cuffs—there is no way out of here. And the elders have warded the castle against portals."

"There are no cuffs or wards that can stop the Dawnstar," said the great dragon. "Destroy the cuffs and let's go—you must warn the Elite about the threat to their queen. Izadora must remain on the throne of Elfi—it is imperative if we are going to defeat Morgana."

I took the Amulet of Auraken from the door and put it in my pocket, its work complete. I didn't need it. The amulet was created to hide the power of the Dawnstar in plain sight, until I learned the true use of my magic. I was the last heir to the ancient house of Eos-Eirendil and I would not hide anymore.

That thought gave me hope.

I searched for fae magic and concentrated all my power on removing the cuffs of blackened iron from my wrists. The cuffs sizzled and sparked as my magic filled them with light, the darkness within clinging to my body like a leech. My hands began to glow as I pushed harder and the blackened iron cuffs fell off, dropping to the floor with a heavy thud.

I healed myself as my fae magic arose. *Aurora Shadow-breaker* was back.

I called forth my powers unbridled and powerful, searched for Tristan, and created a portal leading straight into his room.

Cade jumped when I stepped out of the portal, but smiled when he saw me. Tristan was still lying on the bed, his eyes closed. I could see the black poison in his veins streaking across his neck. I ran over to the bed and knelt down beside him.

"Why hasn't he woken up yet?" I demanded, looking at Cade.

The big red haired warrior shook his head. "I don't know. I think he was bitten twice; there is too much poison in his blood. He's trying to fight it, but even with the antidote the poison is not leaving his body."

"Heal Prince Tristan, Aurora," said Abraxas. *"We need him, and time is running out."*

"But Penelope said it may make it worse," I asserted in my mind.

"If you are going to argue with me every time I tell you to do something, it is going to get very tedious to teach you anything, Aurora," said Abraxas. *"The magic you possess is different from all others. Now do it."*

I put one hand on Tristan's forehead, the other over his heart.

"What are you doing?" Cade whispered, but he didn't stop me.

I ignored him and plunged my magic into Tristan. Calmly, I searched for the poison. I could see it, tiny specks of darkness moving through his blood. I pulled more magic from the well inside me and pushed it into him. It roared through Tristan's body in a wave of white light, swallowing up the darkness within. The werewraith poison shrieked in fury and fled in the radiance of the Dawnstar.

Tristan opened his eyes and smiled when he saw me.

I told him everything that had happened as quickly as I could. Cade listened with his mouth open, and Tristan pushed himself up as soon as he heard about the threat to Izadora and his grandmother.

"You're the Dawnstar?" Cade looked at me wide-eyed.

I nodded. And then explained what we had to do.

In a few minutes Tristan and Cade were ready. The door opened and Aiden stood before us blocking the way, his sword in hand.

"What are you doing here?" the prince and heir of the

Day Court growled, looking at me. "You are supposed to be confined to your room."

Tristan's eyes narrowed and he moved to stand beside me. "Hear her out, Aiden."

"I don't want to hear the lies that come out of that *half-breed's* mouth," spat the blond warrior.

Tristan put his hand on his sword. "Stand down, Aiden," said the Dark Prince. "I don't want to hurt you. Izadora and my grandmother are in trouble. We need to go, but we could use your help."

Aiden's eyes shifted to me and back to Tristan. "Tell me."

Tristan gave Aiden a brief explanation of what Andromeda was planning. I had prepared myself to use my magic if needed to get Aiden out of the way, or anyone else for that matter.

Aiden shook his head. "Why am I not surprised?" He lowered his sword. "I was afraid it might come to this. My mother is a power-hungry bitch and if she means to kill the queen, she's probably already dead."

Aiden's reaction was not what I expected at all. I think the news's coming from Tristan made it easier for him to accept. I knew his relationship with his mother was strained, but I never realized just how much. If Aiden helped us, we would have a much better chance of getting my grandmother back.

I stepped forward. "It's not too late. You have to get there before the werewraiths do."

Aiden turned his gaze on me and pointed with his sword. "If you are lying about this, *half-breed*, I will have your head."

I didn't have time to argue with Aiden. "Go, you will see for yourself," I snapped.

Tristan turned to me. "What about you?"

"I can take care of myself." I tried to smile. "Stick to the plan—you know what you have to do."

He gave me a quick hug, which was a surprise. "Be careful," he whispered.

"I will. Just be there on time."

"You can count on it," Tristan growled, and turned to the other Elite warriors. "Let's go!"

Abraxas spoke. *"Good. Now create a portal to Penelope. We will need her help if this plan is to succeed."*

I created a portal straight into the dungeons. Now that I had discovered deeper parts of my magic, with the guidance of the great dragon, I could manipulate it as I pleased. The dowager had said I could not create a portal to a place I had never been before. But with ancient magic, which only I possessed, it was possible to create a portal to a person. And that's exactly what I did.

Penelope didn't look surprised when she saw me. "I knew you would come."

I hugged her and told Penelope everything that had happened as concisely as I could.

"I will need you to remain here and stop Skye from bringing Andromeda's army into the city through the portal in the catacombs," I told her hurriedly, glancing toward the cell door. "Once the wards fall, you will be able to create a portal out of the dungeons at the same time Skye will be opening one in the tunnels."

She nodded and put her hand on my shoulder. "Go, stop Andromeda. I will do everything I can to protect the city."

I hugged her and created a portal to my room. I grabbed my sword; if I was going into battle, I wanted *Dawn* with me. I didn't portal straight to Andromeda and the elders because I was not sure what would be waiting when I got there. They had left the city a while ago and may have already reached the meeting place. With Lucian and the Drakaar so close, I needed to scope out the area first. So I created another portal leading just outside the city gates.

Within seconds of stepping out of the portal, centaur guards surrounded me, their spears ready and pointing at my face.

"No one is allowed to leave the city," stated one centaur.

"Elders' orders," said another.

I raised my hands to show them I was unarmed. I didn't want to fight them, but I would if I had to.

The rising sun glinted off my ring, and one old centaur gasped. "The ring of a dragonlord," he gasped reverently and bowed his head.

To my surprise, the rest of the centaurs did the same and

moved out of the way.

I had to get to Andromeda before she met with Lucian at the Gandren Pass. I closed my eyes and called Snow. I hoped she had returned from the Old Forest.

Within seconds a musical voice filled my ears. *"I'm here, little one,"* called the white pegasus, shooting out of the sky and landing beside me.

"Let's go." I jumped onto Snow's back. "I hope we are not too late."

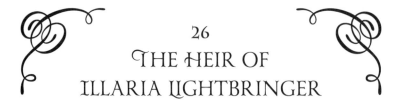

26
THE HEIR OF
ILLARIA LIGHTBRINGER

WE FLEW TO the Gandren Pass in the Wildflower Mountains. It was one of the only mountain passes through which an army could enter the kingdom of Elfi. Abraxas was our only hope to destroy the book. If the great dragon did not come and my grandmother died, Elfi would fall and Morgana would be one step closer to releasing Dragath and destroying the world forever.

If I had to give myself up to Morgana to save Elfi, I would do it. I was prepared for the worst.

I looked at the ring as I flew closer to my doom. "So how do I summon you?" I asked Abraxas, feeling silly as soon as the thought left my brain.

"I can't tell you that," the dragon snapped. *"Don't you think I would have already if I could?"*

"But I don't know how to use the power of the Dawnstar," I argued. "If you can tell me what words I have to say, or if I can understand more about how the Dawnstar works, then I may have a chance."

"It's not the words that are important, Aurora," Abraxas offered. *"It is the will behind them. The stronger the will, the*

stronger the call of a dragonlord. You must have faith in your-self. You are the Dawnstar. You are Illaria's weapon. Your magic is unlike anything this world has ever seen. Certain words do have more power than others, this is true, but the real magic is within you, in a place that has no beginning and no end; a place where no darkness can penetrate. That is where the Dawnstar resides."

I looked at the ring on my finger again as we flew on ahead, doubt creeping into every single thought. What if the summoning didn't work, what if I couldn't break the curse on his prison?

Snow knew where to go. We descended into the valley near the Gandren Pass. I hid myself with glamour and took up a position on a cliff overlooking the meeting place.

Andromeda, the elders, and their army had arrived.

Lucian and a legion of soldiers had already entered the pass and were waiting at the appointed place: a great open field in the shadow of the looming mountains that guarded Elfi from the outside world.

There was no sign of Tristan or my grandmother. I had no way of knowing if the Elite had reached them in time. I closed my eyes and tried summoning the dragon, but Abraxas was silent. I tried everything I could to find the magic within me to break the curse and free him, but no answer came, and time was running out.

As Lucian drew closer, I realized these weren't ordinary

soldiers he had brought with him. They were Drakaar!

I looked around at how many Drakaar he had brought into Elfi and my blood ran cold. The elders were mad to allow this. So many Drakaar in one place could easily summon an army of Shadow demons within seconds. Without the fire-fae warriors, they would be helpless. And as much as I would like to think I could, I could not take on a whole army of Drakaar alone.

I looked up. Although I couldn't see them, I knew their gorgoths were probably positioned overhead in the mountains waiting for their masters to call them down to wreak havoc on the fae.

Lucian didn't need more soldiers; his army was already here.

The archmage sat astride a black stallion in the middle of the field, the Drakaar flanking him on all sides. I glanced around, taking in everyone's positions. Andromeda and the elders stood at the front of the fae army, their faces drawn and resigned to defeat.

Lucian spoke first. "I'm glad you have finally come to your senses," remarked the Archmage of Avalonia, his voice clear and loud. "The fae council is wise. You know you cannot win against my army." He got off his horse and walked closer, his black mage robes billowing in the wind.

"Queen Andromeda." He stressed the word *queen*. "Have you brought the book?'

The others were silent, but one of the elders raised an eyebrow and glanced at Andromeda.

"Queen?" asked the Elder Dyanara. She looked back at Lucian. "You seem to be mistaken, Archmage. Andromeda is not our queen."

"Apologies," he taunted, tilting his head and putting his finger mockingly to his lips. He was obviously not sorry at all. "Was I not supposed to reveal that yet? Well, I'm going to let you all fight that out by yourselves. All I want is what I came for and I shall be on my way."

Andromeda stepped forward and addressed the council and the warriors that stood behind them. "Izadora is dead," she said plainly.

A gasp went up through the ranks. Was it true? Tristan hadn't returned with my grandmother and time was almost up.

"I will be your queen," Andromeda shouted to the warriors. But there were no cries of joy or supportive cheering. There was only the sound of the quickening beat of my heart.

The elders looked startled, but Dyanara narrowed her eyes. "You cannot be crowned queen without the Elder Council's support."

"I don't need your support," snapped Andromeda. "Morgana has already accepted me as queen of Elfi. If any of you don't agree you can spend the rest of your days in the dungeons of the Crystal Castle. Once we are done with this I will be dissolving the council."

"You cannot dissolve the council," countered the Elder Silias. "We will not permit it."

"Fool," replied Andromeda, with a sneer. "I can and I have. You have no choice. As we speak my troops are taking over the capital. Anyone still loyal to Izadora will be killed." Andromeda took out something from the saddlebag beside her and stepped forward. The *Book of Abraxas* rested in her hand.

Lucian's eyes lit up and he held out his hand. "Come," he snapped, "bring it to me. And bring me the girl too. Where is she?"

"Locked in a dungeon, where she belongs," replied Andromeda.

"That was not the deal," Lucian hissed, his eyes narrowing. "There is no dungeon that can hold Aurora Firedrake. I want the girl."

"Deal's changed," smirked Andromeda. "The cuffs Morgana sent me to subdue Aurora's magic have worked very well. She is powerless," she paused. "You can have the book. Once I know Morgana will keep her end of the bargain and I am crowned queen of Elfi with her support, only then will I hand over the Firedrake princess. After you remove your troops from Elfi."

"You will regret this, Andromeda," said the archmage.

"Morgana does not deal lightly with those who try to cross her."

"Take the book," said Andromeda, holding it up. "Remove your troops from my lands and I will hand the girl over to you."

The archmage smiled, white teeth flashing as his obsidian eyes grew darker. "I'm afraid I can't do that," said Lucian. "Without Izadora you are weak, and with the girl locked up, you have no one to defend your puny kingdom. You High Fae think you still rule the world. But I have news for you. You cannot stop me. Look around."

I could see Shadow demons appearing on both sides of the fae army as the Drakaar summoned their hideous henchmen. Gorgoths flew down from the mountains as I had predicted. Lucian never meant to leave Elfi in peace.

"I will take the book and I will take the girl," declared Lucian, "and when I am done exterminating the fae from these lands, I will raze the Crystal Castle to the ground and destroy all trace of the fae from Avalonia once and for all."

It was time.

I flew Snow down to the battlefield and jumped off the pegasus between Lucian's army and the fae; Lucian's eyes widened in surprise when he saw me.

"If you want the book, Lucian"—my hands started to glow—"you will have to go through me."

"Ah! Our little Firedrake," exclaimed the Archmage of

Avalonia. "I'm so glad you decided to join us. You may be dressed like a warrior, but I know under all that swagger is a scared little princess who wants to go home. I gave you a chance to do just that." He paused, assessing me, and his dark eyes swirled with the confidence he had won.

"Now, of course, that offer is off the table," Lucian went on. "You have no friends here; the fae were quite relieved to hand you over to me. And I can understand why. I do know what a handful you can be. That was quite a feat you pulled off in Calos and with the Drakaar in Brandor." He clucked his tongue in displeasure as if I were a child. "It wasn't very nice of you, was it?"

He folded his hands in front of him. "Your family is mostly dead. We know where the rebels are hiding, and the Blackwaters will flush them out soon enough. Silverthorne will give up his key eventually, especially when I torture you right in front of his eyes. I shall so enjoy hearing you scream." He laughed. "Your precious prince Rafael is going to marry another. He doesn't care what happens to you anymore."

I kept quiet and let him talk as I gathered my magic. Lucian was so full of himself and was so sure he had won. But his arrogance made him underestimate me, and I vowed that this was the last time anyone would underestimate Aurora Firedrake.

The immense power within me rose up. I flung it out in a wall of shimmering magic hundreds of feet high, creating a barrier between Lucian's army and the fae, stopping Andromeda from going over to them with the book.

"What are you doing, foolish girl?" Andromeda screamed, hitting the wall of magic that had risen in front of us.

At the same time a portal opened beside me swirling with silver mist and the queen of the fae stepped through, followed by Rhiannon, Tristan, Aiden, Erik, and the rest of the Elite.

"She is doing what we should have done a long time ago," replied Izadora, her immortal face calm, but I could see a strain on her power. She had not fully recovered.

Andromeda stopped in her tracks. "Aiden, what is the meaning of this? Izadora is supposed to be dead."

Aiden ignored his mother.

"What this means," explained the Izadora, holding out her hand, "is that you have lost, Andromeda. Morgana will never get the *Book of Abraxas* as long as I am Queen of Elfi." She stepped closer. "Now give it to me."

I was still holding the wall of magic protecting us from Lucian's army, but from the corner of my eye I could see them moving toward it.

"You won't be queen for much longer," snarled Andromeda. "You will all die here today."

And then it struck.

A huge wave of dark magic hurtled into the shimmering transparent wall I had created, trying to shatter it. I moved backward with the force of it, but my magic was still holding. I closed my eyes and pushed more magic into the wall as the power welling up inside me ignited.

"We have to give the book to him, or he will destroy us," said Andromeda, her eyes frantic, looking at the elders.

But the council stepped away from her.

"We have to," Andromeda pleaded. "Or she will never leave Elfi in peace."

Dark magic crashed into my shield again, and I shuddered with the power it took to hold it. The Drakaar had combined their force and were pounding at it, and it wouldn't be long before one of them broke through.

I closed my eyes and tried to summon the dragon. I used every word combination I could think of, but he did not come.

I gritted my teeth and thrust more power into the shield I was holding. I could not let it fall, not yet. I could hear Lucian and the Drakaar shouting on the other side, trying to break through. Gorgoths flew at the wall of magic, scratching and tearing at it, ready to pounce on the fae when it finally fell.

And it would fall. I could not hold it for much longer against so much dark magic. It was weakening me, and I needed all my power.

Without warning the pressure on my magic subsided. I glanced over to Rhiannon. She had stepped forward, her arms outstretched. Magic was swirling around her, and I realized the Dowager Duchess of the Night Court was adding her magic to the wall, helping me, giving me a chance to breathe and leaving my powers free to do what had to be done.

"The book must be destroyed, Andromeda," said Rhiannon, moving to stand beside me, trying to reason with the grand duchess. "Now hand it over."

Andromeda laughed a feral sound. "There is nothing in this world that can destroy the *Book of Abraxas*. Except Abraxas himself."

"Exactly," I said to Andromeda. The ring glowed as I spoke. "That is why it is time to call him back."

"No!" Andromeda shook her head and clutched the book to her chest. "No one has the power to summon the great dragon."

"The Dawnstar does," I explained as my magic gathered inside me.

Andromeda's eyes went wide as terror crept into them. "You have the Dawnstar?" she asked, slowly enunciating every word.

A hush went over the rest of the council as they waited for my answer.

"I don't *have* the Dawnstar, Andromeda," I said, in a loud, clear voice that could be heard by all the elders and the fae warriors that stood on this side of the wall. "I *am* the

Dawnstar!"

"No!" Andromeda whispered. "That's impossible."

My eyes flashed. "Nothing is impossible," I asserted, as I plunged down deep into the well of unfettered power that lay within me. In my mind stood a great golden door, behind it the magic of the Dawnstar. I knew it was there, waiting to be freed, waiting to rise up and save the world. Gathering my will, I pushed at the door, and it shattered into a thousand pieces. A glow of pure light washed over me as the full force of Illaria Lightbringer's magic awoke.

Illaria's ring glowed on my finger as I pointed it upward, and I knew exactly what I had to do.

I reached for Abraxas with all the magic I had within me. In a loud, clear voice that echoed across the plains, I cried out to the skies. "Hear me, Abraxas, immortal dragon of Avalonia. Rise and fight! Break the chains that keep you from this world. Join me in this battle for Illaria's kingdom. The Dawnstar summons you!"

The wall of magic surrounding us fell as the Drakaar triumphantly broke through.

A great roar sounded across the lands and the mountains shook with the force of it. A massive shadow descended on to the plain, and the army of Drakaar looked up and screamed as the most magnificent dragon, with a wingspan of two football fields, cast his colossal shadow over Lucian's whole army.

"Dragon!" shouted the Drakaar, and all hell broke loose on the battlefield.

The archmage was standing there with his mouth hanging open, staring at the mighty dragon. The Drakaar summoned more Shadow demons and the gorgoths flew out of the sky, hundreds of them descending on Abraxas. The great dragon gave another mighty roar and dragonfire burned them in mid-flight, but more of them swarmed around him like locusts. He had his work cut out for him, I thought, but I was sure he could handle it.

I looked around and spotted Andromeda, who had started running toward Lucian as soon as the wall fell.

"Tristan, she has the book," I shouted as I drew my sword and ran after her. I had to get it back.

Erik still defended his queen, but with a great shout he called to his men. "Elite! Defend the Dawnstar!"

With a mighty war cry all the fire-fae warriors rushed into battle after me.

Shadow demons sprang up around us, blocking the path to Andromeda and Lucian. My sword blazed with silver-fire as I slashed and cut through the melee of Drakaar and their henchmen, but more swarmed. Abraxas was busy fighting the gorgoths and burning Shadow demons to a crisp.

I had to get closer, I had to get the book.

My other hand lit up with a ball of silver-fire. I mixed it with mage magic and shot it at the Shadow demons; they screamed and vanished into smoke. But the Drakaar were harder to kill; a sword of silver-fire to the neck was the only way. I twirled around, slicing through a Drakaar's neck as a black sword came swinging toward me. But Tristan was beside me in an instant, and the Drakaar's sword clattered to the ground as his head rolled away from his body.

I nodded at Tristan in thanks, but he was already engaged in battle with two more Drakaar. How many of them were there?

I rushed forward. If Andromeda got away, we were done.

I pushed myself faster and practically flew through the raging battle, swerving and slashing as I tried to get closer. I nearly caught up to her when a dozen Shadow demons appeared out of nowhere, blocking my path. Dark magic clawed at my shield as the Drakaar who controlled them converged on me, combining their magic as it crashed into me, pushing me to my knees.

I could hear Tristan shout my name as he fought, but there were too many of them and he could not get to me.

I tried to shield myself, but the crushing weight of the Drakaar's combined magic was immense, shrouding my power in a veil of hopelessness. I screamed in agony as my shield shattered and the Drakaar's sorcery started to suck my power out of me.

Flashes of a palace burning and my mother screaming slammed into me as the Drakaar fed me memories of my parents' deaths. They were feeding on my fear and despair and it made them stronger. Their voices rang in my head as they poured their thoughts into my mind.

"We were there, fae-mage," hissed one Drakaar.

"We killed your father," said another.

"And we will enjoy killing you too," chimed the third Drakaar, stepping forward, his sword of blackened iron gleaming in his hands. "The time has come for you to die, Princess Aurora."

I tried to push myself up but there was no strength left, no more magic. I would die here today.

"Help me," I whispered in my mind, and I hoped he heard me. "Abraxas, my magic is not enough."

"Get up," ordered the voice of the great dragon. *"Faith is the greatest magic of all. It can lift the world out of the darkness and bring it into the light. Be the Star of the Morning, the light that fills the world with magic. Be the Lightbringer, the Breaker of Shadows. Believe in yourself, Aurora Firedrake; believe in the Dawnstar. For if you have faith, anything is possible."*

My mother's face flashed before my eyes, giving her life so I could be safe; so I could save her and all of Avalonia. I closed my eyes and plunged down into the depths of my magic, and a wall of darkness rose up to greet me. I pushed at it with all the faith I could muster. I could do this. My kingdom was waiting for me, my people expected me to come home and save them. My mother believed in me and so did Illaria; I was her weapon, I was the Dawnstar. I had to survive; I couldn't give up, not now, not ever.

With the last bit of power I had left, I punched at the darkness with my magic and a small spark ignited within. All my fears and doubt fell away, replaced by an overwhelming feeling of hope and courage; of faith in who I was.

I started to glow brighter than ever before, pushing myself off the ground slowly, as the Dawnstar arose in a fury of unfettered power; my hands flashed with the magic of the ancients.

The Drakaar froze. "You should be dead," said their leader, his black eyes wide. "No fae could survive that."

"That's because I'm not just any fae," I responded as I stood up. "I am a dragonlord of the ancient house of Eos-Eirendil. I am *Aurora Shadowbreaker*, I am the Dawnstar; and you, Drakaar," I growled, "are in my way."

I unleashed my magic in a blinding ripple of power that blazed out of my hands. The Shadow demons shrieked in fury and dissipated immediately as the wall of white light reached out to engulf everything in its path. The Drakaar sorcerers surrounding me screamed in fear and tried to get away, but the light pierced through their bodies and swallowed them up as the magic of the Dawnstar cleaved through the darkness and obliterated them forever.

I scanned the battlefield—Andromeda had nearly reached Lucian. The archmage strode forward, his hand outstretched.

"Give it to me."

I ran toward her. The book!

Andromeda stopped. She clutched the book to her chest.

"What are you doing?" screamed Lucian, his eyes swirling with dark magic. He flung power at Andromeda, but her shield deflected it.

"I don't trust you, Archmage," said Andromeda. A portal beside her opened, and Skye stepped through.

The archmage faltered. "Give. Me. The Book," he shouted, gathering more magic.

"I will give Morgana the book myself," offered Andromeda, flashing me a dark grin and turning toward the portal.

"No!" I screamed, flinging magic at her.

Andromeda took Skye's hand and stepped into the portal just as my magic struck. The portal shut behind them.

The *Book of Abraxas* was gone.

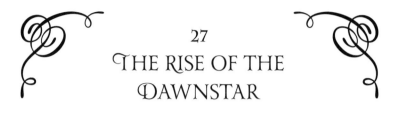

27
THE RISE OF THE DAWNSTAR

I STOOD IN the midst of the still-raging battle, numb. I had failed.

"This is all your fault," screamed the archmage as he stretched out his hand and blasted me with dark magic.

I vaguely felt his power hit me but I didn't flinch as I turned my gaze on him. Lucian's magic could not penetrate my shield. It had become so strong nothing could get through.

From the corner of my eye I saw Tristan charging at the archmage, his gleaming sword raised. Before I could do anything, he swung his sword and brought it down on Lucian's neck, severing his head from his body. It rolled toward me with a thump as the lifeless body of the Archmage of Avalonia fell to the ground.

The remaining Drakaar, realizing their commander had fallen, started to retreat. The field was streaked with blood and black ash, and the terrified screams of death resounded in the air as the fire-fae warriors and Abraxas drove the rest of the Drakaar and their demons back through the pass.

I looked down at Lucian's headless body and felt sick.

Momentarily frozen with the sight of it, I fell to my knees.

Lucian was dead, the battle was over, and Elfi was safe. But we hadn't won yet, not by a long shot. Andromeda had the *Book of Abraxas*, and it was only a matter of time before she gave it to Morgana. I had failed to protect the book and the world would have to pay. I tried my best, but it wasn't good enough.

Rhiannon and the elders came forward to reinforce the wards around the kingdom until my grandmother had recovered fully. The rest of the army was assisting the elite warriors in hunting down any stragglers left this side of the mountains.

There was a beating of massive wings as Abraxas flew out of the sky and landed beside me.

"Thank you, Aurora Shadowbreaker." The great dragon bowed his head to me. *"I will not forget what you have done for me, and for this world."*

A gasp went up from the Elder Council. For a dragon to bow to a dragonlord was unheard of.

The rest of the warriors had started milling around, trying to get a closer look at the legendary Elder Dragon.

"Do not despair," said Abraxas, still talking to me in my head. *"What you have achieved here today was an impossible feat. No dragonlord in five thousand years has been able to break the chains on my prison. We may have lost the book, but Elfi is still standing, and Silverthorne still has his key, so we*

do have hope. You are no longer alone in this. I am here now. I will guide you in the battles to come. If you need me, all you have to do is call."

"Wait! You're leaving? I thought you were going to stay with me," I pleaded in my mind.

"I'm a dragon, Aurora, not a pet," said Abraxas in his deep voice, which reverberated in my head as the others looked on silently. They were probably wondering what we were talking about. "You have the ring. Use it. You can speak to me whenever you wish. I will hear you wherever you may be."

"But what about the book? We still have to destroy it and free my mother from the dagger."

"And we will," answered Abraxas, his purple scales glistening like amethysts in the sunlight. "This is not the end, heir of Illaria Lightbringer. The battle may be over, but the war for Avalonia's freedom has only just begun."

The great dragon roared, a sound that touched the furthest reaches of the fae kingdom. He spread his massive wings, casting an enormous shadow over the fae army, and pounced into the brightening sky.

I turned to my grandmother and the Elder Council. They were all lined up and looking at me with awe and a new-found respect on their immortal faces.

My grandmother stepped forward to stand beside me and addressed the fae. "People of Elfi," she began in a clear voice, the voice of an immortal queen. "For five thousand years we have waited for the heir of Illaria Lightbringer to return and lead us out of the darkness that has descended on our world. Now we are finally on the cusp of a new age, an age where darkness has no place. The war has only begun, and I choose to align myself with *Aurora Shadowbreaker*, Bringer of Light, true queen of the kingdom of Illiador and the Heir of Elfi." She paused, folding her hands together. "Prepare yourselves for the battles to come, for there is hope for this world yet. The Age of the Dawnstar has begun."

There were cheers and delighted cries from the crowd as the word spread through the army. And then the most unexpected thing happened.

My grandmother, the dowager, and the whole Elder Council, including Tristan's father, bowed their heads to me. Behind them, the Elite led by Erik bent their knees, and the rest of the army of fae warriors did too.

I was overwhelmed, but I held back my tears. I couldn't cry in front of practically the whole fae kingdom. They would think the Dawnstar was a blubbering idiot. So I steeled my face and hoped they noticed how truly humbled I was by their acceptance and respect.

Tristan accompanied me as we rode back to the Crystal Castle in a convoy flanked by Erik and the Elite as Snow flew on overhead. We had just received news. Penelope had managed to stop Skye from getting her troops into the castle. But I knew Skye had escaped. Now Andromeda and Skye had the book and Morgana was in an much stronger position than before.

The first thing I needed to do was to get my granduncle out of the dungeons and away from the Blackwaters. His key was all that stood in the way of Morgana opening the book and releasing Dragath on the world. Once we had the key, we would search for the book and destroy it.

The road to my mother and my throne still seemed endless, but at least I had hope.

When we got back to the castle, I went to meet Penelope. She was lying on her bed, her face pale, her blue eyes dim as if the life had been sucked out of them.

"What can I do?" I asked, horrified as I ran to her bedside and knelt down beside her.

She could barely speak, and shook her head slightly. "You cannot heal me, Aurora. I am weak because most of my magic is gone."

"But you will recover?"

A faint smile. "I hope so," she replied. "But it may take a while to regain my powers."

"What happened?"

"While I was busy closing the portal, Skye attacked me," Penelope wheezed. "Tristan had sent reinforcements and I let them into the palace as soon as the wards were down. Night Court warriors drove Andromeda's soldiers back through the portal and secured the city in Izadora's name." Penelope turned her head to the side, away from me. "I should have been able to stop her."

I put my hand over hers. "It's okay, Penelope, you did more than enough. If it was anyone's fault it was mine. I should have been here."

Penelope held my hand in hers and squeezed it gently. "You have to stop blaming yourself, Aurora. Not everything that happens is your fault. You cannot be in two places at once. You did your best, and that is all any of us can ever hope to do."

The door opened and Kildaren walked in, but this time he left his guards waiting outside.

I stood up. "What do you want?"

"I came to apologize," Kildaren answered, to my surprise. His sapphire eyes looked troubled.

"For what, exactly? For trying to get rid of me, for putting Penelope in the dungeons, or for colluding with Andromeda to kill my grandmother?"

Kildaren shook his head. "I didn't know Andromeda was the one who planned to have Izadora killed. I only agreed to go along with her to get rid of you, but I made a mistake."

He came closer and, to my surprise, knelt down next to the bed and took Penelope's hand in his. "I should never have mistrusted you, Penelope, and for that I am truly sorry. When I didn't hear from you for so many years, I thought you had forgotten me. I was so angry I wanted to believe you were a traitor, although I knew you could never be one."

"I could never forget you, Kildaren," said Penelope softly. "I had to leave, and I could not tell you where I was going for a reason."

This was awkward. "Um, I'll leave now," I murmured and started backing away toward the door. There was obviously some unfinished business there, and it wasn't my place to interfere. I shut the door softly behind me. I would have a chance to speak to Penelope later and ask her about it.

I was exhausted and wished I could sleep for a week. I soaked my tired body in the tub, which was already steaming and waiting for me. I barely had any energy as I crawled into my bed and fell into a quiet dreamless sleep.

I woke up to birds chirping high in the trees in the palace gardens. A warm wind signaled the advent of spring and sunlight streamed in through the great arched windows of my room. I realized they had finally been fitted with crystal like the rest of the magnificent fae castle.

Tristan was waiting at the bottom of the steps leaning against the wall, his powerful arms crossed in front of him. He smiled when he saw me, his whole face lighting up. For a moment, I had to catch my breath. The prince of the Night Court was devastatingly handsome. I had realized this before but it was never so noticeable. *Probably because of the perma-*

nent scowl on his face, I thought to myself, and giggled.

"You know you don't have to protect me anymore, don't you?" I teased when I saw him.

His lips curved upward in a wry chuckle. "I thought you could protect me from now on," said Tristan. "I was thinking after we are married, I might retire and leave all the fighting up to you."

I laughed. But cringed inwardly. How was I going to tell him I couldn't marry him? My grandmother had no reason to force my hand. I was sure the fae army would follow me if I didn't marry Tristan. I had to find a way to get out of it without hurting his feelings.

"Izadora wants to see you," said Tristan, pushing himself off the wall. "The Elder Council has called a meeting."

This was my life, council meetings and war strategies. There was no more time to practice being a queen.

"They are waiting for you in the council chamber," Tristan informed me as I fell into step beside him. "I will walk you there."

My grandmother sat at the head of the table in her rightful place, and the dowager sat beside her. All heads turned toward me as I entered the council room; the elders all got up from their seats and bowed.

My grandmother gestured to a chair at the end of the table opposite her. "Have a seat, Aurora," said the queen of the fae.

I sat down on the chair that had been brought in specifically for me.

The Elder Silias spoke. "*Aurora Shadowbreaker*," he began, using my title for the first time. "The council is forever in your debt for stopping Andromeda from destroying everything we have built these five thousand years. As Izadora has rightly said, since the ancient dynasty of Eos-Eirendil disappeared, the fae have waited for the heir of Illaria Lightbringer to return and lead the fae back to their former glory. It is written in the Codex."

I looked at my grandmother. Her face was impassive, her lips set in a thin line. But her golden eyes studied me evenly. Rhiannon was quiet too and sat with her hands folded in her lap, her back ramrod straight.

"What we propose," started the Elder Silias, glancing at the queen of the fae, "is that Izadora steps down and hands the crown of Elfi over to you, thus reinstating the ancient line of Eos-Eirendil to the throne."

What! Were they going to do this now? When the whole of Avalonia stood poised on the brink of war? When they had thought I was a nobody, a *half-breed*, they were ready to throw me to the dogs. They were too scared to stand up to Andromeda and were willing to give the book up to Morgana. Now they were scared of me, so they were willing to push my grandmother aside and give me the throne. I didn't trust them.

"And you are right not to trust them," Abraxas observed in my head. *"A shift in power like this could be detrimental to our plan to retake Illiador and get the Dark Dagger. You need your grandmother on the throne of Elfi to keep the elders and the other noble families in check. You cannot remain here to rule the fae, and once you leave, the council will have absolute power."*

"I agree," I said silently to Abraxas. "I'll handle it." As long as I wore the ring he popped in and out of my head whenever he wanted. But I didn't mind; it was reassuring to know I wasn't alone and had his help and vast knowledge whenever I needed them.

I didn't trust the council to rule Elfi and be there to help when I needed allies. But I could not refuse the throne outright; they would see it as an affront to the fae. I had to choose my words carefully. My grandmother had shown that she trusted me by naming me as her heir in front of the whole council. Now I would do the same for her.

I looked at my grandmother again, but she remained silent.

I cleared my throat, pushed my chair back, and stood up. "Thank you, Elder Silias," I said, nodding at the Elder Fae. "I am truly humbled by your show of good faith and allegiance to my family, the ancient house of Eos-Eirendil." I paused, glancing around the table. "But I cannot accept the title as queen of Elfi, at least not yet."

Whispering broke out around the table.

I cleared my throat again. The whispering died down as the Elder Council gave me their full attention. I could see a smile playing at the corner of my grandmother's lips.

"Elfi already has a queen," I explained, raising the tone of my voice a notch. "Izadora is the rightful queen of Elfi, and I am her heir." I paused, giving them time to take it in. "I am also queen of another kingdom. One now ruled by an evil tyrant. I will not allow one kingdom to fall into chaos because I am too busy looking after another. My grandmother is a great ruler, her power is unmatched in Elfi and beyond."

I walked slowly to where my grandmother sat and stood at her side, putting my hand on the fae queen's slender shoulder. "The time has come for me to leave Elfi and take my place as queen of Illiador. Izadora will rule Elfi in my name, until such a time as she is ready to hand over the crown to me or to my children. The Elder Council will only support the queen with advice, but will no longer be concerned with choosing a new queen every thousand years. Izadora is your queen and always will be, until I say otherwise."

A gasp went up from the council. I had effectively taken away all their power.

My grandmother stood up.

"Now that that's settled," she said crisply, her gold eyes flashing and her lips curving up in a feral grin, "this council is dismissed. Until such a time as I decide I want your advice."

The elders' eyes went wide and Silias stood up. "You don't have the power to dismiss us."

"But I do," I asserted, crossing my arms, just as the enormous shadow of Abraxas fell on the council table as he flew past the castle outside.

Immediately, the whole Elder Council got up, bowed, and scurried out of the council chamber. Only the dowager and my grandmother remained.

"Nicely done," said Abraxas.

I smiled looking out of the window. "Thanks for the fly-by."

"Anytime," said the great dragon.

"You have grown into a fine young lady, Aurora," my grandmother said unexpectedly, stepping closer and holding me gently by the arms, her gold eyes shining. "I couldn't be any prouder to have you as my granddaughter and my heir."

"Thank you," I said simply.

"It is I who should thank you, for saving my life and my kingdom."

I shook my head. "I didn't save the book," I murmured softly. "I'm not worthy to be Illaria's heir."

The queen looked at me sharply. "What is destined is already written—you cannot change that. The world has been awaiting you for a very long time. That is the reason I brought you here, to give you the chance to realize that and to uncover who you are. The Dawnstar was prophesied to save Avalonia from darkness, and you are finally ready for the task ahead. The time has come to take back your father's throne and end Morgana's rule for good." She paused and her voice softened. "The time has come to get your mother back, and make sure Dragath never rises again."

I nodded. This time I would not fail; this time I would do it right.

"They will plot against you once you are gone," said the dowager, turning to me.

"Let them try." The queen sat back down in her chair.

"Izadora will need a strong ally among the fae if she is going to hold the throne in your name," the dowager continued.

"She has you," I said, still smiling.

Rhiannon's lips twitched, but she didn't smile. "Be that as it may, an alliance with the Night Court will greatly help matters here," the dowager said plainly. "Now that Morgana has the *Book of Abraxas* we must act fast. You must take an army to Illiador and retrieve the book as well as the Dagger of Dragath."

I knew what she was getting at. But I let her talk. How was I going to tell her I didn't want to marry her grandson?

"I don't want to force you into marriage," said my grandmother, to my surprise. "But Rhiannon is right. Right now the fae will follow you because they are afraid of your powers.

But a marriage to a fae prince will make them trust you. In battle you must have an army you can depend on."

"But what about Tristan's father? He doesn't want the marriage to happen. He was willing to give me over to Morgana just to get rid of me."

The dowager nodded. "That was before. Now that your true lineage has been revealed, my son is more than happy to overlook your mage side and has given his blessings for this marriage."

I'm sure he has, I thought to myself, but didn't say it out loud. He knew marrying his son to me would ensure his line took the throne. To have the magic of the ancient queens bred into your family was the most prestigious thing that could ever happen to a High Fae.

"Think about it, Aurora," said the dowager. "A betrothal is not a marriage, although it is a contract. You can still take your time to figure things out and get to know each other better. You don't need to marry immediately. A betrothal will show the fae they can trust you, that you are one of them. Once you have taken back your kingdom and are ready to settle down, then you can get married if you so choose."

"I know you have been pining over the Prince of Eldoren," interrupted my grandmother, but her tone was not unkind.

How did she know about him? Had Penelope told her about Rafe?

"I also know he is marrying another." My grandmother's

eyes softened. "My most trusted spies have informed me Prince Rafael was seen in Brandor recently. They have also informed me that the Red Citadel in the port city of Sanria had a big royal wedding."

My face fell. He had finally accepted the Emir's proposal to marry Katerina. Why else would he go there? He had made his decision, and I wasn't part of it.

"He has put his kingdom before you," explained my grandmother, voicing my thoughts. "And you must do the same." Her tone was still soft, but that didn't make her words any less harsh or true.

I realized she pitied me and my stupid dreams of love. I was slowly starting to realize how blind I was, waiting and hoping against hope that Rafe would not marry Katerina and come back for me. But that was the stuff of fairytales, and this was the real world. I had been only sixteen when I met him, and he had been my first love. At seventeen I wasn't much older, but I was a tiny bit wiser. Maybe I thought I was in love because I didn't know any better. But a small part of me was screaming this wasn't true. That the love Rafe and I had was real. I brushed it aside. It was obviously not to be.

Rafe was married, and he was never coming back. If he had only waited, I would have given him an army. I would have helped him get his kingdom back if he had only come to me. But my grandmother was right; I had to do what was best for my kingdom. Marrying Tristan would help me gain the trust of the High Fae, and when the time came to fight Morgana I would have an army at my back.

I made my decision. I had to take my life into my own hands and move on.

I was *Aurora Shadowbreaker*, bringer of light, and dragon-lord of the ancient house of Eos-Eirendil.

I was the Dawnstar. And I was going to change the world.

28
THE WINDS OF CHANGE

THE HALL WAS abuzz with stories of the battle of Abraxas, as it was now being called, and I walked into the grand hall on Tristan's arm wearing a dress of silver that flowed down to my ankles and hugged every curve. A hush fell over the room when they all noticed I had arrived.

The dowager had sent a flock of house sprites to my room with an array of dresses and jewelry to choose from. I wore long ropes of silvery gray pearls wound a few times around my neck. Glamoured clothes were nice, but they never matched the look and feel of hand-stitched dresses. My gown was beautifully embroidered with tiny white flowers and small pearls stitched into the fabric. The house sprites fussed about me and did up my hair in an elaborate design entwined with small, white diamonds that sparkled in my hair as I moved.

Rhiannon had also sent me a variety of jeweled crowns to choose from, but I refused them all, choosing instead a small diadem of pearls. When I put a crown on my head, it would be in the throne room of the Star Palace in Illiador.

The High Fae bowed as I passed. Everyone had heard

what happened, and they all knew who I really was: the Dawnstar, last heir of the ancient house of Eos-Eirendil.

The grand hall was suitably decorated for a betrothal feast. House sprites moved about refilling glasses and serving bite-sized snacks on large silver platters. I popped one in my mouth as they passed by.

The High Fae were dressed to the hilt, sparkling with jewels and swathed in lengths of colorful fabrics. My grandmother sat on the dais with the dowager beside her. Penelope had recovered enough to come for the feast, and she smiled when I caught her eye. I had gone to see her earlier, but she had been resting and I didn't want to disturb her. At least she was feeling better. I was glad to have her back.

"Where's Cade?" I asked Tristan, looking around. Some of the elders were noticeably absent, but I didn't care. Tristan's father had sought me out to let me know how pleased he was I had accepted. I didn't remind him about how he had spoken to me earlier, but I would never forget.

"He's not coming." Tristan's eyes were troubled. "Cade has taken Skye's betrayal quite badly and blames himself."

I shook my head. Poor Cade. "He shouldn't blame himself. We all got taken in by her act."

"I know. But Cade feels he should have realized sooner."

"Nonsense. Where is he? I'll go talk to him."

Tristan caught my hand. "Leave it, Aurora. He'll come when he's ready."

"But . . ."

My grandmother stood up, and the hall went silent.

She called Tristan and me up onto the dais. "My dear people of Elfi," she began. "I am pleased to announce the betrothal of Prince Tristan of the Night Court to my granddaughter and heir, Princess Aurora of the ancient house of Eos-Eirendil."

Cheers and claps went up from the crowd as my grandmother raised her silver goblet.

I turned to look at Tristan, who had his eyes fastened on me. He bent his head and kissed me in front of the whole room. My head swam as his lips touched mine. It lasted only a second, but it was not only a kiss. More like a promise of something else. I blushed as he moved back. Maybe being married to him wouldn't be so bad after all.

"To Aurora and Tristan," cheered the queen of the fae.

The crowd echoed, "To Aurora and Tristan."

I turned to glance at Penelope, who was looking at me with a shocked expression on her face. *She didn't know!* Why had my grandmother not told her?

High Fae started milling about to congratulate us, and I didn't get a chance to talk to Penelope. Dinner was served and I sat beside Tristan, trying to make sense of the conversation around me. But I was failing miserably; my mind was elsewhere and I couldn't concentrate on what Tristan was saying.

This was it. I was engaged. There would be no more waiting for Rafe, no more wishing he would come back. It was
over, he was gone, and I had to move on.

After dinner the tables were moved away for the dancing
to commence, and the musicians started up a lively melody
as couples milled onto the dance floor. I went up to Penelope, who was seated on a chair in the corner of the great
hall talking softly to two High Fae ladies. They bowed and
moved away when they saw me.

"How are you feeling?" I perched myself on the armrest
of the high back chair on which she sat.

"Tired," Penelope replied, glancing at me briefly, then
studying the dancing couples. "I shouldn't have come down
for the feast, but Izadora insisted. Now I know why."

"I can take you back to your room if you want."

She shook her head. "You cannot leave your own betrothal feast until everyone has left." Penelope was always so
proper. "It would be considered rude."

I sighed. "I saw your look when my grandmother announced the betrothal. I thought you knew she was going to
announce it today?"

Penelope shook her head again. "No. I didn't know. I was
surprised, that's all. I thought you were still in love with
Rafe. I didn't expect you to say yes, now that Izadora cannot
force you to do anything you don't want."

I hung my head. "What use would that be? Rafe and Katerina are married. He's never coming back for me."

"What?" Penelope demanded, her blue eyes narrowing into ice chips. "Who told you that?"

"My grandmother." I told her everything Izadora and the dowager had said.

She shook her head as I was talking.

"This time Izadora has gone too far," said Penelope. "She may be my sister, but she can be a real bitch when she doesn't get her way."

"Penelope!" I gasped. I had never heard her use such a word before. Penelope was always so soft spoken and gentle. "Why are you so angry? What did she do?" But a slow dread had started creeping into my heart.

Penelope shook her head. "It's not what she did, but what she didn't do that is the problem."

My eyes narrowed. "I don't understand."

"I was the one who received the information about Rafe," explained Penelope. "I've been keeping an eye on him since I got back. When I passed through Brandor I positioned at least a dozen spies all over the kingdom. I told Izadora about it when she came to see me because I thought I could help her understand why you don't want to marry Tristan, and why you shouldn't be forced to."

I nodded. "Go on."

Penelope wrung her hands. "What I didn't know was that she would only tell you a part of the information and let you jump to conclusions."

"What conclusions? Penelope, what are you saying? Izadora told me he was in Brandor and the Brandorians had a royal wedding at the Red Citadel, the palace of the Emir of Sanria, Katerina's father. What other conclusion could there be?"

"Rafe was in Brandor," said Penelope patiently, "that part is true, and there was a wedding." She paused and looked me in the eye. "But not his."

"What!" I stood up. Heads turned and I lowered my voice. "How can this be?"

"What Izadora failed to tell you was that the wedding in Brandor was Santino's. Not Katerina's and Rafe."

My mouth fell open. I felt like I was being suffocated. I couldn't breathe.

"Then why was Rafe going there if it wasn't for Katerina?" I was so confused.

"Santino married your aunt, Serena Silverthorne."

"What?" I shook my head. *No! No! It couldn't be possible.*

She nodded. "Yes. Apparently when Santino was at Silverthorne Castle in Eldoren, negotiating with Rafe for his father the Emir, the Pirate Prince met and fell in love with your Aunt Serena. Rafe was escorting Serena and Erien to Brandor to make sure they reached it safely."

"And Katerina?" I whispered, barely taking a breath.

"Rafe has rejected the Emir's offer to wed Katerina."

"But what about his kingdom?' I asked. "He needs Santino's army to take back his throne from the Blackwaters."

"He knows that," said Penelope, "but he has rejected the offer all the same. My informant also sent word that Prince Rafael has announced he will not marry until he regains his throne."

I couldn't breathe. How could my grandmother do this to me? She knew how much I loved Rafe, and she fed on my insecurities and let me believe he had accepted the Emir's offer and gotten married. She knew that if I found out Rafe was not marrying Katerina, I would have waited for him. I would have never agreed to get engaged to Tristan, whatever my grandmother might say.

What had I done?

Izadora had tricked me, and I had fallen into her trap. She knew she couldn't force me to do what she wanted anymore, so she made me believe she had my best interests at heart. Maybe she did believe this was best for me, but that didn't make it right. She had not changed, she was still the cunning manipulator she always had been, and I fell for her act.

Tristan came up behind me. "May I have a dance with my betrothed?" he breathed into my ear, his breath warm on my bare shoulders.

I turned to face him and nodded, trying to force a smile when my heart was breaking in two. Poor Tristan deserved better than this; he deserved someone who would love him and no other. But that person wasn't me, for I would always be in love with Rafe.

Tristan's sapphire eyes sparkled as he smiled at me and took my hand. I plastered a smile on my face and followed him to the dance floor.

The musicians played a haunting melody as Tristan swept me up in his arms and twirled me round the dance floor. Onlookers smiled at us, probably thinking we were the happiest couple in the world. They would never know I was slowly building a wall around my heart and one day no one would be able to get through. I had been hurt enough, but no more.

As we danced I saw a figure in a black cloak standing at the far end of the hall near the great arched doors leading out to the garden. He was watching us intently, leaning nonchalantly against the doorframe.

The music stopped and people clapped. But I stood frozen on the dancefloor.

My breath hitched in my throat as the figure removed his hood and my hand flew to my mouth.

It couldn't be!

Rafe! He was here. He had come back for me, like he said he would. But it was too late. I was already engaged to someone else.

Our eyes locked across the crowded hall and his lips

curved up in a half smile. A smile that held all the promise of being the last one I would ever see. I couldn't move, couldn't breathe, as I gazed at the devastatingly handsome figure of the Prince of Eldoren.

Rafe bowed, his dark gaze never leaving my face. I could see the hurt and betrayal in his eyes; eyes I could get lost in for a thousand years. He knew what had happened, he knew I had consented to marry Tristan.

My heart broke all over again as Prince Rafael Ravenswood turned on his heel, his obsidian cloak billowing around him like a dark shadow, and disappeared into the moonlit night.

ACKNOWLEDGMENTS

I AM SO grateful to so many wonderful individuals for their support, help, and guidance throughout this whole process, without whom this book would have never reached its full potential.

To my family: my rock, none of this would be possible without you.

To my phenomenal assistant Kate Tilton, I would be completely lost without you. Thank you for your help and unwavering support.

To my amazing mentor Laura Zats and the wonderful team at Wise Ink Creative Publishing, especially Dara Beevas, Amy Quale, Patrick Maloney, and Roseanne Cheng, as always it has been great working with you. Thank you for believing in me and my books, and helping me to realise my dreams.

To my superb editor Amanda Rutter, for your keen insight, patience, and guidance, which have helped me improve my writing and create a book that is the best possible version of itself.

To my awesome cover designer Scarlett Rugers, for your

magical touch in capturing the essence of the book and creating a spellbinding cover.

And finally a big thank you to all my lovely readers and fans who have supported The Avalonia Chronicles from the very beginning. You are the reason I write.